THE GREAT

Their lips touched, and it was like hot coals landing in a drought-stricken forest. Heat surged through her. She felt weak in the knees. She leaned against him, her arms circling his neck. His lips moved across her cheek and down her throat. She drew a ragged breath.

"Oh, Colt, hold me. Hold me forever," she whispered. She loved him. She felt as if she'd always loved him. Long before they met, she had loved him. And now, here in his arms, she couldn't stop the words from slipping forth, confessing her need for him.

His mouth paused. She couldn't bear it. Any moment he would come to his senses. He would step away from her, and once again, he would belong to Althea. Her fingers tangled themselves in his sandy mane, and she tried to bring his lips back to hers. She wouldn't think of what she was doing. She wouldn't let him stop. Not yet. Not yet.

Other Leisure Books by Robin Lee Hatcher:

STORMY SURRENDER
HEART'S LANDING
THORN OF LOVE
HEART STORM
PIRATE'S LADY
GEMFIRE
THE WAGER

Passion's Gamble

ROBIN LEE HATCHER

LEISURE BOOKS **NEW YORK CITY**

To
my friends in the Idaho Writer's League,
for
their support, their affection and their enthusiasm,
and
To Idahoans everywhere,
Who know and Love
the rugged majesty of God's country.

A LEISURE BOOK®

October 1989

Published by

Dorchester Publishing Co., Inc.
276 Fifth Avenue
New York, NY 10001

Copyright©MCMLXXXVI by Robin Lee Hatcher

All rights reserved. No part of this book may be reproduced or transmitted in any form or by any electronic or mechanical means, including photocopying, recording, or by any information storage and retrieval system, without the written permission of the Publisher, except where permitted by law.

The name "Leisure Books" and the stylized "LB" with design are trademarks of Dorchester Publishing Co., Inc.

Printed in the United States of America.

Passion's Gamble

1

Alexis Ashmore pushed a stray wisp of hair back behind her ear and glanced over at her father. "Seems like an awfully long way to come, just to marry a man. I suppose there's just not enough men left to marry with a war on and all."

"Could be. Or it could be he's someone special."

"Humph. I've yet to meet any man *that* special." She looked away, her ice-blue eyes staring down the dusty trail.

Jonathan's mouth gave no evidence of the smile he felt inside, though his gray eyes twinkled. There she sat, his favorite daughter, astride her flashy palomino, her willowy form clad in tight buckskin trousers, her white shirt open just enough at the neck to catch a tempting glimpse of creamy-skinned cleavage. Her long blonde hair, the pale yellow of a wheat field, was caught back in a brown ribbon at the nape of her neck, the crown of her head hidden beneath a dusty slouch hat. Though her clothes were masculine, they did nothing to hide her natural feminine beauty. She was more lovely in this unlikely attire than most women were when bedecked in their finest silks and satins. Alexis could have had her pick of a dozen men or more, yet none had ever piqued her interest.

Perhaps it's my fault, Jonathan mused. She's never met the right kind of men, following me around the country this way.

Alexis looked his way again. "What do you suppose Althea's like, Papa? It's been so long since we've seen her."

"I imagine she's just what you'll want in a sister," he replied. "You two were always a lot alike."

"Only in looks, Papa. We weren't ever alike inside."

It was true. Alexis and Althea Ashmore had been near enough alike to pass for twins when they were youngsters. There were differences— Althea, the older by ten months, had darker blue eyes than her younger sister and her hair was a more golden blonde—but their physical resemblance was still striking. The real difference lay in their personalities. Althea was always the perfect little lady, and Alexis was always the tomboy. Althea loved the things that money could buy, while Alexis took pleasure in such things as the breeze in her hair or watching a young colt romping in the pasture.

"I wonder if I did you right, taking you away

from home when you were so little," Jonathan said aloud.

Alexis jerked on the reins, drawing her horse to a sudden stop. Her eyebrows drew close in a frown. "That's enough, Papa. You've been saying that ever since you got Althea's letter. Well, I don't want to be like Althea. I never wanted to be like her. I *like* my life. I *like* the way I've grown up. I like being *me*. Mother never could understand me anyway. I would've been miserable if you'd left me in Virginia."

"But if you'd grown up there, it might be you who was getting married."

"Oh, Papa," she sighed, exasperated. But the smile returned to her rosy lips. "Are you trying to get rid of me?"

Jonathan reached over and squeezed her arm. "You know that's not true. I'd rather keep you all to myself. But you're a woman now. You ought to be living a better life than the one you've got, following your vagabond father from one boom town to another."

Alexis shook her head. It was pointless to argue with her father. He was determined to believe he had made a mistake in dragging her out west, and nothing she could say was going to change his mind, at least not at the moment.

"Come on, Papa. We'd better be on our way. Althea could arrive in Boise City any day now, and we would never escape Mother's wrath, even clear out here, if we aren't there to meet Althea when she gets off the stage."

Boise City, born along a river and nestled

against rolling brown hills, was an oasis in the high desert country. Rising above and stretching beyond the barren foothills were majestic mountains, mountains that cradled the site of what would be the richest gold strike in America, though that fact was still to be proven. Boise was an ambitious town with big plans for its future; it had been created as a service center for the more prosperous and much larger mining towns of Idaho City, Placerville, Silver City, and others, but it already had its eye on becoming capital of the young territory. Officially still less than a year old, Boise was already a thousand people strong. It was here that Alexis and Jonathan Ashmore were to meet sister and daughter, and where Althea was coming to join her intended.

As they rode into town, Jonathan stopped his horse in front of the first saloon on Main Street. "I could use a whiskey, Alex. Mind if I get myself a drink before finding a room?"

"You go ahead, Papa. I'll take care of the horses and meet you at the hotel down the street." She pointed as she spoke, indicating the whitewashed building with its false front, *HOTEL* written in large black letters across the highest boards.

"Well . . . if you don't mind . . ."

"Go on. I'll be fine."

Her father dismounted and entered the saloon. Alexis knew it would probably be several hours before she saw him again, at least if there was anyone inside who looked like a good candidate for a game of cards.

Handsome and likable, Jonathan Ashmore

was an adventurer and a gambler. Never happy with his life as lord and master of a great Southern plantation, he had given in eight years ago to the lure of the West. He had parted amicably with his wife, Madonna, leaving the ruling of Willowind in her very capable hands, a circumstance which no doubt had pleased her more than she would have admitted. Jonathan had never meant to stay away so long, but there had always seemed to be a new place to visit, new country to explore. They roamed the West together, father and daughter, experiencing different lifestyles—one year they worked on a cattle ranch in Texas, another they trapped furs in the Pacific Northwest—but all trails eventually led to towns in the vicinity of a gold strike, where the gamblers were plentiful and Jonathan was among friends. As more and more time passed, his genteel life as a Virginia planter seemed foreign to him and much too tame, and so he had never returned home.

As Alexis rode toward the livery stable, she thought of her mother and smiled wryly. Wouldn't Madonna Ashmore be horrified if she could see Alexis now, a daughter of hers dressed in trousers and boots? Actually, Alexis couldn't remember very well what her mother looked like—she had only been ten when she left Willowind with her father—but she could remember the scoldings her mother had given her every time she behaved in a less than ladylike fashion. Alexis wondered how her sister would react when she saw her.

She swung down from the saddle in front of

the stables, her spurs jingling faintly as a puff of dust rose around her boots. It was dry for April. She wound the reins around a post and stepped toward the open doors of the livery.

"Hello," she called, staring into the darkened interior. She waited a moment for her eyes to adjust to the dim light, then stepped inside. "Hello?" she said again.

"What can I do for you?"

Alexis jumped and swung around, startled by the deep voice so close behind her. She stared up at the burly fellow, a giant silhouette with the light at his back.

"Well?" he asked gruffly. "I don't have all day."

The moment of surprise passed, and when she spoke, it was with a firm voice. "I've got two horses outside that need to be stabled."

The man stepped aside, letting the light from outside spill over her. "Well, I'll be jiggered. It's a girl." He lifted a finger and chucked her under the chin. "Where'd you come from?"

"That's no concern of yours, I'm sure. Just tell me where to stable my horses and what it will cost."

"Feisty, ain't ya?"

Alexis hadn't grown up around saloons and mining camps without learning how to handle men who got out of line. Normally, women were so few that anyone of the female gender was treated like a queen, but there were always a few who stepped beyond the bounds of acceptable behavior. This fellow seemed to be one of them.

"I bet you'd be real pretty without that hat,"

he said as his hand reached toward her.

"Keep your hands to yourself, mister," she warned evenly. She stepped to the side, her goal to get the light at her back.

He was a little quicker than she was, however. His long arms shot out and grasped her below the shoulders. "Hey, now. No call to be unfriendly . . ."

"Martin. I suggest you leave the girl alone."

The voice that came from the back of the livery left no room for argument. Both Alexis and the man called Martin looked quickly in that direction. Martin's hands dropped from her arms.

"I wasn't doin' nobody no harm," he protested.

"Just be on your way," came the reply.

Martin frowned, hesitating only a moment before walking out of the livery. Alexis watched him go, then turned her eyes back toward the shadows, waiting for her unseen protector to show himself.

He stepped from one of the stalls, unhurried, and came toward her with a sure step, his rolling gait proclaiming the many hours he had spent in the saddle. Alexis was about to thank him for his aid, but the words died in her throat as he came into view.

He was tall—a good six inches taller than Alexis, and she was nearly five feet eight—but it wasn't his height that drew her notice. It was the rugged handsomeness of his face—the square line of his jaw; the darkened skin, browned by many hours in the sun; the mouth that seemed both strong and tender at the same time, the hint of a smile nestled in each corner; and the deep brown eyes that studied her in a most disconcerting fashion.

"Sorry, miss. Martin doesn't always know his manners."

He exuded strength and confidence, the deep timbre of his voice sending tiny chills down her back—all in all, a most pleasant sensation.

"It's quite all right," she said at last, finding her voice again. "I wasn't afraid. I could have handled him myself."

He lifted an eyebrow and smiled. "Oh? My mistake then."

His gaze slid lazily down from her face, tracing slowly the rounded contours of her blouse, the narrow, belted waist, the trousers that fit snugly over her shapely hips and legs. When his eyes returned to meet hers, she could feel the heat in her cheeks. She had never felt so uncomfortable in her life, yet for some reason, she had no desire to escape his scrutiny.

His smile was echoed in his brown eyes as he placed a battered hat on his head. "You'll find Gus in the shed out back. He runs the livery. He'll tell you where to put your horses." With a quick nod, he turned and went out into the street.

Alexis watched him go, standing still for the longest time, absorbing the strange sensations she had felt, trying to sort out what it was that had made her feel the way she did, and wondering why she'd never felt that way before.

There was nothing too fancy about her room,

and the washtub they brought up to her was little more than a tin bucket, but Alexis sat down in the tepid water with a pleased sigh as if it were the most luxurious of baths. She took a washcloth and began to soap herself, washing off the trail dust that had been gathering for almost a week. She let her head fall backward as she squeezed the cloth just above her throat. The water trickled down between her breasts and across her stomach. Alexis closed her eyes, wishing she could recline in the water. Perhaps she should have slipped out of town and bathed in the river. Maybe she would still do it before they left Boise.

That thought made her wonder how long they would be here. Althea's letter had been a bit vague about when the wedding would be. Actually, with the war going on between North and South and the vast distance between Virginia and the Western territories, it was lucky that her letter had reached them at all. Another day and it probably would have missed them, for the signs had been clear that Jonathan was ready to move to greener pastures and better pickings. Alexis began to soap her hair as she remembered her father's reaction to Althea's news.

"Well, I'll be," he'd said as he finished reading the letter. "Althea's gone and got herself engaged to a Westerner. A rancher. She's going out to Boise City up in Idaho Territory to marry the fellow. Says Madonna would only let her come if she could assure her that I'd be there to see that everything's done properly." Jonathan had fallen silent, perusing the letter once more. Suddenly, he'd grinned. "I've been thinking I'd like to see what's going on up there anyway. What do you say, Alex?"

What *could* she have said? She'd been following her father all around the country for too many years to be surprised when he wanted to go someplace else. Besides, she was more than a bit curious to see her sister again after so many years, and it would be nice if they could be friends.

Alexis rinsed the suds from her silky blonde hair, then stepped out of the murky water and dried herself. Draped only in the towel, she sat on the corner of the bed and began combing the snarls from her long yellow tresses. Reaching nearly to her waist, her baby-fine hair was her only real vanity. She would never think of cutting it, no matter how much of a bother it could be sometimes.

"Alex? You in there?" A rap followed her father's question.

"Yes, Papa. I'm just finishing my bath. Just a moment."

Alexis reached for her nightgown and slipped it over her head, then padded barefoot across the wooden floor and opened the door.

"Town's a bit quiet," he said as he stepped by her. "Ready for some supper?"

Alexis looked down at her nightgown, then back at her father. "I think I'd rather just turn in, Papa. I'm not really hungry, and I'd rather not get dressed again."

Jonathan yawned as he scratched the light stubble on his chin. "Maybe you're right. I could use some sleep myself."

"Did you check on the stage? Has Althea arrived?"

"Yes, I checked. She hasn't made it here yet." Jonathan sat down on the only chair in the room and began to pull off his boots. "Just as well. We need a day or two to get ourselves spruced up. I don't have a clean shirt left to my name, and you probably don't either. Wouldn't hurt us to buy some new clothes in honor of Althea's marriage, don't you think?"

"I'd like that, Papa," Alexis replied. She bent forward and kissed the top of his head. "We'll look around in the morning."

She went to the bed and crawled between the covers, turning her face to the wall. She listened as Jonathan moved around the room, spreading his bedroll on the floor and blowing out the lamp.

"Good night, Alex."

"Good night, Papa."

Days later, Alexis left the house of a local seamstress, clad in a new outfit. Her blouse was the blue of a summer sky, only slightly darker than her eyes, and was stitched with white thread and trimmed with silver braiding. It was open at the neck, revealing a blue silk scarf tied around her white throat. Her hair was tied back with a matching blue ribbon. Her new trousers were made of a pale blond buckskin, and they seemed to be molded to her trim figure. She wore leather boots that reached almost to her knees, her best silver spurs jingling on her heels. Her gun belt was slung low, the holster riding on her right hip.

She walked briskly toward the stage station where her father was meeting her. For some reason, Alexis was certain their waiting was over. Althea was going to be on that stage today.

"If she's not, Papa's going to drive me crazy," Alexis muttered under her breath.

Boise was too quiet for Jonathan Ashmore. The days of waiting, not knowing for sure when Althea would arrive, were making him grouchy. Alexis knew they wouldn't stay in the area long once her sister was safely wed. And that was all right with her. She'd never been any place before where she'd been stared at as much as she had been since arriving here. You'd think it was a crime for a girl to wear shirts and pants.

They ought to try riding fence in a dress, she thought, and then smiled. Truth was she would rather wear trousers even if she stayed home all day and mended socks. She had always thought they were more comfortable and much more practical than all those petticoats and skirts.

"Hey! Watch it there."

Not paying attention to where she was going, Alexis had turned the corner and walked right into him. She felt his hands catch her arms and steady her as she tried to step quickly backward. His eyes were an even deeper brown than she remembered; they seemed warmer in the full light of day than they had that day in the livery. The corners of his mouth were turned up in a lazy smile. Her pulse quickened as she returned his gaze, his hands holding her arms much longer than was necessary.

"Sorry," she said hastily, pulling free.

"Quite all right." He touched the brim of his hat and stepped aside so she could pass.

Alexis hated feeling so awkward and unsure of herself. She didn't even know why she felt that way. Quickly she began walking, only to find that the handsome stranger had fallen into step beside her.

"We seem to be going in the same direction," he said.

"Looks that way."

He was still smiling, and it bothered her. She wasn't sure if he was just being friendly or if he was laughing at her. She had never given much credence to what other people thought about her, but she definitely didn't like the idea of this man being amused by her.

She stopped suddenly and looked up at him. "If you don't mind, I have to meet a stage," she snapped, immediately sorry for the irritation that had crept into her voice.

To make matters worse, his smile grew even bigger. "No, I don't mind. Go on ahead."

Alexis could feel the color rising in her face as she wheeled around and hurried toward the station.

Colter leaned back against the board siding of the general store and tipped his hat away from his forehead. He continued to smile as he watched the girl stalking away from him, her back stiff. He would never have thought a woman could look so good in a pair of men's trousers—and without losing any of her feminine charms either. He had thought about her a lot since seeing her in Gus's livery. He couldn't help thinking that they had met once before. There was just something about her...

He pushed himself off from the building and began to walk in the direction of the Wells Fargo station, forcing his thoughts back where, by all rights, they should have stayed. After all, his fiancee could be on this very next stage.

Colter hadn't been very pleased when Althea had written that she was coming out to see him. He thought he had made it clear enough that they weren't going to be married until he had the ranch going smoothly and the new house built. Not that he wouldn't be glad to see her. It seemed like forever since they'd parted back on her plantation in Virginia. In fact, he sometimes had a hard time remembering just what she looked like, which made him feel a bit guilty. Not exactly the image of the eager bridegroom.

As he neared the station, he caught sight of the girl again, standing beside a man with light brown hair and gray eyes. Judging by the man's age and a slight resemblance, Colter guessed him to be her father. Again he marveled at how attractive she was in her male attire. He'd seen women in trousers before—it wasn't unheard-of out here—but none that looked like her. He would have remembered if he had. Still, he had the feeling that they had met before. Yet he had to be wrong, for it was obvious she didn't recognize him.

She looked up just then and their eyes met. Colter knew she must be thinking he had followed her. He watched as a hint of pink colored her high cheeks, making her lovely face even lovelier. Her seeming innocence was definitely contradicted by the holster strapped to her thigh. Once again the corners of his mouth turned up. In a flash, the blush left her face, replaced by an angry spark in her cool blue eyes.

Colter sauntered to a bench in front of the station and sat down. He leaned back and closed his eyes. The stage would probably be running late, and this seemed like a good opportunity to catch a few winks. He had been up most of the night with his favorite mare, helping to deliver her colt. It had been a difficult birth, but when he left this morning, mare and foal were doing fine.

Colter was proud of his little spread. Someday, it would be a great cattle ranch. He had already made a good start. He had over five hundred head, some of the best stock he could buy, brought up from Texas. His barn was up and the corrals, and he had a winter-tight cabin to live in until the big house was built. He had a good feeling about this town, too. It was going to be more than just a stopping point on the way to the gold mines. He'd felt that way the first time he'd laid eyes on it when he came out to Idaho Territory with his father.

MacKenzie Stephens had made his money in the mines of Black Hawk and Central City in Colorado. He'd built his wife a large mansion in Denver and had invested wisely and diversely, ensuring a life of ease for his large family. Colter was the eldest of the six Stephens children and had worked for a while in his father's mines, but his real ambition was to own a large cattle ranch. When he came to Idaho with his father not long after the strikes were discovered in the Boise Basin, he had known this was where he wanted to stay, not to manage his father's new claims, but to build his cattle empire. He'd chosen a site about fifteen miles northeast of Boise. His temporary home was nothing more than a one room log cabin, but he had already drawn up plans for the ranch house he meant to build from which to rule the Circle S Ranch.

Colter's father had sent him back east to buy horses for the Circle S, not an easy task in the midst of a civil war. "You start with some of them high bred stock, Colt," he'd said. "If you're going to have yourself a ranch, do it right. No skimping, you hear. We've got the money. You do it up right."

It was on his buying trip that he'd met Althea.

As delicate as a magnolia blossom in bloom, that was Althea. A rustle of petticoats beneath a voluminous hooped skirt. Golden hair gathered in intricate curls atop her head. Fluttering eyelashes. That special Virginia drawl that made her sound so utterly helpless and in need of his strength and protection. She was unlike any woman he had ever met before, and when he left Willowind, it was as the future husband of Althea Ashmore. To this day, he wasn't quite sure how it had happened.

The rumble of the stagecoach coming down Main Street interrupted his musings. Colter opened his eyes, yawned and stretched, then got to his feet. He stepped down off the boardwalk and waited for the stage to roll to a stop in front of him. Creaking springs and wheels and the rattle of harness filled the air. A cloud of dust enveloped the stage and everything else nearby. For a second more, the contraption rocked back and forth, then settled as the dust blew on down the street.

The driver hopped down from his lofty seat and pulled open the door. "Here we are, folks."

Two men in dusty suits got off first. They glanced up and down the street, then headed for the nearest saloon. An older woman was next to disembark. Her face was marked by weariness, but she smiled as her eyes lighted on her kin waiting for her. For a moment Colter thought he had made another futile trip to Boise.

"Colter, aren't you going to help me down?" Althea's face appeared at the door of the stage, and she held out her hand to him.

Colter stared at her a long moment before helping her to the ground. Despite the dusty trail, she looked fresh and beautiful. Her golden curls were hidden beneath a bright yellow bonnet. Her linen dress of the same lemon color swayed lightly over several crisp petticoats. He caught a whiff of the delicate fragrance of her cologne and remembered how lightheaded it used to make him feel when they strolled together in the gardens at Willowind. He wondered how he could have so nearly forgotten her face.

She stood close, turning a pretty pout up at him. "I've had a perfectly dreadful time, Colter. Why didn't you tell me how awful it was to travel out here? I thought I would never survive the last few weeks." She turned a cheek toward him and waited for his kiss.

He tried to look stern as he scolded her. "If you'd waited, Althea, I could have brought you out here myself... *after* we were married. You really shouldn't have come alone, you know."

"Oh, I didn't." Althea turned back toward the stage. "Cherry, aren't you going to get out?"

Another face appeared, this one rather pinched and dour and very black.

"This is Cherry, my servant and companion." In a stage whisper, she added, "Ever since the Union conquered our soil, I've been told I can't call her my slave." Her eyes widened, as if she'd suddenly thought of something. "My goodness, Colter. You didn't think Mother would allow me to come all this way alone, did you? Why, my reputation could have been tarnished. You would have been forced to marry me at once." Her eyes dropped and her cheeks turned a bright pink color. "Perhaps I should have left her at home, if it would mean we could be together now."

"Althea?"

She turned her head in response to her name. Colter looked too, wondering who could possibly know her so far from home.

"Father?"

Alexis stayed back on the boardwalk, watching as her father enveloped Althea in his arms and hugged her tightly. At this moment, she couldn't believe anyone had ever thought they could be twins. Althea was beautiful—very beautiful. No wonder she was engaged to *him* . . . Alexis' gazed moved to Colter.

Colter, she repeated in her mind. *The name fits him.*

They made a striking pair—Colter, tall and tanned, his sandy hair streaked with golden highlights and his coffee-colored eyes so expressive; Althea with her fair complexion and hair the color of spun gold, adoring dark blue eyes looking up at him as a soft blush painted her cheeks.

"Father, this is my fiance, Colter Stephens. Colter, this is my father."

Colter held out his hand. "Mr. Ashmore, it's good to meet you. I had no idea. I thought you were . . ." He broke off suddenly.

"Quite all right. I suppose most folks back home think I'm dead." He studied the tall young man for a moment, then smiled as he grasped Colter's hand. "I'm glad to meet you, son. I hope you'll call me Jonathan."

Jonathan turned back to Althea. He lifted her chin with his finger and gazed at her face. She didn't look much different than the day he'd left Willowind. Older, yes. She was a woman now. She was a real beauty, too. And he'd be willing to bet she was as clever as her mother at getting just what she wanted. He lifted an arm and motioned to Alexis.

"I trust you remember your sister?" he asked.

Alexis stepped quickly down into the street. Before Althea could even turn around, Alexis was hugging her and saying, "It's good to see you again, Althea. I want you to tell me all about Willowind and about Mother. I hope we're going to be good friends." She kissed her sister's cheek and then released her, feeling just a little bit silly at her display of emotion.

Althea's smile froze on her lips and she looked at Alexis. "Good heavens, Alexis! What *is* that you're wearing?"

Before she could reply, Colter cleared his throat. "Althea, aren't you going to introduce me to the rest of your family?"

"Of course," she replied, her eyes never leaving Alexis. "This is my sister. Alexis, this is my fiance, Colter Stephens."

Colter held out his hand once again. Alexis looked up into those brown eyes of his. She felt funny in the pit of her stomach as he took hold of her hand and lifted it to his lips. "It's a pleasure to meet you, Miss Ashmore. I had no idea Althea had such a charming family." The corners of his mouth lifted in that lazy smile she had already come to recognize in their previous brief encounters. "And might I add, I like whatever it is you're wearing."

He released her hand and turned back to her father. "I'm afraid I haven't made arrangements for anyone but Althea. I asked my friend Sadie Houston to put her up during her visit, but I doubt that Sadie will have room for everyone."

Jonathan's eyebrows lifted a little at the mention of Althea's *visit*. "Don't worry about us. We're used to fending for ourselves, aren't we, Alex? We're just glad Althea wrote to us to come and meet you. I may not be much of a father, but

I do prefer to get to know my future son-in-law before the wedding day itself."

"Well, we should have plenty of time..." Colter began.

"Really, Colter darling. Don't you think we could go someplace away from all this dust?" Althea interrupted, hooking her arm through his and leaning against him. "I'm really quite thoroughly exhausted." She looked as if she would crumble to the ground at any moment.

Colter's arm slipped around Althea's back to support her, an expression of tender concern in his eyes. "I'm sorry, Althea. I should have been more considerate." He lowered his voice. "I'd nearly forgotten how fragile you are."

Her head against his chest, Althea raised her eyes to him. "But you're strong enough for both of us, my love."

Alexis looked away, strangely bothered by this exchange between lovers.

2

Colter walked down Grove Street with a sister on each arm and Jonathan following behind. "You're going to love Sadie," he told them. "She more or less adopted me when I came here from Colorado. She likes to think I'm still a boy, and so she tries to mother me whenever she can." He turned his head toward Althea. "She's anxious to meet you."

"Well, of course, Colter darling. If she's such a good friend of yours, I know I'm going to like her, too."

"There. That's Sadie's place."

The house was a large, two-story brick with a shaded porch on the east side. A white picket fence circled the yard, and a large flower garden bordered the street.

"My goodness, Colter. I thought you said this Sadie's house was small," Althea said.

"No, I said she wouldn't have enough room for everyone."

"But . . ."

Colter urged them forward. "You'll see why."

He pushed open the gate and escorted them up to the front entrance of the house. He knocked and waited.

The knock seemed to stir up a great deal of activity inside—chairs scraped, voices shouted, feet ran. Suddenly, the door flew open and a large, smiling woman stepped into the doorway, and from all around her, children's faces peered at the guests.

"Landsake, I was beginnin' to think you weren't ever comin'," she cried. Her voice was deep and booming, befitting her immense size. Sadie Houston was easily six feet tall and two hundred pounds. Her face was creased by the sun and the years, but her smile brightened her natural homeliness.

"Sadie, I'd like you to meet . . ."

Sadie turned her dark eyes on Alexis and her thick eyebrows drew close together. "You needn't tell me, Colt, my boy. I would've picked her out as the gal for you from a hundred girls." She took Alexis' chin in one hand and twisted her head to one side and then to the other. "Yes sir, you've got spark, that's what you've got. It takes that to make it out here."

Colter looked from Sadie to Alexis, feeling temporarily at a loss. "Sadie, you . . . that's not Althea."

Sadie's hand dropped. Her eyes widened,

and the look she gave Colter clearly said she thought he was the one who was wrong.

"This is Althea Ashmore," Colter said, a trifle belatedly.

Althea's color was high as she spoke. "Pleased to meet you, Miz Houston."

Sadie didn't answer at once. She just went over Althea with a critical eye that deepened the heat in Althea's cheeks. Finally, she replied, "I'm glad to meet you, too. Sorry about my mistake." Then her gaze slipped back to Alexis. "And who might you be? By the looks of you, you must be her twin, though I'd bet you next Tuesday's laundry that there's more difference betwixt you than there's likeness."

Alexis held out her hand, feeling an immediate kinship with this outspoken woman. "I'm Alexis Ashmore. The little sister by ten months. And this is our father, Jonathan Ashmore."

"Pleased to make your acquaintance, Mr. Ashmore. Landsake, you'll all be thinkin' I haven't any manners. Come in. Come in." She started to turn around, clearing a path through the curious children as she did so. "Excuse my young'uns. They do love to meet new folk."

Althea looked horrified. "Good heavens, Miz Houston. You don't mean to say that *all* of these children are yours?"

Sadie laughed, a sound that filled the parlor and seemed to ricochet off the walls. "That they are. All ten of them. There'd be thirteen but three of my boys were stillborn. Safe with the Lord now, so I try not to fret for them much." She turned toward the nearest girl, who looked to be about fifteen years old. "Helen, you take the little ones upstairs and leave us grown-ups to ourselves."

"Yes, ma'am."

Once the children had disappeared, everyone sat down. Sadie brought out a teapot and china cups. One by one, she filled the cups and passed them around, then settled back in her own chair.

"How long do you plan to stay, Althea? You don't mind if I call you Althea, do you? And you're to call me Sadie. I do hate to be called Mrs. Houston by folks that are my friends, and I mean for us to be friends if you're plannin' on marryin' my boy here."

Althea's smile seemed just a little tight. "Of course we'll be friends. I wouldn't want it any other way." She glanced at Colter who was seated by her side. "I'm not quite sure how long I'll be staying. Of course, if you don't have room for me here, I can take a room at the hotel."

"Not stay here? Just you try! Why, this is Colt's home whenever he comes to Boise. It'd be silly for you to stay anywhere else. And your sister, too," she added, looking toward Alexis.

"Oh, Sadie . . ." Alexis began to protest.

Sadie frowned at Colter. "Haven't you warned these girls how stubborn I am? Now you tell them they're both stayin' with me."

Colter shrugged. "Althea. Alexis. You're staying. Jonathan, why don't you join me out at the ranch? It's nothing fancy, but it would give us a chance to get acquainted."

Althea was surprised. "You mean you won't be staying in town?"

"You forget, Althea. I've got a ranch to run."

Althea lowered her voice, but was unable to completely disguise her pique. "But, Colter, when will we see each other? After all, that's why I've come."

"Don't worry. We'll see plenty of each other. For one thing, I want you to come up to the ranch and see where I'm going to build the house. Maybe we can even go up to Idaho City and see a show at the Jenny Lind Theatre. It just opened, and I hear it's something special."

Althea's expression softened as she leaned against his arm. "All right, darling. Whatever you want."

The room Althea and Alexis were to share was bright and cheerful. There were windows on two sides of the room, French lace curtains draped around the edges. A large canopied bed stood against one wall and, on either side, were heavy oak wardrobes. A washstand was placed in the corner between the windows, the matching porcelain pitcher and bowl set in its center and a tall mirror on the wall above. A rose patterned wallpaper covered the walls, the design varying slightly from the paper on the ceiling.

Alexis sat on the edge of the bed, watching as Althea pulled gowns out of her trunk and hung them in the wardrobe. It felt strange to look at this young woman and know she was her sister and yet so much a stranger. There were so many things she should ask her, things she truly wanted to know, but one above all pressed to be asked, and finally she could contain it no longer.

"When are you going to be married?"

Althea turned from her task, pushing her skirts off to one side. "Before the end of next month . . . if everything goes well."

"Althea? Does *he* know that?"

Her sister came to sit beside her on the bed. She reached forward and placed her hand over Alexis' where it rested on the coverlet. "My dear Alexis, how very little you must know about men. Most of them never know what they want or what they're going to do until a woman helps them realize it."

Alexis' eyes widened. "You mean he really does think you've just come for a visit? Then why did you write to Father and ask him to meet you here for the wedding?"

"Well, I wouldn't have written if we weren't going to get married. It's just that he doesn't know it yet." She frowned. "Don't look at me that way, Alexis. You could never understand. It all became so complicated. I don't know if I can explain it to you. The war and no men anywhere unless they're riffraff. Mother thinks of only one thing. Willowind. What Willowind needs, that's what we must have. And Willowind needs a man right now." She paused and stared across the room toward the window. "So here I am to get one."

It was hard to follow her sister's thinking. Alexis was confused, and it showed in her expression. "But what about his ranch? I thought he said you two were going to live out here?"

"Good heavens, Alexis! You can't really see me living out in a place like this, can you?" Althea got up from the bed and returned to her trunk. She lifted a pale lavender gown from its depths. As she stroked the creases from the shiny satin skirt, her eyes softened, and she seemed to slip away from the room as she lifted it to her cheek. "Oh, you don't know what it was like. You were too young when you left. The parties we used to have. The great balls. There were so many young men. I was surrounded by them, all wanting to dance with me, all swearing to love me forever if they could just steal one kiss in the shadows of the garden. There was no hurry for me to find a husband. There were so many to choose from."

Sadness washed over Alexis as she watched and listened.

"But they just keep dying. Dying in places I've never heard of before. And Mother needs help, and there's no one to help her."

Alexis got up from the bed and went to stand beside Althea. "But what has that to do with you and Colt?"

"It has everything to do with us," Althea snapped. "All I've ever been trained to do is win a man. The *right* man. A man who can rule Willowind at my side when Mother's no longer able. A man Mother approves of. Well, Colter is that man, and I mean to marry him and get him back to Willowind just as soon as I can."

Alexis decided not to ask any more questions. She was disturbed and needed some time to sort out what her sister had told her. "I think I'll go down and see if Sadie needs any help with supper."

"Send Cherry up to me," Althea called after her as she opened the door. "I'm going to lie down awhile and I want her to put away the rest of my things."

Colter and Jonathan were not at supper. They had returned to the Circle S to check on the new foal. Althea was more than a little put out at Colter's less than enthusiastic attention on her first day here, but Alexis had to admire her for the good front she put on before Sadie and her husband.

Jasper Houston was a short, slight man with a bald head and a long, handlebar mustache. He was certainly not the man Alexis would have pictured as the husband of Sadie and the father of such a large brood of children. But she liked Jasper the moment she met him. He was soft-spoken and didn't smile as openly or as easily as his mate, but there was a gentle affection that showed in his expression whenever he spoke to Sadie.

During supper, Alexis kept the conversation lively, asking a myriad of questions about Boise, *Houston's Mercantile*, and the discovery of gold in the Boise Basin. Jasper answered every question, enjoying her eager quest for information. When supper was over and the children had been sent to bed, Althea, protesting fatigue after her tiresome journey, also went upstairs. Jasper retired to his study to smoke his pipe and read. Sadie's oldest girl, Helen, started to help her mother with the dishes, but Alexis forced her from the kitchen, wanting a chance to talk with Sadie some more.

"Sadie, can I ask you a question?"

"Anything you want."

"What made you marry Mr. Houston? I mean, you two seem so . . . different."

"We are different. Different as night and day in a lot of ways, I reckon." She plunged a dish into the hot, soapy water. "But when we met, we knew we were right for each other." She looked over at Alexis. "Some folks'd call it love at first sight. Guess that's what it was. When it happens to you, you'll know it."

Alexis didn't like the way Sadie was watching her. She sniffed. "I've yet to meet a man who interested me that much."

"You haven't, huh?"

"No."

Sadie handed her the dripping dish. "You will, honey. You will."

Alexis just kept shaking her head, partly in denial . . . and partly to get the image of Colter Stephens out of her thoughts.

Althea wasn't the best of company the next day, especially when Colter failed to return to Boise City early in the morning. She sat in their room, her pretty mouth turned in a stubborn pout, thunder in her stormy blue eyes. Alexis tried several times to coax her out of her mood, but then gave up and decided to explore.

She walked up Grove Street, then over to

Main. She could hear pounding hammers echoing further down the street as temporary structures gave way to more permanent buildings of lumber and adobe and brick. There were several general stores, a butcher shop, two breweries, the liveries, and at least five saloons in town. There was even a private school, evidence that this was a town built with families in mind and an eye for the future. Despite her earlier impressions, she was beginning to feel quite comfortable here. Perhaps it was because she had made a friend and no longer felt so out of place.

Alexis went to the livery and saddled her palomino mare, Nugget. She swung up into the saddle and rode slowly down Main Street until she reached the edge of town. Then she nudged her horse into a canter, turning the mare in the direction of the foothills to the north. She eased Nugget back to a walk as they began to climb. Once they reached the first ridge, she stopped and looked back into the valley.

To the south, beyond Boise, stretched a vast, sagebrush-covered desert. The tree-lined river valley was an oasis in a semiarid land. The Boise River country had been extolled decades before as an enchanted land, a land where mountain and plain mingled in unique grandeur and beauty, a land of bubbling brooks and streams and grassy meadows that waved in the breeze, but it had taken a gold rush to bring settlers who would stay to build a city with a future. Many farmers had raced to the Boise Basin in search of gold, only to discover that they had a better chance of success if they stuck to farming. The easily irrigated river bottom land around Boise City had quickly been taken up, and farms now dotted the area up and down the river.

Alexis turned her horse again, this time facing north. The brown foothills rose gently, but steadily, before her until, near the peaks, they became a tree-capped shade of purple. Alexis knew that beyond those mountains lay the Circle S Ranch—and beyond that, the Boise Basin, filled with thousands upon thousands of miners, each with their dreams of great riches.

The sun had climbed high in the sky by this time, and Alexis decided to return to the Houston house, hoping that by now Althea would be in a better frame of mind. She took one more sweeping look at the mountains and valley, then turned Nugget down the hill.

Once in town, she rode leisurely toward the livery stables, her thoughts on nothing in particular. She was unprepared for the sudden hand that reached out to grab Nugget's reins, causing the mare to throw up her head and her front legs to leave the ground, striking at air. Alexis clutched for the saddle horn to keep herself from tumbling backward into the dust.

"Well, here she is again."

Alexis could feel Nugget trembling, and she stroked the mare's glossy neck and whispered, "Easy, girl," before deigning to acknowledge the speaker. As she turned her gaze upon him, she recognized Martin's leer.

"You, sir, had best release your hold on those reins," she said, the softness of her voice belying the hardness of her warning.

"Now, haven't we been through this once before? I'm only tryin' to be friendly. Seems like folks just don't know how to be friendly anymore." As he was talking, he stepped backward, leading Nugget and Alexis into the stables.

"Let go," she demanded again.

"I'll let you go...in a minute or two..." Martin began to grin, but it faded quickly as he stared into the barrel of her revolver.

"Sir, I suggest you never touch me or my horse again." She cocked the gun. "Do I make myself clear?"

Martin released the reins as if they were hot coals. He nodded as he continued to back away, his eyes never leaving the gun that followed him as he moved. He gulped some air and took flight, disappearing around the corner of the next building.

Alexis was returning the gun to its holster when she heard laughter. She turned in her saddle and found Colter no more than twenty feet away.

"I don't think Martin's ever moved faster in his life," he said as he rode forward. Though his smile remained, his eyes were serious as he added, "That was a mighty fast draw. Do you know how to use it?"

"I know how if I have to."

Even the smile disappeared now. "You're not much like your sister, are you?" His voice was low, but she heard him clearly enough.

"No," she replied. "We're not much alike."

There was a hollow feeling in her stomach, and she felt a fleeting regret that she wasn't like Althea.

Colter's smile crept back into the corners of his mouth. "Come on, quick draw. We've got a big day ahead of us. I'm taking you and Althea back up to the Circle S for a few days. Your father's waiting for us at Sadie's."

Jonathan and Althea were standing on the front porch. A horse and buggy waited in the street near the front gate. As Colter stopped his horse, Althea came forward, her face shaded from the sun by a pink parasol.

"What on earth took you so long, Colter? I was beginning to worry."

Colter looked over at Alexis, amusement undisguised in his brown eyes, his glance saying they shared a secret. "No need to worry, Althea. Not so long as Alexis is around."

Althea followed his gaze to her sister, and a frown knitted her eyebrows. She opened her mouth, as if to ask Alexis what he was talking about.

Alexis flushed and hopped to the ground, not wishing to be questioned at the moment. She slipped past them and hurried into the house and up to her room where she poured some water into the washbasin. She splashed water on her face, and as she dried it, she looked at her reflection in the mirror. Again, she wished she were more like her sister with her delicate movements and that soft drawl that made every word sound honeyed.

"The only type of man who'd be attracted to you," she said to her image in the glass, "is one like Martin."

Perhaps it was speaking the thought aloud. Whatever it was, she was suddenly angry with herself. Why would she want to be any different than she was? Hadn't she told her father, only a matter of days ago, that she wouldn't change a thing about the way she'd been raised? And hadn't she told him that there wasn't a man special enough to come cross country for? Well, if that were true, it was certainly true that there wasn't a man special enough to think she needed to change, just to please him.

Without bothering to run a comb through her hair, Alexis tugged her hat onto her head and marched back outside. Althea was seated in the buggy, Jonathan beside her and Cherry in the rear. Alexis thought she still looked a bit perturbed and wondered if she hadn't forgiven Colter for not staying in town the day before.

Colter was waiting with the two saddle horses. When Alexis walked up to him, he passed Nugget's reins to her. "Althea says she doesn't care to ride on horseback as far as the ranch. *You* don't mind, do you? There's room in the buggy if you'd prefer."

Still smarting from her own self-evaluation, she snapped, "Don't be silly, Mr. Stephens. Do I look like I can't handle a little ride in the mountains?" She swung effortlessly into the saddle.

"No, Miss Ashmore. You certainly don't." Mounting his horse, he said, "Let's get going."

They followed the stage route most of the way. The road followed Cottonwood Creek through the mountains. Alexis often rode ahead of the others, enjoying the ruggedness of nature as they passed through the deep canyon on their climb to the summit. From the summit, she beheld the mountain range that seemed to stretch on forever.

"Quite a sight, isn't it?"

Startled, Alexis gasped. She had been so absorbed in the beauty of the country, she hadn't heard Colter ride up beside her.

He smiled. "Kind of takes your breath away? That's how I've always felt about it."

"It is beautiful," she replied, smiling in response. "As many places as I've been with Papa, each is always different than the one before. Even the mountains are never quite the same."

"You see it, too."

Alexis didn't dare look at him. Though his words were ordinary enough, there was something about the way he said them, as if they were sharing something much more intimate than just a mountain range.

The sound of the buggy approaching rescued her from whatever it was—nameless and mysterious—of which she was afraid.

Colter got down from his saddle. He walked over to the buggy and helped Althea to the ground. He took her hand and placed it in the crook of his arm as he led her to the edge of the road.

"It's beautiful, isn't it?" he asked her, pride in every word, as if each mountain peak belonged to him.

Althea gazed around her a moment before replying. "I'm sorry, darling. I don't see any sign of the ranch."

"Not the ranch. We've got a long way to go yet. I meant all of this," he said with a wide sweep of his arm.

"Oh, I thought for sure we must be close. We've come so dreadfully far already without seeing another soul. I'm so tired. Isn't there any place civilized in this country. A place to rest and enjoy oneself." Her eyes widened suddenly. "What about Indians? Are we in any danger out here by ourselves?" She looked as if she would swoon.

Alexis watched Colter's face. The change of expression was minute, yet she detected his disappointment. He had been sharing something dear to him, and Althea hadn't even noticed. Alexis felt a sudden urge to shake her sister until her teeth rattled.

"No, Althea. You're not in any danger." Colter turned her back toward the buggy. "We'd better be on our way, though. It's getting late, and I still have a few things to tend to around the ranch."

"Oh, but Colter, I'm so tired," Althea protested. "Can't we rest awhile longer?"

Jonathan leaned forward. "Listen, Colt. You ride on. Althea and I'll sit here a spell. I know how to get to the Circle S and how long it will take. We'll be there before dark."

"Well, I..."

"Go on, now. If Althea's going to be a rancher's wife, she's going to have to learn that sometimes the ranch comes first. Might as well learn it now." Jonathan glanced at Alexis. "No point you plodding along with us, Alex. You go with Colt."

"You don't mind, do you?" Colter asked Althea.

She sat stiffly in her seat. "Of course not. Whatever you think best." It was said to make him feel guilty for neglecting her, but he didn't seem to notice.

"I'll have the fire lit and supper cooking when you get there."

He leaned forward to kiss her, but she turned her head, and instead of her mouth, his lips brushed her cheek. If he was aware that she'd done it on purpose, he said nothing to acknowledge the fact; yet Alexis, from her vantage point, knew he was bothered by it. He returned to his horse and swung into the saddle.

"If you're coming, let's go," he said to Alexis, and kicked his horse into a canter.

There was no opportunity for conversation as long as Colter kept up the fast pace. Finally, for the sake of the horses more than for Alexis or himself, he eased back on the reins and brought his gelding to a walk. Alexis glanced over at him. He seemed more relaxed than he had when they'd begun their ride down from the summit.

Colter looked over and found her watching him. "You know, I've never seen eyes quite like yours. I feel like they're hiding a lot. Tell me, what *are* you thinking?"

She wasn't sure what she'd been thinking . . . or even *if* she'd been thinking. She had just wanted to look at him, and she couldn't very well admit that to her sister's fiance.

"I . . . I was wondering how much further it was to the ranch," she stammered, looking away.

"You too? Are you worried about Indians?"

"Of course not . . ." She turned to find him grinning at her, an amused twinkle in his eyes. She couldn't resist the look. Her own smile answered his.

Colter lifted an arm and pointed. "Up there. That's all part of the Circle S. It crosses the canyon up ahead and then runs north and east. The new stage route goes right through some of it, but the cattle don't seem to mind, so neither do I." He lifted his hat off and wiped his forehead with the sleeve of his shirt, then put the hat back on, tipping it further back on his head. "I suppose there's better places for a cattle ranch, places not so rugged, easier to get to. But there's something about it . . ."

Alexis thought she'd never seen anyone who looked more content when speaking of his home. She wondered if she would have felt that way about Willowind if she had stayed there. Somehow, as beautiful as it was in her memories, she knew there wouldn't have been the same enchantment.

They stopped a moment to water their horses in a cold mountain creek, the spring melt running high. Then they crossed the stream and began the ascent of the canyon wall. They stopped at the top, and Alexis caught her first real glimpse of what Colter had been speaking of.

Long grasses waved lazily over the gently rolling meadow. The rocky canyon that fell abruptly to the creek had disappeared in the midst of it, a deception that could be dangerous if one became careless. Steep hills, covered in sagebrush and pine trees, rose away from the valley, a reminder of the rugged mountain country that surrounded them. Up a nearby draw and scattered up the hillside, Alexis caught sight of some longhorn cattle.

"We're not far from the ranch house now," Colter said as he nudged his horse forward.

The house was tucked back in a shady draw, surrounded by a grove of cottonwood trees, a small creek running nearby. It was a one-room log cabin with a shake roof. There was a sliver of smoke curling up from the chimney as they approached, as it wafted by them, Alexis caught a whiff of onions cooking.

"That'll be Li Ching," Colter said, noting her surprise. "He's my only hand at the moment."

Just then, the door opened, and a young Chinaman stepped outside. He was smiling and he bowed several times as Colter and Alexis stopped their horses.

"Alexis, this is Li Ching."

"Hello," Alexis said.

Li Ching bowed several more times but made no reply.

When Alexis glanced at Colter in question, he shook his head. "He can't answer. He hasn't got a tongue."

She looked back at the smiling man with the black eyes that shimmered with friendliness. He couldn't have been much older than she was.

Colter hopped to the ground, then looked back up at her. There was no smile on his lips as he told her, "Some damned bigots cut his tongue out."

"Why?" she asked breathlessly.

"Mostly 'cause he's Chinese. They didn't need much more of an excuse."

Alexis dismounted and walked over to Li Ching. She held out her hand to him and returned his smile. "I hope we'll be good friends, Li Ching."

Li Ching's black eyes darted toward Colter before he accepted her proffered hand and shook it briefly. Then he stepped back and opened the cabin door, motioning for her to step inside.

The room was simple and clean, and it had a homey feeling which surprised Alexis, considering it was two bachelors who lived here. Against the wall farthest from the door were two beds, one in each corner. There was a window in the middle of the same wall, the wood shutters open to let in the afternoon light. A sturdy table filled the center of the room, surrounded by four chairs. Across from the door stood a tall cupboard, dishes stacked neatly inside. There was an iron stove for cooking and a large fireplace for heat and light. There was even a bathtub against one wall, partially hidden by a curtain which hung from the ceiling.

"I hung the curtain last night," Colter said from behind her.

Ridiculous though it might have been, Alexis felt as if it were she—and she alone—who would be staying here with Colter. She had a sudden vision of herself in that bathtub with only a curtain hiding her from his view. A tiny shiver ran down her back, and she moved quickly across the room, desiring a little more space between them.

When she turned around, she found him watching her with a curious gaze.

"Is something wrong?" he asked.

She shook her head, wishing that Althea and their father would arrive.

3

Colter sat at the table, watching Althea. Li Ching had prepared a stew for supper, and everyone seemed to be enjoying it except for her. She kept moving the food around her plate with her fork but seldom took a bite. Her expression was one of extreme distaste.

Colter was disturbed about more than just her lack of appreciation for what he considered good grub. She looked so out of place in this room. It wasn't just that she was dressed in a gown fit for a party and the room itself was so plain. Perhaps it was the way she looked at everything and everyone—including him—as if they were beneath her notice. Had she been like this at Willowind? He didn't remember her this way.

His gaze moved to Alexis. She was speaking to her father between bites, and they were laughing as they traded stories of their travels.

Her eyes sparkled; her cheeks were brushed with pink. Along with her hat, she had removed the ribbon that usually tied back her silky tresses, and now her hair flowed freely around her shoulders and down her back. He liked it that way.

He looked back toward Althea and found her watching him. Her mouth was taut and her eyes resembled thunderclouds. The smile that had slipped into the corners of his mouth vanished.

"I think I'll check around before turning in," he said as he rose from the table. "Li Ching, bank the fire for the ladies, please. Jonathan, you and I will sleep in the barn. Good night, Althea." He leaned down to kiss her cheek. "Good night, Alexis."

Althea received his kiss without response.

"Good night, Colt," he heard Alexis say as he closed the door.

As soon as Li Ching and Jonathan had left the cabin, Althea turned toward Alexis with undisguised rage. Hands on her hips, she stalked across the room. "You keep away from him, Alexis Ashmore. Do you hear me?"

Alexis backed away but was stopped by the foot of one of the beds. "Althea . . ."

"Don't you play innocent. I've seen what you're up to. Just remember that Colter is *my* fiance and that he's going to be my husband before too long."

Alexis was mystified. She had done nothing to warrant her sister's anger.

Althea turned away and went to the other

bed, then whirled around. "You were always so tricky, worming your way into Father's good graces, making sure you were his favorite. You didn't fool me, not even then. You were just making sure that it would be you he took with him when he left. And there I was, left with Mother, left with nobody to love me."

"Althea, what are you saying? Mother loves you. She loves all of us, even Papa."

"Madonna Ashmore has never loved anything except Willowind. She married our father to get it, and she drove him away so she could have it all to herself." Althea's hands shook as she tried to unbutton her gown. "A son was what she needed, but when she didn't bear a son, she made do with me. That's what I was raised for. That's what I've been trained for. To marry a master for Willowind. One that, of course, won't mind her ruling until she's no longer capable." She paused before grinding out, "I don't think she'll ever die. Not even the war can kill her."

Alexis was too stunned to speak. There was hate in Althea's voice as she spoke of their mother. Although Alexis remembered more times when Madonna was scolding her than when she approved of her, she had always believed that her mother loved her. And she had always been convinced, even when they were tiny children, that her mother loved Althea much more than she ever could Alexis. Althea was always a little lady, and Alexis was always getting into scrapes of one kind or another—not very ladylike behavior.

"For pity's sake, Cherry, get over here and

undo these buttons for me!" Althea cried, her voice shrill with frustration.

The slave hurried from the corner where she'd been sitting. As her competent hands began to loosen the bodice, Althea's gaze returned to her sister. Her voice was low and as cold as anything Alexis had ever heard. "You mind me, Alexis. You stay away from Colter. He's mine."

"He loves you, Althea," Alexis whispered. "I couldn't come between you."

"Loves me?" There was a long pause. "Of course he loves me."

Alexis couldn't stop herself from asking, "And do you love him, Althea?"

It was as if all the wind went out of her. Althea sagged onto the bed, and Alexis thought she'd never seen anyone look so tired. But it lasted only an instant. The fire returned as her sister turned suspicious eyes her way.

"Let me tell you something, my childish little sister. Love has nothing to do with it. Colter is rich. He can get me things and take me places I want to go. Once we're married, I'll be free. I can get away from Mother. With his kind of money I can do anything."

"But we're not poor. The Ashmores have always had . . ."

"Hush up, Alexis. You know nothing. Nothing, I tell you." Althea lay down, turned her back toward Alexis, and drew the covers up over her shoulders.

Alexis lay down, too. Cherry blew out the lantern, leaving Alexis to stare up at the ceiling as darkness enveloped the room. She felt cold and frightened, afraid of the angry stranger who occupied the bed across from her.

Alexis couldn't sleep. Quietly, she drew on her clothes and slipped outside, walking toward the corral by the light of a waning moon. Nugget's golden head lifted at the sound of her soft footsteps. She whickered and trotted over to the corral gate. Alexis climbed onto the fence, then reached down to rub the mare behind her ears.

"I wish we'd never come," she whispered.

But she didn't mean it. From the first moment she had laid eyes on this valley, she had felt a love for it. It was rough and untamed, the raw beauty of the land challenging man to conquer and survive. Colter would conquer and survive. She knew he would. He was that kind of man.

"Couldn't sleep either, huh?"

Alexis gasped and swung around, nearly dislodging herself from her perch on the fence rail. Colter's hands darted up to steady her, lingering briefly on her arms. Her stomach tightened as she met his gaze. She shivered, but not from the cool night air.

"No," she answered, but the word was barely audible.

Colter swung up onto the fence beside her. "Here. Put this on," he told her as he handed her his jacket.

She slipped her arms into the sleeves and pulled the jacket around her. She felt guilty, sitting here beside him, after what Althea had said to her. Yet she couldn't make herself leave. She *wanted* to be here. She wanted to be here beside him. She felt a flush of color come into her cheeks, and she was thankful that the moon wasn't full enough to expose her feelings.

"Can't see it from here, but there's a perfect spot for the new house up against those mountains. There's a spring and lots of trees."

"But why not build here, where you have so much done already?"

Colter scratched the day-long stubble on his chin. He shrugged. "Just thought I'd like a bit of privacy for my family . . ." He looked at her and smiled a little before adding, "Once I've got one."

Her heart raced in her chest. She couldn't think of anything to say, so she remained silent.

"I'll be taking on more hands soon. Gonna build a bunkhouse here. The cabin can be turned into a cook house and mess for the hands. Once the new house is up, I'll have a small stables up there, but this'll be the main barn and yard right here."

"It's going to be wonderful," Alexis said softly.

His smile faded. "Do you think Althea will agree with you?"

Althea's angry words echoed in her mind. She couldn't tell him what Althea had said. She couldn't bear to repeat her denial of love. "She's a fool if she doesn't." Nugget rubbed her head against Alexis' knee, demanding more attention. Alexis, glad of the distraction, looked away from Colter's searching gaze and stroked the mare's nose.

"I'm asking her to give up a lot. Even once the house is built, it won't be anything like she's used to. She's a lady. She's used to being spoiled and pampered." He was talking to himself now. "Oh, we'll have a few servants, but it won't be the same for her."

"She must have known that when she agreed to marry you," Alexis said, unable to curb her reply.

He nodded, a strange smile returning to his lips. "Yes, I suppose she did." He paused, then asked, "What about you, Alexis? What kind of place would you like to live?"

Just like this, she wanted to say, but couldn't. She shook her head slowly. "I don't know. We've been on the move for so long, guess I never gave much thought to settling anywhere."

"You don't want to get married?"

Again her heart was racing. "Never met anybody that made me want to, but I suppose I will some day. Papa likes to roam, though."

"And so do you?" Colter asked.

She shrugged her shoulders.

"Maybe the two of you will decide to stay around these parts. I think you belong here."

She knew he didn't mean it the way it sounded. He couldn't mean that she belonged here at the Circle S, yet that's the way she felt. That's what she wanted him to be saying.

Alexis swung her legs over the rail and hopped down from the fence. "I think I'll go in." She removed the jacket and held it out to him. "Thanks." She had to get away before she admitted what she was feeling. She couldn't even admit it to herself. "Good night."

"Night," he replied.

She could feel his eyes on her back as she crossed the yard and disappeared into the cabin. She shrugged off her clothes and crept back between the covers to lie, unsleeping, and wait out the night.

The next morning, Jonathan announced he was going to Idaho City. He had a yen to try out a few of the gambling establishments there. Alexis declined his invitation to join him, deciding instead to stay at the ranch and make friends with Li Ching. To Colter's pleasant surprise, Althea asked if she could ride with him as he checked the stock. He was proud of the Circle S, even in this early stage, and he wanted his bride to be just as proud of it. It would be her home, too. He wanted her to be as happy here as he was.

Now, as they rode side by side in silence, he looked over at her. She looked as lovely as he'd ever seen her, dressed in a light brown gown of fine lawn, a matching bonnet covering her hair. She rode sidesaddle, her back straight, her chin high.

She looks... untouchable, Colter thought.

"Come with me," he said, turning suddenly and leading them in a different direction.

The pine trees grew in a half-circle around the knoll. Before it stretched the gently rolling grazing land. In his mind, he could already see the two-story ranch house. It would have many rooms and would be white with a veranda on two sides. There would be lace curtains in the windows and fine furniture in every room. It would be a happy house, a home for laughter, the way his had been when he was a child. Of course, he hadn't grown up in anything like what he envisioned. His childhood had been spent in small shacks in mining camps, his mother working hard to clothe and feed her brood while his father sought that one claim that would turn their fortunes. And it had happened for them. His father had been lucky. But even before that, they had been happy, their house a home, filled with love and laughter—and that's what he wanted for his children.

Colter lifted Althea to the ground. "Here. This is where we'll build our house."

"When? When will we build it?" She moved closer to him.

"Soon, I hope. By next spring, I imagine."

Althea leaned against him. "Oh, Colter. I don't think I can bear it if I have to wait for you much longer." He started to put his arms around her, but she gasped and pulled away. "Whatever must you think of me?" she asked, wide-eyed. "I'd never have thought I could be so bold. I . . . I think we'd better go back. I'm not sure we should be alone right now. I . . . I'm not sure I can resist you as I should."

A hand on each arm, Colter drew her back toward him. He stared down at her, but she dropped her gaze demurely. He brought a finger up to her chin and tipped her head back, then slowly lowered his lips to meet hers. She placed her hands against his chest, as if in protest, but she didn't pull back. Her lips were cool against his. He wanted warmth, and he waited... hoping.

She drew away first. "I knew I couldn't resist you," she whispered. She swayed toward him. "Colter? Colter, come back with me to Willowind. Come back and marry me this summer. I...I don't want to live without you any longer."

She sounded so earnest, breathless, helpless. Yet as he looked down at her, he knew she *had* resisted him, despite her declaration to the contrary. She had been in total control throughout their kiss. Where was the girl who'd made his head spin? Hadn't there been fire, passion, in their kisses? No. No, when he thought about it, there had been few kisses, and those had all been chaste, kisses stolen quickly lest her mother would see them.

He shook his head. "No, Althea. I couldn't ask you to live in that cabin. It will be next summer before I can build our home."

"Then come live with me at Willowind until it is built." She threw her arms around his neck and stood on tiptoe, pressing herself against him.

He looked at her beautiful mouth for a moment, then suddenly took her elbow and steered her back to her horse. "We'd better get back. I've got work to do."

"Oh, Colter. You're being so selfish. Why won't you do what I want? You know we'd be happy at Willowind. Once this war is over, we could have grand parties. Everyone from miles around would come to meet you. Who would come to a party out here? There's nothing here.

No one. No one but the stupid Chinaman you have living with you. At Willowind you could have hundreds of slaves to work for you."

"I don't want any slaves," he replied, his mouth grim.

"You don't want. You don't want. Well, perhaps *I* do." Tears glittered in her eyes. "Do you ever give a thought to what I want? You're taking me away from my home and my mother and bringing me out to this wilderness." She choked back a tiny sob. "I don't know if I'm strong enough for this country."

"I don't know if you are either," he said, lifting her onto her saddle.

The tears vanished. She flashed her most becoming smile. "Then we can go back to Willowind. We can get married there and live there."

"No. We can't."

"But . . ."

His glance quelled her protest. He strode to his horse and mounted. He jerked his head. "We'd better get back to the house."

"I . . . I'm sorry, Colter," Althea whispered, new tears forming in eyes of blue. "I didn't mean any of it. I know I'll be fine once we're married. If this is where you want to live, I'll live here, even if it breaks my heart. I didn't mean to make you angry with me."

"I'm not angry, Althea. I just have work to do."

Alexis saw them riding back to the ranch house together and turned her mare in the other direction. She didn't want to see either of them right now. She was worn out from her sleepless night. Time and again, she had heard Althea's voice, stating that her marriage to Colter had nothing to do with love. She didn't want to believe what her sister had said—not any of it. Surely Althea didn't mean to say those things. Surely she loved Colter, loved him so much she'd come all this way to be with him.

I think I'd ride a long way to be with a man like him.

She remembered how he'd sat beside her last night and the things he had said. She remembered the way she felt.

I'd go to the ends of the earth to be with him.

Her stomach tightened. She felt both hot and cold at the same time.

Alexis kicked Nugget's sides, and they took off like a shot, racing toward the nearby mountainside. As they began to climb, their pace slowed until at last Alexis had to dismount and climb on foot as Nugget lunged up the steep incline. Reaching a ledge, she took pity on her mare. She removed Nugget's saddle, then sat on the ground, her knees pulled up against her chest.

How long she sat there, she didn't know. Time seemed irrelevant. Even her thoughts had no shape, no destination. She allowed the gentle spring breeze to blow away her muddled reflections and ruminations until nothing seemed more important than where she sat.

Was it a sudden movement that drew her eye? She tensed, not sure what was out of place, yet certain something was amiss. Then she saw it. It slinked cautiously along the side of the mountain, its long tail swishing slowly. Alexis got up and moved with care toward the saddle on the ground near Nugget. The mare twitched nervously.

"Easy, girl," she said under her breath as she unsheathed her rifle.

She turned again, her eyes scanning the hillside where she had seen the mountain lion. It seemed to have disappeared. Then she spied it once again. As she leveled her rifle, it stopped and turned its head, yellow eyes boring into her own. She hesitated, lifting her head, awed momentarily by the majestic strength and beauty of the wild animal. Then she gazed down the rifle sight once more and pulled the trigger, but it was already too late. The cougar leapt into the cover of trees a hair's breadth before the bullet plowed into the side of the mountain.

"Damn!" she swore under her breath.

She grabbed the saddle off the ground and swung it onto Nugget's back. Working quickly, she cinched it tight and hopped into the saddle, then kicked Nugget forward, on the trail of the golden mountain lion.

It never occurred to Alexis that she should be wary of tracking the big cat on her own. She had been hunting, with her father or by herself, for the better part of her life. She was confident of her own ability. Her eyesight was sharp and her senses keen, and she could outshoot more than her fair share of bragging men.

Unfortunately, Colter wasn't aware of her extreme competence.

Colter had seen Alexis riding off as he was returning with Althea. He had been half-inclined to leave Althea at the ranch house and follow after her, but he had resisted the temptation, going instead to the barn where he had some blacksmith work to do.

Li Ching was holding the halter rope of the big gelding when the rifle shot echoed through the air. Colter dropped the hoof and ran to the door, looking up into the mountains.

"Alexis is up there," he said, whipping off the heavy apron he was wearing. His saddle horse was still tied to the post outside. He ran toward him and hopped into the saddle, at a gallop almost before he could call back to Li Ching, "Take care of Althea."

His eyes scanned the mountainside. He began to climb at the most likely spot. It was hard to say where she had gone for sure or what kind of trouble could be waiting for her there. Hundreds of men were pouring almost daily into the basin north of here, and with them came trouble. If anyone had harmed her ...

Just then he saw something. It was a hat, lying on the ground. He rode toward it. It looked like Alexis' slouch hat. He jumped down and scooped it up. It was hers, all right. He studied the tracks around him. He could find only hers and her mare's. Who had fired that shot? What had taken her away in such a hurry? Puzzled, he got back on his horse and began to follow after her.

Any relief he might have felt from finding

only her tracks disappeared quickly when he saw what had drawn her rifle fire. He knew those feline prints all too well. Shaitan! The devil himself, as far as Colter was concerned. The mighty cougar, bigger than any other he had ever seen, killed for sport, not just for food. Colter had spent a lot of time tracking him last fall but had failed to find him. The winter had stayed quiet, and so he had thought he was free of the big cat for good. Obviously, he'd been wrong.

"Alexis," he whispered aloud, "be careful."

With as much haste as possible, he followed after her. He continued his climb for a long time, then their path turned, and he was following her back down toward the valley. Perhaps she had given up and was heading for the cabin.

Once again the mountain silence was cracked by rifle fire. Colter spurred his mount, and they scrambled down the side of the mountain. Two more shots sounded, these from a revolver. He whipped his horse forward with the ends of his reins. Was she trapped? Had Shaitan doubled back on her? Would he get there in time?

He saw Nugget first, standing alone, reins dragging the ground. Her nostrils were flared and she shied as Colter burst into view, but she didn't run away. Not far from the nervous mare, he saw Alexis. She was on the ground. He thought he could see blood.

Again he spurred his gelding. His pulse pounded in his temples. As he slid to a stop before her, she lifted her head and looked at him.

There was blood on her face.

"Alexis!" He kneeled beside her. "Where are you hurt?"

The question was barely out of his mouth before he saw what she'd been leaning over. It was Ebony, one of his brood mares. Her throat had been ripped open, and blood still pulsed from the wound.

"I was on his trail," Alexis said faintly. "I saw him take her down. I almost . . ."

Colter stroked the shiny black neck. Air and blood gurgled in the mare's throat as she struggled to breathe. His own throat felt thick. He couldn't swallow. His vision blurred, and he blinked back the tears. He got up and drew his gun.

"Get back," he told Alexis.

"Colt . . ."

"Get back."

Alexis rose and stepped away. Tears streaked down her cheeks unchecked.

Colter pointed the revolver at the mare's head and cocked it. "She was a good horse," he said softly. Then he fired.

They stood for a long time in silence, both of them staring at the dead mare between them. Finally, Colter sheathed his revolver and turned toward his saddle horse.

"She had a foal. He probably got it, too."

Alexis brushed away the drying tears from her face. "No. No, he didn't," she replied, light returning to her eyes. "I saw it. It ran that way." She hurried toward Nugget.

Colter's face was grim as they started in

search of the young black filly. "Even if we find her, she won't stand much of a chance without her mother."

"She'll make it. Orphan colts can survive with the right care."

He only shook his head, his heart still heavy over the loss of the mare.

They found the filly standing amid a rocky outcropping at the base of the mountain. As soon as she saw them, she was off and running, Colter and Alexis in hot pursuit. When Colter's lariat settled around her neck, she fought valiantly, her dark eyes filled with panic. Tired and scared, her fight slowly dwindled until Alexis was able to ease her way toward her, speaking softly, one hand extended.

"Easy girl. It's okay. Easy now. Settle down. Easy girl."

Alexis ran her hand gently over the quivering coat, talking in a soothing tone the entire time. Little by little, the filly's fear began to dissolve.

Colter got down from his saddle and approached Alexis, his eyes on the jittery filly. "She doesn't stand much of a chance," he repeated as he stopped beside Alexis.

Her gaze jumped to meet his—angry eyes, a fire in their icy depths. "She *will* make it. I'll see to it." Her voice lowered as the filly tensed. "If my aim had been truer, she wouldn't be an orphan now. Let me try, Colt. Please."

Her dusty cheeks were streaked from her tears. Her hair ribbon had been lost sometime earlier, and her hair fell in wild disarray about her face and over her shoulders. There was no hint of cologne, no rustle of skirts, no batting of eyes or pretense of weakness. Yet she seemed to him to be more woman at that moment than any he'd ever seen before. She was beautiful. And the way she was looking at him, her pale blue eyes pleading for his consent, he knew he could deny her nothing.

"You can try," he said, a sliver of a smile slipping into the corners of his mouth.

"Oh, Colt! Thank you." She stood on tiptoe and impulsively kissed him on the cheek.

His arms were around her before he knew what he was doing. He pulled her closer and his mouth descended on hers. She swayed toward him as their lips touched, but as the kiss lenghtened, her hands came up to his chest and she pushed at him. He ignored her at first, but as her struggle intensified, he reluctantly released her.

Her eyes were wide as she stepped backward. One hand flew to her mouth, and she felt her lips as if something still lingered there.

"Colt," she whispered.

She whirled away and ran to her horse. Once in the saddle, she looked back at him, a look of tragedy written on her face.

Colter reached out with one hand. "Alexis, wait . . ."

She spun her mare around and was gone.

Alexis galloped up to the cabin and dismounted. The door flew open, and Li Ching and Althea hurried out.

"What's wrong? Where's Colter?" Althea demanded.

"He's coming. Nothing's wrong." Alexis pushed her way past them into the cabin.

Althea followed right behind. "There was shooting! I've been frightened half out of my wits, and you tell me nothing's wrong. Don't you know I was here alone, totally helpless, with only that dumb Chinaman to protect me?"

"Oh, for Pete's sake, Althea. You're not totally helpless." She flopped down on her bed and covered her face with her hands.

All she could think of were his arms around her, his mouth pressing against hers, searching, demanding. And she had wanted to answer his kiss in the same manner. She had wanted to stay there in his arms. Even now, her blood ran hot with wanting him.

"Alexis?" Althea stood over her. "Where is Colter?"

"He's bringing in an orphaned filly," she answered from behind her hands. "He'll be along soon."

Her hands were pulled away from her face, and she found herself looking up at her sister. Althea's eyes bored into her own, questioning eyes, determined to find an answer. Slowly, her features twisted with anger.

Can she tell, Alexis thought as she tried to pull her wrists free from Althea's grasp. "Let go, Althea."

"I told you before. Leave him alone."

"I don't know what you mean."

Althea leaned closer. "You know. But you can't win. Not against me. Not this time." She shoved Alexis' hands back at her face. She turned her back to Alexis and walked over to her bed. When she turned and sat down, her face was serene once more. She smiled and said softly, "You see, Alexis, my dear. I know how to be a lady. And Colter wants a lady. You, on the other hand, are little more than a cowhand. True, you are prettier than most, and he may want to dally with you for amusement. But when he marries, he will marry me. You'll be wise to heed my advice."

They both heard the sound of approaching horses at the same time. Alexis watched her sister smooth her hair as she got to her feet.

Althea didn't look her way again as she walked to the door. "Colter, darling. What happened? We heard shots and then Alexis came back without you."

She closed the door as she went outside.

4

Colter didn't waste a lot of time preparing to track Shaitan. He couldn't afford to lose stock to the big cat. This time he had to find him and kill him.

Alexis watched him as he tied his bedroll behind his saddle. His expression was one of grim determination, and she was worried for him. She had seen the mountain lion in action and knew he was crafty.

"Don't you think you should wait for Father?" she asked. "He'll be back in a few days."

"I can't wait a few days. I can't let that cat kill any more of my horses or cattle. Ebony will be only the first of many unless I stop him now."

"Then let me go with you. I'm a good tracker, and I'm good with a rifle, too. I wouldn't miss him a second time."

He hesitated in his packing, then turned to look her way. "I can't give him a chance to kill you either," he replied softly.

"But you're in much more danger traveling alone."

Colter only shrugged and turned back to his saddle. He pulled his rifle from its sheath and checked the ammunition, then slid it back in place. He took his horse's reins and led the animal toward the cabin. Alexis followed along behind.

Althea was seated at the table when he stepped through the doorway. She looked up as he entered.

"I'm leaving now. With luck, I'll be back in a day or two, but don't worry if it takes longer. I've tracked him before and he's smart. It may take a while to outwit him."

Althea's glance was cool. "And how are we to be safe from this beast while you're away? I would have thought you'd care for me before your silly cows."

It was a long, thoughtful moment before Colter replied. "If you're afraid to stay here while I'm gone, Li Ching can take you into Boise City. You can stay with Sadie, and I'll come for you when I get back."

"I may do just that."

Colter bent slightly forward, as if he would kiss the top of her head or her cheek, but he stopped suddenly. His jaw stiff and his eyes clouded, he turned on his heel and strode out to his horse.

Alexis was standing just outside and had to

step back as he came through the door. She had witnessed Althea's selfish protest. She wanted to somehow make up for it.

"Colt!" she cried, following quickly after him. "If you won't let me go along, what can I do here to help?"

He swung into the saddle. His gaze swept across the valley floor, then dropped to her. "Stay close to the house and . . . keep an eye on the horses."

"I will."

He pressed his heels against his mount's ribs, and they jumped forward and galloped away. Alexis watched him until he'd disappeared from view. When she turned around, she found Althea standing in the doorway, her hands clenched at her sides.

"Li Ching, get the buggy. You're taking me to Boise." Althea whirled around. "I'll show him not to leave me alone in this godforsaken country. Cherry, just leave everything here. Colter can bring it with him when he comes to apologize."

Alexis hurried after her sister. "Althea, you're making a mistake. You should be here when Colt returns."

"Alexis, do you know what your problem is?" Althea asked as she began throwing things into a valise. "You're trying to give advice to a woman, and you don't even know how to be one yourself. Well, here's a lesson for you, just in case you ever *do* wear skirts. Colter will come back, and when he sees that I am gone, he will come all the way to Boise to see me and to apologize for leaving me alone so disgracefully. And, of course, seeing how guilty he feels, I will forgive him."

"You're wrong, Althea."

Althea looked at her sharply.

"I may not have known him as long as you have or as well, but he's not the kind of man that can be manipulated for long. Even love can only stand so much."

Althea picked up her valise and brushed past her sister. "Li Ching, where's that buggy?"

"Don't go!" Alexis cried. "If you love him, don't go."

But Althea wouldn't heed her advice. She climbed into the buggy and sat staring straight ahead while Cherry climbed in behind. Li Ching shook his head as he took his place beside her and snapped the reins. Without a backward glance, they were off.

Alexis leaned back against the side of the log cabin. "You're hurting him, Althea," she whispered, tears coursing down her cheeks, "and you're a fool for doing it."

Alexis kept herself busy working with the orphaned filly. She christened her Lucky—after all, she *had* escaped the mighty lion's claws. If that wasn't luck, she didn't know what was. Alexis coaxed her to eat a bran mash, in addition to hefty helpings of hay. Lucky had a good appetite and thrived on Alexis' attention. It looked as if luck would continue to be with her.

Several times during the day, Alexis saddled her horse and rode out to check on the cattle.

Things remained quiet.

The spring air turned cool early in the evening in these mountains. Alexis stood in the doorway of the cabin, hugging her arms against her breasts. She had been alone for two days, and it looked as if she would spend this night alone too. Jonathan hadn't returned from Idaho City, apparently the willing captive of the card tables. It was not a new experience for Alexis, and she wasn't worried about him. Li Ching hadn't returned from Boise either. Alexis could only assume he was waiting until Althea was ready to come back.

It was thoughts of Colter that caused the tiny furrows in her forehead. Was he all right? She had seen the power and craftiness of the lion he sought. Was it possible that Colter was in danger even now?

Alexis shuddered and stepped back inside, closing the door. She had to quit thinking of Colter that way. She was obsessed with thoughts of him, and she had no right to those thoughts. Colter was her own sister's fiance. He would soon be her brother-in-law.

"Besides," she said aloud, "you couldn't have him if you wanted. Althea's right about that. He wants a lady, not a cowpoke."

A jagged mirror hung on one wall of the cabin, and Alexis went over to it. She ran her fingers over her smooth complexion, failing to see the perfection in her high cheekbones, the look of aristocracy in her straight, slender nose, the seductive fullness of her rosy lips. She only saw a girl dressed in buckskins. A long-haired boy is what her sister had implied.

Could she be a lady?

She went to the clothes Althea had left behind. She looked quickly through the dresses, at last selecting one that appealed to her. It was a soft shade of aquarmarine made of linen, the skirt having several tiers, the bodice snug and daringly low. She tossed off her trousers and shirt, then slipped into her sister's dress. Once it was fastened, she turned again to the mirror. Slowly, she swept her hair up from her neck, catching it with pins into a chignon at the nape of her neck. Pale wisps curled around her face, refusing to be confined.

Is that really me? she marveled as she stared at her reflection. Can a simple dress change so much?

She reached out and touched the cool mirror with her fingertips. Inside, she felt as cold as the glass. She felt as if something was suddenly lost to her. She was empty and alone. She was no longer who she had been before.

Grabbing a shawl from Althea's pile of clothes, Alexis hurried outside. She walked hastily toward the small pen where Lucky was corralled. The black head snapped up as she approached, and wary dark eyes assessed her every move.

"See? Even you don't know who I am," she whispered to the filly. Lucky came over to the rail, and Alexis reached through to scratch her behind her ears. "That makes two of us."

A great sadness washed over her. She wanted to cry, but she wasn't quite sure why. She leaned her chin on the top rail of the pen and closed her eyes, while around her the earth cooled as dusk turned the sky to pewter and then to steel.

Colter rode wearily down the mountain. He had been two days without sleep, but it had been worth it. The pelt of the mighty Shaitan was hanging across the back of his saddle. He had thought of little else but finding and killing the big cat during the long hours he had tracked him, but ever since he had turned his horse toward home, his thoughts had been on matters closer to his heart.

He couldn't figure out what was the matter with him. He had always been the sort of fellow who decided what he wanted and then pursued it with a singleness of purpose. Even his father had said he'd never met any one so dogged and determined when he found something he wanted. Even as a boy, Colter had always seemed to know what he wanted and just how to get it. So why was he confused now about Althea?

He tried to recall how he had felt when he asked her to marry him, but all he could remember was how often he had struggled to remember her face after he returned to Idaho. He had been more angry than happy when he learned she was coming out here. It shouldn't have been so. And once she was here, it seemed that all the little mannerisms that had charmed him at Willowind now rubbed him the wrong way.

Colter leaned back in his saddle as horse and rider slid and slipped their way down the steep path, shale and rocks rolling ahead of them in tiny landslides. Once at the bottom, he dismounted and loosened the cinch to let his gelding rest. He touched the yellow pelt and felt a moment of elation. At least this adversary would stalk him no more. Though there would be other problems for him to face at the Circle S this summer and in the years to come, Shaitan, the devil cat, wouldn't be one of them.

Alexis' image entered his thoughts. She had wanted to come along with him, and there had been times in the past hours when he wished he'd allowed her to come. There had been moments of doubt as he tracked the crafty mountain lion, moments when he could have used another sharp eye, another steady hand with a gun.

But it wasn't really her agility with firearms that he thought of now. It was the way she looked at him sometimes, the way he knew she understood how he felt. It was her eagerness for life. She was vibrant and unspoiled. She looked the world straight in the eye, yet saw it at its best. She could be feisty and she could be tender. She could laugh and she could cry.

Colter knew she would share his triumph over the lion. He could envision her now, standing in those revealing trousers of hers. She would rejoice in his victory and be glad he'd returned safely. She would smile, showing neat rows of pearly-white teeth. Her ice-blue eyes would flash with excitement.

He felt a sudden urge to tighten the cinch and head for home, eager to see in person all that he had imagined. He never once thought of hurrying back to Althea.

"Althea?"
Alexis gasped and whirled around.
"What are you doing out here?"
"Colt." She spoke his name like a caress. "I've been so worried."

He stepped closer. She could sense his eyes trying to see her more clearly in the darkness. Her breathing quickened at his nearness. She wanted this moment to last for an eternity. If it could go on just like this, she would ask for no more. Just to be near him.

He lifted a hand and cupped her chin. She closed her eyes as a tiny sigh escaped her lips. She didn't care about Althea. She didn't care about anything or anyone but Colter. If he could be hers for only a little while . . .

Colter drew nearer, and she opened her eyes again. She could make out his features now and knew his mouth was solemn, his eyes still uncertain as he watched her. She realized she was holding her breath.

When his mouth descended toward hers, she let her neck bend backward, eagerly awaiting his kiss. Their lips touched, and it was like hot coals landing in a drought-stricken forest. Heat surged through her. She felt weak in the knees. She leaned against him, her arms circling his neck. His lips moved across her cheek and down her throat. She drew a ragged breath.

"Oh, Colt, hold me. Hold me forever," she

whispered. She loved him. She felt as if she'd always loved him. Long before they met, she had loved him. And now, here in his arms, she couldn't stop the words from slipping forth, confessing her need for him.

His mouth paused. She couldn't bear it. Any moment he would come to his senses. He would step away from her, and once again, he would belong to Althea. Her fingers tangled themselves in his sandy mane, and she tried to bring his lips back to hers. She wouldn't think of what she was doing. She wouldn't let him stop. Not yet. Not yet.

"Where is everyone?" he asked, his voice hoarse with emotion.

"Gone."

He swept her up in his arms and carried her toward the cabin. The door was still ajar, and he kicked it open before them. The fire had burned low, able to cast only a flicker of light over the room. Colter carried her to Althea's bed where he laid her down, brushing aside the clothes she had scattered across it earlier.

He stood silently above the bed. Alexis could feel him drawing away from her, succumbing to reason. She held out her arms toward him, a plea in her voice. "Colt?"

He eased down onto the bed and gathered her back in his arms. While his lips plied hers, his hands pulled the pins from her hair, setting it free to spill across the quilt. His kisses left her hungry for more. She felt lightheaded, and a strange warmth in the pit of her stomach made her arch her body closer to his. Nothing in her imagination could have prepared her for this moment. She wanted him. She needed him to quench this ache as she knew only he could.

Alexis ran her hands up and down his back, feeling the tight cords of muscles across his shoulders. A soft groan slipped between her lips as his kisses trailed across her cheek and down to her throat. Her breath came in tiny gasps. She was drowning in a sea of pleasure, and the last thing she wanted was to be saved from her fate.

Suddenly, he drew back from her. The flickering light from the fireplace was reflected in his eyes. She saw his question and knew what her answer should be. Yet she could not squelch the passion that he had ignited with his kisses. Reason had no place within these walls this night. With trembling hands she slipped the first button of her bodice through its loop.

Alexis lay awake long after Colter had drifted into an exhausted slumber. Her body still thrilled at the memory of his touch; her lips still longed for the taste of his kisses. But her heart ached with a pain she'd never known before. He wasn't hers. He would never be hers. She had stolen him for a brief moment, and now she must pay for it. When daylight came, he would see her as she was—a fallen woman, one who would bed her own sister's fiance, a woman unfit for the love of a decent man.

A tear slipped from the corner of one eye, dropping to Colter's muscular shoulder. He had thought she was Althea. The words of love he had whispered in her ear had been meant for her sister. He had carried her to Althea's bed where he'd thought he was making love to his bride—prematurely, perhaps, but still his bride. How he would loathe her for deceiving him when he learned the truth with the coming of day. She couldn't bear to see what would be in his eyes. And what if he felt duty bound to make an honorable woman of her? To have him marry her out of obligation would be too terrible to bear.

Carefully, she slipped out of his arms. The air was cold on her nude body, and she sought her clothes and dressed with haste. By the dying embers, she scribbled a note to her father, saying only that it was time she was on her own and not to worry about her. She asked him to give her love and best wishes to Althea and Colter on their wedding day. Then she signed it *Alex* and left it on the table.

Before going outside, she went to stand once more beside Althea's bed. Colter had one arm thrown over his eyes. He was uncovered above his waist, and she could see the steady rise and fall of his chest. She longed to reach out and touch him one more time, to feel the taut muscles of his trim form, to feel the power—his mysteriously gentle power—as he took her to himself.

"I do love you, Colter Stephens," she whispered, turning away. "Please forgive me."

Alexis didn't know where she was headed for sure, but she couldn't risk seeing Althea, so she turned north. She made her way carefully by the gray light of false dawn, hurrying Nugget's pace as the trail became clearer with the rising of the sun. She gave no thought to food or drink. She paid no heed to her tired body. She steeled herself against the aching of her heart, blanking out the vision of Colter's face as he leaned near; shutting out the memory of his lazy smile, his twinkling brown eyes, his confident stance; forcing into forgetfulness all recollection of his searing kisses, his tender caresses. Step by painful step, she shut away the love that burned so fiercely for Colter. As long as she couldn't feel the love, she wouldn't feel the pain either.

It was with a frozen heart that Alexis lay down that night, not to sleep but to stare with unseeing eyes at the starry heavens.

Colter shifted. His arm reached out to pull her against him, but he found nothing but cold emptiness. He opened his eyes and glanced around the cabin. Daylight filled the room. He was surprised that he had slept so late, yet was in no hurry to rise, not when he could lie a little longer with her beside him.

Thinking she had stepped outside to attend to her morning toilet, he closed his eyes once more and smiled as he remembered their hours of lovemaking. What a fire had blazed between them! And she must love him as he loved her. Alexis! Just thinking her name made him long to go looking for her, made him want to hold her in his arms and never let her go, made him want to crush her perfect, naked body against his and feel her passionate response.

Oh, he knew he had problems. Jonathan had trusted him, had thought his daughters would be safe here, and he had betrayed that trust. And then there was Althea. There would be an ugly scene when he broke their engagement. Hell hath no fury . . .

Colter had learned a lot about Althea since she'd followed him to Idaho, one thing being that she wouldn't give him up easily. Not that he believed any longer that she truly cared for him. She had decided to marry him for some reason known only to her, and she wasn't going to cotton to being jilted.

He wondered what it was that he had felt for Althea. He knew it couldn't have been love, now that he knew what love felt like. What had it been that caused him to propose? Was it the unaccustomed atmosphere of the Southern plantation and the fluttering feminity that had surrounded him there? All that paled beside the image of Alexis. She needed no forced feminine airs or frilly clothes to prove she was a woman. And she was *his* woman.

Colter placed an arm beneath his head and stared up at the ceiling. He wondered when it was that he had first known it was Alexis he loved. Was it the time he saw her pull her gun on Martin, or was it when they reached the summit the day they rode up here from town and they shared the special knowledge of the beauty of this land? Was it when he heard the rifle fire when she was alone in the hills or wasn't it until last night when he heard the way she whispered his name?

Colter smiled slowly, then shook his head as he sat up. No matter how much he enjoyed thinking about Alexis and last night, he couldn't lie in bed all day. He had work to do. He threw off the covers and jumped out of bed. He felt an excitement for facing a new day that he'd never felt before. He stretched, then pulled on his trousers as he whistled softly to himself.

He heard the door open and turned with a smile. "Alexis..."

Jonathan stood in the doorway. His gray eyes took in Colter's eager greeting, his bare chest, the rumpled bed. He stepped inside and placed his saddlebags and bedroll on the table. In doing so, he saw the folded paper with his name printed neatly on the outside, the note that had gone unnoticed by Colter. He picked it up and read it in silence.

He lifted his eyes to meet Colter's gaze, then handed him the slip of paper. He gave the younger man a moment to read it before asking, "Do you love her?"

A pained expression filled Colter's eyes. He'd thought she loved him. Yet she'd run away from him, expecting him to marry Althea even after all they had shared.

"Do you love her?" Jonathan repeated.

"Yes," he replied, and waited for the chastisement—and more—that was his due, but it never came.

Instead, Jonathan sat down at the table. He ran his fingers through his hair, then sighed as he shook his head slowly. "Seems to me you've got a few things that need tendin' to before you can go after her. Where's Althea?"

"I... I'm not sure. In Boise City, I think."

"You'll have to tell her yourself that you're

calling off the engagement." He paused before adding, "But I don't think I'd tell her about Alexis. Let her down as easy as you can. She sure as heck isn't going to make it easy on you."

"No, sir, I doubt she'll make it easy."

"She never was the right girl for you, Colter. It's better for the both of you that you learned it now instead of after the wedding. I found that out from marrying their mother. Pretty as they come, but no heart. It hasn't been easy for Althea, and it's not all her fault that she is the way she is. No, she was never the right girl for you."

"I guess I knew that even before she came out here. I just didn't want to admit it to myself. I didn't want to admit I could make such a mistake."

"I've seen it for a long time. You and Alex belong together."

"I don't know, Jonathan," Colter said as he sat down across the table from him. "I'm afraid she'll never forgive me for... for what I've done."

"If you love her, she'll forgive you. But it may take a little time to convince her of that, else she wouldn't have taken off." Jonathan stood up suddenly. "Well, you'd better get dressed and get down to Boise. You don't want the trail growing too cold before you can follow after her."

Colter got to his feet, too. He stood for a moment, looking at Jonathan Ashmore, then held out his hand. "Thanks, Jonathan. I'll make her happy. I promise."

Jonathan accepted the proffered hand. "Yes.

I expect you will. If you don't, you'll have me to tell the reasons why."

Althea met him in the parlor of the Houston home. A gleam of triumph lit her dark blue eyes as she smoothed the billowing skirts of her dress. For a few moments, she let him stand, unacknowledged, in the doorway of the room; then she lifted heavily lashed eyes and raised delicate brows in feigned surprise.

"Why, Colter? I didn't know you'd come to town. I hope you didn't hurry here on my account. Sadie has been just wonderful to me, pampering me most thoroughly. Where is she now? She'll be terribly glad to see you."

"She knows I'm here. I asked if I could speak with you alone."

"Really, Colter? My, that does sound serious." She patted the sofa beside her. "Then come sit down and tell me what's on your mind. I do hope it's not bad news about that dreadful animal."

Colter walked toward her but chose to sit down in a separate chair. "No, it's not Shaitan. I killed him two days ago."

"Well, that's a relief."

Colter stared at his dusty boots. This was even harder than he had thought it would be. How do you tell a woman that you don't love her after all? That you've discovered you never loved her, only thought you did? Especially when the woman who taught you how to love was her own sister. How was he to tell her without being cruel? And even while he wondered how to tell her these things gently, another corner of his brain was remembering how he had lain with Alexis only a few short hours before, how just her breath on his skin stirred a thirst within him that seemed unquenchable. He wanted to tell Althea quickly what he had come to say and then be on his way. He had to find Alexis. He had to find her quickly.

"Colter, darling, whatever is the matter with you? Has something else gone wrong on that little ranch of yours?"

He smiled unconsciously as he remembered just exactly what had happened on "that little ranch" of his.

"Colter?" A sharp edge had crept into her voice.

"Althea, I've never thought myself a coward," he said as he got to his feet and moved across the room, "but right now I'm thinking differently. I don't know how to say what I must."

Something intuitive must have warned Althea of what was about to come. She rose quickly and went to stand beside Colter. She placed her right hand possessively on his shoulder and swayed close, brushing her breasts against him. "My love, you could never be a coward. And besides, whatever is troubling you, we can see it through together."

They were just the right words, just what she should have said at that moment, but they were hollow words—words she had been trained to say—and he knew it. He saw things so much more clearly now than when he had first seen her on the veranda at Willowind.

"Althea, it's time for you to go home. You don't belong here."

"But, Colter, I belong anywhere you are." Her left hand came up to rest on his other shoulder. Her eyelashes brushed her cheeks as she glanced down. "I know I'm not cut out for such a rough country, but . . . but I'm willing to learn if this is where you choose to live. Of course, Willowind will one day be mine and we could . . ."

"No, Althea. You don't understand. I want you to go back to Willowind for good. Without me. I'm calling off the wedding."

"You can't mean that."

"I do mean it."

Althea's fingers tightened on his shoulders. "But you love me, Colter Stephens. You *must* marry me."

He tried to ease away from her, sorry for what he had to say. "I *thought* I loved you."

"Thought! You *thought* you loved me? You *do* love me!" Her voice rose with each word.

"Althea . . ."

She slapped him hard. Her eyes glared pure hatred. "Don't you think you can get away from me so easily, Colter. You've promised to marry me. You've compromised my reputation by bringing me out west. You *will* marry me. My father will see to that."

Colter stood, unflinching, before her. Neither the slap nor her tirade angered him. Mostly he felt sorry for her. He hadn't ever meant to hurt her, and that was, indeed, what he had done. She may have brought some of it on herself, but it made it no less easy to know what his part in this had been.

"Althea, your father knows I'm breaking off the engagement. He agrees it's for the best."

"No! No, I don't believe it. He couldn't. He couldn't do this to me." She backed away from him, her face pale.

Colter lifted his hand toward her in a gesture of compassion. "He's outside. Shall I get him for you?"

With a sudden shriek, Althea reached for the nearest thing at hand—a vase filled with flowers—and hurled it at his head. Colter ducked just in time, and it shattered against the wall behind him, water soaking the wallpaper and pieces of glass and flowers flying everywhere. Before he could right himself, another object was thrown at him. The corner of the picture frame hit him squarely on the forehead, drawing blood.

"You'll not do this to me. You'll not. Do you hear? I'll not be humiliated this way." She reached for another vase.

"Althea, stop. This is insane."

She threw it at him.

"Althea!" Jonathan stood in the doorway.

Tears were streaming down her cheeks as she turned startled eyes toward her father. "He loves me. He *has* to love me. Don't you understand? He *must* love me."

Jonathan went to his oldest daughter and hugged her to him. "Why does he have to, Althea? Do you love him so much?"

"She'll never forgive me if I lose him," Althea replied with a gasp.

"Do you mean your mother?"

"She wanted him for Willowind. She'll hate me, too, if I don't bring him back with me."

"Oh, Althea." It was a statement of sadness. "What has she done to you? What have *I* done to you?"

Althea crumpled against him, succumbing to the bitter tears.

"Hush, baby," her father whispered into her hair. "Ssh."

"No . . . nobody . . . loves me," Althea choked through her sobs. "Nobody . . . has ever . . . loved me."

Jonathan's face was a picture of anguish as he held her tightly and let her cry out the years of pain. Colter met his gaze, then turned slowly and left the parlor.

5

Alexis stirred. Sometime in the wee hours of morning she had drifted into a troubled sleep. Her body was cold, she ached from head to toe from sleeping on the hard ground, and she was hungry. So hungry, in fact, that she thought she could smell bacon frying.

She sat up and opened her eyes...and found herself staring into a bushy, gray beard and dark, studious eyes.

" 'bout ready for breakfast?" a voice asked from somewhere within the beard.

Alexis cast a sly glance to her side, assessing just how quickly she could reach her revolver if necessary. It wasn't there.

"Put your gun up yonder," the man said as he stepped back from her. "Folks tend to wake up a mite suspicious and aren't always too sociable. But now that you've looked me over, if'n you'd feel better with it on, you go right ahead and get it. Me, I'm going to have me a bit to eat. Care to join me 'fore you go runnin' off?" With that he turned his back to her and walked over to the campfire.

She remained still, watching him carefully, but her initial apprehension had waned. He was a short fellow, even shorter than she was, and judging more from his voice and the gray in his beard than from what little she could see of his face, she guessed him to be about fifty, maybe more. He was wearing a blue flannel shirt (several sizes too large) and trousers patched with buckskin. He wore an old boot on one foot and a brogan on the other. A battered slouch hat, part of its brim missing, covered his hair. His creased forehead was blackened by smoke from the campfire.

He swiveled his head around, and she thought he must be smiling at her. He held out a plate toward her, filled with bacon and fried eggs, their yellow yolks runny. "Better join me. I'm not a great cook, but I'm the only one for a ways yet. You don't look too prepared to do much cookin' from what I can see."

Alexis couldn't help herself. She *was* hungry. She got to her feet and walked over to the fire. She accepted the battered tin plate and a bent fork he was holding out toward her and squatted on her heels to eat. "Thanks," she said, taking her first bite without delay.

He took his own tin and settled on a rock near the fire. "Don't usually get much company up this way."

She kept her eyes on her plate, not wanting to answer any questions. He seemed to understand.

"Got me a claim down the trail a ways that I'm workin'. Not much in it, but I scratch out enough to buy me some grub and keep on goin'. Course, closer you get to Idaho and on up that way, the better the pickin's. Sarah—that's my mule over yonder—she doesn't seem to mind that this ain't the richest claim in the basin, so's I don't see no reason why I should complain. Besides, it's quieter this way. Nobody wants to jump a claim that's not payin'."

"Why do you stay?" Alexis asked as she sopped up the last of the eggs with her bacon.

The man's eyes sparkled. "Got gold in my blood, girl. Once that happens to you, you just keep on lookin', always thinkin' the next claim will be a better one." With a sudden sweep of his hand, he removed his hat. "I beg your pardon. I've gone and forgot my manners. My name's Jones. Thaddeus Cyrus Ulysses Jones, at your service." He chuckled. "Most folks just call me Reckless."

"Reckless?"

He got up and put his dirty plate in the pack on Sarah's back. "Seems I get myself into a scrape every now and then that folks say is my own fault . . . 'cause I'm so reckless."

"I see." She was warming to the old fellow with the shaggy beard.

Reckless pulled his hat down over his head again as he leaned against Sarah and stared at Alexis. He cleared his throat. "Listen, girl. It ain't none of my business, and I usually try to mind my own, but it looks as if you've started off from someplace in a mighty big hurry. Could be you're runnin' away from trouble, and you don't have to tell me what it is. Ain't my business, like I said. But something tells me if it's trouble, it's not really of your makin'. Least I'd guess you to be an honest girl. What I'm tryin' to say is this. If you need a place to stay and think you could trust an old geezer like me, you're welcome to stay with me awhile. I ain't got but a shack, but I try to keep it clean, and it's warmer than outside at night."

Alexis eyed him solemnly. For no special reason, she trusted him. She did need a place to go for a while. If she went to Idaho City or Placerville or any of the other bustling towns in the basin, her father or Colter just might find her; that is, if they were looking for her. She didn't want to see anyone right now. This might be just the solution to her problem.

She got up and carried her plate over to Reckless. "My name's Alex. I've been in a few mining camps, but I don't know how to mine. I can hunt, and I can cook. I don't mind working hard, and I could use a place to stay. If you really mean it, I'd like to come help you on your claim for a while, as long as you understand that I can leave any time I want."

"Any time," he replied, taking the plate and dropping it beside the other in the pack.

"One more thing. There might be someone following me that I don't want to see. I'd like to cover my tracks."

Reckless merely nodded and picked up Sarah's lead rope. "You go right ahead and cover 'em up. Sarah and me will move on, and you can follow along behind. Makes no difference if nobody knows where I am."

Alexis watched them head up the trail, then she saddled Nugget and rode in the opposite direction. She did her best to leave an obvious trail, even pulling some strands from Nugget's tail and leaving them on brush near the trail. When it seemed clear that even a blind man could see where she was going, she took Nugget into the creek and turned her back toward the spot where she'd met Reckless. It was hard going. The water was high with the spring runoff, and the rocks were slippery with moss, but Alexis didn't allow Nugget to leave the water until she found a sandy inlet. She rode the mare into the underbrush, then dismounted and returned to the water's edge where she swept all traces of their exit away with a branch. She carefully checked the brush for evidence of their passing but saw none. Satisfied, she remounted and hurried after Reckless and Sarah.

The lead horse shook his head and snorted, then stomped his foot impatiently. Colter lifted another trunk up to the driver.

Behind him, Jonathan stood beside Althea, her hand firmly held in the crook of his arm. Her face was pale. Her eyes were glazed from lack of sleep and from crying. Jonathan's heart ached for this child he hardly knew, and worse, guilt weighed heavily on his soul. Part of him wanted to turn his back on her. She was so many of the things he disliked—selfish, underhanded, devious. Yet, she was his daughter, and much of what she was had been shaped by her parents—her mother by her presence and her father by his absence.

And so here he stood, ready to board the stage with her. He was going back to Virginia, to Willowind, and perhaps even to Madonna. He might never again see this vast, unruly land that had become his true home. Already he could feel the yoke of responsibility weighing on his shoulders.

Colter came toward them, his own expression grim. "They're ready to load up, Jonathan."

Jonathan took a step, drawing a listless Althea with him.

Colter put a hand on his shoulder to stop him. He looked at Jonathan for a long moment, then turned his gaze to Althea. "Althea, I hope someday you'll forgive me. I . . . I truly am sorry."

She looked up at him with blank blue eyes.

Jonathan tugged at her once more, moving them toward the waiting stage. He took her hand and helped her inside, then turned back to face Colter one last time. "She'll be all right, Colt. She just needs a little time. Once she gets back to Willowind . . ."

"I never loved you, Mr. Stephens."

Startled, Jonathan and Colter both looked into the stage. Althea was leaning forward, the blankness gone from her face.

"I don't know if I know how to love. I'm not sure if I've ever loved anyone, and I don't think anyone's ever loved me. But you were so handsome and you were rich and you weren't fighting in that cursed war. You would have been so right for Willowind." Her eyes began to swim with tears. "I'm a lady, Mr. Stephens. I'm what you should want, not that creature in men's clothing. It's all so mixed up." Like a mask, the blank facade dropped over her features once more.

"Althea," Colter said, but there was no drawing her back from the dark recesses of her mind where she had chosen to hide.

Jonathan gripped Colter's arm and turned him around. Softly, he said, "You mustn't worry about her. She'll be with me and with her mother. Remember that this isn't your fault. If anyone's, it's mine. I'm too irresponsible to be a father. Alexis has taken better care of me than I ever took of her." He shook his head, then added, "Now you go find her. I don't want her wandering around out there by herself. She needs you." He swallowed back the lump that threatened to rise in his throat. "You tell her I love her and that I'm thinking of her all the time. And after the two of you are married and start having a family, you come back to Willowind and see me."

"We'll do it, sir."

They clasped hands firmly, gazing at each other with understanding. Abruptly, Jonathan whirled around and hopped into the stage, closing the door behind him.

"We're ready, driver," he hollered.

With a crack of the whip and a shout, the stage jumped forward.

Reckless had not exaggerated. His home was, indeed, nothing more than a shack. The tiny cabin listed to one side, making Alexis wonder if it would hold up under the next gust of wind that might whistle up the draw at any moment. Daylight filtered easily through missing chinks in the cabin walls. There was a cast iron stove for cooking and heating, which seemed quite luxurious compared to the rest of the place. Her host tied a rope across one corner of the cabin and flung two blankets over it, providing Alexis with some privacy. Their beds were made of straw and blankets, but after helping Reckless pan for gold all day, Alexis had no problem sleeping on it.

Reckless never asked questions, and he seemed to be talking all the time. Yet, it didn't take Alexis long to realize that he already knew more about her than she did about him. He made her feel comfortable, and for no reason she could discern, she would find herself telling him things she had never told anyone before in her life, not even her father.

But she kept silent on the subject of Colter and Althea. She was too ashamed of what she had done to confess it to anyone. How they must hate her, but they couldn't hate her more than she hated herself. And what made her feel worse was knowing she still wanted him. She wanted to be with him now more than ever. It was a feeling she had to fight, had to destroy before it destroyed her. She no longer admitted she loved him—she had stifled that thought the night she had left his side—but her desire for him still burned strong. She could only hope that she would never see him again.

Reckless worked his claim for long hours every day. The winter had been a mild one, the snowfall less than normal. He had to work while there was water available. When Alexis wasn't helping him look for color in his pan, she went hunting for fresh meat for their supper. Reckless would have been just as satisfied on hardtack and gravy—or so he said—but Alexis wasn't. She roamed the mountains and found herself falling in love with the country all over again.

Few traces of the venison steaks could be seen on their plates. Reckless pushed his chair back from the table and patted his stomach. "That was mighty good, Alex."

"Thank you, T.C.," she replied. T.C. was the new nickname Alexis had given him, short for Thaddeus Cyrus.

"Can't say as anyone's ever fixed venison better to my likin', except maybe my ma. Back home, we used to have venison real regular."

"Where's back home?"

Reckless tipped his chair back against the wall. He pulled his pouch of Lone Jack from inside his shirt and filled his pipe. Holding his pipe in his mouth with one hand, he drew a phosphorus match across the sole of his boot. He puffed heartily on the pipe until satisfied that it was burning. His smile was hidden in his beard, but Alexis could tell it was there as a thin ribbon of smoke began to twine its way toward the ceiling.

"Home was Kentucky when I was a young'un. Ma grew nearly everything we ate in a little patch of ground out back of our place, and Pa filled it out with the venison."

"How long has it been since you were there?"

"Long, long time. Ain't home no more. Stopped bein' home when the folks died when I was 'bout eleven or so. Wasn't any other family to keep me there, so I came West." He paused and drew silently at his pipe, then added, "They were good folk. Not perfect, but good."

Alexis cleared the dishes from the table. "Sounds like my father—not perfect, but good."

Reckless waited expectantly.

Alexis leaned against the wall and stared out the open doorway. "You know, Reckless. Most people have dreams about something they want to have or do or be, but they never reach for them. Where I come from, there were rules to follow, and most people just follow them, whether they like them or not. My papa was different. He went after what he wanted. He didn't want much. He just wanted to be free to do what he wanted, when he wanted." She chuckled as she turned to look at Reckless. "I guess what I'm saying, if I'm going to be entirely honest, is that he never wanted to grow up. But he was always such a *good* man."

"Sounds like you miss him."

"I do," Alexis confessed as she returned to her chair at the table.

"Is he dead?"

"No."

"Then why don't you go see him?"

Alexis shook her head with great sadness. "I can't."

"Mmmm."

Silence cloaked the room as Reckless continued to smoke his pipe and observe his blonde guest.

Early the next morning, Alexis slipped from the shack and went to bathe in the creek. The morning air was crisp and the water icy cold, but she shed her clothes and waded into the midst of the roiling stream. She scrubbed herself with the harsh soap, lathering her hair too. Her teeth were beginning to chatter as she scrambled back to the bank and wrapped herself in a scratchy wool blanket.

The smattering of airy clouds that dotted the sky were dyed the prettiest of pinks and lavenders by the rising sun, and Alexis hesitated a moment to appreciate their beauty. She didn't hear the hoofbeats until the horse was nearly upon her.

A long, low whistle slipped from the rider's lips as he drew his horse up short.

Alexis gasped as she gripped the blanket tighter in a futile effort to hide herself from view. The blanket was molded to her wet skin, concealing little from the man's appreciative gaze. Her own eyes fell, and it was then she realized the full state of her undress. With another sharp gasp, she bolted for the shack. Just before she reached the door, Reckless stepped outside, and she nearly collided with him as she rushed for shelter. Once inside, she peered out through the cracks in the cabin's walls.

"Didn't know you had company, Jones," the stranger said as he dismounted, his glance drifting momentarily toward the shack.

"What do you want, Anderson?" Reckless responded. It was the first time Alexis had heard anything less than a pleasant tone in his voice.

"Thought we might talk about the palace."

"You can talk, but it won't get you nowhere." Reckless started walking, and the stranger fell into step behind him.

Alexis grabbed her clothes and dressed in a hurry. She didn't want anyone else to stumble in on her. She had never felt so vulnerable in all her life, and she hadn't liked the way that man's eyes had seemed to devour her while she stood before him.

She ran a comb through her hair, carefully working out each snarl, then tied it back with a piece of rawhide. Now that she was dressed, her confidence was returning. Curiosity was beginning to replace fear. She wondered who the stranger was and what he needed to talk to Reckless about. She decided to follow after the two men, but before leaving the cabin, she strapped on her holster—just as a precaution.

Reckless was standing near the sluice, his back to the stranger, when Alexis arrived. She stopped and watched them, unobserved for the moment.

The stranger was clad in a black broadcloth

suit. His hair was a reddish blond shade, worn just long enough to brush the collar of his coat. He was young, maybe 25 or so, and he appeared to be only a few inches taller than she was, but he had an air of assurance about him that seemed to add to his height and years.

Sensing her presence, he turned, and she was once again caught by his appraising gaze. His hand came up to remove his black hat and he bowed. He was smiling as he straightened. She decided, reluctantly, that he was quite handsome with his neatly-trimmed, reddish blond beard and mustache, his straight nose, and his dark brows over hazel eyes.

"I apologize, miss, for my earlier lack of manners. I hope you'll forgive me." He tossed a look toward Reckless, but the old man was ignoring them. "Let me introduce myself. Derek Anderson, at your service."

She made no reply.

Derek didn't seem bothered by her cool stare. He continued to smile confidently as he turned toward Reckless once again. "We'll talk more about this, Jones," he said.

"We can talk. Won't do no good."

"Good day, miss," he said to Alexis as he walked by her.

"Who is he?" she asked, once he was gone.

"He owns a saloon in Idaho City. He's ambitious. I think he means to own the whole town someday."

"What did he want with you?"

"Like I said, he wants to own it all, even what little I've got."

Alexis looked back toward the cabin. "I hope he doesn't come back. He makes me feel uneasy."

"Oh, he'll be back," Reckless said with a chuckle. "After seeing how pretty you are, I don't doubt but what he'll want to own you too."

Her back stiffened. "Well, that's one thing no one will ever do. I can't be owned."

Colter was beginning to wonder if he would ever find Alexis. He knew the trail he had found had been left deliberately to mislead him. Yet it was his only clue, and so he returned to it again and again, scouring the area for another lead, going both up and down the creek. He was about to give up and turn his horse for Idaho City when he saw the chimney smoke curling through the trees.

He rode into the clearing and stopped his horse. There, in a tiny corral, stood Nugget. Colter dismounted and headed for the ramshackle cabin. He knocked but there was no answer. He was about to push open the door when a voice behind him said:

"Get away from that door."

It was Alexis. He'd found her.

"Turn around. Slow."

A smile was creeping into the corners of his mouth as he obeyed.

"Colt."

His name was spoken in something akin to horror, and his smile quickly vanished.

"What are you doing here?" she asked.

She was standing at the edge of the clearing. She wasn't wearing her hat, and her hair fell free over her shoulders. Her shirt sleeves were rolled up, as if she'd been working, and the legs of her trousers were wet. She held her rifle in her right hand, the muzzle now pointed toward the ground. It was all he could do to stop himself from rushing forward and taking her forcefully into his arms.

"I've come to take you back to the Circle S," he replied.

"No."

"Alex," he began, searching for the right words, "you must come back with me. I . . . I'm sorry for what happened, but I intend to make it right. We'll get married right away."

"What about Althea?" Her voice was barely more than a whisper.

"Jonathan has taken her back to Willowind."

She winced as if she'd been struck.

Colter took a step forward and held out a hand toward her. "Your father wanted me to come after you," he said, hoping Jonathan's approval would convince her to forgive him.

The rifle came up. "Go away, Colt. Go after Althea. It's her you should marry. What happened between us was an accident. It should never have happened and it won't ever happen again."

"But . . ."

"No, Colt. I'm staying right here. We made a mistake, but I won't let us pay for it by making another. Go marry Althea. Make things right. No one will ever know what . . . what happened." As she spoke, her eyes grew colder until he thought he would be frozen by her icy stare.

Colter didn't know what else to say. He had taken her to his bed in a rage of passion. He had known she was hurt, even angered, by his impropriety. But he loved her, wanted to marry her, wanted to make things right. Why wouldn't she let him? Maybe asking forgiveness was the wrong tack.

Colter stiffened his back and said firmly, "Alex, I promised your father I'd take care of you and that's just what I intend to do. You're coming with me."

"In a pig's eye," she snapped back.

"Now listen here . . ." He was starting to get angry.

Like two wrestlers sizing each other up in the ring, Alexis and Colter stared at each other. Into the midst of it, Reckless came walking back from the creek. He stopped abruptly when he saw them.

Colter looked at him and demanded, "Who's that?"

"That's T.C. This is his place."

Colter turned his attention to the older man. "I've come to take Alexis back with me."

Reckless was silent as he returned Colter's gaze, then shifted his eyes to Alexis, standing stiffly with her rifle ready. He began to shake his head slowly and his voice sounded amused as he replied, "Son, from the looks of her, nobody's takin' her anywhere. Now, I get the feelin' you two know each other right well and that you don't mean her no harm, but if Alex says she doesn't want to go, then I don't aim to help anyone take her." He glanced back at Alexis. "Alex?"

"I won't go with him."

Reckless nodded. "Then, son, I'm going to have to ask you to leave."

"I don't know who you are . . ." Colter began.

"I'm her friend," Reckless answered.

A wave of helplessness washed over Colter. He couldn't force her to go with him. He looked at Reckless and was convinced that this man was, indeed, Alexis' friend. At least he could be assured that she was safe.

"All right. I'll go."

Alexis lowered the rifle, and for just a moment, he thought he saw a spark of something in her eyes that wanted him to stay. He started to open his mouth to ask her one last time to forgive him, but he swallowed the words as she turned her back to him.

Disheartened, he stepped up into the saddle and turned his horse back down the trail . . . alone.

Alexis listened as he rode away. Tears glistened in eyes that moments before had shown no emotion at all. It had been worse than she had imagined it would be. He had come for her, and just as she had feared, he had come because he was going to do right by her, not because he wanted her. Her own father was so ashamed, so disappointed in her, he had gone back to Willowind with Althea. But not before making Colter promise to make an honest woman of her.

There had been a moment, when Colter was demanding that she come with him, that she had almost relented. Just to be with him. To be his wife. To lie with him at night. To hear his voice in the morning. But then she had remembered that he loved Althea. She knew she couldn't bear to be with him when he was longing for another.

Reckless placed an arm around her shoulders. "Do you love him so much?"

She stiffened and blinked away the tears. "No. No, I don't love him at all," she lied, almost believing the lie herself.

6

Idaho City, the largest city in the Northwest with over seven thousand residents, had two principal streets, both of them lined with saloons, hotels, restaurants, general and specialty stores. With close to another ten thousand men—and some women too—filling the Boise Basin, many of whom came into Idaho when they took a day off from their mining, the place was the epitome of a "rip-roaring town."

And mining wasn't entirely left behind in the hills of the basin. It went on right in the city, under the houses and businesses and in the streets. Those unfortunate enough to have their buildings collapse after being undermined by placering didn't find it as exciting as those who were panning as much as sixteen dollars a day right in the middle of town.

A smoky haze hung over the mountains,

evidence of the nightly bonfires that burned as the miners worked round the clock, trying to get as much gold as they could before the spring runoff ceased. Missouri wagons blocked many of the side streets, and the streets themselves were gutted with ditches and sluices. The ringing of shovels was audible above the murmur of rushing water. The valley was nearly stripped of trees, the wood needed for the sluices and the many new buildings of the boom town.

Alexis rode along Montgomery Street beside Reckless, her eyes darting from one side of the street to another. It was the first sign of real emotion she had shown in over two weeks, and beneath his grizzled beard, Reckless was smiling at her. There were probably hundreds of reasons why Idaho shouldn't have appealed to her. It was rowdy, filled with men crazed by gold fever and those who preyed on them; murders were frequent; churches were few. But at the moment, Alexis wasn't thinking of any of those reasons. Her pulse quickened and her eyes sparkled as she drank in the sights and sounds of Idaho City.

With the advent of June, the water supply was failing, and with it, the profitability of the placers. Reckless claimed no interest in lode mining. "Can't see no reason anyone would want to go down in the earth before his time," he'd told Alexis. So he suggested a few days in town, "to get supplies and see the sights."

Alexis hadn't really been interested in accompanying Reckless, but he'd been so kind to her that she couldn't find a good enough reason to deny him. Now that they were here, she was glad she had come. She hadn't realized how isolated she had been for the last month.

"Alex, I got me some business to attend to. Why don't you look into a few of these ladies' shops? Buy yourself something pretty."

"What would I do with a dress, T.C.?"

"Bet you'd look right pretty in one," he responded.

"No. It's not for me," she answered softly, remembering all too clearly what had happened the last time she had worn a dress.

With a lot of mumbling, Reckless got off Sarah and shook out his legs. "Dang mule. Don't know why I keep such an uncomfortable animal." He slapped Sarah's rump, then patted her neck. As he wrapped the reins around a hitching rail, he looked up at Alexis, squinting at the sun from beneath the rim of his hat. "Do an old man a favor, Alex. Just go look. If you want somethin', buy it." He handed her bag of gold dust.

"T.C...."

He shook his head firmly and walked off.

Alexis sighed. He'd been too good to her to refuse. She'd go and she'd look, but she wasn't about to buy anything.

She dismounted and tethered Nugget next to Sarah. Stuffing her hands inside the pockets of her trousers, she stepped onto the boardwalk and began walking down the street. Finally, she stopped in front of a narrow, whitewashed building with large glass windows framing the door. The displays were filled with lady's hats and gloves and a manikin with a bright pink dress on it. The letters on the glass said *Rachel's Fine Fashions*.

Taking a deep breath, she opened the door, planning to glance quickly around and depart. That way she could tell Reckless she had gone into a store, looked, but found nothing she wanted.

"Oh, my stars! Oh, this will never do."

A tiny woman hurried from the back of the shop. She couldn't have been even five feet tall. Her gray hair was perfectly coifed, and she was wearing a prim white blouse and dark brown skirt over her slightly plump figure. A pair of spectacles perched precariously on the tip of her upturned nose.

"*Tchk, tchk*," she clucked as she walked around Alexis. "No, this will never do." The woman stopped and bent her neck back so she could look up at Alexis. "My dear young woman, you have certainly come to the right place. You are desperate for some motherly advice. This may be a long way from what those in the states consider civilization, but we still must keep up a pretense of it. We can't have lovely young women such as yourself running around displaying themselves in such ... *Tchk, tchk*. My heavens, no." She grasped Alexis by the arm and towed her toward the back of her shop.

Alexis was in shock. She didn't know what to do—laugh or be angry at the woman's protestations.

"I'm Rachel Cane. I'm a widow, but I simply forbid anyone to call me Widow Cane. You may call me Mrs. Cane. I think you're much too young to call me Rachel. Now, let's get you out of that dreadful garb."

Nimble fingers immediately began to unfasten Alexis' clothing. Before she knew what had happened, Alexis was standing naked except for her drawers. She clasped her arms across her bare breasts, speechless at how quickly and effortlessly Mrs. Cane had accomplished her goal.

"My dear, I wasn't wrong. Those dreadful clothes were displaying a very lovely figure indeed. Now, while it's perfectly all right to tantalize the men, we must remember that we are ladies."

"Mrs. Cane," Alexis responded, finally shaken out of her mute state, "I have no desire to *tantalize* the men, no matter what I'm wearing. Now, please excuse me. I'm going to get dressed and leave."

Before she could reach for her clothes, however, Mrs. Cane scooped them up and tossed them out into the middle of the empty shop.

Mrs. Cane faced Alexis, clutching behind her back the curtains which separated the two rooms. She drew herself up as tall as possible and declared indignantly, "Would you have me ruined with the ladies of Idaho? Dear child, I am only a poor widow woman who must make a living in this town. And it's not easy, I'll tell you, not with only a handful of women living here. If those women don't buy from me, I'll starve." Her face had taken on a truly stricken appearance. "If you walk out of here wearing those dreadful clothes, what woman of fashion is going to come to me for advice again? Please, I beg of you, take pity on me."

Alexis thought she had never seen anyone who needed pity less than Rachel Cane. Suddenly, the whole preposterous scene struck her funny and she began to laugh. "All right, Mrs. Cane. Dress me up. Please."

"I knew you'd come to your senses. The moment you walked in the door, I said to myself, Mrs. Cane, there's a bright but very misguided young woman. Underneath those trousers is a beautiful flower waiting to blossom. That's what I said to myself."

"I'm sure you did, Mrs. Cane."

The door of *Rachel's Fine Fashions* opened, the tiny bell tinkling softly, and Alexis stepped outside. She felt dazed. She had no idea how long she had been in the shop, but in that time, Mrs. Cane had thoroughly transformed her from the girl who had first refused her help.

The blue and white striped foulard underskirt was full, its yards of fabric covering several stiff petticoats. The short overskirt, looped with two long lapels, was of blue and white figured alpaca, trimmed with a pinked frill of blue silk, as was the matching scarf fichu. The attractive white lace bonnet was tiny, little more than a decorative headdress, her pale blonde hair falling in tight ringlets from beneath it. Under her arms, she carried more packages, including one hiding the clothes she had worn into the store.

Alexis felt unsure of herself, and Mrs. Cane's assurances that she was the picture of loveliness and would have men falling at her feet didn't help matters any. She decided her best course of action would be to wait for Reckless with the horse and mule. She would change back into her old clothes as soon as they got back to the cabin.

Encumbered with her armload of packages, Alexis didn't see the extra step in front of her and tripped. Her parcels scattered before her, and she would have fallen headlong across the boardwalk if it weren't for the strong hand that suddenly grabbed hold of her arm and hauled her back.

Her face was flushed and she was gasping for breath inside the unaccustomed corset. Flustered, she turned to thank her rescuer.

"I wouldn't have believed it," he said. "You're even more beautiful than I remembered." Derek Anderson still held onto her as his eyes traveled the length of her new gown.

"Please, Mr. Anderson," she replied, tugging her arm free.

She bent to pick up her packages, but he quickly gathered them up for her. "I'll carry these. Let me walk you to where you're staying."

Alexis glanced up the street. She didn't know where they would be staying, and she didn't think she would want him to know if she did. She picked up her skirts and started down the street without her packages.

Derek was beside her in a flash. He was grinning as he took her arm in a familiar manner. "At least tell me your name so I don't have to keep referring to you as that girl with Reckless Jones."

She gave him an icy glance and removed her arm once more.

He stepped in front of her, halting her progress. "Please, miss. You're being unfair. What have I ever done to harm you? Why don't you like me?"

"I'm not sure, Mr. Anderson," Alexis answered honestly.

Instead of looking upset, this brought another smile to his face. "Well, at least we're getting somewhere. I don't know your name but I know you don't like me."

She almost smiled.

"There. That's better. Look, I know you're new here. Let me show you around town—especially the Golden Gulch. You shouldn't miss seeing it. It's going to be the showplace of the territory some day soon."

Alexis raised an eyebrow in question.

"It's my saloon." He stepped backward and lifted his free hand as if she were holding a gun on him. "I promise. No funny business. I'd just like you see that I'm a businessman in this town. And, in case you're not aware of it, I might add that owning a saloon is a totally respectable business."

Alexis hesitated, and that seemed to be all Derek needed for encouragement. He took her arm once more and led her down the boardwalk, right past Nugget and Sarah, not slackening their pace for several blocks. Suddenly, he pulled her right out into the middle of the street and turned her to face the two story building. *The Golden Gulch*, a sign proudly proclaimed, but Alexis couldn't see much else different about it than most of the buildings lining Montgomery Street.

"Someday this is going to be the greatest saloon in Idaho City, maybe even the whole Northwest," he said with pride.

Curious to see the inside of this "great" saloon, Alexis moved willingly beside Derek as he escorted her through the swinging doors. Though she had peeked more than once into the saloons and gambling establishments that her father had patronized in California, he had never allowed her to enter one. She was greatly disappointed, then, when the first one she was allowed to enter looked hardly more impressive than a hotel lobby might. There was sawdust on the floor. Plain kerosene lamps hung from the ceiling over the tables.

"This is only the beginning. Anyone who really wants to can make it rich here. And I want to. The Golden Gulch is doing enough business now that I'm ready to expand. I've ordered materials to build a heavy bar, and I've got a large mirror coming up the Columbia. We're going to knock out that wall and make the place twice as big. I already own the building beside us."

Alexis was trying to be polite as she answered with reserve, "That's all very interesting. I do appreciate your showing it to me. Now, I must be going."

"The lady doesn't want to be here, Derek.

Isn't it clear to you?"

Alexis looked in the direction of the feminine voice. A young woman, about her own age, was standing on the stairs leading up to the second story. The first thing Alexis noticed was her hair. It was a flaming red shade, and her dress was the same color. Her face was artfully painted, bringing out her high cheekbones and full mouth. She came down the stairs slowly and wound her way through the tables until she stopped in front of Alexis. Her bright green eyes flicked over Alexis before her mouth twisted in a sarcastic smile.

"It takes a real woman to exist in a place like this. I think this one's too much of a lady to make it. You'd better look elsewhere, Derek."

"Shut up, Stella," Derek hissed.

But Alexis didn't need his help. She fixed a frigid glare on Stella. She was utterly expressionless except for the coldness of her eyes. After a moment or two, Stella faltered and turned away.

Alexis determinedly removed her elbow from Derek's grasp. "I do thank you for offering to show me around, Mr. Anderson, but I really must leave. Thank you for carrying my packages." She held out her arms for them, and reluctantly, he passed them to her.

"Please. At least tell me your name."

Although he had more than once shown a proprietary air toward her, she had to confess that he had behaved in a gentlemanly fashion. He had stared at her rather boldly up at Reckless's camp, but then she hadn't exactly been overdressed at the time, either. She decided to forgive him for that indiscretion and to give him the benefit of the doubt.

"All right, Mr. Anderson. I'll tell you. My name is Alexis Ashmore."

"Where are you staying?"

She shook her head and started for the door. He beat her there, swinging it open wide. She stepped through without glancing at him. It was then that she noticed the building on the other side of the street for the first time.

The building was made of board and stone. The front had windows all the way across, but these were covered on the inside with white draperies, hiding the interior from view of passersby. The massive entrance in the center of the three-story building had four doors, and above these, the words *Ice Palace* were spelled out in pieces of cut glass and mirrors, making every letter sparkle as brilliantly as diamonds.

She stopped so suddenly, Derek almost bumped into her as he followed her out the door.

"Is that a theatre, Mr. Anderson?" she asked him.

"No. No, it's just a saloon like mine."

It was hardly "just" like his, but she wasn't about to tell him so. Whereas she hadn't cared much if she went into the Golden Gulch except for Derek's proclamations of its grandness, she was filled with curiosity about the interior of the Ice Palace. Anything so beautiful outside, had to be exquisite inside. She was about to ask him if he might be able to escort her through it, but when she glanced at him, she knew it would be a foolish request. There was undisguised envy and anger written across his face.

She turned suddenly on the heel of her new shoes and began walking away. "Good day, Mr. Anderson." She was relieved that he didn't try to follow her again.

Reckless was sitting on a bench near the animals. When he saw her coming, he got to his feet and removed his hat from his head. "Well, I'll be. If you're not the most beautiful gal in all of Idaho, I'll eat this hat of mine, and that's a promise."

Alexis was getting a little tired of everyone's exclamations over how she looked in a dress. She wished she'd just ignored Reckless and stayed in her buckskins and boots. Still, she gave him a warm smile.

"Thank you, Mr. Jones. It's kind of you to say so."

Reckless offered his arm to her. "If you'll hang on, Alex, I'll show you where we'll be stayin'." As they began to walk, Reckless added, "I hope you don't mind, but I've asked a friend of mine to join us for supper tonight."

"Of course I don't mind, T.C."

Reckless chuckled. "One thing's for sure. Sam isn't going to expect my fellow miner to be anyone as pretty as you are."

"Thank you, Mr. Jones," she said one more time.

Samuel Wainwright didn't look the type to leave a thriving law firm in a civilized city to search for adventure in the wilds of the West, but that was exactly what he'd done a few years before. He was a thin man, almost spindly, with receding black hair and an aquiline nose, a nose his close-set eyes seemed always to be looking down in haughty disregard. This appearance, however, was an unfortunate act of nature. Sam Wainwright was, in fact, a very affable fellow, when someone gave him the chance to exhibit other qualities than his excellent ability with the letters of the law.

In Philadelphia, he had grown tired of the dreary cases the partners of the firm kept shuffling his way. One day, he woke up and knew he was leaving. He packed his bags, called on his mother and father, and then left Philadelphia without a backward glance. He arrived in Idaho City a year ago, and he decided to stay there as quickly as he'd decided to leave the East. Thaddeus Jones was his first client in Idaho. Sam was probably the only person in these parts who called Reckless by his given name, but when an attorney has for his client one of the wealthiest men in the territory (albeit the client's wealth being a little known fact), he finds it a little difficult to call him "Reckless."

Sam had been surprised when Reckless dropped in on him earlier in the day, requesting some changes in his business holdings and, more importantly, changes in his will. He had been alarmed to learn that Reckless had acquired a woman partner on his new placer and that he intended to leave her much of what he had in the event of his death. Sam was, therefore, most anxious to meet this Alexis Ashmore and find out just what her game was.

When Reckless stepped into the doorway of the dining room, clad in a broadcloth suit, his hair slicked back and his beard washed and combed, Sam was speechless. He'd never seen the man in anything but a miner's garb. Then Reckless held out his elbow and he was joined by the loveliest creature Sam had ever seen. Without even being aware of it, he rose from his chair, watching as Reckless escorted the young woman across the room.

"Sam, you can close your mouth now," Reckless said, chuckling, as they arrived at the table. "Alex, this here is Samuel Wainwright, Esquire, my very capable attorney at law. Sam, this is the delightful young gal I was telling you about, Alexis Ashmore, my partner."

"Miss Ashmore," Sam managed to reply.

"I'm very pleased to meet you, Mr. Wainwright."

Coming to his senses, Sam pulled out the chair next to him for her. She sat down and smiled her thanks up at him. He was finding it hard to remember his former suspicions of the lady, but he forced himself to think about them again as he took his seat.

"What brings you here, Miss Ashmore?" he asked.

Reckless shook his head at Sam. "That is a subject she prefers not to talk about, Sam. Ask her instead how she likes it here."

Sam looked at Alexis with the question written in his eyes.

"I've seen very little of Idaho City. It would be hard to say if I like it or not, but it is certainly lively enough for anyone's tastes. But of all the places I've traveled with my father, I like this territory the best."

"And why is that?" Sam wondered aloud.

Alexis' gaze moved to Reckless and she smiled fondly. "Because I've made such good friends here."

Sam couldn't help but believe her feelings were genuine. Still, Reckless would be bestowing great wealth someday on this stranger, and even though he had been sworn to secrecy by Reckless, Sam intended to protect his friend from this young woman if she gave him the slightest reason to believe she was a fortune hunter, set on deceiving a friendly old eccentric. Besides, who could really believe that a girl as pretty as Alexis would choose to live in an old shack in the middle of nowhere just because she'd made friends with a miner such as Thaddeus Jones. Unless, of course, she was keeping an eye on her future.

Sadie Houston snapped the whip over the horse pulling her buggy. She wasn't one to waste time lollygagging along the way. She had business at the Circle S.

Li Ching had been in town the day before and had indicated to her, through elaborate sign language, that things were not well at the ranch. Since she was aware of Jonathan and Althea's departure and that Colter had been going to follow after Alexis, she could only assume that Li Ching's message was that Colter hadn't found her.

Sadie trotted the buggy right up to the ranch house. She hopped down from her seat just as the door swung open. Li Ching's anxious face appeared in the doorway.

"Hello, Li Ching. Is Colt around? I've come to pay a visit, since he hasn't been to see me in so long." She tried to sound cheerful. She didn't want Colter to know Li Ching had asked her to come up.

Li Ching stepped aside, but instead of following her in, he hurried off toward the barn.

The scene that greeted Sadie was even worse than she had expected. Colter was seated at the table, bare to the waist and unshaven, one leg up on the table, the other on the chair beside him. A full glass and a half-empty whiskey bottle were on the table in front of him. He looked up at her with drink-glazed eyes.

"Sadie! What are you doing here?"

"Colter Stephens, I just might ask the same thing of you." She marched over and slapped his foot off the table. "Look at you. I've never seen anything so pitiful in my life."

"It's none of your business, Sadie," he replied, reaching for the glass filled with the dark, golden liquid.

"The heck it ain't!" She knocked his other foot off the chair and sat down. With a quick hand, she grabbed the whiskey bottle and set it on the floor behind her. "Now, it's time you tell me what happened, boy. Landsake, Colt Stephens, don't I think of you as one of my own? You keep this up, and I just might turn you over my knee and give you the paddlin' you deserve for actin' so stupid. Now you tell me what's going on and you tell me right now."

"She turned me down," he answered flatly.

At least Sadie knew now that he'd found Alexis and that she was all right. With that off her mind, Sadie could deal with the immediate problem with a little more concentration. "So? She turned you down. Is that any reason to become a sot?"

There was a spark of anger in his eyes now, and he straightened in his chair. She could almost see his mind beginning to clear. She glanced toward the corner of the room and spied the coffee pot on the stove. She got up and went over to the stove where she grabbed a cup from a nearby shelf and filled it to the brim with the hot, thick brew.

"Drink it," she ordered as she set the cup before him.

Colter stared at it for a moment or two, then obeyed. Sadie waited in silence until the cup was drained, then carried it back for a refill.

"Now," she said, passing him the second cupful as she sat down again, "tell me everything."

"I found her staying with an old miner. I think she's helping him work his claim. Don't worry, Sadie," he said, noticing her sudden alarm. "I think it's all okay. He seemed to be a true friend to her."

"Go on."

"I told her I'd come to take her back with me, that I was going to marry her."

"What a wonderful proposal," Sadie

mumbled under her breath, but he didn't seem to hear her.

"I told her I'd promised her father I'd take care of her. After what happened between us . . ." He stopped abruptly.

"I'd guessed as much," Sadie admitted. "Go on."

"Well, after that, I didn't see how she could refuse me. After all, I was just trying to do right by her," he finished, his indignation proclaimed in every word.

Sadie stared at him, her mouth set in a grim line. When at last she spoke, it was not with a voice of conciliation but one of irritation. "I'm surprised she didn't fall right at your feet with gratitude."

Colter's expression was mystified.

"Tell me, Colt. Did you bother to tell the girl you loved her? Did you bother to *ask* her to marry you?"

"Sadie, she must have known I love her. After all, we . . ."

"And does that always have anything to do with love?"

"But why else would I traipse all over these mountains if I didn't love her?"

"Out of sense of guilt. Out of some code of chivalry. Because you're an honorable man. Because Althea wouldn't have you anymore or because Jonathan Ashmore had threatened to kill you if you didn't."

Colter got up from the table. He rubbed his forehead in a gesture of confusion. "But those reasons had nothing to do with it, Sadie," he protested. "I went because I wanted to find her. I love her. I want her here with me."

Sadie got up too. She had accomplished what she'd come here for. "I know that, and you know that. Seems to me you need to tell Alexis that." She headed for the door.

Colter followed her outside. She was already in the buggy by the time he reached her. He squinted up at her, his eyes unaccustomed to the sunlight. "Thanks, Sadie."

"Don't thank me, Colt. Just bring your bride to see me every once in a while."

"I'll do it, Sadie."

7

Alexis had had a wonderful stay. She'd fallen in love with Idaho City. It was bawdy and naughty, yet it also had charm and an air of growing respectability. Besides liking the town in general, she had made friends during the few days she and Reckless had been here—Mrs. Cane, who had already made her two more dresses; Sam Wainwright, who had taken her to the Jenny Lind Theatre one night; and perhaps Derek Anderson, though she still had reservations about him.

They left town early in the morning, hardly before the sun was up, yet they were not the only early risers. They could hear the pounding and hammering of the carpenters as Idaho City gave birth to new buildings, the temporary canvas structures giving way to more permanent ones as the town expanded its boundaries.

Noting her wistful expression, Reckless

assured her, "We'll come again."

"T.C."

"Hmmm?"

"Thank you for bringing me here. I feel better than I have in a long time."

"Wasn't anything."

She pulled back on the reins, stopping quickly. "You're wrong. It's helped a lot. I . . . I wanted to do something special to thank you." She pulled a small package from inside her shirt. "Here."

"Well . . ." Unable to find more words, he accepted the gift and removed the brown paper wrapping. Inside was an American Horologe watch with a gold hunting case, adorned with an etching of a mighty stag, and a heavy gold watch chain.

"Look inside," she encouraged him.

Reckless popped the cover open and read aloud, "To my true friend with love, Alexis." There was a threat of tears in his dark eyes as he looked over at Alexis. "I've never had a nicer gift, Alex. I thank you."

They smiled at one another, an easy camaraderie shared between them, as if they'd known each other for years instead of weeks. In unison, they clucked to their mounts and turned again for their home in the mountains.

Several days later, Sam found an excuse to visit Reckless's cabin, bringing with him a bundle of papers needing his signature. Alexis was out hunting when he arrived.

As he handed Reckless his new will, Sam

couldn't repress his look of chagrin. "I guess I'd better confess it, Thaddeus. I was skeptical of Alexis at first. I couldn't believe a young, beautiful woman would choose to live out here with an old geezer like you unless she knew he was rich and trying to snare him for a husband. I want you to know I think I was wrong. She genuinely cares for you."

"She's not to know about this, Sam. I know you've always kept a confidence, but I can see you're a bit smitten with her yourself, so be careful." He began signing his name. "She doesn't have any idea about . . . well, about what I own in Idaho. I don't want to spoil the ease we have with one another by her thinkin' she's got to treat me different."

"I don't know how else she could learn about it. Nobody knows about your assets but you and me."

"Anderson knows about the Ice Palace. He's been after me to sell it to him for months."

"Derek Anderson?"

"Yup."

"Don't do it, Thaddeus, and keep your distance from him. I don't trust that fellow."

Reckless chuckled. "Sam, sometimes I think you're just an old woman the way you worry and fuss about the littlest things. Anderson's just an ambitious pup who likes to throw his weight around every now and then."

"I don't think so," Sam countered, a deep frown creasing his forehead, his eyes darkening.

Reckless was just putting the final swirl on his last signature when the door flew open and

Alexis burst into the room, holding a rabbit by his hind feet.

"Here's supper," she announced before realizing they had a guest. "Sam!" she exclaimed.

Sam had never seen her in her buckskin trousers and leather boots, nor was the slouch hat on her head like any of the bonnets she had worn in Idaho City. Once again he was caught with his mouth agape because of her.

"Hello, Alexis," he said hesitantly.

She sensed his surprise over her attire and laughed. "Oh, Sam. I'm sorry if I've shocked you. I'm afraid this is what I'm more accustomed to wearing than any of Mrs. Cane's creations."

He'd recovered himself enough now to deny her need for explanation. "I think you look terrific, Alexis. I wouldn't change a thing."

She knew he was lying. Sam might have thought he left all the little rules of polite society behind him when he left Philadelphia, but in truth, he brought a good many of them along with him, one of them being that a lady *never* wore trousers.

"Tell you what," Reckless interjected, seeking to dispel the awkward moment. "Why don't you two youngsters go for a little ride while I skin this critter, and when you get back, we'll have us a bite to eat."

Sam turned hopeful eyes to Alexis. "I'd like that. Will you go with me?"

"Of course Sam. That is if you don't mind my wearing britches." Again she chuckled and led the way out of the cabin.

* * *

Reckless was glad to see Alexis looking happy. Oh, he knew she still cried at night. He often awoke in the dark to hear her sniffling. Poor gal. She was still very much in love with that fellow who'd come for her. He wasn't sure why she was so stubborn about refusing him, especially when he'd come a long way to get her. If he wanted her and she wanted him, it was hard to understand why the two of them couldn't get together.

Anyway, for now Alexis' mind was on happier things. Reckless was thankful to Sam for helping out, but he hoped Sam wasn't fixing to get his own heart broken in the process. Reckless grabbed the rabbit off the table and headed outside, but he had no time to begin skinning it before another guest arrived.

Derek brought his fancy black to a halt and tipped his hat. "Jones."

"Anderson."

Derek dismounted. "Is Alexis around?"

"No, she's gone for a ride. I'll tell her you were here."

"Well, it wasn't really her I came to see. I wanted to talk to you about the Palace again."

Reckless laid the hare on a nearby tree stump. He shook his head, wondering what it was he would have to say to Derek to convince him he wasn't going to sell him anything.

Derek moved closer. "Listen, Jones. I know you own lots more than the Ice Palace. So you're eccentric and don't want anyone to know. Well, I've never told anyone, and if it's so important to you that it stay a secret, why hold onto the saloon?"

"I've got my own good reasons for keeping the Palace, and it's none of your concern what they are," Reckless replied a bit gruffly.

"Aren't you rich enough?" Derek asked, spitting out each word with frustration.

Reckless reached slowly into his pocket and pulled out the watch that Alexis had given him. "You see this watch, Anderson. All my real wealth is right here. This is what has made me a truly rich man."

Angry, Derek grabbed for the watch, but Reckless wouldn't let go.

"Turn loose," he snarled.

"Not a chance," Reckless responded.

Suddenly, Derek released his hold and gave Reckless a harsh shove. Thrown off balance, Reckless stumbled backward, tripping over the tree trunk. He twisted as he fell, trying to catch his balance, but he landed awkwardly on his neck and shoulder. There was an audible snap, then nothing.

"You old fool," Derek mumbled as he stepped over the miner's still form.

He took the watch from his hand, but Reckless made no move to stop him. It was then that Derek took a close enough look to discover the old man was dead. It shouldn't have happened. It hadn't been a bad fall. Reckless shouldn't even have been hurt, let alone killed. Yet, he was undeniably dead.

"You old fool," Derek repeated as he looked at the watch. It wasn't an expensive watch, certainly nothing to fight over. *All his wealth*, he had said, and for it, Reckless had died.

"Over a stupid watch," Derek muttered as he stuffed the time piece into his pocket, then hurried for his horse and galloped away.

Colter's sorrel gelding was winded, his neck glistening with sweat, as they cantered up to the cabin. He had pushed the horse hard to get here as quickly as he did, but once he'd decided he was coming, there was no stopping him. He hopped down from the saddle and was already rushing for the door, ready to call out her name, when he spied the old man's body in a heap on the ground.

Instantly alert, his eyes scanned the area for signs of trouble, then he hurried toward Reckless. He knelt beside him but knew at once that he was dead. Touching his hand, he also knew he hadn't been dead long.

Alexis!

He was ready to rise and go in search of her, his heart pounding in his ears—What if something had happened to her, too?—when he heard the approaching horses and looked up.

Alexis rode into the clearing, her tinkling laughter preceding her. The angular fellow with the black hair riding beside her was first to see Colter. It was his startled look that alerted Alexis of something amiss. Her gaze swung around and clashed with Colter's. Then she saw Reckless on the ground beside him. She flung herself out of the saddle and hurtled herself across the space separating them.

"T.C.? T.C., what's wrong? It's Alex, T.C."

Colter placed a gentle hand on her shoulder. "He's dead," he said simply.

Eyes wide with horror, she replied, "He can't be. We . . . he was fine when we left. T.C.? T.C.?"

Colter took her firmly by the shoulders and pulled her to her feet, forcing her to meet his gaze. "Alex, he'd dead. His neck's been broken." Softly, he added, "I'm sorry." Then he pulled her against him, seeking to provide a haven for her sorrow.

She didn't cry. She was too stunned to cry. Reckless had become her friend, a surrogate father. He couldn't be gone so quickly. She still needed him. He couldn't be dead. He couldn't be.

Sam spoke for the first time. "How did it happen?"

At the question, Colter released his hold on Alexis enough so they could both turn to look at Sam. The lawyer's glare was accusing. Colter felt Alexis stiffen as the horror of Sam's suggestive look dawned in her mind.

Almost angrily, Colter responded to her thoughts. "I don't know how it happened. I just rode in a little before you and found him where he is. He must have fallen over that stump somehow."

She relaxed, the thought forgotten. "I know you didn't hurt him," Alexis said, raising her blue eyes to meet his. "I know you better than that." She pulled away from him and knelt down once more beside Reckless, cradling his head in her lap, the tears beginning to flow.

They buried Reckless behind the ramshackle

cabin he had called home in recent months. Afterwards, Sam led Alexis back inside, Colter following behind them. Alexis was too caught up in her own grief to be aware of the subtle tension that was passing between the two men. She sank down onto one of the rickety chairs by the table and laid her head on her arms.

"Alexis, we need to talk."

"Not now, Sam."

"I'm afraid so. It's important," he insisted.

Alexis raised her head, tyring to ignore the pressure at her temples, the pain behind her eyes.

Sam stepped over to the satchel of papers he had brought with him earlier in the day. He carried it to the table and began to sort through it.

"Alexis, I came up here today for Thaddeus to sign his new will. He has left the bulk of his estate to you."

"I don't want his claim. I only helped him mine it because he was my friend. Let anyone who wants it have it. There's not much gold there anyway."

"You don't understand," Sam replied. "Thaddeus Jones was a very wealthy man. He wanted you to have what was his."

"Reckless? Wealthy?" She looked at him as if he had lost his mind.

"Very."

Alexis shook her head. "I don't believe it. Why did he live like this if . . ."

Sam sat down in the chair across from her. A wry smile turned the corners of his mouth.

"That's simple. He liked the adventure of looking for gold, trying to find the next big strike. I don't think he ever cared about having the wealth. He gave a lot of it away to needy folks." His smile vanished as he turned serious again, clearing his throat for emphasis. "Now, there are some matters that need to be taken care of before you take control of . . ."

"Sam I really don't want anything. Isn't there someone else who should have T.C.'s estate?"

Colter stepped forward, dropping a hand onto Alexis' shoulder. "Especially since I came here to ask Alexis to go back with me as my wife."

Sam's head jerked up in surprise.

"What do you say, Alexis? Will you marry me?" Colter asked as he hunkered down beside her chair.

Alexis stared at the table for the longest time before answering. "We've been through this before, Colt. I'm not the one you should marry."

"You're the one I want."

Again there was a long silence before she replied, "Now is not the time."

Sam coughed again. "Indeed it is not," he mumbled, shoving the document across the table. "I must be on my way, but before I go, you must know that Thaddeus especially wanted you to take a hand in the management of the Palace."

"The Palace?" she echoed.

"The Ice Palace in Idaho City. It's now yours. Thaddeus Jones was awfully proud of that place, though he made sure no one knew it was his. He liked to come and go as he pleased, so he left the running of it to others. But I know he wanted you to watch over it for him yourself. That is, if you want to."

"The Ice Palace . . ." Her voice drifted off as she remembered the beautiful exterior of the building. She had wanted to see the inside of it, and now it was hers. Dear Reckless . . .

Colter frowned. "Alex, you aren't seriously considering trying to run that place, are you? It's the biggest saloon and gambling hall in the whole territory, and some rough characters pass through those doors."

"I could handle them," she protested lightly.

"It's out of the question," he responded.

Alexis stiffened her jaw. "No, it is *not* out of the question. After all, didn't Sam just say it does belong to me. I can run it if I want to."

"But you're going to marry me and live on the Circle S." This was not a proposal. It was a command from a higher authority.

"I'll marry you when snow falls in August and not one minute before." Alexis hopped up and turned her eyes on Sam. "I'm going back with you to Idaho City. I may as well get a look at the Palace right away. I assume there are living quarters above the saloon."

Sam nodded mutely, feeling like a spectator at a fight who has suddenly been pulled into the ring.

Alexis stomped passed Colter and began throwing her few articles of clothing onto her bed, then rolled them up and shoved them under her arm. "I'm ready," she announced, pulling her familiar slouch hat onto her head.

"Wainwright," Colter said ominously, "leave us alone for a minute."

His tone left no room for argument. Sam picked up his satchel and skittered out the door.

Alexis made a move toward the door herself, but Colter was upon her instantly, his hand grabbing her wrist. He pulled her close, forcing her to look up at him and meet his harsh gaze. Then he lowered his lips to hers. The moment they touched, a spark of pleasure ran the length of her body. She closed her eyes, ready to surrender to the ecstasy of his kisses, but he pulled suddenly away.

"I came a long way for you, Alexis," he whispered. "I'm sorry about what happened to the old man. I know he was your friend, and I'm glad he was here for you when you needed him. This isn't the right time for me to say all I wanted to say to you, but I'm going to say this much. You may think you're not going to marry me, now or ever, but you'd better get ready for snow in August, because that's just what you're going to do."

Alexis swallowed hard and turned once more for the door.

"I'll be coming for you, Alex."

Alexis stayed at a hotel the first night. She asked Sam to see that the Ice Palace was closed for two days out of respect for Reckless. He was to tell the employees that the new owner would speak to them the morning they reopened for business, but they were not to know who she was. After he was gone, she lay down on her bed, still fully clothed, and stared at the ceiling.

I'll be coming for you, Alex.

Her body betrayed her. Every nerve was alert, as if waiting for his imminent arrival. Her heart yearned for him, yet she was infuriated by his pronouncement that she *would* marry him. He wanted her but he didn't love her, and she refused to settle for less than love a second time. His passion could comfort her body but not her heart. It was not enough.

She sat up and turned toward the mirror on the dresser. "I let my heart rule my head once," she said aloud, "but it won't happen again. I don't need Colt's gallant gestures. I won't be his second choice." She stood and approached her reflection. "And I won't be told what to do by him or any other man." She tossed her head defiantly. "Alexis Ashmore can't be owned."

Early the next morning, Alexis went with Sam to the Ice Palace. They entered through the rear door to avoid being seen by people in the street. From the first moment she had seen it, Alexis had suspected that it would be elegant inside, but she hadn't imagined how truly spectacular it would be.

The main room was immense with four white columns supporting the floors above. Along the entire length of the back wall was the bar, the dark mahogany polished to a high sheen; there was a brass foot rail and spittoons on the customer side of the bar. The wall behind the bar was covered in mirrors, framed by crystal candelabras. Above the mirrors was a painting of a woman. She was reclining the length of the twenty foot canvas, her nude breasts barely detected beneath a multitude of diamond necklaces. Overhead hung enormous crystal chandeliers, and Alexis could imagine how they must look when they were all ablaze with lights.

She walked into the center of the room. She was surrounded by gambling tables, yet it was uncrowded. The walls were all covered with a blue and silver foiled wall covering, an abundance of lamps ready to shed light on the activities within. The four main doors were straight ahead of her. On either side were wide windows. The heavy, white velvet draperies were tied back with strings of clear glass beads and were fringed in silver braiding. A filmy, white fabric covered the windows, but no light streamed through them today for the shutters were closed and black wreaths had been placed on the outside of each window and door.

To her right were the cashier cages. Over these booths curved an elegant staircase leading to the second floor. Alexis went over to the stairs.

"Is anyone up there now?" she asked Sam.

"No. No one's ever lived in the Palace. Thaddeus had it furnished, but he never stayed here. In fact, I imagine the only one that's ever seen it has been the maid, unless one or two of the girls have slipped up there with their ... a ..." He stopped in embarrassment.

"I see," she replied, beginning to ascend the steps. "Is there another entrance other than these stairs?"

"Yes, there's a private entrance from outside so guests don't have to come through the saloon. And there are servants' stairs up from the kitchen."

She paused midway up the staircase and glanced down at the great gambling hall once more. Everything added together, it was easy to see why Reckless had named it the Ice Palace—the chandeliers, the crystal candelabras, the blue and silver wall coverings, even the painting above the bar. It was as if the room were filled with ice crystals.

"I'm going up," she said. "Do you want to come along, Sam?"

He nodded and hurried after her.

The first rooms along the corridor were obviously meant to be used by guests. It was the last door that opened upon the living quarters of the Ice Palace.

If the gambling hall was elegant, this suite was no less so. The theme of light blue, white, and silver had been carried over into these rooms. Thick white carpet covered the floors. The sofas and chairs were all covered in white and silver brocade, and more chandeliers hung from the ceilings.

The door opened onto a small alcove, beyond which was the parlor, an immense room with a fireplace, a piano, several groupings of chairs and sofas, and large windows with heavy draperies. Off to the right of the alcove was the dining room, filled with an enormous maghogany table and heavy, straight backed chairs. Beyond the fireplace and off to the left was a short hallway leading to the suite's only bedroom.

Alexis opened the bedroom door and looked inside. There was a large, white wardrobe against the far wall. Beside it was a mirrored dressing table, and another full-length mirror stood in the corner. There was a cozy sitting area near the fireplace. But it was the bed that drew her real notice. The four-poster was curtained with sheer white fabric, the material drawn back with satin ribbons of silver and blue. She smiled, thinking of Reckless ever spending the night in that bed.

"I've seen enough, Sam. Let's go," Alexis said abruptly. She hurried down the stairs, Sam in her wake, and out the back door. "Give me the key," she told him as he finished locking the door behind them. As she pocketed it, she added, "I'll see you here in the morning. Use the front doors. They'll be open."

Alexis spent the night alone in her new suite in the Ice Palace. While some women might have been bothered by the vast emptiness of the building, she was undisturbed and slept like a baby.

Before sunrise, she was up and getting ready. This was a big day for her. She would be introduced to the employees of the Ice Palace as the new owner, their boss. Would the men take kindly to a lady proprietor? She would have to make sure that they knew she was their boss, whether or not they liked the idea. And the women? They would have to know right off that she'd have no carrying on in the guest rooms.

Their job was to socialize downstairs, to make sure the men enjoyed their evening of drinking and gambling. If they wanted more, they could visit the cribs on the edge of town. The Ice Palace was going to be respectable.

Alexis got out of bed and washed with the cold water in the pitcher on the night stand. Then she took her brush and began to unsnarl her long, pale hair. Sam had told her she should have a maid, and as she worked with her hair, she decided he was right. She would find someone to live here with her, someone who could be her friend as well as her maid. Her lush tresses gleamed when she'd finished. Carefully, she gathered the fine mass of hair on top of her head. When all was secure, she stuck a light blue feather on top. Around her throat she wore a strand of diamonds and sapphires which Reckless had left to her. Diamond earrings dripped from her ear lobes.

Alexis stared at her reflection in the mirror. She hardly recognized herself. In a flash of unwelcome memory, she thought of the night she had dressed up in Althea's clothes. How strange she had felt then. And now look at her.

She shook off the images of the past. Everything had changed since that night, and for better or worse, this was her life now. She had vowed never to give in to her heart again. She would be ruled by her brain from now on, not by her emotions.

She turned from the mirror and went to her wardrobe. A single dress was waiting for her. Mrs. Cane would be bringing others to her as fast as she could. For now, she only needed this one. Mrs. Cane had done a remarkable job in a short time.

The skirt was a sky blue grosgrain, trimmed with pinked flounces of the same material which extended up the front. The overskirt was made of point lace and was draped behind by means of two ribbons, tied in a large bow, in the same shade of blue as the dress. The low-cut bodice with vandyked bertha opened at the front over a white lace underwaist, confined by a cluster of blue satin roses.

She slipped into the dress and was just finishing with the last button when the knock sounded at the door.

"Come in," she called.

Sam opened the door and stepped inside. "Alexis, everyone's downstairs waiting for . . ." He stopped as she turned from the mirror.

Tall and shapely, her pale blonde hair piled in a mass of curls on her head and her long throat accentuated with the cool glitter of diamonds and sapphires, Sam knew he had never seen a more beautiful woman in his life.

"Alexis . . ." He was speechless.

She leveled an expressionless gaze on him, her icy-blue eyes leaving him feeling cold. Suddenly, she smiled, and warmth returned to the room. "Tell me, Sam. Do you think I can rule this palace?"

"I'm at your command," he responded, sweeping a low bow in her direction.

"Thank you. Now, if you will, take me to meet my subjects."

Alexis took Sam's arm and walked with him down the corridor. She was quaking so hard inside, she felt as if she were falling apart, but she exhibited none of her nervousness on the outside. Her face was serene, her walk casual. They paused at the top of the stairs, and she looked down below.

About fifteen employees waited at the base of the stairs. They were all looking up at her. The air was alive with tension as they tried to size up their new boss. Alexis held her head a little more erect and began the descent. On the third step from the bottom, she stopped once more. With a slow, purposeful gaze, she met the eyes of every person there before speaking.

"I'm Alexis Ashmore, the new owner of the Ice Palace. Thank you for coming in this morning so early. I want everyone to know that, for the moment, no jobs are in jeopardy. I'm sure you have all done a fine job in the past and will continue to do so. I don't expect to make any changes in the operations, but I want to make one thing very clear. I expect the Ice Palace to have a reputation for being honest and fair. My dealers will never cheat, and my girls will not whore on my time. Your jobs are to entertain here in the hall. That is all. I hope that is understood."

She allowed a moment for them to exchange glances among themselves before adding, "Sam Wainwright, whom I believe you all know, will continue to be my legal advisor—as he was to Thaddeus Jones, the previous owner. I have asked Sam to bring each of you into my office during the day so we might become better acquainted. I hope we will all work well together."

On that final word, she turned and climbed the stairs, leaving them to discuss their new employer among themselves.

8

It was in the wee hours of the night, long after the last customers had gone home and the doors to the Ice Palace had been locked, but Alexis was unable to sleep. Over and over again, the events of this evening played in her mind. The grand reopening of the Ice Palace has been an enormous success. Rafe, one of the bartenders, had told her the Palace had never been so full of people, many of them coming for the first time to catch a glimpse of the new owner who, rumor had it, was a real beauty.

What made it even more special to her was that she felt as if she truly belonged. She hadn't found a single person among her employees whom she distrusted or disliked. Some were rougher around the edges than others, but all in all, they were a decent bunch.

With a sigh, Alexis tossed off the blankets

and reached for a bedrobe. Slipping her arms through the satin sleeves, she picked up the lamp beside her bed and left her suite. She was still living alone in the building, although she had informed her employees that anyone interested among them could have a room on the third floor. Rose and Gertie, two of the saloon girls, had told her they would be moving in at the end of the week.

Alexis went down to the main gambling hall. She paused for a moment and let her gaze sweep over the room. A smile brightened her face as the excitement of the evening washed over her once again. She wished her father could have been here. For that matter, she wished Althea could have been here to see her triumph. Would her sister have believed that she, Alexis, could have been transformed into the lady in blue that her guests had seen tonight?

She shook off that thought for she knew beyond it would come thoughts of Colter, and she didn't want to think of him. Not tonight.

She moved across the gambling hall and opened the door to her office. She lit another lamp, then moved to the wall of books that filled the far end of the room. Sam had told her that Reckless had loved books and had gathered this library over many years. After he finished reading a book, he would give it to Sam to add to this collection. She was surprised at how diverse and how extensive his reading habit had been. She was tracing her finger along the book spines, searching for one she thought might interest her, when she thought she heard something. She held her breath, listening. There was someone, or something, in the alley outside her office.

She moved cautiously toward the window. The heavy drapes were down, so she knew her presence had gone undetected. She paused and listened again. Yes. There it was. It was the unmistakable sound of someone crying. Without hesitation, she picked up a lamp and headed toward the rear entrance to the saloon. Before opening the door, however, she reached under the bar and drew out the pistol that was hidden there.

She unbolted the door and opened it. "Who's there?" she asked softly, lifting the lamp high.

The sobs were choked back, but Alexis had already spotted the woman and was hurrying toward her. She recognized the flame-red hair even though the woman's face was hidden. It was Stella from the Golden Gulch. Alexis had only seen her once before, but she knew no two women in Idaho City could have hair that same shade of red.

"Stella? What's happened? Are you all right?"

Stella was huddled against the building between two empty crates. Now that Alexis was standing over her, she could see that her dress was torn and there were bruises on her arms.

"Stella?" she said again.

The girl looked up at Alexis, and Alexis gasped. The entire right side of Stella's face was black and blue and swollen, the right eye little more than a slit.

"Who did this to you?" Alexis asked in horror.

Stella shook her head.

Alexis reached down and tenderly drew her to her feet. "Come inside. I'll get the doctor for you."

"No. No, I don't want a doctor. I'll be fine."

"But . . ."

"No doctor!"

Alexis nodded as she drew the young woman along. "All right. No doctor. I'll take care of you myself."

She led Stella inside, pausing long enough to bolt the door behind them, then took her upstairs to the guest room nearest her own suite. There, she ordered Stella to lie down. She poured water into a bowl and bathed the girl's face and arms. Stella made no protest, nor any other sound, for that matter.

Putting the cloth aside, Alexis asked, "Would you like me to get Derek for you?"

"No!" Stella shot upright on the bed.

Alexis was surprised by her vehemence. She had been certain, that day they met in the Golden Gulch, that Stella was Derek's woman. Surely she would want him to know someone had harmed her this way.

"No," Stella repeated, more calmly this time. "He . . . he mustn't know this happened. It . . . it was all my own fault, Miss Ashmore."

"Won't he wonder where you are?"

"I . . . I'm not working at the Golden Gulch any longer." Tears welled up in her eyes. In a whisper, she said, "I'm going to have a baby. I can't work anywhere." She sank back on the bed again, closing her eyes.

Alexis was thoughtful. She hadn't especially liked Stella when they first met. She had seemed so bold, so hard. There was none of that boldness now. She was just a frightened girl in trouble.

"The father did this to you," Alexis said with certainty.

Stella nodded, a tear slipping from beneath her swollen eyelid.

"Then he'll be no help to you." She paused. "Stella, would you like to stay here with me in the Palace?"

Stella opened her eyes. "Stay here? But . . . but I couldn't work. I mean, no men would . . . What man would want a face like this for company?"

"You wouldn't have to work. At least, not in the saloon. You could help me in other ways as long as you were able, and when your time comes, you could have as long as you need before resuming work of any kind."

"Why are you being so nice to me?" Stella asked, suspicious of this unexpected kindness.

"Because I think you need a friend. And so do I."

Alexis frowned as she stared at the tiny figures in the ledger. Not that what the numbers spelled out wasn't good news. They attested to what everyone suspected—the Ice Palace was an enormous financial success. It was the smallness of the neat handwriting that made her head throb as she studied the pages, determined that if she was going to own this business, she was going to understand every detail and run it herself. She wasn't going to be a pretty figurehead while Sam Wainwright, or someone else like him, made all the real decisions.

The knock that sounded on her office door was a welcome interruption.

"Come in," she called.

The door opened and Derek's handsome face poked in. "May I disturb you?"

"Of course, Mr. Anderson. Please come in."

He chose the heavy leather chair near the bookcase, settling into it with a satisfied sigh. "Last night was quite a triumph for you, wasn't it? I wish you would have told me *you* were the new owner. I would have done whatever I could to help with your reopening."

"Thank you. That's very kind of you, Mr. Anderson, but I wanted to do this on my own, not with the help of someone who's been here longer than I. I hope you understand." She turned a charming smile on him. "And I hope we can be friends, even though we're in competition with each other."

"Please. Won't you call me Derek?"

She gazed at him for a thoughtful moment, then gave a slight nod of her head.

"And may I call you Alexis?" He raised a hopeful eyebrow.

Again, she nodded.

"You know, Alexis," Derek said as he stared at the rows of books on the desk in front of her, "you may find this place too much for you to operate on your own. I wonder if you'd consider selling the Palace to me. I'll give you a good price for it."

"The Palace! Why, that's what you came to speak to T.C. about that first day I saw you." She remembered wondering at the time where around Idaho City anyone would have a palace for folks to talk about. It hadn't occurred to her until this moment that the Ice Palace was what Derek had been talking about.

He got to his feet and approached her desk, his dark brows drawn close. He rubbed his beard thoughtfully before speaking. "Alexis, I've wanted to buy this place from the day the first stone was laid. What makes it worse is that Reckless had finally told me he would discuss a price, that he was ready to sell, but he died before we could work out the details. I won't try to fool you. I still want to own the Ice Palace, and I hope I can convince you to sell it to me."

As he spoke, he leaned toward her over the desk. She looked directly into his hazel eyes, aware of his dashing good looks without being properly affected by them. She felt again her initial uneasiness about him. Why was it, when he had always been friendly toward her, that she felt so much apprehension around him? He seemed honest about his offer of friendship. Why couldn't she just accept it?

Alexis got up from her chair. She walked around the desk, carefully arranging her features to disguise her negative thoughts. When she stopped in front of him, she held out her hand. "Mr. Anderson, I sincerely want us to be friends, but I have no intention of selling you the Ice Palace. It was left to me by someone I loved very dearly, and I intend to take care of it the best way I know how."

There was a flicker of something behind his eyes, but it vanished before Alexis could decide exactly what it was. Derek took her hand and shook it as he would have any fellow businessman. "All right, Miss Ashmore. I accept you as my competitor." He flashed a broad smile.

"Friendly competitors?" she wondered aloud, responding to his smile with a grin of her own.

The handshake slowed, but he didn't release her hand. Instead, he drew her closer. He took her fingers to his lips, then turned a serious gaze on her. "I hope we can be more than competitors," he said, his voice low.

The sudden opening of the door saved Alexis from having to decide how best to retrieve her hand from his grasp.

"Alexis, I was wondering . . ." Stella stopped. She clutched the door handle for support as she stared at them.

Alexis pulled her hand quickly away.

"Stella, what are you doing here?" Derek demanded.

Alexis could see that the girl was too upset to answer. She moved away from Derek and went to Stella, smiling her encouragement. "She's come to work for me."

"Working? At the Palace? Doing what?"

Alexis didn't like the tone of his voice. She took hold of Stella's free hand and squeezed it.

Still holding on, she turned a cool glance in Derek's direction. "Does it matter? It's my place, after all."

But Derek wasn't looking at her. He was staring hard at Stella. Alexis realized he must be looking at Stella's bruises.

"Stella had an accident, but she's healing up quite nicely." She looked at the girl. "What was it you needed, Stella?"

"I . . . I'm sorry. I've forgotten." She was returning Derek's gaze. The hand that had been on the door came up to cover her swollen face.

Alexis squeezed her fingers one more time. "That's all right. Why don't you go on up to your room and lie down? You've probably done too much today anyway." She gave Stella a little shove to start her on her way.

Derek tapped his hat against his leg. "You'll be sorry you've brought her here, Alexis. That girl is nothing but trouble."

"I'm surprised, Derek. I got the feeling that you and she . . . Well, never mind. I think Stella and I are going to get along fine."

"Suit yourself," he replied. He walked toward her and stopped nearby. "Well, I've got my own place to run. I'll see you again soon."

She nodded but kept silent. She watched him walk through the gambling hall, winding his way through the tables that were already beginning to fill as the afternoon lengthened.

It had taken Colter longer than he had wanted to hire the right men to take care of the Circle S in his absence. They had to be men he could trust, especially since he didn't know how many months it might be before he was able to return. Li Ching could come to Idaho City if the need arose, of course, but that wasn't the same as being there himself. Still, Alexis was more important to him, and that's what had brought him here. He would stay, no matter how long it took, until he convinced her that she belonged with him.

Colter rode slowly down the street, studying the buildings and watching the faces of the people on the boardwalks. He was drawing more than a few stares himself, especially from the women in town. He cut a fine figure astride his prancing white stallion. He was wearing a black suit and hat, contrasting smartly with his horse. He tipped his hat and smiled at the ladies, playing the part he was expected to play.

He turned his horse aside from the Ice Palace, tied him to the post, and entered the Golden Gulch. Although it was making strides toward grandeur, this saloon wasn't much in comparison to its neighbor across the street, but Colter was hoping to learn some news about Alexis before going over there himself. He didn't have long to wait.

"Did you see the way she looks at folks when she thinks they are gettin' out of line? It's enough to freeze 'em in their tracks. Cold, I tell you. She's cold."

"Naw. It's those peculiar blue eyes of hers. No woman can be that beautiful and not know how to please a man, if you know what I mean. After all, she runs a saloon, don't she?"

"I wonder where she's from. She looks like she could be royalty or something."

"She's royalty, all right. The Ice Queen in her Ice Palace."

"Well, if she's made of ice, I'd like to be the man who gets to thaw her out, if you know what I mean . . ."

Colter threw down the rest of his drink, swallowing his desire to mash his fist into that fellow's vivid imagination. He didn't want anyone else imagining what had haunted his thoughts now for weeks. But at least he had learned something about Alexis. She was running the Ice Palace—and she had caught the attention of every red-blooded man in Idaho City while she was at it.

He went back outside and paused on the boardwalk. The July sun was beating down overhead, causing the glass lettering to sparkle and glitter festively. Colter could hear a piano playing and loud voices, laughing and talking, as they filtered through the doors. He wondered if one of those voices could be hers. He quelled the urge to rush in and find her. This time he was going to do things right. This time he was going to court her, right and proper. He was going to win her trust and her love.

He turned and walked away from the Ice Palace, glancing at the display windows of the shops as he went by. At last he saw something that piqued his interest. A perky little hat of sky blue—the same color as her eyes—adorned with long white and blue feathers. It looked just right for Alexis.

Either that, he thought, or a new pair of chaps. He smiled to himself and opened the shop door.

A bespectacled, gray-haired woman came through the curtains at the back of the shop as he entered. A smile immediately lit up her plump face. "May I help you, sir?"

Colter removed his hat. "Yes. I'd like to buy that blue bonnet in the window."

"That's a very fine choice, sir. She's a lucky lady. So many men have poor taste in women's clothes. They bring home the most outrageous and unsuitable gifts and can't imagine why their wives aren't thrilled to receive them." As she spoke, she went to the window and retrieved the hat. Turning toward him again, she said, "If you'll give me just a moment, I'll put it in a box for you."

Colter followed her toward the back of the shop. She pulled out a stool and was about to step up on it to reach the hat boxes on the top shelf. "Let me," he said, easily reaching a box without the use of the stool. He handed it to her, realizing now just how tiny the woman was. She barely reached his chest.

She looked up at him. "Thank you, sir. I'll have it ready in a moment."

"If it's not too much trouble," he told her as he pulled out some coins. "I'd like to have it delivered instead of taking it with me. Just let me know what I owe you."

The woman paused long enough to assess him. He could almost see the gears in her mind working.

She was thinking—Here's a man with money and good taste in women's clothes. He'll probably return if he's treated right. Giving him a little extra now will show me a greater return later.

"There'll be no charge for delivering it, sir. I'm glad to be of service. Just tell me where and to whom this pretty little gem goes, and she'll be admiring it very shortly."

"It goes to Miss Ashmore at the Ice Palace. I'd like to put a card in with it."

"Miss Ashmore, is it? Well, you couldn't have chosen a better hat. I happen to be making a large number of her gowns, and she has a preference for this shade of blue. She looks very pretty in them, too, I might add. My, you should have seen the state she was in when I first saw her. *Tchk, tchk*. The poor girl was in need of my guidance, I'll tell you." She looked up at him over the glasses on the end of her nose. "You're mighty handsome, young man, but don't go getting your hopes up too high. That lady doesn't seem to have any interest in the men around here, and she's got two of Idaho's most eligible businessmen doing their darndest to court her, too. Not that there wouldn't be hundreds trying, but most of the men in town are riffraff. No one for her to worry her pretty head about." As she talked, she handed him a card.

Colter scribbled a message, then handed it to the sales woman. He could tell it was all she could do to keep from reading it right while he stood there, but she resisted, placing it in an envelope and slipping it into the hat box.

"I'll get that to her right away, sir."

"Thank you." He placed ten dollars on the counter.

"Sir, that's too much."

He waved off her protest, put his hat back on and touched the brim in a farewell, then sauntered out of the shop.

Alexis sat at her dressing table, waiting patiently as Stella arranged her hair. The two women had fallen into a daily routine, beginning in midmorning. Stella would bring breakfast to Alexis' bedroom, and they would eat together. Then Alexis would go to her office to go over receipts from the previous day and cover any other business that needed attention. After a late lunch, Alexis would lie down and rest. When she awoke, Stella was always there to help her dress and arrange her hair before going down to the saloon for the evening.

Alexis glanced at Stella's reflection in the mirror. Her face was no longer swollen and the bruises were slowly fading, although it would be a long time before all traces of her wounds had disappeared. Alexis was more concerned with the scars that Stella carried inside. It couldn't be good for the baby growing inside her to be so unhappy all the time.

Stella never volunteered any information about what had brought her to the alley the night Alexis found her. In her own mind, Alexis had put together all the events. Stella, she was certain, was in love with Derek, but apparently he hadn't returned her affections. She had entertained another man, perhaps out of despair. When she discovered she was pregnant, she couldn't stay at the Golden Gulch and let Derek see her humiliation, so she had gone to the baby's father, only to be beaten and, most likely, scorned and ridiculed for thinking he would be of any help. After all, she was nothing but a cheap saloon girl, there for the entertainment and amusement of men.

Her theory about Stella's feelings for Derek seemed confirmed by the girl's unwillingness to be around whenever Derek found an excuse to come calling on Alexis. Alexis felt bad and often made a point of stating that she felt nothing more for Derek than a mild friendship.

"Alexis?"

She turned on her stool and looked toward the door. "We're in the bedroom, Rose," she called.

The barmaid entered the room, carrying a hatbox. "This just came from Rachel Cane's. I thought it might be something you wanted to wear tonight, so I brought it right up."

"Thank you," Alexis said as she took the box into her lap. She couldn't remember ordering another hat. She slipped off the ribbon holding it shut, then lifted off the lid. "Oh." She drew out the perky little bonnet. "Look, Stella. Look, Rose," she whispered as she placed it on her head.

The felt bonnet had a high peaked crown covered in sky-blue grosgrain. The brim came to a point in front just above her forehead and was laid in a box pleat in the back. On the right, the broad chip brim was turned up, on the left, turned down. Blue and white feathers were held in the brim on the right side by a blue satin ribbon, and a spray of white rose buds and blue satin ribbons were set under the brim at the back.

"I wonder who sent it?" Alexis whispered as she admired her reflection.

"Maybe this will tell you," Stella replied, reaching into the box.

Alexis accepted the envelope. It was probably from Sam or Derek. They were, after all, two very persistent suitors. Yet, as she glanced once more at the hat in the mirror, she couldn't help thinking that this didn't look like something etiher one of them would think to send to her.

She pulled out the card and read, *Life is a game of chance and everyone hopes to win. Some men gamble for money. I'm gambling for love. C*

Alexis stared at the cared for a long time, not quite sure what it meant. And who was "C"? The only "C" she knew was . . . *Colter*!

Her heart thundered in her breast. Colter. He was here in Idaho City. She felt as if her corset were squeezing the air right out of her. She was cold and flushed at the same time.

I'm gambling for love. C

If only that were the truth.

"Alex, are you all right?" Stella asked.

She folded the card in half and placed it beneath the bodice of her gown, next to her heart. "I'm fine," she answered, so softly it was barely audible. She rose from her dressing stool.

"Are you going to wear the hat tonight?"

"Yes, Stella. I am."

"Alexis?" Stella touched her bare arm. "Be careful."

The words of warning brought Alexis back to the brink of reality. Yes, she must be careful. She must be sure. She didn't want to ever again feel the pain she had known that night. She could not allow her love to resurface, only to be dashed by the harshness of reality. She would not take second place to her sister.

She hugged Stella. "Don't worry. I'll be careful." Then she glided out of the room, once again protected by her cool facade.

Derek was seated at the table nearest the stairs. He knew the moment Alexis paused at the top; men throughout the room stopped what they were doing to stare up in her direction with undisguised admiration. But she was so damned sure of herself, so confident of her own abilities. He would love to be the man to put her in her place. Especially if that place were his bed.

He got up from his table and moved to the base of the stairs, awaiting her arrival with a proprietary air.

She looked particularly beautiful tonight. Her blue eyes seemed brighter than normal, and her cheeks had a warm glow. She descended the stairs with her usual grace, yet there seemed to be an added elegance tonight that he'd never seen before.

He wanted her more than ever.

"Hello, Derek," she said as she reached him,

but her deliberate gaze was studying the people filling the saloon. "Are things all right at the Golden Gulch? You've been here every evening this week."

He held out his arm to her. "The Gulch can manage without me for a few hours a day while I come to see you."

She gave him an absent-minded nod as she moved past him, ignoring his proffered elbow as she began to move around the room in her nightly routine of greeting her guests. Already she knew a great many by name, and she spoke to them as if they were old friends.

Derek remained by the stairs. He leaned against the bannister in feigned relaxation, but his insides were in a turmoil. How dare she act as if he weren't even there? Who was she to come into town and take over the Ice Palace without so much as a "Can you help, please?" Did she think she deserved to own this showplace? It should be his, and there she was, lording it over him. Someday, he would put her in her place. He would show her who was really boss.

He saw the sudden stiffening of her back. She was looking over the heads of the men at the gaming tables toward the far corner of the room where five men were playing poker. Derek saw nothing unusual about them. Still, there was no denying that something there had sparked her attention. He pushed off from the bannister and began to work his way toward that table, while keeping his eyes on Alexis. She was speaking to the men around her again, but it was easy to see that all her senses were alert to every motion, every nuance at the far poker table.

Derek leaned against the nearest white column and turned his attention to those at the table. Three of the men he knew. They were businessmen in town. The fourth was obviously a miner who had had some good luck on his placer and was now bent on losing it all to someone else. The fifth man was a stranger to him. He had the look of a professional gambler. He was dressed in a black broadcloth suit, a black tie knotted under his stiff white collar, but it was an air of confidence that Derek sensed that told him this man was experienced at what he was doing. He wore a friendly grin that told nothing. He sat with casual indifference in his chair, yet Derek would have bet that he was prepared for anything.

Even from a man's point of view, he could see that the stranger was handsome in a roguish sort of way. He wondered if it was just the man's looks that had drawn Alexis' interest.

He glanced away from the stranger just as Alexis paused one table away. "Hello, George. Having any luck tonight?"

"Not too bad, ma'am. Not too bad."

"Good. I'm glad to hear it."

The stranger laid his cards on the table. He gave his winnings little notice as he scraped his chair backward on the floor and got up.

"Hello, Miss Ashmore. I'm delighted to see you again."

"Thank you, Mr. Stephens. How do you like my place?"

Derek thought he noticed a slight heightening of color, a small tremble in her voice. It was unlike her.

"It's grand, but then, I never would've expected anything less from you." A warm, lazy smile moved all the way up from his mouth to his deep brown eyes.

"Wouldn't you?" Alexis responded, a hint of irony in her words. "Some men wouldn't think a woman capable of managing a saloon like the Ice Palace."

"Any man who would think that of you would be a fool. I'd be the first to tell him so."

Alexis seemed unable to say anything more.

"Will you allow me to buy you a drink later, Miss Ashmore?"

She nodded silently.

The stranger turned back to the game. "Deal me in, fellas. I feel lucky tonight."

9

Alexis was on edge all evening, waiting for the moment when Colter would leave his game of poker and come looking for her. Where were all her thoughts of caution? How was she to keep him at a distance when her entire being was tuned to his movement?

Derek tried several times to draw her off into a private corner, but she shrugged him off every time. She was glad when he finally gave up and left. She didn't like the way he tried to monopolize her, especially when Colter was so near. Derek's hand on her arm made her feel somehow unfaithful, though she knew that was silly. She didn't belong to Colter. She didn't belong to anyone.

"Miss Alexis? We have a fellow over here that wants us to use his mining claim as a wager against the house."

"Where is he, Jessie?"

The dealer pointed the man out to her.

Alexis nodded. "It's all right. His claim's good for it. He wanted to use it the other night, and I've done some checking with Sam since then."

Jessie moved back toward his table.

"Miss Ashmore, may I buy you that drink now?"

Colter's breath on her neck when he spoke sent shivers—delightful shivers—down her spine. She turned with as much poise as she could muster.

"I'd like that," she answered.

He turned toward the bar and she studied him with hungry eyes. His black suit fit his broad shoulders and trim waist to perfection. He had removed his tie and opened the collar of his shirt, revealing a light sprinkling of chest hair, giving an added dash to his handsome appearance. He turned, drinks in hand, and caught her staring at him. That slow smile of his returned.

"Is there somewhere we can sit in private?"

"My office." It seemed much safer than her suite.

A lamp burned dimly in one corner, but Alexis left it turned low. She went automatically to her desk and sat in the chair behind it.

"Is that far enough away to be safe?"

She couldn't help but return his smile. It did seem silly to have that big desk between them, as if she were his employer. She got up and motioned with her hand toward the chairs near the bookcase. "Please. We'll be more comfortable over there."

After they'd settled into their chairs, shadows reigning in the darkened office, Colter handed Alexis her drink. He continued to watch her with a tender gaze. There was so much she wanted to read into that look, but she was afraid to trust her normally good instincts. When it came to Colter, she was a poor judge of anything.

"Thank you for the bonnet," she said, grabbing at the first thing she could think of to say to break the spell. "It's very pretty."

"It's you who makes the hat pretty." He set his glass on a nearby stand. The smile vanished. His eyes became solemn. "Alexis, I keep making mistakes with you, and I don't want to make another one."

"Colt . . ."

"Hear me out. We both know what my first mistake was."

She blushed and dropped her eyes, reliving in a flash their one night together.

"My second mistake was trying to force you to be my bride." He paused. "My third was telling you you couldn't handle this place."

She looked up again.

"I've already told you I was wrong about the Palace. You're doing a great job. Everyone's talking about you." He frowned, but there was a halfway earnest smile on his lips. "Some more than I'd like them to. There are too many men in this town."

Alexis felt like she needed to say something. "Not too many for the owner of the Palace. It's how I stay in business, you know."

He continued as if she hadn't spoken. "I can't undo my first mistake. I'm sorry for the hurt I caused everyone, but I can't undo it." He reached for her hand. "Alexis, I'd like to have a chance to rectify the second. I won't try to force you to marry me, but will you give me the chance to try to win you over to the idea? Let me court you. I'd be only one among many here. Just give me a chance."

She felt breathless. How she wanted to fall into his arms and surrender completely. "Colt . . ." she whispered, looking away from him once more, this time to hide the swelling tears.

"Alexis . . . please."

How could she deny him anything? "All right, Colt."

"Will you go riding with me tomorrow?"

"Yes," she answered without looking up.

"I'll go now. I don't want to wear out my welcome. I'll come at noon if that's all right."

"That's fine."

He walked away, drawing her gaze to his back like a magnet. He opened the door, paused as if he would turn and say something more, then went out and shut it behind him.

Alexis sagged in her chair, allowing the tears to fall down her cheeks. She didn't care. No one could see the Ice Queen crying in this dark room. And she had no desire to return to the bright lights and noise of the saloon. A broken heart was better concealed from the eyes of others.

She'd been so sure she had put him behind her, that she had frozen her heart against him.

How foolish. How utterly foolish she was. She would never be free of Colter. Never in a million years. She belonged to him as surely as if she were his slave, as if she wore his brand.

But it hurt so, knowing he was still trying to do right by her, still trying to make amends for their night of lovemaking, still trying to fulfill his promise to her father that he would marry Jonathan's wayward daughter. Yet the pain of being with him under those conditions was not nearly as bad as the pain of not being with him at all.

"Alexis? Are you okay?"

She blinked away the tears enough to recognize Stella standing over her. She sniffed and nodded.

"Can I help?"

Alexis shook her head, choking on a sob. Then Stella gathered her into her arms as a mother would a child, and let her cry out her sorrow into the comforting arms of someone who cared.

Clothes lay scattered across her bed and the floor. Despite the many outfits she had acquired since Reckless first brought her to Idaho City, Alexis had nothing suitable to wear riding with Colter. Why hadn't she thought to order some riding habits?

She hadn't ordered any because she hadn't ridden in anything except buckskin britches since she was a child. It was Althea who had always dressed for riding as she would for any other occasion.

"Well, I won't be my sister, even if I do wear dresses around the Palace," she muttered aloud.

She returned to her chest and rummaged deep to find her buckskin pants and a roomy blouse with long, rolled-up sleeves and an open collar. Her boots were in the back of her wardrobe.

"Just waiting for me to regain my senses, weren't you?" she said to them as she pulled them from hiding.

She dressed in a hurry, then glanced in the mirror and laughed. "Wait until the folks of Idaho see their Ice Queen today."

Stella was suitably surprised when Alexis came out of her bedroom. "Alexis!" she cried.

"Believe it or not, Stella, up until I came to Idaho City, these are the kind of clothes I wore every day."

"I *don't* believe it."

Alexis laughed again. "I guess I should tell you about it some time." She grew thoughtful. "Come to think of it, Stella, neither one of us talks much about the past."

"There's not much to tell about me," Stella replied, her mouth set in a stubborn line, her green eyes wary.

Alexis touched her shoulder. "Don't worry. I won't pry." Just then the mantel clock chimed. "Come and help me with my hair, will you? He'll be here any moment."

The afternoon sun kissed the earth with warmth, while a gentle breeze ruffled the tree branches and kept an uncomfortable summer heat at bay. The hillsides were brushed with the vivid colors of wild flowers. The gentle ripple and splash of the mountain creek created a friendly song of its own. A doe and her fawn paused in their grazing to watch the two riders cross the far end of the grassy clearing.

Alexis felt a peace she hadn't known in months. *Not since Althea got off the stage and I knew he belonged to her*, she thought now, glancing at Colter.

He, too, was dressed casually. Gone was the fancy gambler's suit. In its stead were buckskin trousers to match her own and a white shirt with sleeves rolled up. A wide-brimmed hat shaded his eyes from the sun. She wondered what he was thinking about as they rode so quietly.

As if reading her thoughts, he turned his head to meet her gaze. "It's been a long time since we've been riding together."

"How is the ranch? And Li Ching?"

"Things were quiet when I left. I hired some more help for while I'm away. Good men, too. I'll probably keep them on. The Circle S needs them. Li Ching and I can't do it all alone anymore." He looked up the trail, adding, "We're starting work on the new ranch house."

"That's wonderful, Colt."

"I'd like you to help me with the decorating. You know. Ordering the furniture and the wall coverings and the carpets. I don't know much about such things."

Alexis was pleased by his request, but was struck by its incongruity all the same. "And I *do* know about them?" She laughed, her blue eyes warming. "Colt, you seem to forget that I've spent most of my life on a horse."

"I haven't forgotten. That's one of the things I love about you," he responded. "Besides, I know whatever you choose, I'll be comfortable with." His brown eyes twinkled with mischief as he added, "Even if you choose saddles for chairs and straw for carpets."

"Oh, what a novel idea. And you could have a bed made of horse blankets and a pit for your cook fires right in the middle of the kitchen floor."

Colter pulled back on the reins, stopping his mount. "Rocks for chairs around the dining room table. I knew I could count on you, Alexis. What else?"

"I'm not sure I should share my ideas with you any further, Mr. Stephens," Alexis responded, removing all traces of mirth from her face. "It has just occurred to me that I should open my own shop in Idaho City. There are many, many people who would pay very handsomely for someone of my expertise to decorate their homes."

"I will meet your price, Miss Ashmore. Any price. Ask and it shall be yours."

Despite his continuing jest, Alexis was suddenly saddened by their banter. She knew just what she would wish from him. Something she couldn't have. His love.

Colter saw her drawing away from him again. He didn't understand what he'd said to make her withdraw, but he was unwilling to lose these last precious moments they had shared. He hopped down from the saddle and approached her horse. He held his hand out for her.

"Let's walk," he said.

She took his hand and dismounted. She tried once to pull her hand away, but he held on. He led her across the creek and up another hillside, not sure where they were going, only knowing he couldn't allow her to get away. There were no sounds in the forest. They had left the noise of the city far behind them. There was no one else for miles around. Only two people. Two people in search of each other.

With a sudden fierceness, Colter stopped and pulled her against him. His arms tightened like steel cords around her back, one hand supporting her head as it fell back, exposing the soft white skin of her throat. The longing, the wanting inside him threatened to explode, blowing into pieces his carefully laid plans for wooing her. He wanted to pick her up and carry her away, forcefully if necessary, taking her where she could never run away from him again.

He stared at her, his eyes hot with an almost angry passion. Long sooty lashes brushed her pale cheeks. Her lips were parted. He longed to taste her sweet breath on his own. But somehow, in the midst of his blind desire, he felt her quivering. She was frightened, frightened of his taking her right here on the forest floor. And he knew he was close to doing just that. With an iron will, he released his hold. Her eyes fluttered open, a myriad of emotions displayed in their swirling blue depths.

"I'd better take you back to town." The ache

of his self-denial made his voice gruff.
She nodded.

The Golden Gulch was closed. Derek drove the workmen to a near frenzy in an effort to complete the remodeling ahead of schedule. Even as the interior went through its metamorphosis from simple boom town bar to showplace saloon, he knew it was no competitor for the Ice Palace. Nor could he, a mere man, pretend to compete with the drawing power of the Ice Queen. If only he could merge the two. If only he could make her see what a force the two of them joined could be. And most of all, he wanted to see her cool aloofness crumble before him. How he'd love to hear her begging for his mercy.

A smile twisted his mouth as he imagined her, lying in his bed, pleading . . .

He saw them ride up to the Ice Palace and dismount. He was unsure at first that it was even her. Her silken hair fell loose down her back, and she was wearing pants and men's boots. Yet it *was* Alexis, and she couldn't have looked more desirable. He stepped to the edge of the boardwalk and leaned against the post holding up the awning.

She was with the stranger he had seen last night. Derek hadn't liked the looks of the man then, and he liked him even less today. He was horning in on someone that Derek already considered his.

He watched as Alexis said a quick farewell, then disappeared inside. Neither of them had looked any too happy. The stranger removed his hat and stood on the walk outside the Palace, twirling the rim through his fingers, his face a mixture of thoughtfulness and misery.

Derek grinned. It looked like he had nothing to worry about after all. The Ice Queen had shown no more warmth to the stranger than she had to him.

Stella let the curtain fall back across the window. She felt cold and hugged her arms against her. She wished she had left Idaho. Anywhere would have been better than here. She was a prisoner. A prisoner without a prison and only she knew she was held captive. She felt the stirrings of life, and her hands dropped to touch her rounded stomach.

"How foolish you are to want to live," she whispered. "There's so much pain. So much pain."

She remembered how glad she'd been to get away from her father's farm. She was tired of being poor. She was afraid of being married off to some big oaf of a boy or, even worse, an old man with no hair and no teeth. She was pretty. Everyone had told her so all her life. Flaming red hair, thick and curly. Emerald green eyes with tiny flecks of gold. Her body developed early, and she learned the power of making a man want what he couldn't have, though even she hadn't understood what it was they wanted, not really.

And so she ran away and came here. Here where she was desired by men by the thousands, men who were satisfied just to be in her company, who treated her like fine china. Here where the gold flowed like water into her hands, and all she had to do was laugh and smile and be pretty. Here where she could have nice things—dresses and hats and jewels. Here where all her dreams could come true.

She shivered again as she pushed the curtain aside once more. He was still standing there, leaning against the post, grinning. She'd been so innocent, such a child, the first time she turned and found him smiling at her. She had thought him so handsome. She had thought he cared for her. She had thought she could go on, laughing and smiling and being pretty, and never give anything more.

But he wasn't a man to be teased and charmed, and so he had taken her—she cringed even now at the memories of his takings. He'd taken her virtue and destroyed her dream-vision of the little world she had made for herself. He had owned her body and soul. Confused, frightened, she had tried to be what he wanted her to be, but nothing she did seemed to please him. Nothing except... she pleaded and he laughed... she cried and he triumphed... she...

No. She didn't want to think of it anymore. She was safe here. Safe with Alexis.

There was movement in her womb again.

How much you must want to live, she thought. *I will love you. No one will ever try to take your life again.*

Alexis received two gifts that afternoon. A bouquet of roses came from Derek with a note asking her to attend a play at the Jenny Lind Theatre, followed by supper with him afterwards. A spray of forget-me-nots arrived from Colter. His note said only: *Yours, Colt.*

Alexis held the blue flowers against her face as tears trailed down each cheek. She was so confused by him. One moment he courted her. The next he was angry at her. One moment she thought he might really care. The next she was certain he hated her for ruining everything.

Yours, Colt.

What did it mean? Did it mean nothing she did would send him away? Was he that determined to honor his promise to her father?

She sniffed the floral spray, then dried her cheeks with the back of her hand. She mustn't have puffy eyes when she went downstairs. It wouldn't do for her patrons to think she sat up in her room and cried. She had carefully manufactured a regal facade, and they must go on believing in it.

Why don't I just marry him? she wondered. Perhaps he really would learn to love me in time.

But she knew she couldn't do that. She could never take second place. She had to be loved for who and what she was, not out of a sense of duty. Alexis straightened her back. No, he would have to want her for her own sake. And if he didn't . . . Well, if he didn't, she still had the Ice Palace. She still had the legacy Reckless had left to her. She could still be a part of this bawdy, bustling city.

Colt had said he wanted to court her, that he would be only one suitor among many. Then she must give him some competition. She must see how he truly felt. She reached for her stationery box and wrote a hasty reply, accepting Derek's invitation.

Stella came into her suite as she was folding the note. Alexis passed it to her.

"See that this is taken to Mr. Anderson."

Stella looked surprised and hesitant.

"Don't gawk at me, Stella. I'm merely going to the theatre with him." She had spoken more sharply than she intended. "I'm sorry," she said, getting to her feet. "I know you still care for him. Maybe, once the baby's born, he'll forgive you and ask you back."

The girl shrank away from Alexis. "Never! I would never go back."

"But if you still love him . . ."

Stella's eyes burned fiercely. "I *hate* him," she ground out.

Alexis was stunned.

Stella grabbed Alexis by the arm. "Be careful with him, Alex. He's not the man you think he is." Her face was pasty white.

Alexis feared Stella was about to faint and sought to calm her. "None of us are who others think we are, Stella. Please. Come sit down. You are much too distressed. I have no interest in Mr. Anderson. He is . . . he is just a friend, an acquaintance really. Nothing more."

Stella sat as she was told, but she refused to release her grip on Alexis' arm.

"Please, Stella. Tell me what's troubling you."

But Stella only shook her head. "Don't go, Alexis."

* * *

The Jenny Lind Theatre, named after the famous Swedish nightingale, was Idaho City's most elegant theatre. Derek led the way to their box, guiding Alexis to her plush velvet seat. She thanked him, then glanced about her. She returned a few smiles and waves from people she knew as the boxes around her and the room below filled to capacity. She admired the frescoes on the ceiling and walls and wondered aloud at how beautiful everything was.

"I'm glad I could be the first to bring you here," Derek said, his voice low and intimate.

"Oh, but I *have* been here before. Mr. Wainwright brought me during my first visit to the city."

"Then let me hope that the performance tonight will outshine the other, so you will remember this night even more fondly."

It was a handsome speech. She returned it with a polite nod and a smile, but she suddenly wished she had listened to Stella and stayed home. There was something about Derek, something she couldn't quite put her finger on, but that left her feeling uncomfortable. Echoes of Stella saying, "I hate him," reverberated in her mind.

"Excuse me, Miss Ashmore, but you look absolutely stunning tonight."

"Not enough women around with your looks, Miss Alexis."

"You're a lucky devil, Anderson."

"We heard you'd be here tonight, Miss

Alexis, and decided there wasn't any point in going to the Palace if you weren't going to be there."

Alexis allowed the flowery compliments and idle chatter of those around her to brush her uneasiness away. What point was there in going out with Derek this evening if she wasn't going to enjoy herself?

The theatre grew dark. The curtain went up, and Alexis was transported to another time by the writings of Shakespeare through the artistry of the Irwin Troupe.

As in any boom town, the women in Idaho City were far outnumbered by the men. Since she had become the owner and proprietress of the biggest saloon there, Alexis had not had the time or the opportunity to meet many of the women, especially those of the elite and proper social order of the town. The women, however, had made it their business to learn about Alexis Ashmore, and they had learned enough to know that she didn't dally with her male customers (their own husbands being of primary concern) nor allow the girls in her saloon to do so either. They were naturally curious about her, and tonight was their chance to meet her in person.

The curtain dropped. The lights went up. Derek offered his arm as she rose from the chair. Suddenly, they were surrounded by people, women introducing themselves, chattering noisily, asking her questions and insisting that she join them for some activity or other. Carried along with the tide, Alexis descended the stairs and flowed with the crowd out into the street.

A gloved hand touched her elbow. The women's faces around her shone with open admiration. She looked to her side.

Colter removed his top hat. "Excuse me, ladies. I would like a few words with Miss Ashmore."

"Of course," someone said, followed by envious murmurs as Alexis was drawn away from the crowd.

"Colt," she protested weakly. "I'm here with someone else. He'll be looking for me."

"I know. I just didn't want an evening to go by without seeing you. You weren't at the Palace. Did you know nothing sparkles in that place when you're not there?"

He was so close. Could he hear her racing heart?

"Have you ever seen how a crystal catches the sun and throws a glittering rainbow onto the walls of a room? That's what you're like, Alexis. They call you the Ice Queen because they think you're cool and removed from them. But you and I know better. You're not the icy crystal they see on the outside. You're the warm, bright colors of the rainbow."

She watched his mouth as he spoke. Such a perfect mouth.

"Pardon me, but I believe you are intruding on Miss Ashmore's evening with me."

The spell was broken, and she wanted to turn and wreak vengeance on Derek's head. Instead, she smoothed her face into indifference as she faced him.

"Mr. Anderson, I would like you to meet a friend of mine. This is Colter Stephens of the Circle S Ranch. He is . . . a friend of my father's."

Neither man offered a hand.

"Are you here for long, Mr. Stephens?" Derek asked.

"I'm not sure. My plans are a little sketchy at the moment."

"Circle S Ranch, huh? I would've guessed you to be a gambler by profession. I've seen you in action at the Ice Palace."

Colter looked at Alexis and gave her a warm, meaningful smile. "Gambling is merely a hobby of mine. Unless I'm playing for something that truly matters."

Alexis felt weak beneath his gaze.

I'm gambling for love. C.

Everything in her wanted to believe he cared as much as his look told her he did. If only they could go back in time. If only she could be sure. If only . . .

"Please excuse us, Mr. Stephens. Our supper is awaiting us." Derek took her arm, his fingers pressing hard into her flesh.

"Derek," she protested, "I'm afraid I'm not feeling up to supper. I'd prefer you just take me home."

Colter was immediately concerned. "What's wrong, Alex?"

"Nothing. Really. Just the heat and the excitement of the play."

Derek glowered at her. "Don't you think you'll feel better once you've eaten something?"

"She wants to go home, Anderson," Colter

said, his tone brooking no argument.

Sullen, Derek motioned for his buggy to be brought over. He handed Alexis up, then went around to the other side and got in beside her. Colter stepped toward the buggy, but Derek slapped the reins sharply across the horse's back and they shot forward before he could reach them.

"My cook's prepared quite a meal for you." His voice was low, almost threatening.

"I'm sorry, Derek. I'm really not feeling up to it."

"You'd change your mind once we got there."

The uneasiness that she'd felt earlier in the evening returned with a rush. "Derek," she demanded, "take me home." She was afraid to look at him, sensing that in the shadows of the buggy he would appear sinister, and she didn't want to be frightened by shadows.

Derek jerked the reins and turned the horse down a side street, cracking the buggy whip across the animal's flanks, whipping it into a frenzied gallop. She thought for a moment that he meant to take them right out of town, but he turned again, this time onto Montgomery and they raced recklessly toward the Ice Palace. When he hauled brutally back on the reins, Alexis gripped the side rail to keep from being tossed forward, perhaps hurtled into the street.

Out of breath, she sat motionless as the dust settled around them. Derek hopped down and hurried around to her side of the buggy. She stared straight ahead, wanting a moment to compose herself before looking at him.

"I'm sorry, Alexis. I shouldn't have pushed the horse like that. Not when you're feeling ill. We'll have our supper together another time."

It sounded more like a threat than an invitation. She wanted to get away from him. She was as close to sheer panic as she'd ever been in her life.

"Of course, Derek. We must do that. I'm sorry I spoiled the evening for you."

Seeing no other choice, she accepted his help out of the buggy, but she wasted no time in heading for the door to the Ice Palace.

"Another time," he called after her.

She turned her head to glance back at him, and it was then that she saw Colter, sitting astride his white horse, watching from across the street. Her fear vanished. She was being silly. Derek was no threat to her.

"We'll see, Derek," she replied. "I can't make any promises tonight."

She turned and went inside before he could speak again.

10

"You understand? Stir things up in there. She's only a woman. She'll need a man's help if there's real trouble. Make sure she realizes she can't manage on her own. Things'll get out of hand. Just too much for her. Understand? I don't care if a few tables get broken but don't damage that bar or that mirror."

"What about the woman?"

"Don't let her get damaged either. I'll take care of her in my own time in my own way."

Alexis stood in front of her mirror. She was wearing another new gown, but she wasn't really looking at it. She was looking deeper, trying to see right inside herself.

He was going to ask her to marry him again tonight. She knew he would, and she wondered if she could say no to him one more time. If only he would say that he loved her, all would be well, but even without those words, she doubted she could deny him any longer. A feeling stronger than she'd ever known burned inside her, refusing to be ignored. Her pride was quickly faltering beside her growing desire to be held in his arms. What good was pride anyway, if it kept her from the man she loved?

"Alexis Ashmore," she whispered, reaching out to touch her reflection in the looking glass, "who are you anyway?"

Was she the girl she'd once been, riding astride, wearing a gun and holster? Or was she this woman she saw here, dressed in an elegant gown, diamonds sparkling at her throat?

She heard the knock on her door. "Come on in, Stella," she called, not moving away from the mirror.

"You grow more beautiful every day."

She whirled around, feeling a rush of heat at the sound of Colter's voice. He was wearing a white suit tonight with a ruffled shirt. He looked every bit the part of a riverboat gambler, too handsome to be trusted.

He stepped closer. "I wonder sometimes how I ever could have thought you and Althea looked like twins. You're really not much alike at all."

Alexis would have turned away, but his hand, placed lightly on her upper arm, stopped her.

"Your hair is much finer. It's like silk." He caressed her hair between his fingertips.

"Colt, I must go downstairs," she said with

difficulty, not really wanting to stop him, yet knowing she must end this intimate moment or lose whatever shreds of control she still had.

"Then let me escort you to your subjects, Your Majesty." He swept a dramatic bow, then offered his elbow. He led her toward the door. "Wait," he said suddenly. "I nearly forgot. Every queen should have a crown." Out of his pocket he drew a diamond and sapphire tiara.

Alexis was left speechless.

"I wish they were brighter. They pale beside your brilliance," he whispered in her ear before placing the tiara on her head.

Alexis blinked back a sudden rush of tears. Why was it he could make her cry so easily?

Colter turned her toward a gilt-framed mirror near the door. "Well? Do you like it?"

"It's . . . it's wonderful, Colt. I . . ."

Tenderly, almost chastely, he kissed her cheek. "Let's go down. You look too beautiful tonight to cry."

Once they were downstairs, Colter left her side and joined the game at a poker table. Alexis moved by rote, following a routine that was so well established she needn't think about what she was doing. She moved from table to table, greeting the customers, dropping a friendly word here and there, observing her dealers. She smiled automatically at the men's teasing, yet without really knowing what it was they said. She was wishing the whole while that she had never come down this evening. That Colter's kiss would have been more than friendly, more than tender and chaste.

"You've cheated me, mister. I saw you deal from the bottom of the deck."

Distracted by her own musings, it took the man's words a moment to sink in. By the time she looked his way, the burly man had pushed himself to his feet and was glaring ferociously at the much shorter dealer. Heads throughout the saloon were turning to see what was happening. Alexis hurried toward them.

"What seems to be wrong, sir?" she asked.

"Your dealer's trying to cheat me, that's what's wrong?"

Alexis looked at the dealer. "Jessie?"

"I never cheat. You know that, Miss Alexis."

The big man slammed a fist down onto the green felt table. "I say you *did* cheat."

"Sir," she said, trying to avoid the fracas that seemed about to break loose, "if you'll step into my office, I think we can discuss this in a calm and sensible manner. I'm sure if we try we can come to an agreement on what is fair."

"You're not going to talk me out of what I say happened." He swept his eyes over his audience. "What do you men expect from a place that lets a woman run it? You think these men are going to play fair with us when they've got no real boss." He sneered at Alexis. "That dealer's been cheating me, and he's going to get what he's got coming."

The derringer she always carried, hidden in a pocket of her dress, was suddenly aimed at the bridge of his nose, almost before she even knew she was reaching for it herself. She was tempted to echo his sneer as his ugly threats turned to surprise.

"Mister, I'll have no trouble in the Ice Palace. We run an honest saloon here. I'll stand for no cheating, on either side of the table. Now, since you refused to discuss it with me, I can only assume the best course is for you to take your sport elsewhere. Pick up your money and get out."

"But . . ."

"Get out."

He swept the coins into one meaty palm, then shoved them into a pocket. "You won't get away with this," he threatened.

Alexis kept the pistol pointed at his head the entire time. The man's face was clouded with dark rage as he pushed his way through the silent crowd. Alexis followed him, pistol in hand, to the door. Once he was gone, she sighed and pocketed the derringer. As she turned around, a cheer erupted, startling her before bringing a smile to her lips and a rosy glow to her cheeks.

Her smile was short-lived. Colter appeared suddenly at her side, his face clouded with anger. Strong fingers clasped her arm, and he hauled her unceremoniously up the stairs toward her suite, leaving behind a stunned and silent crowd.

Colter pushed the door open with force and propelled her inside the room.

"Colt, what on earth . . ."

"You idiot!" he exploded. The full force of his rage was turned on her. "What did you think you were doing?"

"What do you . . ." she began, confused and a little frightened. She had never seen Colter like this.

"You think that man was joking? He won't forget that a woman threw him out of here, that you threatened him with a gun and humiliated him in front of so many. Why didn't you let someone else take care of him? I was here. I would have stopped him."

Her own anger flared. "It's my *place* to protect my property. Do you think I'm just another stupid female, able only to bat my eyes and simper before a man?" She jerked free of his hand and stalked to the fireplace. She stared at the cold hearth, trying to calm her ragged nerves.

Colter paused, also reining in his anger. "Alexis, what if he'd drawn his gun?"

She turned a steady gaze his way. "I would have shot him."

"Have you ever shot a man before?" His question unnerved her.

"No."

He followed her across the room. He didn't touch her. He just stood before her, his eyes boring into hers, searching, probing. She felt her reason melting before his gaze.

"I don't want you hurt, Alexis."

"I . . . I'll be all right, Colt. I know how to take care of myself. I have to know how."

His throaty reply was almost a whisper. "Do you?" His hands took hold of her shoulders and drew her closer. "Why not let me do it for you? Let me take care of you, Alex."

Alexis looked up and saw the smoldering

glow in his brown eyes. She was powerless to resist his descending lips, even if she'd wanted to. She closed her eyes, ready to savor the taste of his mouth against hers and the texture of his lips. The kiss was restrained, yet she could feel the heat of his desire in the touch of his hand on her back. Her heart beat erratically in her breast. She waited, unable and unwilling to stop him from taking more than just a kiss. Her thoughts were blurred by her own wanting.

Their mouths parted, but they didn't draw away from each other. There was a breathless waiting.

"Marry me, Alex."

Her eyes opened slowly. She knew he could see the fire of her wanting in them. There was no hiding it. She was his woman. She would always be his woman, whether or not he loved her. She was branded by her own uncontrollable passion for him. She was shamed by her weakness. What power did he have over her? She had been a virgin, ignorant of the ways of love, yet she had drawn him to her that first night with a boldness, instinctively knowing that only he could fill the strange emptiness he stirred inside of her.

Now she stood on this precipice again. Where was her pride, her independence? She had stolen him from her sister. Wasn't that bad enough? Would she now settle for a life without real love, just so she could taste his kisses and linger in his embraces?

Yes. Yes, she would settle for anything just to be with him.

"I can't say no to you anymore," she

whispered weakly. Her head dropped to his chest, and she fought her rising tears. "I'll hate myself forever, but I can't say no."

She felt his lips brush her hair. "Why? Why will you hate yourself?" His words were soft, tender.

"Because of what I did to you ... and to Althea. If I hadn't let you go on thinking it was her that night, we ... you and I ... never would have ..."

Colter tilted her chin with his finger, forcing her to look at him. "Alex, I knew it was you."

"But ... but you called me Althea," she replied, unbelieving.

"That was outside. In the dark. You had on her dress and your back was toward me. As soon as you turned around, I knew it was you. Alex, it was you I made love to, not Althea." He paused, his gaze saying as much as his lips. "It was you I loved that night ... and have loved ever since."

Her heart flipped, and she felt herself go pale. She wanted to believe him, but how could she? "Then ... why did you take me to her bed instead of mine?" Her voice quivered.

Calloused fingers stroked her cheek before cradling her chin. He kissed her forehead lightly, then kissed the bridge of her nose. She could feel his breath warm on her skin as he spoke softly. "You silly girl. That was *my* bed. Althea was just using it as a guest in my house."

"Colt." She spoke his name as a caress, an expression of wonder and of surrender.

Colter drew her up, his arms tightening, his mouth claiming hers in a fiery kiss that made her blood run hot in her veins. Her skin tingled with pleasant sensations. She pressed herself closer against him, wanting to become a part of him, to be forever one with him, to be consumed by his love and his body. She could feel the thunder of his heart beating in his chest, an echo of her own.

Firm hands fastened around her arms. Reason warred with passion in Colter's eyes as he removed her to a safer distance. "No, Alex. Not again." He shook his head. "I won't have you wondering about my motives a second time."

He lifted her hand to his lips, kissing each finger, then turning it and kissing the palm. The tender caresses were almost more than she could bear.

"We will marry first," he whispered, "and then we will have forever to love each other."

"Yes. Oh, yes."

Alexis went around in a daze in the days that followed. An announcement of their engagement appeared in the *Boise News*, and she was suddenly making small talk with nearly every woman who lived in Idaho City as they paid visits and extended their congratulations.

"They're just glad to see anyone as pretty as you are get married," Stella whispered to her as one particularly dour matron left Alexis' suite one morning. "Lessens the temptations for their husbands, you know."

"Stella!" Alexis protested, but she laughed, her joy bubbling over.

Derek Anderson paid her a visit one afternoon when she was alone in her suite. Colter had reluctantly returned to the ranch for a few days. He had wanted her to go with him, but Mrs. Cane had forbidden her to leave. The wedding was only two weeks away, and Alexis had to be close at hand for the many fittings. There was the bridal gown and the many dresses for her trousseau to be finished. They would never be done in time without Alexis nearby. Stella had left for Mrs. Cane's with more fabric choices only minutes before Derek's knock sounded on her door.

She was seated at her desk. With great difficulty, she was trying to pen a letter to her father.

"Come in," she called absent-mindedly.

She heard the door open and close but didn't look up until she heard a man clearing his throat. She turned, placing her hands on the polished wood back of the chair.

"Derek. I'm sorry. I thought it must be someone from the saloon."

She hadn't seen him since the night he'd taken her to the Jenny Lind. She felt a rush of anxiety, as if she were once again racing through the streets of town, out of control. Then the scene changed, and she remembered the first time she'd seen him, and the way he had looked at her, wrapped in her clinging blanket. Now she wished he would just go away so she could forget she'd ever met him.

"I hear congratulations are in order," he said, setting his hat on the table near the door.

"Thank you, Derek." She rose from the desk, shaking off her apprehensions. "Please forgive me. Come in and sit down."

He crossed the room and stood by the blue sofa, waiting for her to take her seat before he sat down. Alexis smiled, her mind grasping for small talk to fill the silence that stifled the room.

"Would you like some tea or some coffee?"

"No, thank you."

She smoothed the fabric of her day dress, then glanced at the door as if willing Stella to return.

"I won't pretend to be happy about this," Derek said abruptly. "You must have known I had hoped... Well, you must know I care for you."

"Derek..."

"Are you sure you know what you're doing?"

Alexis stood up, her hands clenched before her. "Mr. Anderson, I think you presume too much. We have never been more than casual friends. Our one evening at the theatre hardly gives you the right to question my plans for marriage."

Derek was on his feet too. "I'm sorry, Alexis. I..."

"I think you'd best call me Miss Ashmore."

His mouth tensed as he nodded. "Miss Ashmore." Then he flashed her a conciliatory smile. "May I try again? Miss Ashmore, I hope you will find every happiness with Mr. Stephens. Please allow me to host a small gathering for you and some of the leading citizens of Idaho City at the Golden Gulch. We'll be reopening this week, and I can't think of a better way to celebrate it."

"I don't know..."

He offered his hand. "Truce?"

Her anger melted. She was being unfair. He hadn't really done anything to earn her distrust. Hadn't he always tried to be friendly and helpful? And, if he had been carrying a torch for her as he'd just said, then shouldn't she forgive him his ill-considered intrusion into her private affairs?

She took his hand and shook it firmly. "Truce."

"And the party at the Golden Gulch?"

"I'll have to check with Colt when he returns."

"Is he gone for long?"

Alexis pulled her hand away. "No. I'll be able to let you know quite soon."

"Good day then," Derek replied.

He bowed formally, then turned on his heel and strode away. He picked up his hat, opened the door, and stepped into the hall, but before he closed it, he glanced back at her one more time. The look left her feeling uneasy as he closed the door.

She shook herself mentally. She had to stop being so melodramatic when it came to Derek Anderson.

She turned back to her writing desk and sighed. This was what was truly bothering her. This letter to her father. This *unwritten* letter to her father. She had been struggling over the blank sheet of paper for hours.

"No more excuses," she muttered aloud as she sat down and picked up her pen.

Dear Father, I hope this letter finds you soon and that it finds everyone well at Willowind. I am fine. I've been living in Idaho City for the past several weeks. Much has happened in my life, more than I will attempt to tell in this letter. Colt has followed me here and has succeeded in persuading me to marry him. I know you know all about my shameful behavior and have been concerned that Colt should do right by me, but that is not why I agreed to become his wife. It's because I love him and he loves me. I never thought I could be so happy. But there is still a sadness—that my happiness should have caused my own sister such sorrow. I hope someday Althea will be able to forgive me my part in all of this. I'm glad you could be with her.

Though you may find it hard to believe, I am the owner of the Ice Palace in Idaho. I know you must have patronized it while you were here and will know what a splendid saloon it is. Colt has agreed that we can stay here until next summer. The new ranch house will be complete and furnished by then, and in the meantime, I will be able to prove to myself and to Colt that I can manage the Palace with continued success, something he told me once that I couldn't do.

I think of you and Mother and Althea often, wondering what is happening with the war. The news we receive is always so sketchy and so old. Feelings run high here and most everyone is a Confederate sympathizer. When you and I were in California, I never thought much about the war, one way or the other. Even Althea's descriptions of what it's been like didn't affect me much. But now, as I listen, I begin to wonder how anyone can sit on the fence and not react to what is happening in the states. Perhaps my sudden concern is because my family is there, right in the middle of it all.

Papa, I miss you and wish you could be here with me now, to share my happiness. I would wish all of you here, away from the dangers of the war. By the time you get this letter, if you get it at all, I will be Mrs. Colter Stephens. Please know that I have remembered you on that special day and thank you for all you have been and done for me.

Love,
Alexis

It was inadequate. She couldn't put onto paper everything she was feeling. Her joy was bittersweet. If only Jonathan could have been here on her wedding day. He would have understood her happiness and her confusion. He had always understood her.

Derek rubbed his beard thoughtfully as he walked along the boardwalk. She was going to marry someone else. She'd never even given him a second glance. Derek didn't like to lose.

But marriages didn't always last. Sometimes two people weren't happy with each other. Sometimes one of them died before the other. Life was filled with circumstances that could separate a man and woman, even once they were married. Derek hadn't lost yet. He meant to have the Ice Palace, and he meant to have its Queen. Now all he needed was a plan.

Derek was cautious. He had a reputation to uphold in this town. He meant to own it all one day. Perhaps he'd even be governor of the territory—or even the state, when that day finally came. His future depended upon his careful assessment of every situation.

He caught sight of the bright red hair beneath a subdued sunbonnet and halted. He leaned against a post and watched as she smiled and spoke her good-byes to Mrs. Cane. Her arms were filled with packages, undoubtedly for Alexis. Her swelling form was concealed beneath the ample skirt of her gown.

Derek clenched his teeth. He didn't like to make mistakes any more than he liked to lose. Mistakes could cost him dearly, and Stella was a mistake. He had been so certain that she would leave town, but here she was—and not even with enough good sense to stay hidden away while she grew big with child.

She walked toward him, the remains of her smile still tilting the corners of her mouth. He straightened, blocking the walkway. She glanced up and the smile vanished for good. The green eyes widened as her cheeks lost their color.

"Hello, Stella. It's been awhile since I've seen you. Here. Let me help you." He took the packages from her arms and took hold of her elbow. He tilted his head toward hers as he propelled her along the walk. "You really shouldn't avoid me so much, my dear. We've been friends for a long time."

"Please let go, Derek."

"But we have so much to talk about. After all, we share something special, you and I." His voice hardened on his last words as he steered them into an alley, stopping behind some large crates stacked against the wall of a saloon.

Stella resembled a trapped animal. Her eyes darted from side to side, seeking a way of escape. He could feel her trembling.

"Why are you still in Idaho? What are you doing at the Palace?"

"I had nowhere to go, Derek. I . . . I was hurt and . . . and Alexis found me and took me in."

"What have you told her?" He leaned closer, his tone menacing.

"Nothing," she whispered. "I've told her nothing."

Derek's smile returned. He stepped back from her and tapped the brim of his hat. "My dear Stella, I can't tell you how pleased I am to learn you have some good sense after all. Allow me to impart a little more wisdom to you. You do *not* know who the father of that child is, and don't you forget it. You are a whore, dear Stella. Whores never know who it was that fathered their bastard children." He reached out and stroked the side of her face. "Even in this town, people believe the word of a respected citizen over a whore. I'm a respected citizen, Stella. People look up to me. Be careful what you say and who you say it to. I would hate to see anything happen to you or that child of yours."

He handed the packages back to her and, with a jaunty step, walked away. He would have to keep an eye on Stella, but he was certain she would keep her silence.

11

As chance would have it, Alexis was standing by her parlor window, looking down on Montgomery Street, when the wagon pulled up in front of the Ice Palace.

"I don't believe it." She pulled the drapes aside. "It is! It's Sadie!"

She whirled away from the window and raced from her suite, fairly flying down the stairs on her way to greet her friend. Sadie was still unloading her brood when Alexis whisked through the front doors.

"Sadie!"

The woman's homely face was brightened by her broad smile. She handed two-year-old Summer, the youngest of the Houston clan, to Helen, then held her arms wide open for Alexis. Alexis ran into them as naturally as if she'd been doing it all her life.

"Oh, Sadie, I'm so glad you've come," she said into the woman's massive breast.

"Landsake, girl. Did you think I'd miss this wedding? Who was it that said you were the girl for my Colt from the moment she laid eyes on you? That was me, and I haven't forgot it even if you have." She released her bear hug and held Alexis at arm's length. "Look at you. All the spunk that was there before and then some. And right pretty in your new clothes."

"Thanks, Sadie. Come on everyone. Let's go inside."

She led them to her private entrance, bypassing the saloon. It gave her a happy feeling, thinking of all the guest rooms being filled for a change. Chances were the Ice Palace would never be quite the same after the Houston invasion. Once the children were settled, Alexis took Sadie into her own suite and sat her down on a sofa. She rang for a tea tray, then settled on the sofa beside her friend.

"I'm so glad you could come," she repeated. "You're the closest I have to family who could be here. I wrote to my father, but I'll be lucky if he even gets the letter. Will Jasper be able to come?"

"He'll be here, love. He's got a soft spot for you, just like the rest of us." She patted Alexis' hand. "Now, tell me everything. I want to hear it all."

Sam leaned back in his chair and rolled his pen back and forth between the palms of his hands. He was grinning to himself, his thoughts a thousand miles from the notes he should have been thinking about.

It was odd how a man's life could change so suddenly. One moment he thought he knew exactly what he wanted and then... Boom! Things changed, and what should have made him unhappy turned out to be for the best. It wasn't the least bit logical, but there it was. Sam Wainwright was in love, and he intended to marry the girl. If he had to, he'd throw her bodily across a horse and cart her off to the mountains as his captive. The thought made him laugh aloud.

He dropped his pen and closed his open brief. There was no point in wasting any more time here in his office. He had more important things with which to concern himself. He was going to propose to her today.

He got up from behind his desk and went over to the small mirror on the wall near the door. He ran a hand over his thinning black hair, then straightened his tie. He wished he was taller. He wished he was more handsome. He swallowed, making his Adam's apple bob.

"Well, I won't take no for an answer," he mumbled.

He squared his shoulders as he placed his bowler on his head. As an afterthought, he reached for his walking stick. He might as well go all out in trying to impress the lady. With a determined step, he left his office and turned in the direction of the Ice Palace.

The day was hot, the August sun beating relentlessly down on the pine board and pitch mining town. Anything that moved in the street stirred up a cloud of dust that lingered in the still air long after the cause had disappeared from view. The saloons were filled with idle miners. Water was low and the town was full. It was a good day for trouble of one kind or another.

Sam wasn't aware of any of this, however. He was rehearsing his speech over and over again as he hurried along.

Reaching the Ice Palace, he used the back entrance. As a matter of routine, he checked with the cashiers, took a cursory glance at the books, then headed up the stairs. He could hear laughter coming from several of the rooms as he walked toward Alexis' suite and wondered what guests had arrived early for the wedding. He knocked on her door.

Alexis opened the door for him. "Why, Sam. I didn't expect you here today. Were we supposed to be going over some things? I'm afraid in all the . . ."

"No, Alexis," Sam said, stopping her. "There's nothing that needs attending to until after your honeymoon. This is purely a social call."

She stepped back. "Come in. There's someone here I'd like you to meet." She took his arm and led him into her parlor.

A very large woman was seated on the sofa near the window. Her face was plain, yet friendly, and he knew even before they were introduced that this must be Sadie. Alexis had described her to him once. Only one woman could fit that description.

"You must be Mrs. Houston," he said before

Alexis could introduce them. "Alexis has been worried you wouldn't be able to come."

"Sadie, this is Sam Wainwright, my attorney and a very dear friend."

"I'm pleased to meet you, Mr. Wainwright. If you've been a friend to Alexis, then you're a friend of mine."

"I consider that an honor, madam."

Sam took a nearby seat and proceeded to pass the next few minutes in exchanging pleasantries, but his eyes kept moving toward the door. Finally, Alexis asked him what was wrong.

"Wrong? Oh, nothing's wrong. I was just wondering if . . . well, if Stella is around today. She's usually here with you." The words all came out in a rush.

Alexis looked surprised, then puzzled, then pleased. "Sam," she said softly, "I always thought it was me you came to see."

He was flustered. "It was. At first. I mean, we had business together, you and I."

Alexis stopped him by placing a hand on his arm. "Sam, does Stella know how you feel?"

"Not yet. But she's going to," he replied, his determination strenghtening his words.

Alexis's eyebrows drew together in concern. "You do know that she's . . . that Stella is . . ."

"In the family way?" he finished for her. He smiled wanly. "I'd guessed. It doesn't make any difference to me." He felt as if he needed to explain himself further. "I don't care about what she might have done in the past, Alexis. The last few weeks we've spent a lot of time together, in your office, talking. I want her to marry me."

"Then, Sam, I don't think it's me you should be telling. It's Stella. She's in her room lying down. Let me call her for you."

Sam got up. "Wait. If . . . if you don't think it would be too improper, I'd like to go myself. We could be alone that way."

Alexis hooked her arm through his and drew him across the room. "No one will ever know whether it's improper or not." She opened the door and pointed down the hallway. "She's moved into the last room at the end. It's a little cooler in the afternoons. She's been suffering from the heat lately." She gave his arm a warm squeeze. "Good luck, Sam." She kissed his cheek.

Sam looked at her in surprise.

Alexis laughed. "Sam, it's the prerogative of every bride to want everyone else to be in love and as happy as she." She gave him a little shove. "Go on."

Stella had drawn the curtains against the stifling heat, shrouding her room in shadows. She was lying on her bed, wearing her most sheer dressing gown, when the knock sounded at her door. Mona, the new maid Alexis had hired, had gone for something cool for her to drink only moments before, and Stella assumed it was her.

"Come on in, Mona."

Sam stepped inside, blinking against the dimness of the room as he looked for her.

"Sam!" She tugged at her dressing gown above her swollen breasts.

"Hello, Stella."

"Sam, what are you doing here? I'm not dressed to see anyone. Please..." She had always tried to hide her pregnancy from Sam. He had always treated her so square, as if he didn't know the way she had lived before she came to the Ice Palace. She wasn't ready for him to know the truth about her.

"It's all right, Stella. I don't care what you're wearing." His eyes had adjusted to the lack of light, and he was looking right at her now.

She smoothed her hair away from her face. She could feel the color rising in her cheeks. She was going to lose him as a friend. He would see what she was, and then she would never see him again. Or worse, he would expect to see her no longer as a friend but as what she was. She wanted to die.

"Stella, I've come to say something to you. I'm not very good at speeches, unless they're before a judge and jury, but I'm going to do my best. I came West because I wanted to get away from the sameness, from the routine. Maybe I'm still rather stodgy in my own way, but one of the things I like out here is that a person's past is his own business. People have a new chance at being just what they want to be. There's a freshness, an excitement. Every day's a challenge. It takes special people to meet the challenge. I think you're one of those people, Stella. I think you're special."

He took a few steps toward her. Sweat was trickling down the sides of his face. He pulled his handkerchief from inside his coat and dabbed at his forehead, hoping she wouldn't guess that he was perspiring more from nerves than from the heat of the room.

"You and I, we've talked a lot. I think we've become friends. I mean, I think you like me, at least a little. What I'm trying to say, Stella, is that . . . I'd like us to get married. That is if you wouldn't mind being the wife of a lawyer. It's not very exciting. Not like living over a saloon with someone like Alexis, but I'd be good to you and I do care for you and . . ."

Sam's voice trailed off into silence as Stella stared at him, her eyes wide with surprise. He took two more steps in her direction and then knelt down on the floor.

"What do you say, Stella? Will you marry me?"

"Sam," she whispered, "I'm not good enough to marry you."

"Don't be silly."

This was worse than if he'd seen for himself and then rejected her. She was going to be forced to tell him and watch his disgust as he learned the truth.

"I can't marry you. I . . . Sam, I'm going to have a baby."

"I know."

She felt a little lightheaded. "You know?"

"Of course. If you're worried about how I'd feel about it, don't. It will be a Wainwright. My own child."

"But, Sam . . . You don't even know who . . ."

"And I don't want to know. Don't need to know. All I want to know is . . . Will you marry me?" He cleared his throat and then raised his voice. "I love you, Stella."

She thought back to all those hours they had spent in Alexis' office, after the business was done, after Alexis had gone to see to other things. Sam had taken time to help her choose good books to read. Some times he had talked about his childhood. Mostly he had just made her feel good about herself, made her forget the mistakes she had made, at least for a little while. She had never thought that he might really care for her, had never dared hope that he might. It wasn't until this moment that she realized just how much she cared for him.

"Sam," she offered as one last protest, "you don't even know my last name."

He reached forward and took her hand. "Then tell me. What is your last name?"

"Barnes. Stella Barnes."

"Will you marry me, Stella Barnes?"

"Yes, Sam Wainright. If you want me, I'll marry you." She felt the threat of tears rising in her emerald eyes as she added, "I love you, too."

Between the Houston family's arrival and Stella's sudden marriage (the private ceremony was held in Alexis' suite), Alexis' thoughts were distracted from her own approaching wedding, at least for a couple of days. But when sunrise cast its golden glow over the mountains on the morning of her special day, Alexis was awake to see it.

She was standing at the window of her bedroom, looking out over the silent town. For the moment, all was still in the street below. It was hard to believe she'd been living here two months already, yet somehow she felt she'd always been a part of it. Maybe it was because the town wasn't even two years old itself. Everyone here had a part in making it what it was. She was going to miss it when she returned with Colter to the Circle S, yet she missed the ranch, too, and was looking forward to being there again.

She leaned her head against the window frame and closed her eyes. Funny, she thought, how special days always make a person want to look back at the past. She was no different from most. Her thoughts carried her back in time to other special days. Like the birthday when she was eight and her father gave her her very own pony. How she loved that little horse. Gray with a white mane and tail and full of punch. Ignoring her petticoats and pantaloons, she'd throw her leg across his back and race up the country roads and across the many acres of Willowind. Oh, how her mother would scold her.

Her mother. Would Madonna be pleased that she was getting married? No. Not since she'd expected Colter to marry Althea and live at Willowind. But then Alexis had never been able to please her mother, try as she might. Still, she felt a strange emptiness that her mother wasn't with her on this day, to share in her joy and to understand her jitters.

And her father. Jonathan wouldn't know until long after they'd been married, but then, he had left here knowing that this was what Colter wanted. If only he knew that she loved Colter, too, that she was sorry she had let it happen the way it did. But she wouldn't have changed the outcome for anything in the world.

She was going to be Colter's wife. Nothing could stop her from wanting that now. She remembered that April day when she and her father rode into Boise City. She had told her father that no man was worth coming all the way from Virginia to Idaho. How wrong she'd been. She would cross the seven seas to be with Colter. Strange that she hadn't known it the first moment she laid eyes on him in that livery.

"Maybe I did know it. Even then," she whispered, opening her eyes to gaze down at the sleepy town once more.

"Thought you probably wouldn't be able to sleep much."

Alexis turned from the window. "Good morning, Sadie. No, I couldn't sleep." She let the curtain fall back in place as she stepped away from the window. "Did you know, on your wedding day, even the canvas saloons look pretty special? And there's not a single wagon stuck in the middle of the street."

Sadie laughed. "Oh, you've got them for sure."

"Got what?"

"Starry eyes. Happens only to very lucky brides who're in love with the man they're about to marry. You don't know just how few they are."

Alexis sat down on her bed and patted the spread, encouraging Sadie to join her there. "I *do* know how lucky I am, Sadie. I know how close I came to losing him because of my pride. I'm glad he was more stubborn than me."

"He's stubborn, all right, but it's a good stubborn. Like my Jasper."

"How did you meet him, Sadie?" Alexis settled back against the headboard and drew a pillow into her lap, hugging it to her breast.

"Met him on my way West. My first husband, Mr. Humphrey, died in St. Jo just before we were to come out this way. Headed for California. Lookin' for good farm land. When he died, I decided to come out myself. Figured I could farm good land just as good as he could've. I met Jasper on the train out. His wagon was just two behind me. It must have been fate. Well, we got married before we reached California."

"What about Mr. Humphrey? Did you love him too?"

Sadie sighed as she shrugged. "I don't really know, Alex. He was a good man, quite a bit older than me. He was a friend of my father's, and I grew up around him. When he asked my father for my hand, it seemed agreeable enough, and I can't say we were ever unhappy in those years we were married." She smiled. "But I loved my Jasper from the moment I laid eyes on him."

Alexis rested her chin on the pillow in her lap as she drew her knees up toward her chest. "What happened when you got to California?"

"There was a lot of excitement. Gold was discovered at Sutter's Mill. Men were leavin' the soil and rushin' for the gold fields. Jasper figured the best way to make money was to sell the goods to all those miners, and so we opened our first store. Did right well, too, but I don't think either one of us was very happy in California. Just didn't suit us somehow. So we sold everything and came up this way when the time seemed right. Glad we did, else I wouldn't have met Colt and then I wouldn't be sittin' here right now with you."

"I'm glad you did, too, Sadie. I'd be a nervous wreck without you here."

Sadie laughed. "If you're like most women, you'll be a nervous wreck no matter who's here with you. It's all part of the plan. An unwritten law. A bride must be nervous on her wedding day, no matter how much she loves the groom." She got to her feet, placed her hands on her ample hips and winked at Alexis. "I knew you were the girl for my Colt the minute I laid eyes on you. Now, we'd better rustle up some grub for you or you won't have a bite to eat all day. Can't have you fainting for lack of nourishment right in the middle of the ceremony."

Colter jerked at his tie. He just couldn't get the knot right. His fingers seemed to be in knots themselves.

"Relax, Colter. It won't be much longer now," Sam said from behind him.

Colter turned away from the small mirror on the wall. "All thumbs," he said by way of explanation.

"It's to be expected." Sam grinned.

Colter had been staying with the attorney since his return from the Circle S. It seemed he'd hardly had a minute alone with his bride for weeks. He had begun to wish that he'd dragged her away by her hair, stood her before a judge, and then carried her back to the ranch, even if they would have had to live in the cabin with Li Ching until the house was built. At least they would be married by now and he wouldn't be so nervous.

"Not having second thoughts, are you?" Sam asked, noting Colter's frown.

"About marrying Alexis? Not a one. It's all this fuss that's driving me crazy."

Sam laughed. "It's the price a man must pay to have the woman he loves."

Price to pay? There wasn't *anything* he wouldn't do to make Alexis his. Suddenly, Colter relaxed. Why was he being so silly? This was just a ceremony after all. His love for Alexis was what truly made them married. This wouldn't make him any more hers than he'd been before, or her his. It just made sure that everyone else knew they belonged to each other.

"You know what, Sam? It's a very small price."

He turned back to the mirror. The tie went together perfectly this time. Colter reached for his high hat and placed it over his sandy hair.

"I think it's time to go," he added as he tapped the crown of the shiny hat, a cocky grin replacing the frown that he had worn only minutes before.

The Ice Palace had been transformed from a saloon into a cathedral. Yards of satin fabric covered the bar and the wall behind it, hiding from view the liquor bottles, the mirrors, and the reclining, bare-breasted woman on the twenty foot canvas. Blue and white flowers were everywhere, their perfume adding a sweetness to the air. Candles flickered merrily in candelabras, and the chandeliers glittered and shone as never before. The gaming tables had disappeared. In their place were rows and rows of chairs which were already beginning to fill as guests arrived.

Upstairs, another transformation was taking place as women buzzed around Alexis. She stood nearly naked in their midst, clad only in a chemise and pantaloons. Sadie held the satin and lace wedding gown in her arms with care as Stella helped Alexis into several stiff petticoats. Mrs. Cane observed and ordered as she circled the bride, frowning and muttering to herself as if everything was wrong. But when the gown was slipped over the bride's head, each tiny button carefully fastened, the seamstress stopped. A slow smile dawned on her lips as she observed her creation.

"*Tchk, tchk*," she clucked, but in awe, not in disapproval. "I said you were too lovely to be wearing those trousers, but I had no idea. My dear, you have done wonders for that dress. You are a truly beautiful bride. Take a look."

Alexis obeyed, catching a glimpse of herself in the full-length mirror for the first time.

The cream-colored satin gown had a snug bodice with off the shoulder sleeves. Tiny pearls traced the neckline, both front and back. Below the tiny waist, the skirt blossomed into fullness, the many yards of satin glistening over crackling petticoats.

Stella brought several strings of pearls and

clasped them around her throat. Alexis touched them almost reverently. They were another of Colter's gifts sent to his bride before the wedding.

Sadie brought her a crown of pearls with a whisper-fine veil. Before setting it on Alexis' head, she bent forward to kiss the bride's cheek. Her dark eyes were misty.

In deference to Colter's wishes, Alexis had left her hair loose, pulling it back with combs at her temples, then letting the pale yellow tresses fall in gentle waves over her bare shoulders and down her back.

Sadie stepped behind Alexis and set the crown in place, smoothing the veil over Alexis' hair and face. "All the happiness in the world. That's what I'm wishing for you and my Colt," she whispered.

"Thank you, Sadie." Alexis discovered that her throat seemed swollen. Her words were barely audible.

Even Mrs. Cane was brushing away tears as she searched her reticule for a handkerchief. "My goodness. I don't ever cry. This will never do." She dabbed at her damp cheeks, then stood on tiptoe to peck Alexis' cheek through the veil. "You're a mighty lucky girl. I liked him the first I saw him in my shop. To buy you that pretty blue hat."

"I like him, too," Alexis whispered, hoping she wasn't going to start crying too.

The two older women left the bedroom, and Alexis turned around to face Stella.

"Well . . . it's here," she said, sounding breathless.

Stella stepped closer, a quivering smile on her mouth. Her cheeks were pink; her green eyes sparkled with what looked suspiciously like tears. "Alex, I want to say something. I'm so happy with Sam, and if it hadn't been for your kindness, it never would've happened. I never would've met him. Not . . . well, we just wouldn't have. I don't deserve to be as happy as I am, but you deserve all the happiness that life can give. You've been so good to me. I . . . never had a friend until I met you."

"Oh, Stella, you're wrong about me deserving to be happier than you. I don't suppose anybody deserves happiness. Some of us are just lucky enough to stumble into it. I'm glad we're friends."

They hugged and then Stella hurried from the room.

Alexis turned once more toward the mirror, gazing at her reflection with wonder. She couldn't believe that the bride in satin and lace who was staring back at her with round, almost bewildered, blue eyes was really her. Her stomach was all aflutter. Her hands felt clammy. What if he changed his mind? What if he didn't really love her but still felt obligated? What if she made him miserable? What if . . .

"May I come in?" Jasper stepped into the room on the echo of his question. "Sadie told me you were ready."

Alexis turned. "I'm ready," she answered in

a soft voice.

He smiled, wiggling his handlebar mustache. "Not nervous, are you?"

She shook her head.

Jasper chuckled at her pretense and held out his elbow for her to take. "Awfully honored that you'd ask me to do this, Alexis. Sort of puts me in practice for a few of my own. Besides, I like to think of you and Colter as being a part of our family."

"Thank you, Jasper. It's I who am honored. I'm so glad you could be with me today. Papa would be glad, too, if he knew. He did like you and Sadie so much."

They stopped talking as they left her suite. They walked silently down the hallway toward the curving staircase. There was a moment, as they paused at the top and she could see the saloon packed with people, that she nearly panicked and bolted for her room again. Then her gaze met with Colter's, and she was calmed. Here was her strength. Here was everything she had ever wanted, even when she hadn't known she wanted it.

Colter. Her eyes spoke his name in silence.

She could read her love returned in his eyes of brown. They told her how much he cherished her. They promised he would be beside her always. They promised trust and companionship and devotion. And they promised the warmth of his embrace, the passionate taste of his mouth, the demanding ecstasy of his love. Her face took on a radiance that could be seen by everyone, even through her veil.

"Like an angel," someone whispered.

"Still a queen," someone else replied.

No one was envied more than Colter Stephens at that moment. He had won the prize so many had coveted. He alone had known that the Ice Queen had a heart of fire and he had made it burn for him. There was more than one man in the room who had dreamed that this woman would one day look at him in the same manner she was now gazing at her groom.

With a heart filled with love, Alexis descended the stairs, certain that they carried her toward a lifetime of happiness.

The delicate song of the violins drifted on the gentle summer breeze that entered through the open doors. Like colorful butterflies circling a flower, the dancers twirled around the room, the women's ball gowns billowing out behind them.

Colter held Alexis close against him, his hand in the small of her back guiding her in perfect unison with his every step. Her head was thrown back, and she gazed up at him with adoring eyes. They could have been waltzing alone for all the notice they paid their guests.

"Happy?" he asked.

Her smile brightened as she nodded. She didn't have the words that could express her happiness. A thousand emotions seemed to fill her heart, all crying to be shared with him, yet she could only speak them with her eyes and hope he would understand.

"Is it snowing outside?" he asked suddenly.

"Snowing?" What a silly question. "Of

course not. It's August."

He chuckled and his eyes twinkled with mirth. "That's my point, my darling bride. You once said you'd marry me when it snowed in August. And it's August and we're married . . ."

"So it must be snowing," she finished for him, her smile matching his. Her smile faded and her blue eyes grew serious as she added, "I wish it had started snowing sooner."

The music stopped, but Colter didn't release his tight hold on her. Alexis could feel the heat of his hand through his kid glove as it rested on her bare shoulder. It made the rest of her—anywhere he wasn't touching—feel cold in comparison. She shivered and drew herself even closer against him.

Something in his gaze changed. She could feel the muscles in his back and neck tighten.

"I think it's time we left the party," he said in a controlled voice.

A possessive arm around her waist, Colter guided her across the room toward the stairs. Alexis sensed they had drawn the attention of many, and a warm blush spread to her cheeks. They all knew where she and Colter were going.

"Have the orchestra play another waltz," she asked quickly.

He obliged by waving his hand at the conductor, and the music started once again, but before he could lead her up the stairs, Sadie appeared before them.

"Colt Stephens, don't you take another step. Aren't you going to let her have some help with this dress of hers?" She shooed him away with her hands. "Men. They never use their heads." She took Alexis' arm and pulled her away from Colter, tossing back over her shoulder to him, "You give us a few minutes. I'll let you know when you can come up."

Alexis felt bereft without him by her side. It seemed there hadn't been even a moment all evening when they hadn't been touching. She glanced back at him as if afraid he would disappear forever.

"Alex, my girl, watch where you're going," Sadie ordered. "One minute you look as if you'll die of embarrassment before all these folks, and the next you're turnin' a look on Colt that could melt iron."

Alexis reluctantly turned her eyes back at the steps as they began to climb. "I really don't need your help, Sadie. Colt could have..."

"Trust me, Alexis. That wedding gown of yours has too many buttons for an eager husband to deal with."

Alexis' cheeks flamed. "Sadie!"

"Pish posh," Sadie replied with a snort. "I didn't have ten children without knowing what goes on betwixt a man and his wife."

Candles flickered on either side of the bed, casting a warm, golden glow across the turned back covers. Alexis stood on the far side of the room, waiting. Sadie had brushed her blonde hair to a high sheen. The pale gold tresses caught the shimmer of the candlelight and held it there.

The door opened slowly, light from the parlor spilling across the floor. Alexis couldn't see Colter's face as he stopped, his tall form framed by the doorway, but she knew his eyes were drinking her in. She lifted a hand to nervously touch the ruffled bodice of her nightgown. The fabric felt so flimsy. She knew it revealed every curve of her body, and she felt shy beneath his gaze.

The door closed. He came toward her, skirting the bed. Only inches separated them, but he didn't touch her. She felt mesmerized by his smoldering umber eyes. She could scarcely breathe. Her skin tingled in anticipation of his caresses. A sweet warmth emanated from deep inside, growing into a burning need to be one with him.

With deliberate slowness, he pulled at his tie. He removed his coat, his vest, his shirt. His body was hard-hewn, his chest broad. She resisted the urge to reach out and run her hand lightly across the sprinkling of curly chest hair, afraid to move, afraid to break the wonderous spell that held her in its grip.

"Alexis."

"Yes."

One arm encircled her and drew her toward him. His mouth descended to meet hers, and she closed her eyes in expectation. The kiss was light, barely there at all. A soft groan sounded in her throat. His lips moved across her cheek and down her throat, tasting her skin. She shivered in delight and frustration. Every nerve ending in her body was alert to his touch, waiting for that moment of surrender.

"Colter," she whispered, but she wasn't sure

if any sound actually was heard from her lips.

Suddenly, his arm slipped behind her knees, and he scooped her up from the floor, carrying her toward the bed. He laid her down, then stepped back, as if to admire her once more from a distance.

She couldn't bear it. "Colter..." It was a plea from the depths of her soul.

He shed the last traces of clothing and joined her on the bed. He stroked her hair as he kissed her eyelids, the tip of her nose, her ear lobes. Her own arms traced the muscled hardness of his chest and back.

"I love you, Alexis Stephens," Colter breathed into her ear.

Her reply was strangled in her throat as his mouth took hers once more, this time with a fiery passion that set her ablaze with wanting, and she abandoned herself to the pleasures to come.

12

Alexis awoke to a room bathed in morning sunlight. She was nestled against Colter's side, her head on his shoulder, her arm draped over his chest. She almost purred with satisfaction, knowing she had a right to be there. She snuggled even closer.

"I wondered if you were ever going to wake up," he said softly, his hand coming up from his side to rest on her head. His fingers gently tangled themselves in her mass of golden hair.

"Mmmm. I'm not sure I'm awake yet," she replied, kissing his throat.

"You're awake. And you'd better stay that way. We've got a full day ahead of us."

Reluctantly, she agreed and pulled herself away from him. They were riding to the ranch that morning and planned to spend a few days there, overseeing the work on the new house and giving them a chance to escape the intrusions of the Ice Palace on their time together. Besides, Alexis knew how much Colter missed being at the Circle S. She wondered sometimes at her stubborn insistence on staying here for the next year. She loved the ranch, too, and she really wouldn't have minded living in the small cabin. She had lived in less. Yet, she refused to change her mind about leaving the Ice Palace until next June. She wanted to finish what she had begun there. Reckless, in one of his last gestures of love and friendship, had left it to her and had wanted her to run it herself. It was important that she stay, at least until June, as a way of repaying him for all his kindnesses to her.

She pushed her hair away from her face and sighed. "All right. I'll get up, but I'd much rather stay here with you for the whole day."

"Mrs. Stephens! What would people think?" He widened his eyes in mock surprise.

"They'd think I'm in love with my husband," Alexis answered, a wicked lilt in her voice.

Colter laughed and threw his legs over the side of the bed. "I'm starved, and something tells me if I linger around here any longer, it'll be awhile before I get anything to eat." He reached for his trousers which lay on the chair beside the bed. Swiveling around, he found Alexis still lying in bed, watching him, the sheet molded to her shapely figure. "Come on," he ordered, swatting her bottom lightly. "Get dressed, woman, or I'll have my breakfast without you."

While she was dressing, Colter rang for Mona and ordered their morning repast. When the maid returned with the tray heaped with food, Stella followed carrying another tray, this one piled high with gifts.

"I'm sorry, Alexis, Colter, but I just had to bring these up. They're all gifts for Alexis that arrived this morning."

Alexis picked up a large hatbox and tugged at the string tied around it. "For me? But everyone has given us so much already." She lifted the lid and found a black Marie Stuart bonnet with a deep purple feather and matching satin bow to tie under the chin. "Oh, look!" she cried as she lifted it out of its box. She perched the small hat on her head and turned from side to side to show the others. "What do you think?" she asked.

Colter spread some preserves on a thick slice of bread, but his gaze remained on her. "I think it looks quite captivating with what you're wearing. You should wear them together often." His voice was warm and suggestive.

Glancing down at her flowing morning gown of black satin, Alexis felt the color rising in her cheeks.

"I don't see any cards," Colter mentioned as he glanced at the array of boxes. "Who are they from, Stella?"

"I don't know, but they were delivered all together. The boy that brought them said they were for Mrs. Stephens. I gave him a penny and he left. I don't know who he was."

"Seems you have a mystery admirer, Mrs. Stephens. Care to reveal any secrets that I, your devoted husband, should know about?"

Alexis frowned, taking his question

seriously. "I can't imagine . . ." she began.

Colter had to laugh. "I was merely teasing, my love. You've made a lot of friends and many conquests in Idaho in the time you've been here. Even the good ladies of this fair city have taken you to their hearts, despite the fact that you run a saloon and are far too beautiful for their husbands to be around. Anyone could have sent you those gifts." He reached forward and cupped her cheek with a brief caress. "Whoever it was has great taste in bonnets. It looks lovely on you."

Seeing the loving glance exchanged between the newlyweds, Stella said, "Well, I'll leave you two alone," and hurried out of the room.

As Colter began eating his breakfast, Alexis opened her packages, revealing a pair of soft kid gloves, a black *poult-de-soie* parasol, several lady's handkerchiefs embroidered with the letter A, a periwinkle blue fan, and even a diamond and sapphire brooch. Colter raised an eyebrow at the expensive jewelry, but said nothing about the impropriety of such a gift. He wiped his mouth on the cloth napkin and rose from the table as she put the brooch with the other gifts.

"While you finish opening your treasures," he said, "I'm going to shave. I won't be long."

Alexis watched him go into their bedroom, then brought her eyes back to the gifts before her. If she knew who had sent them, she would package them all up and return them at once. Despite his nonchalance, she was certain Colter was bothered by them.

Still, she couldn't stop herself from opening

the last box. Inside the lid, she found a note, the first clue of who had sent her the gifts. The note was written in a neat, precise hand.

> *Mrs. Stephens,*
>
> *I bought this from your husband just after you reopened the Ice Palace. I didn't know at that time who the Alexis of the inscription was, or for that matter who your husband was. Now that the two of you have married, I'm sure you'll want this back. The quarrel that caused its sale must have been forgiven and forgotten. I wish you all the best in your marriage.*
>
> *A friend*

Her fingers trembled as she lifted the tissue paper that lined the box, revealing a gold watch and chain. Her breath caught in her throat as she drew it out. She turned it over and over in the palm of her hand, delaying as long as possible the moment she knew must come. At last, she popped open the hunting case with the etching of a stag on the cover and read the inscription: "To my true friend with love, Alexis."

She glanced toward the bedroom, then back at the watch, and finally at the note lying on the table, a jumble of questions resounding inside her head. And the obvious answers were there as well.

No. No, she wouldn't think it. It wasn't possible.

But think it, she did. She could see Colter as he was that day, standing over Reckless's lifeless body. Samuel had all but accused him of being responsible, but Colter had denied it and she had believed him. Of course she had believed him. Colter wouldn't hurt a harmless old man. He wouldn't . . .

She heard the door opening and quickly shoved the watch into the pocket of her morning gown. Almost too late, she remembered the note. She picked it up and held it in her hand as Colter came across the room.

He paused beside her chair. "Well, is everything open?" he asked, dropping a kiss on top of her head.

"Yes . . . yes, I'm through," she replied. She looked up at him. He was so handsome, so strong, so good. She knew him as he was, as he must be. He would never do what the note implied.

"Is something wrong?"

Alexis brought her hand up to cover his where it rested on her shoulder. She laid her head to the side, pressing their hands together. She closed her eyes to hide the glimmer of tears. "No," she whispered. "Nothing's wrong. I'm just incredibly happy."

Colter kissed her hair one more time and squeezed her shoulder gently. "I'm glad, my love. All I want is to make you happy."

Alexis stood up and turned to face him, her pale blue eyes urgently seeking some kind of assurance. "I love you, Colt. I'm so glad to be your wife."

His hands ran up and down her arms. "And I'm proud to be your husband." He searched her face, his own eyes serious. "I would have done anything to make you mine." Then he pulled her into his embrace and kissed her, never knowing that the words he spoke in love could strike terror in Alexis' heart.

I would have done anything to make you mine.

It had been too long since Nugget had had any real exercise. All she wanted to do this morning was run. Alexis kept a tight rein until she was worn out by the mare's constant crow-hopping. The palomino's golden neck was lathered with white foam as she bobbed her head up and down and strained at the bit. Finally, Alexis relented. She let the reins slip through her fingers and leaned forward in the saddle. The mare jumped forward as if she'd been fired from a cannon.

"Hey!" Colter called after her. He spurred Titan, and the white stallion galloped after the mare and her rider.

Alexis pushed her bonnet off her head and let the wind tug at her perfectly arranged hair. She wished she hadn't worn her riding habit. Her buckskin trousers would have been more comfortable, and she would have been able to leave this wretched sidesaddle behind, too.

She heard the stallion's pounding hooves approaching from behind. "Come on, Nugget," she cried, willing more speed into her mount.

"Alexis!"

She ignored Colter's protest. She wanted to go faster and faster. She wanted to run away from the doubts and suspicions that were threatening to destroy the happiness she had found. She leaned low, her hands close to Nugget's neck. "Run, girl. Run," she whispered, her words snapped away on the wind.

The two horses raced along the dusty road, the steady rhythm of galloping hooves the only sound to break the quiet of midday. The tall stands of timber were a mere blur of greens and browns to Alexis. Her clouded thoughts began to dim in the thrill of the race, and for a while, Alexis thought Nugget might actually have a chance to outrun Colter's stallion. But it was not to be. Steadily, the white horse closed the space between them until, at last, he had drawn up beside the golden mare.

"Alex," Colter called to her, "ease up."

She glanced over at him.

"Ease up," he called again. "You're pushing her too hard."

He was right, of course. Nugget had spent her initial energy and was now laboring just to obey her mistress. Alexis pulled lightly on the reins, and Nugget's pace slowed at once. Colter reached over and touched Alexis' arm. She met his gaze, then continued to tighten the reins until they had come to a complete stop.

"Mind telling me what the was all about?" he asked.

"She needed a run. So did I."

Colter's face clouded as he continued to watch her. "Alex, is something wrong?"

She shook her head, her eyes dropping from his. "No, Colt. It's just been a long time since I've been for a good gallop. I guess I just lost my head over it."

There was a long, thoughtful pause while he studied her. She could feel his gaze upon her. He knew her well. Would he press her for the truth? And if he did, what would she tell him? Would she ask him if he had killed Reckless? Was she ready to hear his answer?

I love him, she thought. How can I even wonder about him? I *know* he couldn't do anything so horrible, so why am I torturing myself this way? Colt is decent and honest. I know that about him better than I know it about myself. I will not doubt him. *I will not.*

She glanced back up at him. His eyes were concerned, puzzled. He had no idea what troubled thoughts wrestled with reason beneath her tousled blonde hair. And she didn't want him to know. He must never know that her faith in him had wavered.

Alexis smiled. "I'm sorry, Colt. You must think I don't have any sense at all, running a horse like that. I didn't mean to worry you. May I write it off to being cooped up too long at the Ice Palace?"

His frown was replaced by relief, and his eyes warmed. "Let's just take it a little slower. After all, we don't have to be in such a hurry to get to the ranch. I'd like to enjoy just being with you. Alone."

It had been three months since Alexis left the Circle S in the gray morning light. She never would have believed when she left that she would return so soon. Or that she would return as Colter's bride.

Her eyes swept over the outbuildings and corrals. There was a new bunkhouse for the hired hands, and the barn had received a fresh coat of paint. In the distance, she could see the rising lines of the new house. As they approached the cabin, the door was flung open and Li Ching came outside. His eyes nearly disappeared as his face crinkled up in a joyous smile of welcome.

"Hello, Li Ching," Alexis said as she dismounted.

He bowed several times.

"I think he's trying to tell you how pleased he is that you've returned." Colter put his arm around her waist and squeezed gently.

Li Ching nodded. He held out his hands for the reins, then motioned with his other arm for them to go inside while he attended to their horses. Colter and Alexis obliged.

For Alexis, stepping inside the cabin was like stepping inside a memory. All her guilt, all her shame, came rushing back. She was keenly aware of Colter's nearness. Her gaze darted to the bed in the corner, and she felt the color rising in her cheeks.

"I love you, Alex," her husband whispered near her ear. "Stop feeling guilty for what happened."

"Oh, Colt . . ."

He pulled her into his arms and held her tightly against his chest. He rubbed his cheek against her silken hair. "My silly, silly Alexis. When will you realize that nothing you did or didn't do would have kept us apart? We were destined to be together."

She lifted sooty lashes to reveal brilliant orbs of blue. "Tell me one more time how much you love me," she asked.

'More than time or space can fathom." He kissed her forehead. "More than one man has ever loved a woman before." He kissed the tip of her nose. "More than my own life." He kissed her chin. Then, meeting her gaze again, he asked, "Does that tell you what you need to know?"

Alexis nodded, feeling the heaviness lift from her heart.

"Good. Now, what is it you want to do with the rest of the day? You can get out of those fancy clothes and into something fit to wear around a cattle ranch or . . ." he leered, "you can get out of those fancy clothes and into nothing else."

This time it was her own pleasurable thoughts that brought the color back to her cheeks. With the expertise of a practiced coquette, Alexis batted her long lashes and tilted her head to one side. "Whatever do you mean to suggest by that remark, Mr. Stephens?"

"Just what it sounds like, Mrs. Stephens," he answered, his voice low.

They heard Li Ching's footsteps behind them and jumped apart like children caught in the cookie jar. They glanced at Li Ching, then turned sheepish looks on each other before joining in laughter.

"Li Ching," Colter said, "let's you and me leave Alexis alone so she can change. I want to show her the new house before the day gets clear away from us."

She was left alone in the cabin. Her eyes traveled over the familiar room—two beds, a table and four chairs, the tall cupboard, the fireplace and cast-iron stove, the bathtub with the curtain for privacy. It was like coming home. It felt good. It felt right.

With a sudden burst of energy, she removed her riding habit and donned her pants and shirt. She tied her long hair back from her face with a ribbon and set her slouch hat on her head. She grinned to herself. She felt as lighthearted as a child. Not a care in the world.

Maybe. Just maybe. Maybe she would change her mind and decide to stay here, not wait a year. Colter would rather be here than in Idaho City. She knew that for certain. It would make him happy if she gave up the Palace now so they could stay, and she did want him to be happy. Well, she could think about it. If that's what she decided to do, she'd tell him later. Surprise him with the news. It would be all the more special that way.

The days flew by. They spent their days riding about the ranch and their nights in each other's arms. Alexis met the new ranch hands and was reintroduced to a black filly called Lucky. She walked through the rooms of the new Circle S ranch house, envisioning each one as it would be when it was all finished. With the passing of each day, she thought more and more often of ending her reign as Queen of the Ice

Palace now instead of waiting, of staying right here where their love began and where it would grow even greater.

It was evening. Alexis stood outside the cabin, staring at the mountains to the west. Pink and lavender clouds had been finger-painted across the edge of the sky, colors both fragile and vibrant. She felt warmed by them, as if they promised her continued good fortune. She sighed her contentment as she leaned back against the log cabin.

"May I join you?" Colter had come around the side of the house.

She held out an arm as he stepped near and closed it around his waist. His own arm circled her shoulders, and she rested her head against his chest.

"Beautiful, isn't it?" he asked, echoing her thoughts.

"Yes."

"We're leaving tomorrow."

Now. She should tell him now that they could stay. That they need not ever go back.

"I'm going to miss the ranch."

"Colt . . ."

"I'll miss it, but I'd rather be with you. I know how important the Palace is to you. I admire your determination, Alex. And, after all, Reckless did want you to run it yourself."

"Yes. Yes, he wanted me to run it."

By his own words, he had stopped her from choosing to stay there now instead of returning to Idaho City. In her happiness and contentment, she had nearly forgotten about Reckless and what he had wanted. She'd nearly forgotten that he had willed it to her just before his death. Her thoughts darted to the watch. She hadn't thought of it since they'd arrived at the ranch, but now it intruded on her happiness once more.

"Wait here," she said abruptly.

She hurried into the cabin. She wasn't going to let suspicions ruin her life. She was going to get this out in the open, once and for all. She found the watch and carried it outside where her husband was waiting.

"Here," she said to Colter, dropping the golden case and chain into his hand.

He might have thought it was a gift if it hadn't been for the strange way she presented the watch to him. He glanced at the object in his hand, then back at Alexis, then back at the watch, a puzzled frown knitting his brows. He rolled the watch case over in his hand several times before snapping open the cover. He held it closer to his eyes in order to read the inscription in the dying light of day.

Alexis waited anxiously, watching his every expression, trying to read his inner thoughts.

"I'm not the friend in this watch," he said, glancing up.

It wasn't a question, but she answered it as if it had been one. "No, you're not."

"Why are you giving this to me?"

"Have you ever seen it before, Colt?"

He looked at the watch one more time. He closed the cover and turned it over again before shaking his head. "I don't know. I can't say I've ever paid much attention to time pieces or fancy watch fobs. One looks the same as the other." He lifted his gaze to meet hers. "Why? Why is it so important that I know if I've seen it before or not?"

She couldn't see his face well in the gathering dusk. "Come inside, and I'll tell you."

His consternation was clear in every angle of his body as he sat at the table. Alexis took a moment to turn up the lantern before taking her seat across from him. Her mind scrambled for the right way to tell him about the watch and about the note that had arrived with it the day they left the city to come here. Colter opened the watch cover once more, then laid it in the middle of the table between them, his dark glance demanding an explanation to the puzzle.

"I gave that to T.C. before he died. It was my way of thanking him for all he'd done for me. He was a good friend when I needed one."

"I know."

"He always had it in his pocket after I gave it to him." She touched the watch chain with her index finger. "But he didn't have it when we buried him. I was too upset to think about the watch being missing. Somehow, it didn't mean anything to me then. But it does now." Alexis brushed away an insistent tear. "Do you remember all those presents I received the morning after the wedding?"

"Of course."

"This was among them."

"The watch? But . . ."

Alexis leaned across the table, her face tight. "It came with a note saying *you* had sold it to that person and, now that we were married, the giver wanted us to have it back."

"But how was I to have had the watch, and why would I sell it to anyone?"

She didn't answer his questions. She watched as he answered them himself. She read the realization, then the anger in his deep brown eyes.

"And you, Alexis? Do you believe it?"

She would never tell him of her moments of doubt. "I know with all my heart that you didn't do what the note implied." Never had she been more earnest about anything.

His face was clouded with suppressed rage. "I'd like to do more than it implied to the writer of the note."

Alexis reached across the table and took hold of his hand. "Colt, I didn't understand at first why anyone would want to do this. I was shocked and... and confused. I just wanted to forget it. But I've realized something this evening. Just as we've been talking. Something important. Whoever sent this to me wanted me to believe the worst about you, and the only way he could know what that would be is if he had something to do with T.C.'s death. He had to have taken the watch before any of us arrived there."

"But why show his hand? We thought the old man's death was an accident. Why take the chance of raising suspicions?"

"I don't know." There didn't seem to be any answers. "But, Colt. I've got to find out. If T.C. didn't die accidentally, if he was murdered, I want to know who did it. I want to see him punished for it."

Colter picked up the watch from the table. "This isn't much to go on, Alex," he said gently.

"It's all we have."

Colter nodded grimly as he snapped the cover shut. There was a long silence before he said, "Sam Wainwright."

"Sam? But he was with me..."

"No, I didn't mean he had anything to do with Reckless's death. I meant we need to talk to him, see if anyone has anything to gain from causing trouble between us. I don't see what, but there might be something. Maybe something in Reckless's will about if you marry and should ever divorce... Maybe you would lose your inheritance if that happened." He shook his head. "It's not much of an idea, but someone had a reason for doing this. If we can just find out what it was..."

Alexis suddenly felt very tired. She wished she was still standing outside, savoring the rich colors in the sky and the warm happiness that had filled her soul. She wished she'd never thought of the watch again. She wished they didn't have to leave this ranch. They were so happy here.

Colter must have sensed her mood. He rose from the table and came around to stand before her. He drew her to her feet and tilted her chin with the tip of his finger, forcing her gaze to meet with his. "We have each other. We can be happy anywhere."

A tiny smile crept into the corners of her mouth. He was right. It didn't matter where they lived, as long as they were together.

Colter's head descended toward hers, and he kissed her smiling lips, a long, languorous kiss that made her forget anything but the sweet ecstasy of his touch.

13

The cinnamon September sun kissed the horizon and then sank gracefully beyond the mountains. The bustling mining town cooled in the autumn shadows and the saloons began to fill.

Alexis sat at her dressing table, observing her reflection in the mirror. She touched the emerald and diamond choker that decorated her white throat and smiled as she remembered the night Colter had given it and the matching emerald earrings to her.

She shook her head resolutely, clearing her thoughts. If she started recalling all the pleasant moments of her marriage, even as brief as it was, she would never be ready to go downstairs. She rose from her chair, petticoats rustling beneath her green and white striped silk dress. She reached for her light shawl to drape across her back and through her arms. She turned toward the door to find Colter lounging in the entrance, watching her with a hungry gaze.

"You're a vision, my love," he said softly. "Must we pass the evening with the patrons of this fine establishment tonight? Wouldn't the night be better spent with just you and me, alone?"

He would never know how tempted she was to agree with him, but she could only shake her head. "We must go down, Colt. I'm expected to be there."

His shoulders heaved with an exaggerated sigh. "We'll both be sorry." Brown eyes twinkled suggestively.

"No doubt," she replied with a chuckle as she joined him in the doorway. She stood on tiptoe and kissed his cheek. "Come along, Mr. Stephens. It's time we were downstairs."

Colter offered his arm and they traced the familiar path to the saloon below.

Alexis' routine had been well established before her marriage and had not changed since their return from the Circle S. Throughout the evening, she circulated around the room, speaking to the men, laughing at their jokes, keeping an eye on the tables and a lookout for troublemakers. Sometimes Colter stood beside her. When not there, he could usually be found at one of the poker tables.

The marriage of the Ice Queen had not dimmed her popularity among the men who visited the Palace. Her beauty was extolled far and wide, and new arrivals to the basin made it a point to visit the saloon as soon as possible.

There were many who envied Colter Stephens for his good luck . . . and there was at least one who hated him for it.

Derek didn't visit the Ice Palace as often as before, but when he came, he never failed to join the poker table if Colter was in the game. Alexis happened to glance up just as he entered that evening. She watched as his eyes swept the room, stopping as they met with hers. He tipped his gray top hat in her direction, then turned toward the poker table where Colter was seated.

She didn't know why he insisted on coming to the Ice Palace. His own saloon had done well since its reopening. True, it wasn't as popular as the Palace, but in a town with over thirty-five saloons, he couldn't be displeased with the prosperity of the Golden Gulch. Try as she might, she couldn't rid herself of the apprehension that troubled her whenever he was around. Again and again she had reminded herself that he had never really done anything to make her feel this way, but it changed nothing.

Alexis excused herself as soon as possible and made her way through the tables. She nodded silently at the six men, Colter and Derek among them, who were playing poker at a corner table.

"Evenin', Miss Alexis," one of the men said in greeting.

"Good evening, Mac. I haven't seen you in awhile."

"My back's been ailin' me, but I'm myself again."

"I'm glad to hear it."

Derek scowled at the old miner called Mac. "Can we get on with this game?" His hazel eyes darted to Colter. "Stephens, it's up to you."

Colter's mouth turned up in the lazy smile that was so characteristic of him. Derek's face darkened as he waited impatiently. Then Colter laid his cards down.

"I'm out, men," he said, rising from the table. "It's just not my night for cards." He put his arm around Alexis' waist. "Maybe my luck will be better elsewhere."

All the men at the table chuckled and poked each other in the ribs. All except Derek. Alexis felt the color rise in her cheeks, but she couldn't stop the laughter that rose in her throat as he guided her away from the poker table. They both stopped when they heard a chair tumble onto its back. They turned in unison to see Derek throw his cards onto the table and stalk darkly out of the saloon.

"I don't think he likes me much," Colter commented.

Alexis didn't find it as amusing as her husband did. "Colt, please be careful around Derek."

"Do you think I can't handle the likes of Mr. Anderson?" he chided her.

She turned blue eyes upward. "I don't think he's as harmless as you do. There's something about him..."

"Alex," he whispered, "you're looking for danger. Derek Anderson's only problem is that he still wants you. I've checked on him, just like I've checked on nearly everybody else in the basin since we came back, and nothing I've found shows he's ever broken the law or been a threat to anyone."

"But . . ."

Colter squeezed her arm against his side. "You'd better smile, my love. People are beginning to wonder at that worried look on your face."

She forced herself to obey, but she still wasn't convinced he was right. She didn't trust Derek.

It was true; Colter had done a lot of background checking on residents of Idaho City, trying to find a clue to who might have had something to gain by killing Reckless. He had come up empty-handed so far. Oh, there were many unscrupulous characters in the basin. Murders weren't uncommon. In fact, a man could just about count on his fingers the number of people buried in the city's cemetery who were there of natural causes. But nothing he had learned about the ambitious Mr. Anderson indicated he was dangerous in any way.

Stella could have told them differently. But when Colter had approached her for information, she had vividly remembered Derek's threats and had little to say about her former employer. Besides, if she'd told all she knew about him, her own marriage might have been threatened.

Stella had never believed she could be so happy. Suddenly, she had become a married woman with a home to run and a man to care for.

She learned to cook his favorite foods, and she waited eagerly for his return home at the end of each day. She didn't miss the excitement of the saloon or the fancy clothes. That old way of life seemed little more than a dream to her now. This was what she wanted. To be Sam's wife. This was all she would ever want.

And dear Sam. He treated her like fine china. He brought her little trinkets almost every day. He even brought gifts for the baby. He never mentioned the fact that the child was not his. In fact, he acted just the opposite. He talked about "their" child, already planning where "he" would go to school when the time came.

Sam kissed his wife and headed back to his office after his noon meal. Stella cleaned up the dishes, then donned her coat and hat and went out herself. A brisk breeze caught at her skirt and wrapped the fabric around her ankles. Curds of white scudded across the brilliant blue sky. Stella leaned into the wind and hurried toward the Ice Palace. She had seen little of her friend since Alexis and Colter returned from their honeymoon at the ranch, and she had decided this morning to remedy that.

She found Alexis in the parlor of her living suite. She was seated on the sofa, still wearing a satin dressing gown, surrounded by fabric samples. Mrs. Cane was standing behind her, nodding as Alexis touched first one, then another.

"Oh, Stella. I'm so glad you see you. Come here and help me make up my mind. The Irwin

Troupe will be at the Jenny Lind next week, and I don't have anything appropriate to wear. All my gowns are for summer and suddenly winter is upon us."

Stella tossed her coat across a nearby chair, then stood opposite Mrs. Cane and studied the fabric. Finally, she picked up a burgundy and white striped foulard and held it up against Alexis' cheek. "I like this one."

"Then this one it is, Mrs. Cane," Alexis announced, relieved to have the decision made.

"I'll start on it right away, Mrs. Stephens. And the coat?"

"Yes. In the black velvet, I think."

Mrs. Cane gathered her samples and departed, talking to herself as she went.

"Poor Mrs. Cane. I'm not an easy customer," Alexis commented as the door closed.

"But I've never known you to look anything but lovely," Stella protested.

Alexis laughed. "Oh, I wear some of the most elegant gowns in Idaho, and I guess I do enjoy the compliments, but it was so much simpler when I just wore my buckskins. There wasn't all this fuss over fabrics and styles." She gave an exaggerated sigh. "I guess it's the price I must pay for deciding to stay in Idaho for the winter."

"Once winter sets in, you won't need as many new gowns. I promise you, it'll be a lot quieter around here. The miners won't have any gold dust to spend in the saloons. They'll all stay huddled around their stoves in their little shacks trying to keep warm. Your customers will be the townsfolk and the professionals." Stella wrinkled her forehead. "Of course, *they* can be more trouble than the others."

"Enough about that, Stella. Tell me about yourself. Are you happy? You must be. You look wonderful."

Stella blushed to the roots of her flaming tresses. "I didn't think I'd ever be this happy. I don't deserve a man as good as Sam."

"Of course you do," Alexis responded indignantly. "You deserve happiness as much as anybody I know." She patted Stella's hand. "And the baby? How are you feeling?"

"Like a barn, and the baby isn't due until January. I wonder how I'll manage if I get any bigger." Stella ran her hand over her rounded belly.

Alexis watched the gesture, then smiled wistfully. "I hope I have the same complaints soon."

"Alex, are you . . ."

"No. Not yet. But I hope Colt and I won't have long to wait. I'd love to have his baby." The mantel clock chimed the hour, and Alexis looked up in surprise. "Good heavens, I didn't realize it was so late. Come into the bedroom with me and we'll chat while I get dressed."

Stella wandered idly around the room while Alexis searched her wardrobe for a dress she wanted to wear. Stella had always liked the airiness of the room and had enjoyed her mornings here with Alexis before they were both married. Now, she wouldn't trade her cozy little bedroom in her house behind Sam's office for anything.

She paused by the dresser, glancing at the

array of combs and brushes and jewelry scattered across its surface. A shaving mug and brush had been added to the feminine paraphernalia since she'd last seen the dresser. She smiled thoughtfully, thinking of how much she enjoyed watching Sam shaving in the morning.

It took her eyes a moment to focus on the watch and chain lying behind the mug, but there was something about it that drew her attention.

Alexis saw her looking at it. "Stella? Have you ever seen that watch before?" she asked, walking toward her.

"Seen it? I don't know. I don't think I've ever noticed Colter checking his watch."

"It's not Colt's."

Stella glanced at Alexis. "Then why is it here?"

"It's a long story." She touched Stella's shoulder. "Think hard, Stella. Have you ever seen it before?"

"A watch is a watch," Stella answered, her eyes dropping to the gold cover again.

Alexis turned away too soon to see the sudden expression on Stella's face. She did remember seeing the watch before . . . or at least one just like it. It had been in Derek's room. She'd seen it the day she waited for him to tell him she was pregnant with his baby. She had been nervous and had walked a steady path around his room. The watch had been tossed into a nearby bookcase. She remembered now how she'd thought the craftsman had done an excellent job; the great buck had looked very real, etched in the gold hunting cover.

"Why is it so important that you know whose it is?" Stella asked softly.

"Because whoever it belongs to hurt a very dear friend of mine and has tried to hurt me too."

Stella felt suddenly lightheaded. She turned away from the dresser and went to sit on the edge of the bed. When Alexis glanced her way, she forced a smile and said, "I like that dress on you, Alex. You should have Mrs. Cane make you another one in the same style."

She should say something about the watch. She knew she should. She knew Derek was capable of doing anything, and she seemed to be the only one who did know it. But if she accused Derek, he would get even. He would hurt her; he might even kill her. Or worse, he might harm Sam or the baby. If she said nothing, the watch and the story behind it would be forgotten. No one need be hurt again. Besides, the watch wasn't *that* unusual. She could be wrong about it being the one she saw in Derek's room. Many men had hunting cases for their watches, and there must be plenty with deer on the covers.

"Alexis, I just remembered I promised to bake Sam a pie this afternoon. I must get home and get started or it won't be ready for him." She jumped up from the bed and headed for the door.

Alexis' laughter followed her. "My, how domesticated we've become, Stella. I was just thinking about Colt's dinner. He's gone up to see the operation of Raymond's Pioneer mill in Placerville, and when he gets back, he's going to be tired and hungry."

Alexis caught up with Stella, hooked her arm

through her friend's, and walked with her to the private stairway and the rear entrance.

"Why don't you and Sam plan on going with us to the theatre next week? We really would like to have you join us." Alexis kissed her cheek.

Stella nodded. "I'll ask him. I'm sure he'd like to, if he's not too busy."

"You tell him I insist."

"I'll tell him. Good-bye, Alexis."

Stella hurried away, rushing toward the safety of her tiny home behind the Wainwright Law Office.

The saloon was less than half full. The clear sky of midday had disappeared behind dark gray clouds, and the wind had a decided bite in it as it whistled in under the closed doors. The lanterns on the outer wall flickered as gusts of air attacked the burning wicks.

Alexis was in her office, going over an order for supplies, when the door burst open and Rafe entered. He stood staring at her for a moment, then said, "Miss Alexis, I think you'd better come out here. There's someone to see you." He shook his head. "I thought you'd lost your mind. Now I think I have," he muttered as he turned away.

Alarmed, Alexis jumped to her feet and followed him out of her office. It wasn't hard to discover what had caused the stir. All eyes were turned to the center of the room.

"Althea?" she whispered, not believing it herself.

Her sister was seated at a table in the middle of the saloon, her coat and bonnet travel-stained and covered with dust, one small valise on the floor at her feet. Her gloved hands were clenching a shot glass, and she flung back her head to drain it of the golden whiskey inside.

"Althea!" Alexis repeated, rushing through the maze of tables. "Althea, what are you doing here? Where's Papa?"

Althea set her glass on the table and looked up with glazed eyes. "Alex? Is it really you? I didn't think I'd ever find you. That Houston woman told me where you were, but I just didn't believe her. She wanted me to stay with her, but I wouldn't hear of it. I was so afraid I wouldn't really find you and then I'd have to keep looking and I'm so terribly tired. Night and day on that dreadful coach. Men snoring and smoking and spitting their chew. Old women falling asleep against my shoulder. And I was so alone. No one to care for me. Cherry's gone, too. It's been weeks, you know, since I've had a good night's sleep." She brushed a bedraggled lock of golden hair away from her cheek.

Alexis wanted to grab her sister by the shoulders and shake her until her teeth rattled. She wanted to know what had brought her back here, where their father was, but she could see it would do her no good. Althea was in a near stupor, whether from lack of sleep or from the whiskey she had quickly consumed, Alexis couldn't be sure.

"Rafe, help me get my sister upstairs."

She put her hand under Althea's arm and drew her to her feet. Rafe was quickly on her other side with a steady arm around her back.

They had taken only a few steps when Althea began to crumple in a dead faint. The bartender caught her before she fell. He gathered her in his arms and followed Alexis up the stairs. Alexis opened the door to the bedroom nearest her own suite of rooms, and Rafe laid Althea on the bed.

"Have Mona bring me some warm water and a cloth, Rafe."

"Right away, Miss Alexis."

Alexis removed her sister's bonnet. She smoothed the snarled hair. It was so unlike Althea to be unkempt in any way. She remembered the day Althea got off the stage in Boise. She had been traveling a long time then, too, but she had appeared totally unruffled. Something must be terribly wrong. She unfastened the buttons of Althea's coat and struggled to remove it, rolling Althea first to one side and then to the other. She had just begun loosening her sister's gown when Mona arrived with the water.

"Help me get her out of her clothes," Alexis told the maid.

Together, they managed to sit Althea up enough to pull the soiled traveling dress over her head, leaving her in her corset and petticoat. Gently, Alexis began to sponge the dust and dirt from her sister's skin, the thoughts inside her head tumbling with possible explanations.

The room grew dark as the afternoon became evening, and still Alexis sat at Althea's side. Mona returned to the bedroom and lit a lamp, but Alexis paid her no heed. Mona doubted her mistress even knew she was ever in the room.

What's happened, Althea? Alexis wondered in agonized silence, praying that whatever had happened was not as bad as what she was imagining.

The atmosphere of the saloon was subdued when Colter returned from Placerville. His instincts were instantly alert. Rose left her customer at the bar and hurried toward him. Even as she came, his glance darted toward the stairs.

"Where's Alex?" he demanded.

"She's okay. It's her sister."

"Althea? Here?"

"She's in a bad way, Mr. Stephens."

"Where is she?" he asked, already moving toward the stairs.

"The one next to your own," Rose called after him.

Colter took the steps three at a time, racing down the hallway toward his own suite. He paused at the next to the last door and forced himself to knock. There was no reply, so he opened the door.

Spider-web shadows laced the room. A lamp, turned low, sat on the table near the door, casting a pale glow on the room's occupants. Alexis sat on a chair beside the bed. He could see her profile as she held Althea's limp hand. Her face was drawn and anxious. He knew she was unaware of his entrance.

"Alex?" He moved across the room and placed a comforting hand on her shoulder.

"Something terrible has happened," she told him woodenly, not looking away from Althea.

"What is it?" he asked.

Alexis raised tortured eyes. "She came *alone*, Colt. Papa's not with her. Not even Cherry. And she brought none of her clothes."

"Did she tell you why?"

She shook her head. "No. She fainted before she could tell me. She's exhausted."

"Maybe you're jumping to conclusions. It may be that nothing's wrong," Colter said, trying to soothe Alexis, though he didn't believe it himself. "Why don't I get Mona or one of the girls to sit with her? She looks as if she'll sleep through the night."

"No! No, I'm going to stay right here. She might need me, and I don't want her waking with strangers."

"All right, love. We'll stay with her. We'll stay together."

"Thank you, Colt," Alexis replied in a weak voice, turning her gaze back to Althea's pale face.

Colter pulled another chair across the room and sat down to wait out the night.

Morning was nearly gone when Althea opened her eyes again. Colter had gone for some coffee, so it was only a drowsy Alexis she saw as she blinked the slumber from her eyes.

"I wasn't dreaming?" she said as she pushed herself up on the pillows.

Alexis straightened with a start. "No. You weren't dreaming, Althea," she replied, a relieved smile removing the fatigue from around her eyes. "How are you feeling? Are you hungry?"

"I think I could eat something a little later, but not yet."

Alexis leaned forward. "What's happened, Althea?"

Her sister turned her face toward the window. Outside, the sky was dark. The storm that the skies had promised to them yesterday had arrived, and shards of sleet struck the window panes with force. "It gets cold early here, doesn't it?"

"Althea! What's happened?" Alexis' nerves were stretched to the breaking point.

"The end of the world," came her ominous reply.

Colter entered with the coffee tray in time to hear her answer. "What do you mean, Althea?"

"Colter? Whatever are you doing here?" A hand flew up to touch her hair, then moved to finger the collar of her nightgown. There was a spark of renewed life in her eyes. "Really, Colter. You shouldn't be in here. I'm not dressed. I must look a sight." She cast accusing eyes toward Alexis. "Did you send for him? Was I so ill?"

Alexis looked over at Colter *She doesn't know we're married*, her glance told him as she gave a light shake of her head.

"It was good of you to come, Colter," Althea continued, "though after the way we parted, I must say I'm surprised. Perhaps you've missed me just a little . . ." Her voice drifted into a coy silence.

Colter poured a cup of coffee and offered it to Althea. He gave her a tight smile as she accepted the cup. "I'm glad to see you're feeling better, Althea, but I must disappoint you on the reason I'm here. You see, I live here."

"Live here?" Her dark blue eyes widened. "But Sadie said it was Alexis' saloon. Do you mean to say my sister merely works for you?"

"Not hardly," Colter said as he handed a steaming cup to Alexis.

"It *is* my saloon, Althea." Alexis paused uncertainly, then blurted, "Colt lives here because . . . because he and I are married."

The spark in Althea's eyes flickered and died as they watched. She sank down once more into her pillow and pulled the blankets up to her chin as she turned her face away from them.

"Althea, please tell me where Papa is?" Alexis pleaded, seeing her sister retreating into herself once again.

"Later, Alex. I'll tell you later. Right now I'm just too tired. Too tired for words . . ."

"She's had a terrible shock of some sort, Mrs. Stephens. She's suffering from a trauma and complete exhaustion." Dr. Barker closed his black leather bag. "You let her sleep and see that she drinks lots of fluids, and she'll be herself in a few days. Maybe even a week or so. And don't press her to tell you what has happened," he warned. "The mind is a funny thing. Right now it's protecting her from something she can't handle. In time, she'll be able to face it, and then she'll tell you."

Alexis nodded as she walked with the doctor down the hallway. "I'll do as you say, Dr. Barker, but it's not easy. Something has happened to my father, and I don't know what it is."

The doctor stopped and looked at her. He took her chin between his fingers and held her steady while he pulled up on her eyelids. "Now, don't go getting yourself so worked up that you get sick," he said as he released his hold, "or that husband of yours will be down on me in a fury." He smiled. "You get some rest yourself."

Alexis returned his smile. The doctor was right. Colter was worried about her. Not that he wasn't concerned for Althea. He was. But he saw how Alexis was neglecting herself while caring for Althea. He had to remind her to eat and to sleep.

"I'll behave, doctor. I wouldn't want Colt mad at Idaho's best physician."

Dr. Barker scoffed. "Now you're trying to flatter me, Mrs. Stephens, and I'm too old for such nonsense. You just do as I say."

Alexis shivered at the cold blast of air that entered through the open door as the doctor went out. It matched the cold apprehension that dwelled in her heart. She turned and headed wearily for Althea's room. Maybe today Althea would be able to tell them something. All Alexis could do was sit in her room and wait.

14

"No! Mother! No! No!"

The screams split the blackness of night. Alexis was up and running from their bedroom before the words could fade in the air. She flung Althea's door open and found Mona struggling to hold Althea back on the bed.

Althea's eyes were wide open, her face as white as a sheet. The screams had quieted, but she continued to shake her head, muttering, "No . . . no . . . no . . ."

Alexis hurried to the bedside. "Althea? Althea, honey, what is it?" she asked as she took her sister by the shoulders and pressed her back toward her pillows. "You've had a dream. That's all. A bad dream."

Colter entered the room then. He'd pulled on a pair of trousers, but he was barefooted and bare-chested. Mona saw him enter and excused herself, Colter taking her empty place on the other side of the bed.

Althea reached out suddenly and clasped Colter's hand. "You won't let them come back, will you, Colter?"

"Who?" He glanced up at Alexis for explanation.

Alexis shook her head. "She's had a nightmare," she answered softly.

"No, Alexis. It wasn't a nightmare. It happened. It all happened." Althea's voice was deathly calm.

"Do you . . . feel like talking about it?" Alexis said, afraid to hear and afraid not to hear.

Althea looked from her sister to Colter, then let her gaze drift to the far wall. She continued to stare, as if her eyes could see through the wall of her room and beyond, miles and miles beyond.

"Everything was gone from Willowind when we got there. In just those few weeks I was away, everything had changed. Everything was gone. Our people had left us. The army had taken all of the horses. Mother was always so sure they wouldn't bother her breeding stock. Poor Mother. She thought the war was over for us. She'd taken no side. All that mattered was Willowind. She would have sold her soul for Willowind . . ." Althea fell silent. She continued staring beyond the darkness at something only she could see.

The night winds of October rattled the window glass, and Alexis shivered. A great terror threatened to overwhelm her as she waited . . . and waited.

"Father didn't know where to begin. There were only a few hands left. The old people who were afraid to leave and the lazy ones who didn't want to work. They stayed so someone else could feed them. And there wasn't much food. Father didn't know where he could get enough food. That's where he was when they came. He was hunting. Of course, there wasn't much left to hunt." Althea's eyes grew wide. She looked intently from Colter to Alexis, then back. "I was down by the creek washing my dress. That pretty pink one with the white ruffles. You remember it, don't you, Colter? You told me how lovely I looked in it the first time I wore it for you." She clutched his hand as if it were a lifeline.

"I remember, Althea," he replied as he squeezed her fingers.

"Mother shoved me into the bushes and threatened to kill me herself if I so much as poked my nose out. There were six of them. Six stinkin' blue bellies. Unshaven and dirty and their horses the sorriest you've ever seen." Althea brought her gaze back to the present and shifted it to her sister. "Mother hadn't ever been afraid before. Not with the Union soldiers, not with the Confederates. I'd seen her meet them before and she wasn't afraid. But she was afraid this time. I could feel it. Fear was thick in the air." She was beginning to tremble.

Alexis stroked her arm and crooned, "It's all right, Althea. You needn't talk anymore if you don't want to."

But Althea didn't seem to hear her. "I'd never seen Mother afraid of anything. I don't know what she said to them. I couldn't hear from where I was. They laughed at her. One of them... one of them grabbed her and kissed her. Then they pushed her out of the way as if she were nothing. They went inside and Mother followed them in. I could hear things breaking. They were breaking things and breaking things. And laughing. I can still hear them laughing." She covered her ears and closed her eyes. "And I thought I could hear Mother. Alexis, I think they..." But she couldn't say what she thought they had done to her mother.

For a long time, she was silent, but at last, she lowered her hands. She kept them clenched in tight fists, lying tensely at her sides. Her eyes opened, and she looked directly at Alexis with a fierce blue gaze.

"I don't know how long they were inside. It seemed like forever. When they came out, they were dragging Mother with them. Her hair was loose. I'd never seen her hair down before. And I remember the sleeve of her dress was torn. I felt bad because it was the only decent dress she had left. The others were hardly more than rags. She was fighting them to let her go, kicking and screaming at them. She was always such a lady, Alexis. But she was kicking and screaming like some poor white trash... Then I saw why. They'd set the house on fire. I could see the flames through my bedroom window. I could hear it crackling and popping as it spread through the upstairs." Althea closed her eyes again. Her voice grew softer and she seemed to shrink from the tale she was telling. "That's all I could hear. The crackling and popping and the laughter and Mother's screams. It went on and on and on."

Tears streaked Alexis' cheeks as she watched and listened. She bit her lower lip until she could taste her own blood, but she scarcely knew she had done it.

"They shoved her again and she fell. One of them kicked her and laughed. She lay there so still. I thought she was dead, and I couldn't do anything. Then they got on their horses and rode away. I started to get up, to come out of hiding. I was so afraid. And then she got up. She was all right. She wasn't dead. She didn't even seem to be hurt. She was all right. I called to her, but she didn't hear me. She just . . . she picked up her skirts and ran into the house. She went in to put out the fire. She couldn't let Willowind burn. It was the only thing she ever wanted, ever loved. She couldn't let it burn. Oh, Mother. Mother, why couldn't you let it just burn . . ."

"Althea," Alexis whispered. She gathered her sister into her arms and began to rock her as tears streamed down her face to dampen Althea's golden hair. Her mother. Their mother. Gone. Such a grisly way to die.

"I couldn't go in, Alex. I couldn't go after her. I called and I called, but she didn't come out."

"I know, dear. There was nothing you could do."

"I thought Father would go mad."

"Papa." Alexis breathed his name. She had forgotten he had even been there. She sat back from Althea. "What happened to Papa?"

"He must have loved her a little, Alexis. He blamed himself for not being there to stop them."

"They would have just killed him if he had been," Alexis muttered. Then she repeated, "What happened to Papa?"

"I don't remember how he got me on the train. He shoved a bag in my hand and hid some money in my dress lining and sent me to you. Cherry was with me, but she ran away. After all the time we've been together, she ran away; right in the middle of Union country, and she deserts me. Ungrateful chit. After all I've done for her. The Yankees will be sorry, treating those darkies like white folk. They'll learn they can't be trusted."

Alexis could see that Althea's thoughts were beginning to wander. "Papa, Althea. What about Papa?"

Althea's gaze cleared again. "He said he was going to join up with the Confederates. He said he was going to go fight."

"Fight? But, Althea, where? Where did he go to join the army?"

"I don't know, Alexis. He just put me on the train and left." Althea drooped back on the bed and closed her eyes. "I was so alone," she whispered. "So alone . . ."

Alexis sat stiffly beside the bed for a long time. Then Colter's hand under her arm lifted her to her feet.

"She's asleep, Alex. Come on."

"Maybe I should stay . . ." she began.

"No," he answered firmly. "You're coming to bed. Althea's going to be okay, but I'm not so sure about you."

With that, he swept her into his arms and carried her toward their suite. Alexis slipped her arms around his neck and rested in his strength. She knew that beyond her immediate numbness lurked blind hysteria, waiting to sweep over her like the rising ride. As long as she held onto Colter, she would be all right.

He laid her on the bed and stretched out beside her, pulling the covers over them. He held her close against him. He kissed her forehead time and time again and whispered "I love you," in her ear.

At last, she slept.

She was still in his arms when she awoke before dawn. His chest rose and fell with the steady breathing of deep sleep, and she tried not to move and disturb him. In fact, she didn't want to move. She didn't want to move out of the warm safety of his embrace. She still felt shaken by the story her sister had unveiled. Perhaps she would never be over it, and if it was so bad for her, who hadn't been there, how much worse it must be for Althea, who had been there.

Brief memories of Willowind drifted in and out of her thoughts. Funny. She could only recall the good times now, times when the house was filled with laughter and they were a whole family. She knew those times had been few, yet they were all she could see. She even remembered Madonna holding her on her lap and brushing her hair. Alexis had been wearing a new yellow frock and her mother was tying matching ribbons in her tight ringlets. Madonna had kissed her cheek and told her to be careful with her clothes, then she'd hugged her and set her down.

Was that the only time she kissed me? Alexis wondered silently. She couldn't think of any other time.

But instead of making her feel worse, it made that single kiss all the more precious. More precious because now her mother would never be able to kiss her again. Madonna was a stranger to her. Had been for years. But she'd still been her mother. Alexis felt the loss in the deep recesses of her heart.

And what about her father? Jonathan gone to fight in the war. But he didn't belong in a war. He belonged out here. Out in the West where there was lots of land and few people. He needed to be able to come and go as the mood struck him. Jonathan didn't belong in the war.

Alexis smelled the rich aroma of coffee and opened her eyes. The storm that had buffeted the city the previous day had blown itself out, and the bedroom was bright with morning sunlight. She was surprised. She thought she had just closed her eyes for a moment. Apparently, she had fallen into another deep sleep.

Mona stood by the side of the bed, holding a serving tray with the silver coffee pot and two china cups. Colter was propped up in bed beside Alexis, wearing the satin dressing jacket she had given him a few weeks before.

"I thought I'd better ring for my morning coffee whether you were awake or not," he said as he added some cream to his coffee. "The way you were sleeping, I might not have got it otherwise."

Alexis pushed her tousled hair away from her face and sat up, stuffing a fluffy pillow behind her back. "Thank you, Mona," she mumbled as the maid handed her a steaming cup. "What time is it?"

"Almost noon, Miss Alexis."

"Noon! Good heavens, Colt. The day's half gone, and I haven't been in to see how Althea is."

"No need for that," Mona volunteered. "She'll not be needing you this morning."

"But last night . . ."

"Whatever else that nightmare did for her," Mona said, picking the tray up and heading for the door, "it put some color back in her cheeks. She's up and dressed and gone out to look over our fair city."

"She's what?" Alexis couldn't believe it.

"She borrowed one of your dresses, Miss Alexis, and went out. She didn't say where she was going, though she did ask who your dressmaker was." Mona opened the door and left the bedroom.

Alexis set her cup on the stand next to the bed. "Colt, I'd better go find her," she said as she pushed the covers aside.

Colter caught her arm and pulled her back. "Not a chance, Mrs. Stephens. If Althea feels good enough to be asking about your dressmaker, she doesn't need you to chaperone her. You'll stay right here and drink your coffee, and then you're going to eat a hearty breakfast . . .

And I'll have no arguments out of you, either."

"But . . ."

"I said no arguments."

Alexis sighed heavily, but she didn't mind. Not really. It did sound as though Althea was feeling better, and it was nice to have Colter pampering her. She had had so little time for him since Althea arrived, and when they had been together, her thoughts had still been on Althea and the unknown disaster that had brought her to them.

She settled back on her pillow and wiggled into the crook of his arm, then picked up her cup again and sipped the hot brew. For the moment, she refused to let thoughts of her father or mother or Althea intrude. She was not going to think of anything except Colter until they were up and dressed and getting on with their day.

"I've missed you," he whispered into her hair.

"And I've missed you," she answered.

"Shall I ring Mona for our breakfast?"

She lifted her eyes to look into his. "Not yet."

He reached for her cup and set it on the table beside his own, then wrapped her in his arms and kissed her. She felt protected and sheltered here in his arms. His kiss was warm and tender, yet demanding too. It demanded her response, and respond she did. Her hands came up to run through his hair. She could feel her pulse pounding against his lips as his kisses moved down her throat and to the gentle swell of her breasts.

"Alexis . . ." The door flew open and Althea bustled into the room.

The lovers were torn apart by her sudden appearance.

"Oh, my. Colter. I didn't think I'd find you here this time of day."

Alexis could feel the blood rushing to her face as she gathered the sheet up close to her shoulders. A glance toward her husband told her he was more angry than embarrassed.

"Why shouldn't I be here, Althea? It *is* my bedroom," he said, the words grating through clenched teeth.

Althea blinked innocently. "Well, you needn't be so rude. It's not my fault if you're so lazy you're not out of bed before noon."

Colter turned his head toward Alexis, his eyes asking her for help before he did or said something they would all regret.

"Althea, would you be kind enough to wait for me in the parlor?" Alexis asked. "Give me just a moment to get dressed."

"Oh, of course. How silly of me. I'll just go out to the parlor." She smiled sweetly at Colter. "And Colter, my dear, you really must try not to be so grumpy with people. We are family now, after all."

Alexis and Colter both watched her leave and continued to stare at the closed door. Then, in precision, they turned to each other with twin looks of dismay.

"This isn't going to be an easy winter with Althea staying with us," Colter said.

"I think it's going to be a very long one," Alexis responded. She touched his chest for just a moment, a look of apology in her eyes. Then she got out of bed and dressed hastily.

"I'm going over to Sam's this afternoon," Colter told her as she reached the door. "Let's plan an early evening."

She nodded. The Ice Palace could do without her for one more evening. Tomorrow would be soon enough to return to her role as the Ice Queen.

"I love you, Colt Stephens," she said softly as she went out of their bedroom.

Althea was seated on the couch, an impatient look on her face.

"I'm glad to see you're feeling so much better, Althea. You had us terribly worried." Alexis crossed the room and took a chair opposite her sister.

"Really? Well, you wouldn't know it by the concern you've shown today. You didn't even stop by my room this morning. Lying in bed with a man until this time of day. I couldn't believe my eyes. You and Colter . . . and you with no clothes on. Why, it's positively *common*. One might think you were just white trash with no moral breeding whatsoever."

Alexis calmed her anger and spoke in a soft but firm voice, her gaze frigid. "Althea, Colt is my husband. What we do is in no way any concern of yours."

Althea was taken back. Her dark blue eyes grew round, and she replied in a wounded tone, "Well, I certainly didn't think it should be."

"Then let's talk of something else, shall we?" Alexis asked in a sweetened tone. "Mona tells me you took a stroll around town."

"Yes, and I wasn't too impressed. Alexis, a lady can't walk on the street without sharing the sidewalk with trollops and hoodlums. I saw a painted woman, as bold as brass, talking to the sheriff as if she were a lady of consequence."

Alexis grinned. "That's Idaho, but it's growing up. I'm told there's more law now than there was last year, and it'll be better next year than it was this. We've got new theatres and new churches and more wives and children arriving. They all make a difference. They're making it a town to be proud of."

"Pooh," Althea responded. "How can you be proud of a town made of boards and dirt? Surely you can't mean you prefer this place to a real city like Richmond?"

"I do, Althea. Because this is *my* town."

"Well, I certainly wouldn't stay any longer than I had to."

Alexis' eyes narrowed. "If there's someplace you'd like to go, Althea, we'd be glad to buy you a ticket on the first stage that can take you there."

Althea saw her error and tried to remedy it by appearing suddenly frail. "You know I have nowhere else to go. I'm totally at your mercy, and there you sit making me feel like a pauper, relying solely on your charity. I do so hate to take charity. I do have a little pride, Alexis. You might think of that."

"It's not charity, Althea. You're welcome in our home." Alexis felt guilty now, remembering all that Althea had been through. "We want you with us, Althea. Really, we do."

Althea leaned back on the sofa with a

satisfied grin. "Well, let me tell you what I did this morning. I went to visit your Mrs. Cane. What a strange little woman she is. But she seems to be a good enough seamstress for you."

For the first time, Alexis realized that Althea was wearing one of her favorite dresses. Shorter and somewhat thicker around the waist than Alexis, the bodice was being strained to its limits.

"I've ordered several new dresses and told Mrs. Cane to put everything else on hold while she gets them finished. After all, I can't be seen around town in your hand-me-downs. You and I have such different tastes in clothes. You and your trousers." She shook her head. "Although I must admit, you seem to have improved a little. This dress has some charm, though I wouldn't wear it if I had any other choice."

Alexis' nerves were quickly fraying at the edges. She stood up. "Please excuse me, Althea. It's getting quite late, and I must get dressed and go downstairs. My work has piled up since I've been sitting with you. If I don't try to wade through some of it this afternoon, there'll be no getting through it." She took a few steps, then added, "Please make yourself comfortable. There are some books in the case. Perhaps there's something you'd like to read. Or I could ask Mona to bring you some needlework."

"Don't bother with me, Alex," came Althea's stiff reply. "I'll find something to occupy my time. I certainly wouldn't want to interfere any more than I already have on your precious work."

Alexis bit back her retort as she hurried

toward the safe refuge of her bedroom.

Alexis was shut up in her office most of the day, digging through the paperwork that had accumulated during her seclusion with Althea. Several of the Palace employees dropped in to discuss how things had been going and to express their good wishes for her sister's complete recovery. Everyone seemed eager to meet Althea, and Alexis assured them that Althea would soon be feeling well enough to do so.

When Rafe came by in the late afternoon, he asked if she would be down in the saloon that night. "Everybody's been askin' for you, Miss Alexis."

"I've missed being there, Rafe," she replied, "but Althea needed me more." Remembering her promise to Colter, she added, "But I won't be down tonight. Tomorrow night, Rafe. Tell everyone I'll be back tomorrow."

15

Derek stood at the back of the Golden Gulch and stared at the near-empty saloon. He was angry. He longed to hit something . . . or someone. Why did they all flock to the Palace when he offered them everything *she* did? His saloon now boasted the same refinements as the Ice Palace, yet they still went across the street first. Oh, sure. He had a few regulars, but not as many as the Palace had. What more could he do to woo them away?

The rumor had spread through town like a wildfire that day. The Ice Queen would be back in her saloon tonight. One would have thought a monarch had been lying near death and had had a miraculous recovery for all the hoopla that was being made of her appearance. And, of course, there was the added speculation about her sister and just how soon the town would get a good glimpse at her.

Derek had heard that Althea was nearly as beautiful as Alexis. He found that hard to believe. No one could be as beautiful as the queen herself. And someday, he would make her pay for scorning him. He could be patient. He would wait until he found just the right method of payment, and then she would pay. He would have her as he'd always wanted to have her.

He looked down at his hands and found that he had crumpled his felt hat between his clenched hands. He tossed it into the corner beneath the stairway. He would go without it. He smoothed his reddish-blond hair with one hand while he reached for his walking stick with his other.

His thoughts moved from Alexis to Colter as he headed for the door of the Golden Gulch. Tonight he was going to play poker and win. He was going to make Colter Stephens leave that table empty-handed. He was going to get even with the man.

It wasn't just that Colter had a way of always beating him at the gaming tables. He was being a nuisance to Derek in other ways. Colter had gained the confidence of many of the businessmen around town, men who used to come to Derek for help when they needed it. Colter was also investing in new buildings and businesses, some of them in partnership with Sam Wainwright. None of these activities coincided with Derek's goal of owning Idaho City, lock, stock and barrel.

Derek looked up at the sky as he stepped out onto the sidewalk. It was clear again, but there was a cold edge to the night air. A lazy yellow moon, cut in half and rocking on its back, illuminated the rooftops, temporarily transforming the rough-and-tumble mining town into a fairyland. Winter was almost upon them. For the most part, mining would grind to a stop, though there were always a few who continued their search even in the worst weather. As soon as the snow started to fall, construction would be brought to a standstill, too. There would be more time for socializing among the townsfolk, but business would slacken in the saloons. It was always the same.

Derek stepped into the street. The Ice Palace was ablaze with lights. Laughter and loud voices spilled through the entrance, and he could hear the piano playing in the background. He pushed open the door and stepped inside, perusing the room quickly to ascertain if he had arrived before Alexis made her appearance. He had.

He moved to a far corner and sat down. One of the girls approached him to see if he wanted a drink, but he waved her away. He wanted nothing until Alexis came down. He would watch and admire and desire—and then he would play his game of cards with Colter and destroy him. This was going to be his lucky night. He could feel it.

Like a sheet ruffled by a gentle breeze as it hangs on the line, a hush moved over the crowd and all eyes turned toward the staircase. There she stood, her arm through her husband's.

Damn! but she's beautiful, Derek thought—and he hated her for it.

Her wheat-colored hair was worn up with soft wisps escaping to curl around the nape of her neck. Her gown was made of teal velvet that clung revealingly to her high breasts, narrow waist, and shapely hips. Derek licked his lips as he watched her regal descent.

The men in the saloon began to talk again, calling out to her, welcoming her back, asking about her sister. She moved among them, still on Colter's arm, thanking them for their kindnesses, asking about their families or their claims or even their old burros. If they were businessmen of the town, she inquired about their stores or offices or hotels. She seemed never to be wrong, never forgot a face or a name. It was one of the secrets of her popularity among these men, aside from the fact that she was simply a pleasure to behold.

Her special promenade of welcome complete, Colter kissed her cheek and headed for his favorite table. He hadn't quite reached it when another silent wave moved over the crowd, and once more all eyes turned to the head of the stairs. No one had to wonder who she was. She had to be the sister.

Derek stared along with the others. He could scarcely believe it. She could be Alexis.

Althea was wearing a gown made of the same teal velvet as her sister's, but the style was her own. The belled skirt was fuller than most of the men had ever seen. Her golden hair was gathered to the back, then fell in tight ringlets. Her gaze swept over the room without actually looking directly at any of them. A secretive smile turned the corners of her full mouth. She laid a hand on the banister, then began her own descent.

Before Colter could move to meet his sister-in-law, Derek hastened through the crowded saloon to the base of the stairs. He held out a hand as her feet touched the last step. He bowed. "Miss Ashmore, if I may be so bold, it would be a great honor for me if you would allow me to escort you to a table."

"I'm not sure that I should, Mr. . . ." Her pause was an unspoken question regarding his identity.

"Anderson. Derek Anderson. I'm a friend of your sister's. I own the Golden Gulch across the street."

"Really? How interesting." She accepted his hand. "Is it such a good thing out here to own a saloon? So many people do, you know."

"It can be a good thing, Miss Ashmore."

He drew her with him through the crowd. She carried her head high, looking neither right nor left. He stopped at a small table and, with a glance, told the men there to leave. Once the table was empty, he pulled out a chair for her.

"May I get you something, Miss Ashmore?" he asked solicitously.

"Nothing, thank you," she replied, looking up at him through long lashes.

Derek pulled out the chair beside her and sat down. "May I be the first to tell you that you are a very beautiful woman?"

She was pleased, but she protested. "I'm afraid you are being much too forward, Mr. Anderson. If you don't stop at once, I will be forced to leave your company."

"I beg your pardon. I'm going too fast, but you don't know what you've done to me."

"Me? Done to you?" she asked in feigned innocence. "Whatever can you mean? We've only just met."

Derek would have said more, but he saw Alexis approaching their table and swallowed his response as he rose from his chair.

"Althea, I didn't expect to see you down in the saloon tonight," Alexis said as she stopped beside her sister's chair. "Are you feeling up to it?"

"Of course, I am," Althea snapped. Then, realizing Derek was watching her, she added softly, "Please don't worry about me, Alex. I won't overdo. I promise."

"Alexis," Derek interrupted, "I believe your sister would feel more comfortable if she and I were properly introduced. Would you be so kind?"

There was an almost indiscernible frown on Alexis' forehead, but she nodded. "Of course. Althea, may I introduce Derek Anderson, a well-known businessman of our city and the owner of the Golden Gulch Saloon. Derek, this is my sister, Althea Ashmore, of Virginia."

Althea lifted a curved wrist up to him. He took her hand and kissed it. Her fingers still near his lips, he looked at her. Her head was dipped forward, and she was returning his gaze through coyly lowered lashes.

"It is a pleasure to meet you, Miss Ashmore."

"How delightful of you to say so, Mr. Anderson. I assure you, the pleasure is mine."

"I see you two have no need of me," Alexis commented. "Please excuse me."

Alexis gone, Derek leaned across the table and spoke in a low, intimate voice. "I believe we're going to be very good friends, Miss Ashmore."

The storm blew in from the Northwest, dumping snow on the western edge of the Rocky Mountains, burying Idaho City in a sea of white overnight. Alexis and Colter had planned a dinner party for a few of their friends for that night, and she worried throughout the day that the weather would keep them from coming. But at the appointed time, the horses and sleighs began arriving, and the Stephens' suite buzzed with friendly conversations.

Derek and Althea spent much of the evening seated in the window alcove. Alexis' dislike for Derek grew with her sister's attraction to him. She wished it were otherwise, but she couldn't shake her distrust of the man.

Dinner over, the men remained in the dining room to smoke while the ladies adjourned to the parlor. As much as she liked the women she had invited to the party, it didn't take Alexis long to grow tired of their small talk—fashions and the weather; their husbands and their children; the hardships of living in the West. Finally, she excused herself and wandered toward the dining room.

"Mark me. Pinkham's going to find a hole through his belly one of these days if he doesn't mind that abolition talk of his," one of the men said as she stepped, unnoticed, into the room.

Colter frowned. "I hope you're wrong, Donahue. Pinkham's a good lawman."

"Good or not, he's a Union man. It's men like him who are making sure that the gold from this territory reaches Union coffers and not the Confederacy."

"If it did reach the Confederacy, it would only prolong the inevitable," Colter said with disgust. "The Confederacy was doomed to lose this war from the very start. It will be better for it to end before thousands more die or are maimed."

Donahue got to his feet. "You're beginning to sound like a government man yourself, Stephens."

Colter ran the fingers of one hand through his hair in a gesture of futility. "Maybe. I see both sides. My wife's family is from the South. They've suffered a great deal. But prolonging the war isn't going to see it end any differently. The South is going to lose the war. Sherman's already taken Atlanta, and he won't stop there."

"But if the South had the money to buy the food and guns and supplies they need..." another man interjected.

"It's too late," Colter replied.

Alexis stepped away from the wall. "Does the gold from these mines really go to help the Yankees win the war?" she asked.

Surprised by her presence, the men rose quickly to their feet, murmuring greetings and apologies, but she waved their words away. She wanted an answer. Her gaze went to Colter as she took a chair at the table.

"Does it?" she asked again.

"Yes," her husband answered. "That's probably the biggest reason Idaho became a territory, so that the Union could get the wealth from these mountains."

"But . . ." her eyes swept over the men in the room, "most of these men are Confederate sympathizers. Why don't they do something?"

Colter's hand touched her shoulder. "It isn't that simple, Alexis. And even if it was, it really is too late to change anything."

"Is it? Is it too late, or is Donahue right? Would you just like to see Sherman and his ilk wipe the South off the map?"

Alexis saw Colter's jaw tighten and knew she was being unfair, especially in front of his friends. "I'm sorry. I didn't mean that, Colt. But after all that's happened to . . . to my family . . . Is there really nothing we can do out here? My father is fighting to save the Confederacy," she ended weakly.

"Alex, I'm as fond of your father as any man I've ever known. I don't want to see him killed or wounded any more than you do, but the surest way to prevent that from happening is to see this war finished and done with as quickly as possible. The ending will be the same no matter how long it takes."

Colter turned his gaze away from her. "Gentlemen, I know how most of you feel, and I hope what I've said won't damage our friendships. I mean what I said. I *can* see both sides. I *do* sympathize with you. But I believe the only answer is a speedy finish if we don't want to see every man and boy in the South killed. Or worse, missing their arms and legs." He got to his feet. "Now, if my point of view hasn't entirely spoiled this evening, why don't we rejoin the ladies? They are bound to brighten things up again."

Alexis glanced up at Colter as he stepped over to her chair. "If you don't mind, Colt, I think I'll just sit here for a moment."

"Angry with me?"

"No. Just confused."

He leaned down to kiss her cheek. "I know it isn't easy for you. You've lost a lot in this war."

She nodded, and he left the room.

Alexis *was* confused. How could she not support the Confederacy when her father was fighting with them? How could she not do everything in her power to help them win this war? Yet she understood what Colter was saying. Even she understood that there was little chance the South could regain their losses. The news that reached them was not good for those who stood by the Confederacy. Atlanta had fallen; most of it had burned. The Rebel soldiers were fighting in rags. The men of their cavalry units had no horses. Food was in scarce supply. But they fought on, and if they kept fighting, shouldn't those not fighting do everything they could to help?

"Miss Alexis?"

She looked up at the tall Irishman who had returned to the dining room.

"There are a few men here in Idaho City who

are going to try to do something to help our people in the South."

"What is that, Mr. Donahue?"

"I don't think we should talk about it now."

Alexis glanced toward the parlor and nodded her agreement.

"Come to my store on Wednesday morning at ten if you'd like to help." He paused, then added, "But I don't think you should tell your husband."

Alexis nodded again as she got to her feet. She placed her hand through the merchant's proffered elbow, and they returned to the parlor together, Alexis' head swirling with questions.

Wearing a fur coat and hat and carrying a fur muff, her hands tucked deep inside, Alexis stepped outside the following Wednesday morning and turned north on Montgomery, then east on Wall. It was still early, and the snow-covered streets were quiet. Her breath hung frozen in the air as she hurried along the sidewalk. She bypassed the office that faced the street, going directly to the small, whitewashed house behind it.

Stella opened the door in response to her knock. "Alexis, whatever are you doing here so early? Come in quick." She shivered as she shut the door.

"I haven't come at a bad time, have I?" Alexis removed her hat and coat and threw them across a nearby chair.

"Of course not. You're welcome in my home any time. Come into the kitchen. It's warmer there, and we can talk over a cup of coffee."

Alexis followed Stella into the tiny kitchen and sat on a chair near the cast-iron stove while Stella poured coffee into two cups.

"We missed you at our dinner party the other night," Alexis said as she accepted a cup from Stella. "Why didn't you come?"

"Didn't Sam tell Colter? I didn't want to come out in the snow. I'm so big and clumsy as it is. I don't need ice and snow to make me lose my footing."

"That's the only reason?"

Stella turned puzzled green eyes on her. "What other reason could there be?"

"Well . . . I was afraid you were bothered by Derek being there with Althea." She saw a strange expression pass over Stella's face. "Now, I know you've told me you don't care for Derek, but I know you did. I remember very well the first time we met. You *did* care for him, and I was afraid you still might."

Stella turned away for a moment while she set her cup on the table. When she turned back, her mouth was set in a determined line. "All right, Alexis. You are right. I *did* care for Derek at one time. But it wasn't love. I was a young girl alone in a rough mining town. He took me in and gave me a job. I . . . I was never more to him than another saloon girl. I didn't know what love was . . . and neither does Derek Anderson." She leaned forward in her chair, conveying the importance of her words. "It was Sam who taught me about love, and I don't ever want to know anything else. I'd just as soon forget whatever happened before I married Sam."

Alexis smiled. "I'm sorry, Stella. I didn't mean to doubt you. I guess I'm just worried about Althea. I think she's seeing too much of him and that got me thinking and when you didn't come..." Her voice drifted off.

"Alexis." Stella's gaze dropped to the floor. "Alexis, I don't think Derek knows how to care about anyone but himself. Your sister should be careful."

A tiny alarm went off in Alexis' head, and her pulse quickened. "What do you mean?" She waited for Stella to look up, to confirm with her eyes if not with her words that Alexis' own distrust of Derek was justifiable.

"Nothing special," Stella replied, turning her head to look out the window at the snow-covered yard behind the house. "I... just don't think he'll take proper care of her." As if a thought just occurred to her, she brought her head back around and met Alexis' gaze with round eyes. "He owns a saloon, after all."

Alexis couldn't help but laugh sardonically. "I hope that isn't a good reason for distrusting someone. *I* happen to own a saloon."

"Oh! I didn't mean..." Stella began, flustered by her unintentional insult.

Alexis knew Stella was keeping something from her, but she couldn't force her to tell what it was. "I know you didn't mean it the way it sounded." She reached across the space between them and clasped Stella's hand. "Now, let's talk of more pleasant things before I have to leave."

* * *

A little before ten, Alexis left the Wainwright home and walked toward the Donahue Bakery on Main Street. Light snow flurries stung her face as she leaned into the wind which had risen while she was visiting with Stella. She opened the door to the bakery. A tiny bell tinkled, announcing her entrance, as a wave of delightful odors surrounded her.

"Mrs. Stephens! My, but it's good t'see you. Whatever has brought you out on such a miserable morning as this? Haven't you got servants t'do your runnin' for you? What else good is it t'own the likes o' the Palace if you can't leave such chores t'others, I might ask?"

"Good morning, Mrs. Donahue," Alexis replied, shaking the snowflakes from her muff.

Mrs. Donahue, a rotund woman with a permanently red face, wiped her floury hands on her apron and stepped around the counter. "What can I get for you this morning?"

"I'd like to take some of your rolls home with me when I leave, but first I must speak with Mr. Donahue."

"I'm afraid he's in a meeting right now. I can send him 'round t'you later if you're needin' him."

Alexis wondered if Mrs. Donahue knew what the meeting was about. "I know he's in a meeting, Mrs. Donahue. That's why I'm here."

"You?" Mrs. Donahus chuckled. "Now, what concern could you have with the prospect of a new lumber mill?"

"Your husband asked me to come this morning. He told me to be here at ten this morning." The stiffening of her back stated she had no intention of leaving without seeing the baker.

The large woman peered at Alexis with cautious eyes, then nodded her head against her double chin. "They're meeting in the store room. Come with me."

Mrs. Donahue led the way past the large ovens. She rapped twice on the door, then opened it. "Tip? Mrs. Stephens is here t'see you. Said you'd asked her t'come."

"That I did, Molly. Come in, Miss Alexis. Come in." He took her by the arm and drew her into the crowded store room. "I believe you know everyone here."

Alexis looked around and nodded at each of the four men in the room. She knew them all.

"Have a seat here," Donahue said, pointing at a large sack of flour. "It's the best I have to offer, I'm afraid."

"Enough of the pleasantries," a man named Meyers said gruffly. "We've got business to discuss here."

Donahue frowned at Meyers. "I think we should tell Miss Alexis what's been said between us." He turned toward her. "We've all got family in the South, and we've decided it's time we do something. The best way we know, short of closing our homes and businesses here and going to fight with the army itself, is to get money to the Confederacy. Not that worthless script they've issued themselves, but gold. Something they can bargain with to get the things they need. I won't pretend to you, Miss Alexis. What we're planning is illegal. If you want no part of it, it's best you leave right now without hearing any more."

Alexis returned his gaze with an unfaltering one of her own. "Is anyone likely to get killed as a part of your plan, Mr. Donahue?"

"Not if everything works out the way we hope," he answered.

"And will it rob any of our friends here in Idaho?"

"No. We'll be takin' from the Union government."

"Then I'm with you."

Donahue breathed a satisfied sigh and turned a sweeping gaze over the other men in the room. "There's to be no others than those here today that will know about what's going on. We have the winter before us to perfect our plans. We've got to trust each other to keep silent. Agreed?"

"Agreed," everyone answered in unison.

Donahue nodded. "Then here's the plan."

16

Colter was feeling restless. There wasn't enough for him to do in town, even with the business investments he'd been making. He was a man of action. He needed to be back on his ranch, even in weather like this.

He pushed the draperies aside and looked down from the parlor window onto the street below. There was not a soul to be seen, and it was nearly noon. Ice and snow covered the frozen ground. The wind moaned mournfully, stirring up powdery snow flurries and blowing deep drifts against the sides of buildings.

As he stood there, he saw Alexis coming down the street in the sleigh. She'd gone out early again this morning, saying only that she had some shopping to do and that he would be bored if he came along. Her meaning was clear; she wanted to go alone. But he knew, judging by the recent past, that she would return with next to nothing. Perhaps a loaf of bread or a pair of gloves. Nothing worth going out into weather like this.

Alexis was keeping something from him. He tried not to use the word "lying" even in his own thoughts. He couldn't think of anything that would cause her to lie to him. They loved each other. They shared each other's thoughts. No, she would never lie to him.

He let the curtains fall back in place and moved back to the sofa. He sat down and opened a book, something he had been trying to read for over two weeks and couldn't get more than ten pages into it. He thought it was probably a good book, but nothing he had read so far had gone past his eyes. He was merely looking at words, not comprehending them. How could he concentrate on reading when Alexis was away?

He looked up as the door closed. Alexis shook her muff and laid it on the table near the door. She removed her fur hat and coat next, then turned with a smile to enter the parlor.

"Hello, darling. It's terribly cold out. It's going to be another quiet night in the saloon." She kissed his forehead before continuing over to the window. She pushed aside the curtains as he had only a little while before. "Sam thinks we'll have a lot more snow and cold before this winter is behind us."

"You went by the Wainwrights?" Colter asked, laying aside the unread book.

"Yes," she replied absently. "I stopped by for a moment. I wanted to see if Stella needed anything from the Mercantile."

"Wish you'd told me you were going over. I could have joined you."

The look on her face was unmistakably guilty as she turned toward him. "I'm sorry, Colt. I really didn't think you'd care to go shopping with me."

"What did you buy for yourself?" He hadn't wanted to ask the question, but it slipped out anyway. He wasn't sure he wanted to hear the answer.

"Nothing really. I couldn't find what I wanted."

"And what was that?"

Alexis glanced at the floor, and there was an uncomfortable silence before she answered, "Colt, I wish you wouldn't ask me."

Why? he wondered. What could she be hiding from him?

She lifted her gaze to meet his, and a secretive smile turned up the corners of her mouth. "Hasn't anyone ever told you it's best not to ask too many questions this time of year?"

"What?"

"Christmas is less than two months away," she replied. "Now, don't ask me anything else."

It was as if the world was lifted off his shoulders. His heart lightened, and he smiled his first honest smile in weeks. He got up quickly and walked over to her. His arms shot around her, and he drew her close in a hungry embrace.

"I'm sorry," he said softly. "I won't ask any more questions about where you go or what you're doing."

"Thank you, Colt. I don't like to keep things from you, no matter how good the reason, but sometimes..."

His kiss drowned out the rest of her reply.

Alexis wanted to die inside. How could she lie to him this way? Of course, she hadn't *really* lied. She had gone by Stella's and she had looked, at least a little, for Christmas gifts. Thank goodness Donahue had decided this morning that they needn't meet again until winter began to ease. She was worn out by the strain of deception already. How was she to do her part come spring if Colter were around to observe her actions and ask questions?

"Alex," Colter said, still holding her close against him, "I'm about to go crazy around here. The saloon's nearly empty every night. You don't need me to make any decisions around the place. The mines I've invested in are shut down for the winter. I'd like to go down to the ranch for a week or two. Will you go with me?"

Alexis looked up at him through sooty lashes and felt a leap of joy in her heart. A chance to be alone with him. No business to be handled. No secret meetings with Donahue and the others. No Althea intruding on their privacy. It would be heaven.

"You don't have to come, Alex. I'll understand if you don't want to."

"Don't want to!" She flung her arms around his neck. Her eyes sparkled. "You couldn't keep me from going with you. When do we leave?"

"As soon as you're ready."

"I'm ready now."

Colter felt foolish for doubting her. Her undisguised wish to be alone with him was enough to erase any lingering doubts he had had about her secret outings. He should have taken her away sooner. He knew the last few weeks hadn't been easy for Alexis, what with her sister staying with them and wondering about her father's safety. Time must weigh heavy on her hands, too, for she was no more used to idleness than he was.

He chuckled as he brushed a stray wisp of hair away from her temple. "I think we'd be wiser to take a little time to pack. We need to decide how long we'll stay so everyone will know when to expect us back."

"Let's not tell them. Maybe we shouldn't even come back." Her words sounded almost desperate.

"Do you mean it, Alexis? Would you rather leave the Palace and move to the ranch now?"

The brightness left her cheeks, and she shook her head. "I would if I could, Colt. Sometimes I think it would be so much easier." Her blue eyes pleaded for understanding. "But I can't quit now. You know it as well as I do. Besides, if I don't stick it out, I'd never know if the success of the Palace this far was luck or because of me."

"You know it's you," Colter said.

"It's me in the good times and while I've been a novelty. No, Colt. I want to finish it. If not for me, for Reckless. He wanted me to have it, and I have to do this for him. If I can't find his killer, I can at least do this." She reached up and stroked his cheek with her finger. "But you'll always know I wanted to run away with you."

"I told you before, I don't mind living here with you." He pressed his lips against her hair and whispered, "I love you, Alexis Stephens."

"And I love you, Colt. More than you'll ever know."

It was a difficult trip to the Circle S. Sometimes the horses sank in drifts up to their bellies. At other times, their shod hooves slipped on patches of ice. The sun shone brightly in the cloudless sky, belying the frigid temperature of the day.

Both Alexis and Colter were clad in furs from head to toe, but still their cheeks stung and their feet tingled. They wondered more than once at the wisdom of their journey. But it was worth it when the cabin came into view, a ribbon of gray smoke curling skyward from the chimney. The cattle had been brought in from the surrounding mountains for the winter. Their brown backs and wide horns darkened the valley around the cabin, bunkhouse, and barn, and a gentle lowing could be heard across the silent snow.

Two weeks. Two weeks with little more to do than stay in bed and keep each other warm.

When they did emerge from the seclusion of their tiny cabin, they frolicked like children in the winter wonderland, breaking icicles from the eaves of the barn and throwing snowballs at each other. They tramped on snowshoes to the new ranch house. With its outer shell completed, the interior was almost haunting in its unfinished state.

"It's waiting for us to make it a home," Colter told Alexis.

But the two weeks drew to a close, and once again they were strapping their bundles behind their saddles and preparing to bid the Circle S adieu. It would probably be spring before they could return again.

Alexis pondered again her decision to stay at the Palace. Why did she cling to it so stubbornly? But she wasn't just returning because of the saloon Reckless had left to her, as she had told Colter. At one time, that was true, but no longer. Now, it was also because of her father. She had to do whatever she could to help the Confederate Army. If it would be enough, she would gladly sell all she owned—the saloon, her jewels, everything—but that wouldn't help. They needed gold. Lots of gold.

She glanced at Colter as he checked his mount's cinch. She would have to lie to him again. He would never understand or condone what she was planning. She feared what he would think of her if he found out. Would he ever forgive her? Perhaps the memory of these two blissful weeks would make up for deceiving him. She hoped so.

"Ready?" Colter asked, catching her watching him.

She nodded. "Ready."

The temperatures had warmed slightly over the past few days. A brief thaw dripped melting snow from the bare branches of the aspens and the green needles of the pines. A cobalt sky harbored harmless puffs of white clouds, promising a day free of new snow.

With a wave to Li Chung who stood by the bunkhouse door, they turned their horses to the north.

Althea hated being the poor sister. How she hated it! If the war had never started, she would have been rich. If she had married Colter, she would have been rich. How unfair it was that she must live on Alexis' charity. After all, she was the one who had been raised to appreciate the finer things, not Alexis who had spent her growing years on the back of a horse in this cultural wilderness.

Althea caressed the smooth satin fabric of her newest gown as she considered the injustice of her situation, causing tiny frown lines to crease her forehead. Why was it that Alexis should stumble into this fortune? Wasn't it enough that she had stolen Colter from her own sister? Was it fair that she beguile a stupid old man into leaving his wealth to her, too?

"I deserve it more than she," Althea muttered, standing suddenly and leaving her room.

She hurried into her sister's suite and went into the bedroom. She stopped at the dressing table and pulled the jewelry box from the top drawer. She dumped its contents onto the dresser, searching for the diamond choker she had seen Alexis wear not long before she and Colter left for the ranch. Finding it, she held it up to her throat and admired the cool flame that appeared to flicker in the depths of the gems.

Perfect, she thought.

She fastened the choker around her neck and patted her hair to assure its perfection as well. Then she left the suite and went to the head of the stairs.

In Alexis' absence, Althea had assumed the nightly role as queen of the Ice Palace. A role, she thought, that she was much better suited for than her younger sister.

With a superior sweep of her eyes, she surveyed the customers. Their numbers were still small due to the early onset of winter. There was the usual collection of professional gamblers, hard-luck miners, and businessmen of the town. One man she didn't find among them tonight was Derek. She was surprised. Derek was here every night.

Derek was a mystery to Althea, and her feelings for him were nearly as mysterious. He was quite good-looking, though admittedly not as handsome as Colter. She found his reddish blond hair and beard distinguished and liked his self-confident air. She especially found his attentions toward her attractive. But sometimes she wondered why he came. Was it because he liked her, or was it because he disliked Alexis? Nothing he had ever said had indicated his negative feelings about Alexis. In fact, his words said just the opposite. He spoke only praise for the Ice Queen. But behind those words, Althea felt sure he harbored a deep resentment. Perhaps that was one more reason she felt attracted to him.

Yes, she was attracted to Derek Anderson, but she was also wary of him. He smiled and said all the right things to her, yet beneath his gentlemanly veneer, she sensed something almost frightening, as if, should his careful retraint on his emotions ever slip, he would be dangerous. Despite this, however, he was the one man who seemed to appreciate her refined company over that of her sister, and Althea needed to be appreciated.

The door opened and the subject of her thoughts entered the saloon. His eyes darted quickly to the top of the stairs, as if he'd known she would be waiting for him there. Althea smiled her greeting and began her descent as he strode across the hall to meet her.

"Althea, you grow more beautiful every time I see you," he said as he held out his arm for her to take.

"And you continue to say things you shouldn't, Mr. Anderson."

"Isn't it time you dropped the Mr. Anderson and called me Derek?"

Althea raised her eyebrows, feigning surprise at his request. "Why, Mr. Anderson, you'll make me blush. It just isn't proper for a lady such as myself to address a man she's known only a short time in such personal terms."

"It may not be proper where you come from, Althea," Derek said, leaning his head close to her own, "but I assure you that it would not be thought ill of in our fair city." He held out a chair for her.

"Thank you, sir." She sat down and turned her head up to look at him as she continued her mild protest. "Good manners are in vogue anywhere, Mr. Anderson."

Derek sat down beside her. Slowly, he removed his kid gloves and put them inside his top hat on the chair beside him. When he lifted his hazel eyes to gaze upon her once more, any hint of a smile had disappeared from his face. "Althea," he said in a low voice, "you must know that I hold you in high esteem. My hope is we will become much more than good friends, and I think you know that."

Althea grew warm under his intense gaze. She felt almost frightened by the implications of his words. Yet, he was handsome and he did pursue her most gallantly. He was a wealthy man in his own right, a man of note in this community. He would be a good catch for any girl.

"All right, Mr. Anderson. I will call you by your given name," she agreed in a breathless voice.

He leaned closer. "Then let me hear you say it."

"Derek. I will call you Derek."

A broad smile brightened his face. "Wonderful. I think we should celebrate. How about a drink, my dear Althea?" He waved to Rose. "Bring us two glasses and a bottle of champagne."

"A celebration just because I agreed to call you Derek?" Althea asked, her spirits reviving in unison with his. She dropped her eyes in coy embarrassment. "Whatever must you think of me?"

"I think you are the most beautiful woman in Idaho City," he replied.

* * *

She *was* the most beautiful woman in Idaho City, but only because her sister was out of town.

Derek saw the spark of pleasure in Althea's eyes as she looked at him again. How easy this woman was to maneuver. She played all the little games expected of a woman, and Derek had joined her in them to achieve his goal, but he tired of it all quickly. It was all he could do to control his temper as she simpered and preened before him. But he had need of her, and so he played the game. Besides, it might be fun to make a woman out of this southern belle.

Alexis and Colter stopped to rest their horses. Even in this cold weather, the animals were sweating from their efforts. Colter loosened the cinches on the saddles and gave them both some grain from his saddlebags.

"It's going to be a bad winter," Colter said as he sat on a boulder beside Alexis. "Going to make up for the mild one we had last year."

Alexis snuggled against him. "Can it get much worse than this?"

"It can and it will. This is only November. Winter hasn't even really begun."

"It could be rather dull in Idaho if it stays like this. There won't be much of a crowd in the saloon."

Colter hugged her closer to him. "I guarantee you, it won't be dull for us," he said huskily.

She shivered, but not from the cold.

"Maybe we should hope for another foot or two of snow," he continued.

"Perhaps we should," she replied, lifting her mouth to meet his.

The cold was forgotten as she surrendered to the heat of his kisses. She closed her eyes, lost for the moment to reality. How she loved him. How she loved his touch, his kiss, his voice. She was the luckiest woman alive to have found him. She belonged to him, body and soul. She wondered sometimes, in those awful moments when dire thoughts entered her mind, if she would simply cease to exist if he should die. She was certain she could not live without him.

Colter pulled back from her. "We'd better move on. I'm getting anxious to reach the warmth of our bedroom."

Alexis smiled quickly. "No more than I am, husband." Then she pointed behind him and added, "And if you don't want to walk all the way back, you'd better go after your horse. He's already on his way."

Colter turned to look in the direction Alexis was pointing. Titan had wandered into a stand of trees and seemed intent on disappearing into their midst. Colter got up and hurried after him. Alexis pushed herself up and had almost reached Nugget when she heard the sudden whish and clang, followed by Colter's startled cry. She whirled around.

He was on the ground near a tall pine, his hands prying desperately at the steel trap that was biting into his calf. By the time, Alexis reached him, his blood was already staining the white snow beneath him.

"The man must be after grizzlies," Colter said through gritted teeth. "I can't budge it."

Alexis joined her hands with his, putting every ounce of her strength into the effort to free him. It was no use. Even with two of them, they couldn't pry the bear trap far enough apart for Colter to pull out his leg.

"Let's try to pull the chain free," Colter told her, his breathing labored.

Alexis glanced at him. His face was pale, his eyes glazed with pain. She had to hurry. She grabbed hold of the chain and jerked with all her might. It didn't move. She looked back at Colter, trying to disguise her fear, than yanked at it again.

"Colt, I can't free it."

"I didn't really think you could. After all, it was meant to hold a bear once it was in here. You'll have to go for help."

Panic tightened her throat. "I can't leave you here alone. You're hurt. You're losing blood."

"You'll have to go," he replied, gripping the steel teeth and trying once more to separate them.

"But, Colt . . ."

He gave her a harsh look. "Alex," he barked, "you've got to go for help. You won't do either of us any good staying here. Bring me my rifle and give me the extra blankets. I'll be all right 'til you get back."

Still she didn't move except to place a hand on his cheek. "Colt . . ."

"It's just a little blood, Alex. It's not as bad as

you think. Nothing's going to happen to me if you leave now. You'll be back here before dark." The smile he tried to show her was more of a grimace. "I don't like the thought of freezing to death out here, so get moving."

She realized that he was right. If she lingered any longer, they could both freeze to death. She brushed her lips across his forehead in a hurried kiss, then got to her feet and ran, as best she could, through the snow to Titan. She grabbed his reins and led him back to Colter before drawing the rifle from its scabbard and handing it to her husband. She gave Colter one more long, loving glance, then hurried toward Nugget and swung up into the saddle.

"I'll be back before you know it," she promised.

Alexis pushed Nugget unmercifully. The mare gave her all, struggling against the deep snow that sucked at her every step. Alexis cursed the foul weather, her heart looking backward and her mind imagining the snow around Colter growing red with his blood. And more blood and more blood and . . .

As she neared Idaho City, the snow was trampled from greater road use, and she was able to spur her tired horse into a faster pace. A mile south of town was the Warm Springs, a bathing resort just off the Boise City stage road. Alexis prayed there would be some men there willing to help her. It could save valuable time if she didn't have to ride on into town. In front of the resort, she pulled Nugget to a halt and jumped from the saddle. She raced up the steps and along the porch, pulling the door open with force, and entered the barroom.

"I need help," she announced, her panicked eyes sweeping over the handful of men inside, but none of their faces registered in her mind. Relief flowed over her as she recognized Sam Wainwright as he entered the barroom from the hall leading to the baths. "Sam, I need help."

"Alexis, what's wrong?"

"It's Colt. He's caught in a trap. We couldn't get him free. Sam, he's hurt bad. Come quick." She was shaking. She felt as if her head would burst open.

Sam turned around and spoke to the man behind him. "George, get Doc Barker. Have him meet us at the Palace. Hank, you'd better come with me."

Alexis followed his glance, recognizing one of the dealers from the Ice Palace. She knew then that she had looked without seeing anyone until Sam came into the room. All her thoughts were still back by those trees where the snow was blood red.

"Hurry, Sam," she pleaded.

"How's your horse, Alexis?" he asked.

"Tired. She'll never make it back."

"Johnson, can we borrow your horse?" Sam asked one of the other men in the room.

"Sure," came the reply.

Sam slipped his hand beneath her arm and steered her toward the door. "Are you going to be all right? Can you take us to him?" he asked, watching her with worried eyes.

"I'll be fine as soon as we get back to him.

Oh, Sam, it's getting so late already. He was bleeding and he was in terrible pain. He tried to hide it from me. He's strong, but . . ."

Sam squeezed her shoulder in a gesture of comfort. "We'll get there in time, Alexis. Let's go."

The pain and loss of blood had taken its toll. Colter lost consciousness more than once while he waited for Alexis to bring help. Still, when he was awake, he pulled with what strength he had on the chain, refusing to give in to the weakness that shrouded his mind in a dark haze.

He glanced at the sky, wondering how long it had been since Alexis left. The sky was pewter gray. Was evening almost here or was it cloudy again? He shivered from the cold as he turned his eyes back to his steel jailer. He grasped the heavy chain again and threw all his remaining strength into his attempt to wrench it free. Shards of white lightning speared his leg, and he collapsed back into the snow, succumbing to the black relief of unconsciousness once again.

They found him like that, Titan still standing over him. He looked dead. Alexis was paralyzed in her saddle, afraid to go closer and have her worst nightmares come true.

Sam dismounted and knelt beside him. "Colt?" He touched his shoulder.

Colter opened his eyes. "Hi, Sam," he whispered weakly. "Heck of a way to end a great two weeks."

"Colt!" Alexis cried as she hurled herself out

of the saddle. Dropping to her knees, she cradled his head in her lap. "Oh, Colt." There was nothing more to say. Those two words said it all as the tears welled up in her eyes.

He tried to smile. "I always thought I was tough. Guess I was wrong," he said in an attempt at humor.

Sam shook his head, a grim look on his face. "You're going to need to be tough, Colt." He glanced at Alexis. "Get behind his head with your hands under his arms. When I tell you to, you pull him as hard as you can 'cause you won't have much time."

Alexis did as she was told, watching as Hank and Sam stood across from each other and placed their hands on the jagged jaws of the trap.

"Ready?" Sam asked, and Hank nodded.

With agonizing slowness, the trap opened.

"Pull his foot out, Alexis," Sam yelled at her.

There was no time to be tender. Alexis quickly obeyed. Colter ground his teeth together but stifled a cry of objection.

The steel jaws snapped shut again as Sam tossed it aside. He knelt down beside Colter again. "Let's have a look at this." He tore the ragged trousers away from the wound. "We'd better get this bleeding stopped. Looks like it's broken."

Alexis continued to cradle Colter's head, crooning senseless words of comfort as Sam bound the broken leg, using a rifle for a splint.

"Do you think you can ride?" Sam asked, glancing at the sky. "I don't think we've got time to fix up a travois."

Colter nodded. "I can ride."

Sam and Hank lifted him up and carried him to his horse. Sheer willpower kept him from blacking out again as he straddled the saddle.

"Better strap me in," he said. "It's easier than picking me up when I fall off." He tried to smile at his own small joke.

Alexis stood beside him, her hand rubbing Titan's muzzle. "Colt," she said softly, "I love you."

"And I love you," he answered. "Now stop looking as if the world has ended. I'm going to be fine."

"Your husband's a lucky man, Mrs. Stephens. If that trap had snapped lower, he could have lost his foot." Dr. Barker closed his black bag and headed for the door. "I don't think that leg will cause him much trouble once it's mended. Unless, of course, it gets infected. Mr. Wainwright tells me it looked like the trap had been there several years and there was quite a bit of rust. That might cause him some problems. One never knows for sure." He opened the door and stepped into the hallway. "Now, you go back in with him and quit your worrying."

Alexis nodded, but her worrying didn't cease. She had never seen Colter look anything but strong and robust. When she'd left their room with Dr. Barker, he was lying against the pillows, his face as white as the bedsheets. It frightened her to see him so weakened.

She walked back through the suite and opened the bedroom door. Colter was asleep. She sat beside the bed, taking his hand in her own as she watched the gentle rise and fall of his chest.

17

Mournful winter winds whistled through the mountain canyons, reaching with freezing tentacles beneath doors, between cracks in the walls, and through window glass to grasp the residents huddled inside in a relentless chill. Black storm clouds blew down from the north, dumping snow upon snow and burying the town of Idaho City beneath a heavy white blanket. It would not be a winter soon forgotten by those living in the basin that December of 1864.

At first Alexis was too busy tending to her husband to notice the weather, but now that Colter's leg was mending without threat of infection, she realized how paralyzed the entire region had become. Some men had left for other gold strikes before the weather turned so foul, but those who remained were snowbound inside their mountain shacks. The saloons and gambling halls stood empty much of the time. Alexis wondered about the miners who had frequented the Ice Palace but no longer came into town. Were they all right? Did they have food, wood for a fire? These men were her friends, and she was concerned.

One bright spot was the free time she had to spend with Colter, alone in their suite. With no demands on her time in the saloon at night, she could lie in bed as late as she wanted in the morning, nestled in Colter's arms, and if she wanted to retire early, there were few customers around to wonder at her break in routine.

She and Colter spent their hours talking of the Circle S and the grand plans they had for the ranch. The house would be finished and ready for them to move in by June or July. Colter had a good market for his beef with the miners in the area and wasn't going to drive the cattle east to sell this year. In fact, he planned to return to Texas to buy more cattle to bring to his ranch.

"Someday there'll be trains all the way across this country," he told Alexis. "It'll make it a lot easier for ranchers out here to sell their stock and make a profit." He gazed deeply into her eyes, adding, "It'll make it a lot easier for our sons to operate the Circle S."

Alexis was disappointed that one of those sons he spoke of wasn't already living within her. It certainly wasn't for lack of effort on their part, she thought with a secret smile as she snuggled closer to Colter beneath the heavy blankets, her fingers beginning a lazy tracing over his chest.

* * *

Althea let herself into the suite without knocking. It was nearly noon, and she wanted some company. She thought she would go crazy from the silence that dominated this town. She was surprised not to see Alexis and Colter in the parlor now that Colter was allowed to get out of bed for a few hours a day. She was about to leave when she heard muffled voices coming from the bedroom. Thinking Alexis must be visiting with him at bedside, she went to the door and turned the handle.

She opened her mouth to say something, but the words died in her throat as she spied the two lovers in their bed. Her face blazed with embarrassment as she backed out of the room, thankful that they had been too engrossed in each other to notice her. Hiking her skirts, she turned quickly and rushed out of the suite.

"Disgusting," she muttered under her breath. "It's the middle of the day."

She grabbed her new fur coat, identical to the one Alexis had, and clutched it tightly around her as she left the Palace by the private entrance. Blowing snow stung her cheeks, but she ignored it. She had to get away from there. Even this weather couldn't stop her. Without much choice of destination, her feet turned automatically toward Mrs. Cane's clothing store. She had become the widow's most frequent customer, and now seemed like a good time to order several new gowns, courtesy of Alexis Stephens, of course.

Head down and her thoughts angry, she barreled right into Derek as he left a cigar store not far from Mrs. Cane's.

"What the . . . Alexis, what's wrong?" he said as he grabbed her by the shoulders to steady her.

Her head snapped up and her eyes blazed their fury. "I'm not Alex." She jerked free of his hands.

Derek chuckled as he took a step backward. "I can see that now."

"Just *what* do you mean by that?"

"Nothing, my dear Miss Althea." He bowed, then offered her an elbow. "May I escort you wherever it is you're going in such a hurry?"

Althea glanced around her, not knowing what she wanted to do. Then her expression softened, and she turned a gentle gaze upon him. "Oh, Derek, I just had to get out of that place before I went stark raving mad. Staring at those same walls, day in and day out. Absolutely nothing going on in this town. No theatre. No dancing. Oh, how I'd love to go to a ball like we used to have at Willowind." She slipped her arm through Derek's, and they began walking.

"Would you like to go where there's dancing, Miss Althea? We haven't anything like your balls, but . . ." He paused. "No. You wouldn't like it."

That piqued her interest. "Wouldn't like what?"

"Well, there are the hurdy-gurdy houses."

"Mr. Anderson! Do you realize what you're saying to me?" She tried to look appropriately shocked, but in truth, she was curious and she couldn't hide it.

Derek grinned. "Ah, you would like to go, wouldn't you? Do you know why it appeals to you, Althea? Because you *would* like to know what goes on inside such a place."

"Really, Mr. Anderson," she huffed. "I think we should end this discussion. I have no interest in seeing how harlots and drunks spend their evenings."

He stopped suddenly and leaned his face close to her own. His eyes bored into hers, a dangerous gleam in their hazel depths. "Don't you? I think you're dying to see just that. I think you'd love to know what it is that a harlot does to earn her wages." He laughed at her horrified expression. His hand tightened painfully on her arm. "Don't play the innocent with me, Althea Ashmore."

"Derek, I think you've said enough." She was growing nervous.

The threatening look in his eyes disappeared so quickly, she doubted it had ever been there. His smile was warm and friendly as he said, "Would you allow me to buy you lunch, Miss Ashmore? In case you haven't noticed, we happen to be standing outside one of the finest restaurants in Idaho."

Althea hadn't noticed. She hadn't been paying any attention to where they were going. She realized she was hungry and nodded her acquiescence.

Derek opened the door. "I promise you an interesting conversation over lunch, and I refuse to allow you to return to the tedium of your place until the day is waning. A lovely flower should not have to live in the shadows of boredom, my dear."

"You do say the most outrageous things, Derek," she replied, stepping by him with head high and eyes sparkling.

They had champagne. Derek kept filling her glass and coaxing her to drain it. Her head felt light and everything he said seemed so funny. Althea looked at him across the table and thought what a wonderfully handsome man he was. And he was kind and he cared for her. He found her company enjoyable and sought her out when he could be with others. Surely she was the envy of all the women in town.

The afternoon flew by, and Althea was surprised at how late it was when Derek led her from the restaurant. At the Celestial Laundry, they turned north, walking toward the Ice Palace. Althea was disappointed. She didn't want the evening to end for her so soon. But Derek stopped at the livery and ordered his horse hitched up to his sleigh.

While they waited, Althea leaned her head on his shoulder and closed her eyes. She felt a little dizzy from so much champagne, and it was nice to lean against someone strong.

"Get in, Althea," Derek said to her.

She opened her eyes again. The sleigh was in front of her, the horse blowing frosty clouds through his nostrils.

Derek handed her up, then pulled a heavy blanket from beneath the seat and spread it over her legs before climbing in beside her. "Warm enough?" he asked.

"As long as I'm beside you," she replied,

tucking her arm through his.

Derek picked up the reins and clucked to the horse.

The sudden start made Althea's head reel. Once more, she closed her eyes and leaned against him. She wondered briefly where they were going, but the thought didn't stay long in her head. She couldn't seem to take hold of any thought for too long. Everything was a jumble in her mind.

Derek took the sleigh across Elk Creek to Buena Vista Bar. Ten months before, Buena Vista Bar and Bannock City had been two separate towns. The citizens had been surprised one day to read in the *Idaho World* that, by an act of the Territorial Legislature, the two towns could incorporate and the name had been changed to Idaho City. Still, residents continued to refer to the area across Elk Creek as Buena Vista.

When Derek pulled the horse to a stop, Althea could hear loud music coming from inside the nearby building. She opened her eyes, blinked a few times to focus them, then read the lettering on the front of the building: *Ruby's Hurdy House*.

"Derek? Are you really going to take me inside this place?" She was both insulted and excited.

He got out without answering and went around the sleigh. Excitement won. She took his proffered hand.

The hall was long and narrow. A bar at one end had a large sign behind it. "Champagne $12 a bottle. Whisky 50 cents a drink. One dollar in gold per dance." A small orchestra occupied a far corner of the room. A barrier separated the dancing women from the paying customers until the men had made their selection. Several curtained enclosures lined the far wall, allowing privacy for those who wanted more than a drink and dance and had the money to pay for it.

There were more customers here than she had seen at the Palace for quite some time, though these men were admittedly rougher than those who frequented her sister's saloon. She felt curious eyes turn on her throughout the dance hall and knew she was the only woman there who wasn't paid to be there.

"I don't think I should be here," she whispered to Derek.

"Nonsense, Althea. We'll sit down and have a few drinks and watch the dancing. Then, if you want to leave, we will. Agreed?"

She had the feeling that it wouldn't matter if she agreed or not. Derek wanted to be here and that was where they were going to be.

He left her at a table near the dance floor and went to the bar, returning with a bottle of champagne and two glasses. He smiled at her as he filled a glass, then slid it across the table.

"I'm afraid I've had too much already," Althea protested.

"Drink up. Enjoy yourself." The corners of his mouth twitched. "What else is there to do, Althea? Go back and watch Alexis and that husband of hers make calf eyes at each other?" He lowered his voice, but she could hear him clearly enough. "Are you afraid to be as much woman as she is, Althea?"

She glared at him with burning eyes. "I am more of a woman than she'll ever be," she retorted.

"Are you? Then why is she married to Colter Stephens and not you?"

Fury choked the words in her throat. She grabbed the glass and drained the champagne. Why was he being so cruel?

Suddenly, he was beside her, an arm around her shoulders. "I'm sorry, Althea. I don't know what got into me. It's just . . . just that I want you to be *my* woman."

She looked at him with disbelieving eyes.

"It's true," he said softly, turning away. He refilled her glass and slid it into her hand. "You are the woman I've waited for, but you're so much a lady, always so distant. I guess I'm not enough of a gentleman for someone like you. I . . . I had to try something, say anything, to . . . I guess I just wanted to make you angry. I hurt you instead. I was wrong and I'm sorry."

Althea wished she could think clearly. It didn't seem to make sense, yet the expression on his face was so earnest, so sincere. He must really love her. He wanted her for his own. He must want to marry her. She would forgive him.

He leaned over and kissed her cheek, then moved nibbling lips over to her ear. "I need a *real* woman, Althea. Are you that woman?"

There was an alarming intensity in his voice. She looked at him and read demands in his eyes that frightened her. She looked away, raising her glass to her lips once more. The orchestra had begun playing. Dancers were twirling around the room—men in buckskins with clumsy agility and growing enthusiasm, and their partners with practiced feet and easy grace. An occasional couple slipped into a curtained room rather than joining the whirling on the dance floor.

"I have a curtained hideaway of my own back at my house," Derek whispered in her ear. "You haven't seen my house, Althea. It's the big one up on East Hill. Just right for someone like you. You'd like it. Come with me, Althea. Prove to me that you're more woman than Alexis."

"She didn't come home last night." Alexis stared out the window at the Golden Gulch. "I think she's with him."

"Alex, come eat your breakfast. Althea's a grown woman. She has to make her own decisions."

"He's not the right man for her."

Colter shook his head. "Just who *would* be the right man for her?"

"Oh, Colt, you know perfectly well what I mean. I know she's difficult and selfish. And greedy. But she's also lonely and vulnerable. She's not *all* bad. She's had a very difficult time."

Colter got up and hobbled across the room. He took Alexis by the shoulders and turned her around. "You are not her mother. You can't be responsible for her. She's our guest here, but she is a grown woman and can come and go as she pleases."

Her lips tightened. "I still don't think Derek

is the man she should be seeing."

"What's he ever done to you, anyway, besides being such a persistent suitor?" Colter asked suspiciously.

"Nothing." She sighed. "He's always been a gentleman. But there's something about him. I don't know . . ."

It was Colter's turn to glance out the window. "I suppose we should find out if she's there. If she isn't, something much worse may have happened to her."

Alexis' eyes widened. "I . . . I hadn't thought of that. Colt, I have to go right over."

"You sit down," Colter said sternly. "If anyone has to go over there, it will be me."

"But . . ."

"No arguments. You are not going to the Golden Gulch to check on your sister. Understand me? I'll go."

"You shouldn't go out yet. Besides, it's slippery."

"I can go that far. I'll have Rafe go with me to make sure I don't fall. He can wait in the saloon while I go up to see Anderson. Now eat."

Alexis sat down at the table obediently but made no move to pick up her fork. "What will you do if she's there?" she asked, disturbed eyes watching him.

"I promise not to grab her by the hair and drag her back." He smiled hopefully, trying to make her do the same.

"You mustn't embarrass her, Colt. We must try to keep it quiet. I don't want her to be hurt by gossip."

Colter stooped to kiss her. He stroked her cheek. "I'll be very discreet. There aren't many people out and about this early, anyway."

"You understand, don't you, Colt? She might think she has to marry him if she's seen. I don't want her under any obligation. If no one knows..."

Colter almost asked her if she'd considered the possibility that Althea might be in love with Derek. But the way Alexis felt about Derek, that thought would probably only increase her distress, and he didn't want to do that. Besides, there was the very real possibility that something much worse than spending the night in bed with a man had happened to her. If she were with Derek, they could deal with the complications of the situation later. If not, the sooner he found out the better.

Crutch under his arm, he left Alexis in their suite and hobbled down the stairs. Rafe was behind the bar, visiting with a customer.

"Rafe?" Colter called, and the bartender excused himself and came around from behind the bar. "I need to go have a chat with Anderson at the Gulch. Alexis is afraid I'll take a tumble in the snow with this leg of mine and wants you to come along."

"Sure thing, Colt. Hey, Joe. Cover for me."

A blast of arctic air met them as they opened the door and went into the street. Colter was glad they didn't have far to go. It was difficult, walking across the street with a crutch. Beneath the snow and ice, deep ruts had been carved in the muddy street before the ground had frozen.

Several times his crutch sank through the snow and snagged in one of these ruts, nearly toppling him, but Rafe's hand managed to catch and steady him in time.

Two saloon girls were lounging against the bar when they entered. Except for them and the bartender, the saloon was empty.

"Mornin', Stephens. Out lookin' for customers?" the bartender asked. "You won't find 'em here."

"No, Maxwell. I need to talk to Anderson. Is he around?"

"Nope. Spent the night up in that fancy house of his on East Hill. Sent word he wouldn't be in 'til this afternoon." The man smirked. "Only does that when he's got company. If you know what I mean?"

"I know what you mean," Colter replied as he turned and went outside. "Better get the sleigh hitched up, Rafe. I'm going to have to go up to Anderson's place."

"You want me to come along, Colt?"

"No. I think I'd better go alone." He started walking toward the livery. "After you've helped me with the horse, you go back to the Palace and tell Alexis where I've gone. And, Rafe, tell her not to worry."

Rafe didn't pry into the meaning of Colter's words. He simply agreed to do as he was asked.

The road up to Derek Anderson's private residence was steep and slick, and it took Colter several minutes to coax the horse up the hill. The Anderson place had been pointed out to him before, but Colter had never ridden up close to it.

The two-story Carpenter Gothic had a high pitched roof and lacy, hand-carved decorations around the eaves. A wide porch stretched the length of the front of the house.

Colter drove the horse as close to the front steps as he could get, then climbed out of the sleigh. There were about fifteen steep steps to climb to the porch, but they had been swept clean of the snow and ice so at least he didn't have to worry about falling because it was slippery. He was more afraid of the scolding he would get from Alexis if he fell than the actual fall itself.

Reaching the front door, he rang the bell and waited. When it was opened, he was surprised to find a pretty young Chinese girl staring back at him.

"I'm Colt Stephens. I need to see Mr. Anderson."

She bowed and backed away from the door, opening it wide to let him in. "I will tell him you are here," she said in surprisingly good English. "Will you wait in the parlor, please?"

"Thank you."

Colter went into the parlor and sat on a satin and brocade sofa. "Pretty fancy for a bachelor," he said to himself.

"Mr. Anderson will see you in a moment, Mr. Stephens, sir." The girl stood in the doorway, bowing once more in his direction. "May I serve you some tea or coffee?"

Colter found himself bowing in her direction and replying formally. "No, thank you very much." He grinned, amused at himself.

She smiled too.

"Mai Ling! Take a coffee tray up to my guest."

The girl jumped and disappeared into the back of the house as Derek reached the bottom of the stairs. Colter got up from the couch.

Derek waved a hand for him to be seated, then sat across from him and lit a cigarette. "You're an early visitor, Stephens. What can I do for you?"

"I've come on an errand that's a bit awkward, Anderson."

Derek chuckled. "Let me save you the trouble of trying to find the words. Your charming sister-in-law stayed here with me last night." He paused for effect. "The road was so bad that I couldn't get her home. You wouldn't have wanted me to risk her life on that hill—now would you?—so I provided her with the guest room. Strictly proper, I assure you. Mai Ling was here to chaperone us."

Colter said nothing, but he suddenly understood what Alexis sensed about this man. He hadn't liked him before, but it had been because Derek had been a rival for Alexis' affections—or at least, he had wanted to be a rival. Now Colter felt that Alexis was right. This man was not to be trusted.

Derek exhaled a puff of blue smoke. "That is the story you want others to hear if word leaks that Althea spent the night in my home, isn't it?"

"Anderson . . ." Colter began.

"Before you act too much the irate protector of feminine virtue, let me tell you that I intend to marry the girl." Derek got up from his chair and stepped to the wall where he pulled a cord. Mai Ling appeared almost instantly. "Tell Miss Ashmore her brother-in-law is here to take her home and help her dress."

"Yes, Mr. Anderson, sir."

"Cute little thing, isn't she?" Derek asked as he turned around. "For a Chinagirl, that is. Too bad her people are such a nuisance to have around mining towns. Makes folks prejudiced toward them. Otherwise, I'd have a few of them for girls in my saloons. They can be quite entertaining." He jerked his head toward the empty doorway. "Now Mai Ling is just a house servant, but she's going to blossom into a woman one of these days, and then I'll put her to work at the Gulch."

"Is that what she wants?" Colter asked, thinking how timid and innocent the girl seemed.

"Doesn't have much choice. I own her. She'll work where I tell her to."

Colter frowned. "You can't own her. She's not a negress and this isn't the South."

"Technicalities," Derek answered. "Her father owes me a sizable sum of money, and he sent her to me to pay the debt. Quaint little custom."

Colter was growing angry, but the rustle of skirts on the stairs stopped his retort. He got up from the sofa, his eyes on the doorway. Althea came into the room. Her cheeks were pink, and she kept her eyes on the carpet.

"Alexis was worried," Colter said. "We'd better get home."

Derek stepped to her side and placed an arm around her shoulders. "I will call on you tonight at the Palace, my dear."

She looked up at him, then over at Colter. Her blue eyes seemed confused.

"At eight," Derek added. He placed a chaste kiss on her cheek. "Good day, my dear Althea."

Colter crossed the room to take her arm and steer her out of the house. They went in silence, Colter not even saying good-bye to Derek. But once he had maneuvered the horse and sleigh to the base of the hill, he pulled on the reins and stopped the horse.

He stared straight ahead without seeing a thing. "He says he wants to marry you, Althea. Is that what you want?"

There was a long silence before Althea answered softly, "Yes. That's what I want."

Alexis was helpless to stop the wedding. Her sister said she wanted to marry him and that's all there was to it. Mrs. Cane was put to work designing a magnificent gown of lace and satin and pearls. The date was set for the day before Christmas.

Althea wavered between hysterical tears and obnoxious demands. The only time Alexis knew how she would behave was when Derek came to call in the evening. Then her sister was quiet and reserved. Alexis would watch the engaged couple from across the room, and her anxiety would increase. Was this a happy bride?

Three days before the wedding, she tried to broach the subject of Althea's night with Derek.

"You mustn't feel you have to marry him," she said.

"But, of course, I must marry him," Althea answered, her eyes round with surprise. Then, as an afterthought, she added, "I want to marry him, Alex. Please don't bother me about it anymore."

So, on December 24th, the interior of the Ice Palace was once more decorated for a wedding. It was as elaborate as the first had been, but many of the guests didn't come because of the weather. Still, the bride was beautiful in her voluminous white gown, and the groom was handsome in his dark suit. An orchestra occupied a corner of the hall for dancing following the ceremony. An abundance of food filled long tables. Champagne flowed freely. Especially into Althea's glass.

By the time Alexis helped her up the stairs to change her clothes, Althea was in a liquored daze. She swayed against her sister and giggled like a schoolgirl. Alexis thought she looked happier now than she had since announcing her wedding plans.

"Honestly, Althea," she scolded as she began unfastening the many buttons on the back of the gown. "You shouldn't have been drinking so much. Tonight of all nights."

"You're wrong, Alex," Althea shot back over her shoulder. "This night, of all nights, is the very one I should drink so much on."

"Althea, is something wrong?"

"Wrong? What could be wrong? I have just married the most eligible and wealthiest bachelor in town. He's going to own this town—lock, stock, and barrel—someday. He told me so. And I'm going to own it right along with him."

"Is that why you married him?" Alexis asked sadly.

"Of course not."

Alexis hoped she would add that she loved him, something she had never heard her say, but she didn't.

Althea stepped out of the satin gown and kicked it across the floor. Suddenly, she turned wide eyes on Alexis. "How often must I expect him to . . ." She clamped her mouth shut and turned away without finishing.

Alexis touched her bare arm. "What is it, Althea? What's troubling you?"

"It's so vile. How do you bear it?"

"I don't know what . . ." she began, but then she did know. What could she say? She had only known heaven in Colter's arms. "It will get better," she said, hoping it was true. Yet, wouldn't she feel the same way if she were anyone's wife but Colter's?

Althea whirled on her in a fury. "Don't be so smug with me. Don't you dare feel sorry for me. What do you know? What do you know about anything? You're just a boy in skirts, pretending for all those fools downstairs. Well, you're not the queen of this town any more. I'll show you that it takes a real lady to rule it, and you never were a lady. You've dressed yourself up, but you aren't a lady. That's an art only a Southern gentlewoman can learn from her mama. Your mama didn't teach it to you because she didn't want you. You hear me? She didn't *want* you!"

Alexis backed away as if she'd been struck.

"I hate you, Alexis Ashmore," Althea spat out. "And I hate Colter, too. You stole my father from me, and then you took Colter. Well, I never wanted him anyway. I never loved him. But he wanted me. You remember that. He wanted me before he ever wanted you. He married you because I went away. Because I wouldn't have him."

"Althea, please. Why are you saying these things? All I ever wanted was for us to be close."

"Charity! You gave me charity and expected me to be grateful."

Alexis vigorously shook her head in denial. "You're wrong. I was glad you came to stay with me. You're my sister. You belong here."

"You are a fool, Alexis. Get out of here. Get out of my room."

Alexis fled to her suite, throwing herself across her bed and succumbing to tears. Truth or not, Althea's words had opened deep wounds and revived old insecurities. She'd never found favor in her mother's eyes. Was it because her mother didn't love her, never wanted her? Is that why Jonathan took her with him, because Madonna refused to keep her there? And Colter. Did he marry her because Althea wouldn't have him? Had she turned out to be second choice after all?

Colter found her there. He sat on the edge of the bed, placing a gentle hand on her back. "Alex," he whispered.

She turned tear-blurred eyes toward him

and, with a whimper, moved into his comforting arms, the flood of tears renewed.

"What happened, love?" he asked once the deluge was spent, his shirt thoroughly wet.

She shook her head against his chest, hiccupping.

"Alexis?"

"Do you . . . do you love me?"

He laughed tenderly and drew her even tighter against him. In the gentle shadows of their room, he gazed down into her blue eyes. "I love you, Alexis. I love you too much. I could walk away from everything else, but I couldn't live without you. You are what makes my life happy. I never knew the real meaning of love until you came into my life. You are the stars and moon and the heavens above." His lips against her forehead, he finished. "I love you."

Minutes ticked away on the mantel clock in the parlor, and still Colter held her. In the shelter of his arms, the pain vanished. The cruelty of Althea's words lost their sting. Alexis could look at them for what they were, words spoken in an attempt to hurt as Althea had been hurt.

"Have they left?" Alexis asked at last.

"Yes."

"I feel sorry for her, Colt. She's so angry at life. I hope she finds happiness somehow."

He kissed her forehead again and stroked her hair, soothing her into a peaceful sleep.

18

Donahue dropped in for a few drinks and a game of cards. Alexis was standing by the faro table when he came in. She glanced up and he nodded toward her, then crossed to the bar. She waited a few moments before excusing herself and walking over to him.

"Good evening, Mr. Donahue. How's your wife?"

"She's herself, Miss Alexis, and thanks for askin'." He took a long swallow of beer. He wiped his mouth on his shirt sleeve. "And your husband? Is his leg healin' proper?"

"He only needs a cane now. The doctor says it's mending very well."

"And is he in for a bit of cards for this evenin'?"

Alexis was relieved he hadn't come about their secret project, and her face brightened with a smile. "He said he'd be down in a little while. I'm sure he'd be glad to join you."

Donahue lowered his voice just a little. "Miss Alexis, this weather is going to set our plans back a month or more. The longer we delay, the more apt someone is to find out. Now I like your husband, and I know he's not a true Yankee at heart, but I hope you're bein' careful what you say around him. I've got a feelin' he wouldn't take kindly to his wife bein' mixed up with those of us tryin' to help the Confederacy."

"You're right, Mr. Donahue," Alexis replied, stiffening a little, "he would not like my involvement. But I can assure you I use the utmost discretion."

"There. And I knew you would," Donahue said with a laugh. He threw his head back and drained his glass, wiping his mouth once more on his sleeve. "And speak of the devil. There's your Mr. Stephens now," he said as he slammed the empty glass onto the bar. "Stephens! I've been waitin' for you."

Colter looked his way. "Glad to see you, Donahue. There hasn't been any easy pickings for days."

"Is that so? Well, come down here and try it."

The men sat down at the table, and Rafe brought over a new deck of cards. Colter began shuffling.

"What's your pleasure, Donahue?"

Before the baker could answer, the door of the saloon burst open and Sam Wainwright barreled into the room, looking frantically about.

"Alexis! Come quick! It's Stella," he cried as he spied her near the poker table.

"The baby?"

He nodded.

Alexis looked over her shoulder. "Rose, would you mind fetching my coat for me?" As the girl hurried up the stairs, Alexis turned back toward Sam. "Have you sent for the doctor?"

"Doc Barker's up toward Placerville. There's been a bad accident. His wife didn't think he'd be back 'til late tonight."

"You told her to have him come as soon as he gets back?"

Sam nodded again.

Alexis glanced at Colter. "Why don't you get Sam a drink? Maybe it will calm him down. I'll go over to stay with Stella until the doctor comes." Rose had returned with her coat, and she slipped her arms into the sleeves as she spoke. "Don't worry, Sam. Stella's going to be just fine."

"Do you want me to come with you?" Colter asked quietly.

"No. Not yet. Sam needs you more than I do. But you'd better send Mona over, just in case the doctor doesn't get back when he's supposed to. I've never delivered a baby."

She pulled her coat close and headed out into the night. She tucked her nose down behind the fur collar. The temperature had dipped below zero tonight again. The cold made the short walk from the Palace to the Wainwright house seem miles long.

Alexis let herself in. "Stella?" she called as she stepped into the parlor.

"Alexis? I'm in the bedroom." The reply was weak and strained.

Quick steps carried her to the bedroom door. She opened it and went inside. Stella lay in the middle of the brass bed, blankets pulled up to her chin. Despite the chill of the room, there were beads of sweat on her forehead. Her red hair clung to her face in damp tendrils.

"I was afraid no one was coming. Sam left so long ago."

Alexis took off her coat as she moved toward the bed. She glanced down at her gown and wished she had taken a moment to change. Not that she cared that much about the dress, but the skirt was an excessively full one and would be awkward to move around this tiny room in. With a quick decision, she hiked up the skirt and removed the stiff petticoats, then she tucked a corner of the skirt into the waist band of her frilly pantaloons to keep the extra yards of fabric out of her way.

"I've come to sit with you until the doctor arrives," she said as she arranged her skirt to suit her. "I left Sam with Colter for the time being. Men are only in the way when women are having babies."

Stella grimaced as a pain tightened her abdomen. She bit her lip and held out her hand for Alexis to take. Alexis held on to it, pressing back as Stella squeezed her fingers.

"I . . . didn't know . . . it would take so . . . long," Stella said through clenched teeth.

Alexis pulled the chair beside the bed closer

and sat down. "How long have you been in labor, Stella?"

"Since this morning. I wasn't sure at first."

"Didn't you tell Sam?"

"I didn't want to bother him. He's working so hard right now."

Alexis frowned. "I think you should know that Doc Barker isn't in town right now. He may not be back until morning."

Stella blanched, and her eyes seemed to sink deeper into their sockets. "I don't think I can bear it until then," she whispered.

"I may not know a great deal about this, Stella, but I know this much. That baby of yours will come when it's ready, whether or not the doctor is here."

"I'm frightened, Alex. Really frightened."

Alexis patted her hand as she rose from her chair. She leaned forward and gave Stella a stern gaze. "Now, Stella, I want you to get hold of yourself. This may be a long night for both of us, but we'll come through it just fine. You, me, and the baby. Now, I'm going into the other room and stoke the fire. Then I'm going to put some water on to boil and get some towels and sheets. You close your eyes and rest. It's hard work having a baby. Go on. Close them. That's right."

She moved away from the bed, her eyes still watching Stella. She didn't like the way she looked. Were all women in labor so pale? She wished she knew more about it. She wished the doctor were here.

Alexis went into the kitchen. She shoved

more wood into the stove, then filled a pot with water and set it on the stove to boil. It took a few moments for her to find the linens, but finally she returned to the bedroom with her arms full. Stella was gripping the rails of the bed and moaning softly.

"Stella?"

"Am I going to die?" the girl whispered.

"No!" Alexis snapped. "You most certainly are *not* going to die. You've got far too much fight in you for such nonsense."

"I would hate to die. This baby wanted to live so much. Despite its father. Even when he beat me and tried to make me lose it, the baby was strong. It just wouldn't give up. I want to live. I want to be a good mother."

"You will be a good mother," Alexis assured her. "And Sam is going to be a wonderful father."

Stella hadn't heard her. "I thought it would change things. I really did. I was so happy to be having a baby. Maybe a son. I thought a son would make Derek love me. But it didn't. It just made him more cruel. So cruel. Why would a man want to kill his own child?"

"Stella? Are you saying this is Derek's baby?" Alexis felt herself grow pale.

"I thought he meant to kill me. And I wanted to die. But then you helped me. You were so good to me, and I didn't lose the baby. Then I knew it wanted to live, so I wanted to live."

"But Stella, you told me Derek mustn't know about the baby. I thought . . . I thought . . ." She closed her eyes. "Dear Lord. Althea."

A low moan slipped through Stella's lips,

growing louder as she clenched the brass rails at the head of the bed. Alexis sat motionless, stunned into inactivity. Her sister married to a man who would... It was unthinkable. What might he do? What else was he capable of?

"Alex..." Stella panted. "Help me."

Alexis shook off her black thoughts. She would have to face those questions later. Right now, Stella needed her. She got to her feet and rolled up the sleeves of her evening gown. She didn't know much about it, but it seemed she was going to be the one to bring this new life into the world.

"Hold on, Stella. You're going to be a wonderful mother."

Lusty cries greeted Dr. Barker as he opened the door of the Wainwright home with Sam and Colter hot on his heels. Before they could reach the bedroom door, it opened, and Alexis stepped out. Her face looked tired, but she was smiling.

"Hello, Dr. Barker," she said.

"Sounds like I'm a little late."

"A little. Go on in. I think they're all right, but I'll feel better once you tell me so."

"Alexis, how's Stella?" Sam asked anxiously.

"She's tired, Sam, but she's okay."

Sam sighed in relief. Then his face brightened as he asked, "And the baby?"

"You have a beautiful, red-haired daughter, Mr. Wainwright."

"A daughter?" He beamed. "I have a daughter." He slapped Colter on the back, his voice growing louder. "I have a daughter! Colt, do you hear that? I've got a beautiful daughter."

"I hear. I hear," Colter replied, laughing.

The door to the bedroom opened, revealing Dr. Barker. "If you'll quiet down, Mr. Wainwright, you may come in and see your family."

"A daughter. I've got a daughter." Sam continued to whisper these words as he walked into the bedroom.

Alexis looked at Colter. Her eyes felt leaden, and her head and neck ached. Still, it was a good kind of tired. She had witnessed something wonderful. A new life. She had helped bring a new life into the world. She felt as if a wonderful blessing had been bestowed upon her.

"Alex?" Colter had moved to stand beside her. His arm went around her. "You look exhausted."

"I am." She smiled. "What happened to Mona?"

"She wasn't at her place. Sam and I should have come sooner."

"You couldn't have done anything. Sam would've gone crazy with worry, anyway."

Colter chuckled in agreement. "I know."

"She is so *very* beautiful," Alexis whispered in an awe-filled voice. She looked into Colter's brown eyes. "I would love to have your baby."

His look was tender. "And I'd love it too." He kissed the tip of her nose. "Now, let's go home so you can get some sleep. You've had a full day."

A gray winter light filtered through the window. Alexis curled her body close to Colter, but her thoughts were far from the warmth of this room. She was thinking of Derek Anderson and the child she had helped deliver last night. His child.

Could it be true? She didn't like Derek much, that was true, but was he really capable of trying to murder his own unborn child, illegitimate or not? Perhaps she'd misunderstood what Stella said. After all, Alexis had always believed Stella had been in love with Derek at one time. Perhaps, in the pain of giving birth, she had confused the child's natural father with the man she had once loved. It was possible.

There was only one thing she could do. She would have to go see Stella and ask her outright. She would have to learn the truth.

But if the truth was what she feared, then what would she do?

Stella's bright red hair was pulled back from her face with a white ribbon. The fiery curls fell in gentle waves over her shoulders. Her complexion was pale with just a touch of pink above her cheekbones, and her emerald eyes sparkled despite the gray smudges beneath them, evidence of the long childbirth. She was wearing a white nightgown, the high collar bordered with a bright green ribbon. In her arms she cradled the day-old infant.

"Have you and Sam decided on a name?" Alexis asked.

Stella looked down at the baby, her expression blissful. "We're going to call her Greta, after my mother."

"Will you visit your parents now, to show

them their grandchild?"

"My parents? No. My mother died when I was little, and my father would never forgive me for running off like I did, to become a cheap saloon girl. No, he wouldn't want to see me."

Alexis gazed at the baby and found what Stella was saying hard to believe. "But you're a married woman now. You have a successful attorney for a husband and a beautiful daughter. Surely, he would forgive your running away when he saw all you have."

"You never knew my father," Stella replied. Wistful eyes turned toward the shuttered window. "No. He has no daughter named Stella as far as he's concerned."

Alexis wondered if she'd come too soon to ask what she needed to know, but she couldn't leave without learning the truth. She folded her hands in her lap, squeezing them until her knuckles turned white. Swallowing hard, she plunged in. "Stella, I have something quite serious I must ask you. I know you're still tired after yesterday and all, but I must know the truth, and you're the only one who can tell me." She paused, waiting for Stella's reaction.

Stella cradled Greta higher against her breast, then kissed the downy hair on the baby's head. Tears threatened as she raised her eyes to meet Alexis' gaze. "What is it you need to know?"

"I must know the truth about Derek. Please, Stella." Stella had to see the desperation in her blue eyes.

The new mother sighed as she nodded. "I was a poor man's pretty daughter and I knew I was going to be bartered away, sooner or later, for a new horse or a plow or something else for that little patch of dirt my father called a farm. I ran away from home and eventually I ended up here. It was brand-new. The gold strikes, I mean, and the town was just tents and shacks thrown together in a hurry. I was still such an innocent. The men flattered me and bought me pretty baubles, and I thought I had the world by the string. I never . . . I wasn't a whore." She lifted her head high and cast a defiant look toward Alexis.

"The first time I saw Derek," she continued, "I thought he was the most handsome man in the world, and he made me think he thought the same way about me. He bought me prettier clothes than I'd ever had and real jewels to wear around my neck. I thought he'd just let me look pretty on his arm like all the other men had, but Derek isn't that kind of man." She stopped. Her gaze fell to the baby in her arms.

Alexis waited, giving her friend time to collect herself.

"He . . . he took me to his bed. I thought he loved me. I thought he would marry me. After all, I wasn't some cheap girl, waiting outside my crib for the next customer to come by. He . . . he was the first man to ever . . ." She blushed. "I was a virgin. I was sure he would marry me." Again she paused, this time to wipe away a tear. When she spoke again, there was anger in her voice. "Derek is ambitious. He thrives on power. He has to control people. He wants to control this town. He controlled me. Sometimes, I wanted to get away from him. And then I'd see him looking and smiling at another pretty girl, and I'd be afraid he was tiring of me, that he was going to throw me aside. I had nowhere to go. No money. No family. Men didn't treat me the same as before 'cause they knew what I had become. I had nothing but Derek. So I'd plead with him to love me. It gave him pleasure to see me afraid. He likes to hear a woman beg. He's so cruel, Alexis. He's cruel in so many ways."

"How else was he cruel to you, Stella?"

"People see him only as the handsome owner of the Golden Gulch. They think he's their friend, but he's only a friend to himself. He would kill his own mother to gain more power and more wealth. He's just more careful than other outlaws."

Alexis was alarmed. What Stella was not saying frightened her more than what she'd told so far.

"He was furious when I told him I was going to have his baby. We were up at his house, just the two of us. I told him that now we'd have to get married. He called me a fool. Why would he saddle himself to a girl like me just because I wasn't smart enough to prevent a pregnancy? I told him everyone would know it was his. He laughed and said no one ever paid any attention to a pregnant harlot. It could be anyone's brat." She shook her head. "That wasn't true. I was his prisoner. I'd never been with another man, and folks knew it." Her eyes grew round as she stared into the past and relived that night. "He said, if that was the case, then there couldn't be a baby.

He began hitting me, and when I fell, he kicked me. He kicked me again and again. I thought he was going to kill me. When he stopped, he told me to get out of town if I wanted to live. Then he threw me out in the street. I was in so much pain. I was dazed. I don't know how I ended up behind the Palace where you found me. I was just trying to hide, like any wounded animal."

"Oh, Stella," Alexis said softly, "why didn't you tell me any of this before?"

"I was too afraid . . . I still am."

Alexis closed her eyes as she leaned back in her chair. Now she knew the truth, but what could she do about it?

"Alexis? Be careful what you do or say. He's capable of anything."

"He's my brother-in-law."

Stella wore an agonized expression. "It's my fault. I should have told someone. I should have tried to stop what was happening."

"No. You mustn't feel guilty," Alexis protested. "You had a right to be frightened. He'd threatened your life and that of your child. But now it could be my sister who's in danger, and I must do something."

"Tell Colter. He'll know what to do."

Alexis shook her head. "I can't tell him. Not yet. There is just a chance that Derek's in love with Althea. He might be good to her." She didn't believe it even as she said it. She got up to leave, drawing on her coat as she stepped over to kiss Stella's cheek. "Don't worry, Stella. I'll be careful, no matter what I do." She went toward the door.

"Alexis," Stella called after her, "there's something else I didn't tell you."

She turned around, dreading Stella's continuing confession. Whatever she was adding, it was certain to be more bad news.

"The watch I saw in your room. The one I said I'd never seen before. I lied. I think I did see it before."

"Where?"

"In Derek's room at the Golden Gulch."

"Are you sure?"

"It . . . looked the same."

Alexis turned once more. "Thank you, Stella," she said, too low for the new mother to hear.

Alexis climbed into her sleigh and pondered the news as she gathered the reins. She glanced toward the house on East Hill, her decision made. She had to see Althea, make sure she was all right. It just could be that Althea was happy with Derek, that Stella's experience would never be repeated.

She slapped the reins against the horse's broad rump. With a snort, the horse pulled the sleigh along Wall Street and up the hill to Derek's house. The road was no longer icy. Thick, hard-packed snow made it nearly as easy for the horse as a dry road in summer. She stopped the sleigh at the bottom of the steep steps, glancing up at the house.

She hadn't seen Althea since the wedding. She wondered how her sister would greet her. Would she be welcome in Althea's new home? Not if she knew why I'd come, Alexis thought as she got out of the sleigh and began climbing the steps.

Like Colter's visit before her, the door was opened by the young Chinese servant.

"I am Mrs. Stephens, Mrs. Anderson's sister. Is she in?"

"Yes, madam. Please come in. I will tell her you are here." The girl led the way into the parlor. "Please. Sit down." Then she went up the stairs.

Alexis glanced around the room but was too restless to sit. She twisted her gloves, thinking again about what Stella had told her, still not knowing what she could say or do.

"My goodness. Alexis. What a pleasant surprise. I was wondering if you would ever call on me."

Alexis looked up as Althea entered the room. She was smiling, but Alexis thought it looked forced. *You're jumping to conclusions*, she warned herself as she hugged her sister.

"Mai Ling is bringing us some coffee. Come. Sit down beside me on the sofa. Can you stay and visit or must you rush off?" she asked, waving at Alexis' coat.

"I can stay a little while," Alexis answered as she removed her fur wrap. "I'm sorry I haven't come sooner. I thought you might like some time alone with your new husband."

"Of course." Althea laughed. "You would think that, the way you and Colter are so . . . distracted by each other. Derek is much too busy with the Gulch and his other businesses to spend a lot of time at home with his wife. You don't become as successful as he is without effort."

"Are you lonely, Althea?"

"Lonely? What a silly notion. I'm glad he's busy. I would hate to have him home all day."

Alexis wanted to know the truth about her sister's marriage, but she couldn't come right out and ask the questions she wanted to ask, just like that. So she tried to make small talk with Althea. "Have you made friends with Mai Ling? She seems very sweet."

"She's a servant. A lady does not make friends with her servants. Besides, she's Oriental, and I can't see that she's any different than one of our slaves back home, except her skin is lighter."

"Althea?" Alexis began, deciding to be more direct. "I was wondering..."

"Hello. What a nice surprise."

Alexis glanced toward the doorway where Derek was removing his coat and hat. Her stomach lurched, and she realized she was afraid. Luckily, she was good at concealing her emotions. She gave him a slight smile, but her eyes were cool. "Hello, Derek," she replied.

"What has brought you to our humble home?" he asked as he came and stood beside Althea, placing a hand on her shoulder.

Althea jumped as if startled, her eyes nervous as they looked up at him. He grinned at her, squeezing her shoulder.

"I just wanted to see my sister. We haven't spoken since the wedding." Alexis smoothed her skirt. "Oh, I did have some news to share. Stella Wainwright had her baby. A beautiful little girl with red hair like her mother's." When neither Althea nor Derek said anything, she continued, "They're both doing very well, and Sam couldn't be more the proud father."

"How nice for them," Althea said, sounding insincere.

But Alexis was looking at Derek. "Stella's lucky everything turned out this way. She was in a bad accident last summer. Someone beat her. You remember, don't you, Derek? You saw her in my office. She could have lost the baby. Could have died herself, for that matter."

"Did she ever identify the person who beat her?" Derek asked, a placid smile on his mouth. "I never heard of any arrest."

"There wasn't an arrest. She never even talked to the sheriff."

"Strange. I suppose it was some drunk. Those are the hazards of working a saloon like Stella did."

"You know as well as I do, Derek, that Stella never *worked* the saloon. Not the way you mean." Alexis felt the muscles in her neck tightening but restrained her anger. "I think if anything ever happened to Stella again, or to her family, the man responsible would pay for his crime. I personally would see to that, since she's my friend. But then, I doubt he'd ever make such a foolish mistake twice. Don't you agree, Derek?" She saw his mouth twitch and knew he understood her.

"We can only hope you're right, Alexis," he said.

Mai Ling came in with the coffee tray just

then, drawing their attention away from each other.

Althea, sensing the tension between her husband and her sister, filled the cups, her hand shaking as she passed one to Alexis. "What other news is there?" she asked. "The new baby can't be the only thing happening in the whole town."

Before Alexis could reply, Derek interrupted, "You must excuse me. I have some papers to take care of. Enjoy your visit." He turned on his heel and marched from the room.

"It is late. I really should be going," Alexis said once he was gone.

"No. Please," Althea said, reaching out to touch her hand. "Please don't go yet."

Alexis' heart tightened at the pleading look in Althea's eyes. "All right, Althea. I won't go if you want me to stay."

19

Althea watched Alexis descending the steps to her sleigh. When she looked back, Althea lifted a hand to wave, then stepped back inside and closed the door. The house seemed too quiet. She hated the thought of returning to her room or to the parlor, yet what else was there for her to do? She had no real friends in town, and Derek had made it clear she wasn't to visit the Ice Palace.

"You're my wife, and I will not have you seen going into the Palace without me," he had told her. "Do you understand?"

If his words hadn't convinced her, his bruising fingers on her wrist had. She'd understood.

Althea went into the parlor and sat on the satin sofa, her eyes moving slowly over the room. She remembered all too well the first time she had been in this house, although it wasn't this room she remembered. She had been too intoxicated to remember seeing the parlor, if they'd ever been in here at all. It was Derek's bedroom she remembered—and his bedroom was just one of the reasons she hated this house.

She twisted on the sofa, placing her arm across the back and then laying her forehead on her arm, silent tears coursing down her cheeks as she remembered...

She awoke with an incredible headache. She opened her eyes slowly, afraid that the light coming in her bedroom window would make the headache worse. Only she wasn't in her bedroom. The room was totally unfamiliar. Everything was red and white—the carpeting on the floor, the wallpaper, the canopy above her, even the draperies. She blinked her eyes, confused. She couldn't remember where she was or how she'd gotten here.

Then she felt him watching her, and at the same time, she realized she was naked beneath the red comforter on the bed. She turned her head sideways, meeting Derek's solemn gaze.

"I wondered when you would wake up, my dear," he said.

"Derek, what am I doing here?"

He chuckled low in his throat. "Can't you remember?"

And then she did. In brief snatches, the memory of her night in this room came back to her, and she wished she hadn't remembered. She never wanted to think of it again—the roughness of his hands, her humiliation as he used her body, laughing at her protests, delighting in her struggles to make him stop.

She closed her eyes, not wanting to look at him. "I think I should go home now."

"At this hour of the morning? Why, Miss Ashmore, everyone would see you and know what kind of woman you are. They would look and say, 'That Ashmore woman is certainly no lady.' You wouldn't want them knowing the truth, would you?" He lay back against his pillow, an arm behind his head. "Of course, they'll all know anyway. Things like this have a way of getting around. Talking servants. You know. There won't be a decent man in town who would give you a second glance. Of course, you could ply your new trade at the Palace, except your sister won't allow that kind of business in her saloon."

Althea felt sick to her stomach. She edged away from him, but his hand darted out, clamping on her breast and stopping her escape. She opened terrified eyes. He was leaning over her, his brows drawn together in a thunderous look.

"Don't try to get away from me, Althea. There's only one thing you can do now, and that's marry me. You *will* marry me." His fingers pinched the tender flesh of her breast. "Do you agree?"

"Derek..." she pleaded.

He grinned again as he lay on his back, drawing her along with him to lie with her head on his shoulder, her body held tightly against his. She was rigid with shame and fear.

"Would you really want to go back to the

Palace, anyway, my dear? Living on your sister's charity. It isn't fair. You should be the wealthy one. Instead, every dress you own is charity from Alexis. Of course, I'm sure she and Colter feel quite sorry for you when they think of you, but they're so wrapped up in each other, that probably isn't often. You must hate it there."

Althea was listening and found herself agreeing with him.

"Now, if I were the owner of the Ice Palace, you would be the Ice Queen. You are, after all, a Southern gentlewoman. You are a true lady, raised to rule a great plantation. Someday I will own the Palace, and as my wife, you will be its queen."

"Its queen," she said under her breath, not even knowing she was speaking aloud.

His arm tightened. "You'd like that, wouldn't you, Althea? Yes, you'd like that. That's why you'll marry me." His fingers wrapped through her tangled hair and jerked her head back. "That, and because you know you can't escape me. I own your body now. If you don't marry me, you'll be selling yourself on the street to make a living. You'll have no husband, no home, no money for food or clothes."

There was no escaping him . . .

She had married him, hoping that everything would be all right, that he would learn to be tender and gentle with her, but there was no kindness, no tenderness in the man. He knew what he wanted and took it when it suited him. He enjoyed the taking more when there was a struggle involved. This was true in his business dealings, and it was true in his private moments with his wife.

Althea was trapped—by her own mistake and her own greed. She told herself she'd married him because she had to, because her reputation would have been ruined if she hadn't. But she knew there was more to it than that. She had married him because he stood for wealth and power in this town. Perhaps he was even wealthier than Alexis. And someday, he'd said, he would own the Ice Palace and she would dethrone her sister as queen. She wanted that day desperately, praying that it would make the harsh realities of her life with Derek all worthwhile.

Derek watched Alexis' departing sleigh from the window of his study. His fingers clenched the draperies as his eyes narrowed.

She had threatened him. She had had the nerve to come into his home and threaten him. Someday, he would make her regret it. It was one more payment he meant to extract from her. He would make her pay for marrying Colter Stephens when she should have been his. He would make her pay for stealing the Ice Palace out from under him. And he was going to enjoy making her pay. He imagined her naked before him, begging him to let her go. But he wouldn't let her go. Not until he was through with her. And when he was through, he would squeeze the life from that lovely white throat of hers.

But not before I've collected in full, he

thought, a dark smile spreading across his face.

He moved away from the window and sat behind his desk, continuing to ponder just how he was going to exact his delightful revenge before snuffing the life from her.

He was distracted from these thoughts by the sound of cups rattling on a tray. He glanced toward the closed door of his study, once again frowning. He knew without looking that Althea was still in the parlor. He considered taking her to bed. He wasn't getting any work done anyway. But right now, he didn't want Althea. He wanted Alexis.

He hit his fist on his desk, swearing loudly.

That's why he'd married Althea. Because he wanted Alexis. Althea was almost her double in looks, and he'd thought he could take his pleasure from Althea and believe it was Alexis. It didn't work. He knew it wasn't Alexis, and he knew he wouldn't be satisfied until he had broken that superior aloofness of hers. The day would come. He was already making plans.

Colter found Alexis sitting before a crackling fire, staring into the yellow-orange flames with distant eyes. Even when he sat down beside her, she didn't turn her head. She just kept staring, as if she were looking for something. Instinct told him to remain silent, and so he did, waiting for her to acknowledge him and tell him what was troubling her so.

"I don't know what to do for her," she said at last, her voice barely audible above the snap and pop of the fire.

"Who?"

Alexis blinked, then turned her face toward him. Colter read great sadness in her eyes.

"Althea's in trouble and I don't know how to help her."

"In trouble? What kind of trouble?"

Alexis moved her hand over to his knee, and he covered it with his own.

"I went to see Stella today. She told me some things about Derek. I'm afraid for Althea."

"What kind of things?" he asked gently.

Alexis looked back at the fire. "I don't think Stella would want me to tell even you what he did to her. But, Colt, he's an evil man, and I let my sister marry him."

"She's a grown woman, Alex. No one forced her to marry Derek."

"Yes!" she cried. "Someone did force her to marry him. Derek forced her. I know he did."

Colter's arm went around her shoulder to calm her. "How did he force her?"

"I don't know, but he did." She turned up her troubled face to look at him again. "Colt, I went up to see her today. She's frightened and she's lonely. I know she is."

"And what did she tell you?"

Alexis shook her head in abject misery, then laid her head on his shoulder. "Nothing. She wouldn't tell me anything. She's trying to be so brave. She's so proud. She can't admit she was wrong. Especially not to me. She resents me so, because of Papa and because of you."

"If she won't admit she's unhappy and she doesn't want your help, there's nothing we can do for her," Colter told her.

"If I could just talk to her alone, when he wasn't in the house . . ." Alexis said thoughtfully. "I've just got to get her away from him."

"Alex?"

She lifted her head from his shoulder.

"Alex, what is it you aren't telling me?"

"I think Derek killed T.C. Stella thinks she saw the watch in Derek's office."

Colter was silent a moment, digesting what she'd said. At last, he got up and walked over to the mantel and leaned his arm against it. It was his turn to stare into the fire as if searching for answers. When he turned around again, his look was solemn.

"*You* think. *Stella* thinks. You have no facts, Alexis. I agree that Anderson is an unlikable sort. Just a bit too smooth to suit me. But that's not enough reason to accuse him of murder."

"But he mistreated Stella and I'm sure he mistreats Althea," Alexis insisted.

"Alexis, you've said yourself that Althea doesn't admit she's unhappy. She hasn't told you he mistreats her. Perhaps he's changed since Stella was with him."

She jumped to her feet, her hands in tight fists at her side. "Why are you standing up for him? He's a beast. A cruel beast. Colt, I've *got* to do something. I can't just stand by while . . ."

Colter's hands on her shoulders stopped her protestations. "I'm not standing up for him, Alexis, but there's nothing we can do right now. Althea has to want to leave him. And there *is* always the chance we could be wrong about

Derek and Althea's happiness together. As for the watch, I'll do some checking of my own. Now, promise me you won't do anything foolish."

"I promise," she replied halfheartedly.

Bill Tanner lounged in the chair opposite Derek, twirling his battered hat on one hand. His long mustache drooped past his jaw, and he was in need of a shave. Derek didn't approve of Tanner's unkempt appearance, but he never quarrelled with success. Anytime he asked Tanner to do a job, it was done and done right. No foul-ups. No excuses.

"I'm not in any hurry," Derek said. "Things are too idle right now. It would give the sheriff too much time to snoop around. I can wait for spring."

"Killin' that Stephens fella won't be no problem. Any number of things could happen to him. But what about his wife? How do you want her to go?"

Derek leered. "When I'm through with her, you can do what you please. It's up to you. Just so long as no one ever finds her again."

"And your wife?"

"I'll keep her around as long as it suits me. I think the customers of the Palace expect an Ice Queen now. I'll give them Althea. If I ever change my mind, I'll . . ."

He stopped abruptly, his head snapping toward the door. He was certain he'd heard the floor creaking. As he got to his feet, Tanner straightened in his chair, alert for trouble. Derek walked silently to the door, and with a stealthful motion, turned the door knob. He eased the door open and looked out, his eyes catching sight of Althea's skirt as she slipped into the parlor. Without a sound, he closed the door again and turned to face Tanner.

"Althea," Derek said.

"She hear?"

"I don't know."

Tanner got up and put his hat on over his long, greasy hair. "Want me to take care of it for you?"

"Tanner, you like your work too much," Derek said as he returned to his desk. "No. I have no intention of getting rid of my darling wife. She may prove much more important to me in the future. Call her an ace up my sleeve." He sat down, a thoughtful frown creasing his forehead. "No, I think I have a way to assure her silence without your kind of assistance. Thanks anyway, Tanner."

Alexis was in her office, going over the inventory lists with Rafe, when Derek knocked on the door and opened it.

"Alexis. I was hoping I'd find you here," he said. His face looked haggard, his eyes tired.

"Hello, Derek." She kept her dislike from revealing itself in her voice. She laid down the papers and motioned her head for Rafe to leave them alone. "What can I do for you?"

"It's Althea. She's sick."

Alexis got up from her chair. "What's wrong?"

"We don't know. I've had the doctor up. He

wasn't much help." He stepped toward the desk. "She hasn't been able to keep any food down for days. I thought at first . . . well, I thought she might be pregnant, but then she wouldn't eat anything. She was sleepy all the time. And now she doesn't seem to recognize anyone. She's in a daze. I was hoping if you came up . . . if she saw you . . . I'm worried about her, Alexis. I don't want to lose her."

She didn't want to believe him, yet he seemed truly concerned. "I'll get my coat." She opened the door of her office. "Rafe, send someone for my sleigh, will you?" She looked back at Derek. "I'll be up as soon as I can get there."

Derek nodded, then placed his hat on his head. "Thank you, Alexis. I'll be waiting for you at the house."

Alexis flew up the stairs to her suite, silently berating herself. Had Althea been ill the day she visited? Was that why she'd acted so strangely? If Alexis had paid closer attention, could she have done something to prevent the extent of her illness? She must be very ill, indeed, for Derek to look so tired and drawn.

By the time she was back downstairs, her horse and sleigh were waiting outside. Colter was meeting with Sam that afternoon at Sam's office, so Alexis went there first. As soon as she entered the room, Colter was up and beside her.

"Derek came for me a little bit ago. Althea's sick."

Colter grabbed for his coat and drew it on. "Let's go," he said, already ushering her outside.

Mai Ling opened the door of the Anderson

house to let them in. She held out her arms for their coats.

"Where is she?" Alexis asked.

"Come with me," Mai Ling replied softly.

Althea's room was gloomy. The drapes were drawn tight over shuttered windows. A lamp sat on a bedside table, throwing a yellow light on Althea's face. A fire burned on the hearth, struggling valiantly to add heat to the room. Derek looked up as they entered but said nothing.

Alexis went to the bedside and took Althea's limp hand. "Althea?"

Althea's eyelids flickered several times, then finally opened. Her blue eyes, looking nearly black in the dim light of the room, seemed vacant.

"Althea, what's wrong?"

Her sister continued to look at her without seeming to see her. Alexis looked across at Derek, and he shook his head.

Colter stepped closer to Alexis, his hand on her waist. "What's Dr. Barker have to say?"

"He hasn't seen her," Derek answered. "Dr. Walters is our doctor. He doesn't know what's causing this, but she is a little improved from when he began treatment. She's able to eat a little now."

"Dr. Barker took care of her when she first came to Idaho," Alexis said, her gaze dropping back to Althea's sallow complexion. "Maybe we should have him up to see her too."

"No," Derek answered flatly. "I will not have that doctor in my house."

Alexis was startled by his refusal. "But why not?"

"We have..." he paused thoughtfully "...not seen eye to eye in the past."

"But if he could help her..." Alexis began.

Derek got to his feet. "If I thought he could help her, I'd let even Dr. Barker in. But I don't think he can, so I'll trust Dr. Walters to do what can be done." He turned his back on them and walked over to the fireplace.

Alexis opened her mouth to object, but Colter's hand on her shoulder stopped her. She glanced up at him, and he shook his head.

"It's his right to decide what doctor will care for his wife," he whispered.

Alexis looked back at her sister. She remembered when Althea had first arrived. She'd been ill then from shock. Could this be just a reoccurrence? No, she answered herself. This was different. This wasn't a deep sleep to escape reality. She was really sick this time. She had lost weight, and her eyes were rimmed with dark circles.

"Althea? Please look at me. Althea?"

Again, the eyes fluttered open, a chore that seemed nearly impossible to accomplish. There was no life in her eyes, no recognition of the faces around her.

"Althea, dear. Do you know me?"

Althea stared at her in silence, not blinking, not moving, not acknowledging her presence in any way.

"Colt, what can we do?" Alexis whispered.

Derek turned. "Do you think *I'm* not doing

everything I can?" he cried, his voice rising in anxiety. He rushed back to the bedside. "I know you don't approve of me, Alexis. I know you didn't want your sister to marry me. You seem to think I'm some sort of monster. Well, I'm not. I happen to love Althea, and I would give my right arm to see her out of that bed. I would give my own life . . ." He choked on his words and turned away again.

Tears formed in Alexis' eyes. It was incredible but she felt sorry for Derek. She believed him. "Forgive me, Derek. I know you want her to get well." She turned toward Colter. "She doesn't even see us," she said.

Colter held her in his arms. Over the top of her head, he spoke to Derek. "You'll let us know if there's any change."

Derek nodded, his back still toward them.

"Then we'll be going." Colter tugged at Alexis. "Come on, Alex."

Derek turned suddenly and said, "Come again, Alexis. It might help. It just might help."

"I will, Derek."

Derek grinned as the door closed. By George, he should have been an actor. What a performance!

He strolled back to Althea's bedside and looked down at the woman in the bed. Pity, that he should have to make her look like this. Maybe a little later he could lessen the dosage. He would have to check with Hon Wy. It was amazing what that Chinaman knew about drugs.

20

Winter dragged on with a terrible sameness. The temperature dropped far below zero every night, and the days brought either more snow or frigid winds—or both. It was difficult to get around even in town, but Alexis went almost every day up to the house on East Hill. There was no change in Althea's condition.

She talked to Dr. Barker, asking him if he wouldn't try to see her sister, but he declined, telling her he had no right if Mr. Anderson didn't want him there. He did agree to speak with Dr. Walters about the case, to offer his assistance and express Alexis' concern. There was nothing more he could do for her.

In early March, there was a break in the weather. Derek told Alexis he was taking Althea to Boise City. The temperature were always a little milder in the valley. He was hoping a change of scenery and some warmer air would help her. He could only hope.

Alexis felt at loose ends once Althea was gone. Business in the saloon was still quiet. Colter suggested a trek to the ranch, but she couldn't even be induced to do that. A numbing apathy gripped her. She knew Colter was worried about her but could do nothing to allay his fears.

It was an argument in the Palace that finally stirred her. There were several men at the table that afternoon, Donahue among them, a blue cloud of smoke hanging over their heads. The rest of the saloon was quiet. No one at the faro tables. No one at the roulette wheel. Rafe stood alone behind the bar. Rose, Joe, and Jessie were watching the game from a nearby table. Gertie was standing behind Donahue, leaning against his chair as she watched over his shoulder.

Alexis, breaking her normal habits, had taken a seat at the poker table beside Colter and was playing with the others. She wasn't paying any attention to the conversations of the men. She was staring at her cards but not really concentrating on them when Henry Meyers hit his hand on the table.

"Damn it, Stephens! You can't excuse that devil Sherman for what he's done to the South. Why, he's near wiped out Georgia, I hear."

Colter looked up calmly from his hand. "You're right, Meyers. I can't excuse it. But we're talking about war, and wars aren't fought without people suffering. The South knew at the start that it wasn't able to win this war. If they didn't know, they should have."

Meyers threw his cards onto the table. "I'm out. I can't sit down and play cards with no damn Yankee lover."

"But, Colt," Alexis said in gentle rebuke, ignoring Meyers' outburst, "we're talking about innocent people, not soldiers."

"Innocent people suffer the most in wars," he replied.

Donahue put down his cards and leaned his elbows on the table. "Then what are people, who ask only to have the right to decide how to run their own states, to do? Just lay back and say nothing? I say the South had a right to secede, and I say they can still win this war with the right help."

"Then you, my friend, are a fool." Colter's voice was low as his gaze locked with Donahue's.

Alexis grew cold with anger. "Is my father a fool, too?" she asked in an icy tone.

Colter turned his eyes toward her. There was a long, thoughtful pause before he answered, "Perhaps."

"And you're saying my mother's death was for nothing?" The cards crinkled in her hands.

"I'm saying your mother's death was a tragedy. It needn't have happened. The South can't hold on much longer. The war will be over by summer, and if the South hasn't suffered enough already, they'll be made to suffer as a conquered people."

Alexis rose slowly to her feet. "How can you sit there so calmly and say those things?"

"Because they're the truth and someone has

to say them."

"If I could do one thing for the Confederate cause," Alexis said, "I want you to know I would do it. If I weren't so far away, I'd go fight by my father's side myself."

Donahue scraped his chair backward and got up, too. "Stephens. I've got no quarrel with you. You're only thinkin' of the people who're dyin' and losin' what little they have while the Yankee soldiers rape the land. But if I were you, I'd watch what I say. We haven't much use for more black Republicans in this town."

Colter ran a hand through his hair and shook his head with deliberate slowness before looking at Donahue. "I was born in the states, but I've spent my whole life in the territories, building the kind of life I want. I don't want to tell states they can or can't have slaves, though I've got my own opinion of slavery. But I hate waste, and that's what this war is. Waste. People dying for a cause that was lost the day the first shot was fired." He rose from the table. "I guess I don't know if I'm a Republican or a Democrat, but I know I hate seeing this great country ripped apart, not just between North and South but in towns like this." He picked up his hat from the back of his chair and put it on. "Now, I think I'll take my company elsewhere and stop spoiling your game."

Alexis walked along the muddy planks, her skirts lifted in a futile attempt to keep them clean. The beginning thaw had turned the ground to muck, and it was difficult to keep her hem clean and dry. She nodded at some familiar faces as she hurried toward the bakery, but she didn't smile. She was deep in thought, remembering her latest argument with Colter.

"Why can't we forget that damned war?" he'd asked her, frustrated by her continued efforts to convert him into a supporter of the Southern cause.

"I won't! Not as long as my father is fighting in it. Not as long as my mother died for it."

"Your mother did not die for the South. She died to protect her home from some no good renegades. They weren't soldiers. They were outlaws, just like the outlaws you can meet out here. They rob and kill for the fun of it. Those men were just using the war as an excuse."

"Why can't you understand, Colt?" she'd cried.

He had looked at her for a long, silent time before saying, "I do understand, love. More than you think I do." He'd touched her arm. "Please don't let this come between us. It's so far away."

But it wasn't far away for Alexis. It was something she thought about often. She had to get even with those who had destroyed Willowind and killed her mother. She had to do anything and everything she could to help her father.

Seeing the stubborn glint in his wife's blue eyes, Colter had decided to ride down to the Circle S for a few days. Before he left, he had reminded her that the time for their move was fast approaching. In another two months, the new ranch house would be ready to occupy. She hadn't acknowledged his comment.

Alexis hated the growing schism between them. She knew it was all of her own making, but she was helpless to change it. She couldn't tell him what she was doing to help the Confederacy. Time and again she had lied to him about where she was going when she went out to meet with Donahue and the others. Between their arguments and her deception, she wondered if things would ever be the same between them again.

Alexis pushed open the bakery door. The warm smell of fresh-baked bread enveloped her. She felt a sudden wave of nausea and stopped suddenly, fighting to control her queasy stomach.

Mrs. Donahue looked up from her bread dough. "Is somethin' the matter, Mrs. Stephens? You're lookin' a bit pale now."

"I'm all right," Alexis said as she closed the door. She swallowed several times, the bitter taste of bile still in her mouth. "Are the others here?"

"In the store room. Go on in."

Pressing her lips together, she hurried toward the store room, determined not to succumb to the lingering ill-feelings.

"Miss Alexis, we've been waiting for you," Donahue said as she opened the door.

"I'm sorry I'm late," she replied. "I . . . had a few problems getting away this morning." She thought of Colter as he rode away from the Ice Palace.

"We've had good news. We're ready to go, Alexis. We just got word that the government will be taking out a gold shipment from the assay office in Boise City at the end of next week."

Alexis sat down on a keg. "Next week," she repeated after him.

"Somethin' wrong with that?" Meyers asked her.

She glanced up at him, shaking her head. "No. Next week is fine. In fact, the sooner we get this done, the better."

Donahue nodded, then looked at the others. "That goes for all of us, I think. Now, everyone know what to do?"

"Yes," they answered in unison.

"Then we'll meet in Boise at Chapman's Saloon at noon next Thursday. Watch yourselves until then."

Alexis started to get up but stopped as a sudden dizziness made her see thousands of tiny black spots instead of the room around her. She blinked and took a deep breath, hoping no one would notice her. She was lucky in that respect. The men were talking amongst themselves and weren't looking her way. Her vision cleared and, more slowly this time, she stood.

"Donahue," she said softly, drawing his attention. "I'm going to leave for Boise tomorrow. My sister is there with her husband, and I have other friends there, too. It will give me a good reason for being there. If you need to get hold of me, send word to Jasper Houston at Houston's Mercantile."

"I'll do it."

"Good day, Mr. Donahue," she said as she opened the store room door. "And thanks so much for your help." Her eyes swept the bakery, but there was no one there except for Mrs. Donahue, making her departing performance unnecessary.

She stepped outside and inhaled deeply, filling her lungs with the fresh, crisp air, hoping it would clear her head. She couldn't understand what was wrong with her. She had always had excellent health, but lately, her stomach was upset almost daily and she felt dizzy off and on, too.

Drawing up her skirt, she started walking, turning her feet in the direction of Stella's house. For the moment, she forgot her plans for the gold shipment and her arguments with Colter, her thoughts turning instead to Stella's pretty daughter, Greta. It was difficult to believe that the red-haired infant was nearly three months old already. She loved to slip away from the Palace for an hour or so each day and go over to Stella's. She felt a special closeness to Greta, perhaps because she had helped bring her into the world.

Stella answered the door in response to Alexis' knock. Brushing back a stray lock of hair, she said, "I thought it was about time for your visit. Come on in."

"I'm not becoming a pest, am I?" Alexis asked as she stepped by the young mother.

Stella laughed. "Never. I love your company. You know that." She took Alexis by the arm and drew her into the house. "Greta and I were just starting supper. Come join us in the kitchen."

Greta was lying in a basket on the kitchen

table, staring at the shadows on the ceiling and cooing. Alexis bent over the basket and grinned at the infant. "Hello, Greta," she said.

Greta cooed louder.

Alexis straightened. "See. She knows..." she began, but her words were stopped by another wave of blackness. She grabbed for a chair and sat down with a thud.

"Alex!" Stella cried, reaching her before she could fall from the chair.

Alexis groaned as she came to. Her head was resting on the table. A cold cloth was on her forehead. "What happened?" she asked weakly.

"You fainted."

She sat up, her hands pressed against the table to steady herself. She turned to look at her friend. "I don't know what's wrong with me," she whispered.

"Has this happened before?" Stella asked.

Alexis nodded.

"Often?"

"Well..." She nodded again.

There was a funny expression on Stella's face. "Are you sick to your stomach, Alex?"

"Yes." She felt a little frightened.

"And you have no idea what's wrong with you?"

"No, Stella, I don't. What is it? What do you think it is?" Her voice rose in anxiety.

Stella stifled her mirth as she replied, "Well, Alexis, I'm not a a doctor, but I *am* a mother." She looked at Alexis, waiting for a response, but Alexis only stared at her blankly. Stella sighed. "My guess, Alexis, is that you're going to be a mother, too."

"A mother?"

This time, Stella couldn't stop the laughter. "You really had no idea?"

"You mean, I'm going to have a baby?" She felt faint again.

Stella, noting her friend's renewed paleness, turned toward the stove. "I think I'd better get you some tea." As she reached for a cup, she added, "I can't believe you hadn't guessed, Alexis. Not as badly as you've wanted a baby."

Alexis couldn't believe it either. How could she not have known? All the symptoms had been there. But she had been so distracted lately, first with Althea and then with her secret meetings with Donahue and then her troubles with Colter.

"Colt," she whispered under her breath. Just wait until she told him. He would be so happy at the news. A son for the Circle S.

As if she'd read her thoughts, Stells said, "Colter will be thrilled." She carried the teapot over to the table. "Are you going to tell him right away?"

"He's gone to the ranch for a few days," Alexis answered. *Besides*, she thought suddenly, *I can't tell him until I'm finished with Donahue. He would never let me leave town.* "It will have to wait until I get back from Boise."

"You're going to Boise?"

"Yes. I want to see Althea. I haven't heard a single word from Derek on how she's doing, and I'm worried."

Stella's eyes dropped to the table and her lips tightened, but she said nothing.

Alexis wasn't too distracted by her own thoughts to notice the expression. "Stella, I know you find it hard to believe, but I think Derek really cares for my sister. You have good reason for hating him, Stella, but I wish you could have seen him with Althea. He's tender and attentive. He left his own business affairs just to take her to a milder climate in hopes she'd improve." She sighed. "I found it hard to believe myself at first. I've suspected him of murder, and I admit I still don't like him much. But that doesn't change what he's doing for his wife. I have to support him in that."

Stella looked up. "He's a performer, Alexis. People see what he wants them to see. Just be careful."

"I will be." She rose slowly from her chair. "Now, I must be on my way. I have things to pack before I can take the stage."

The stage pulled out of Idaho City early the next morning. There was only one other passenger besides Alexis, a banker from Placerville who was more inclined to snooze than to visit. Alexis was relieved. She didn't feel like making small talk during the daylong trip to Boise City.

As the stage jounced along the winter-rutted road, Alexis gripped her seat for balance, but her thoughts were on Colter and their baby. She'd thought of little else during the long night. All these months she had been hoping she would get pregnant. Now, her hopes had come true, and she should be happy. She *was* happy, but there was a shadow hanging over her, dimming her joy. She wished she'd never gotten herself mixed up with Donahue now. What if something went wrong? What if she lost the baby because of what they were going to do? She would never forgive herself. Colter would never forgive her.

She shook her head, trying to rid her mind of those negative thoughts. Think instead about what it's going to be like, she told herself.

It was time to sell the Ice Palace. She had thought she might want to keep it and let others run it as Reckless had done. Now she knew she wanted to let it go. It held nothing for her. She had proved she could run it. She had taken something successful and made it even more so. Reckless would have been proud of her. She had made many friends, and she would miss them, but something better called to her.

She remembered the first time she had seen the Circle S. She remembered Colter's pride in his ranch. She thought of the cattle and the horses and the new ranch house. These things were real. There was no glitter and gold to blind a man's eye like there was at the Ice Palace. Just honest work. Hard work. Work that made a man sweat. That was the kind of man Colter was—honest and hardworking. Those were some of the reasons she loved him.

"I should never have taken him from the ranch," she said to herself.

"What?" the banker asked, opening his eyes.

Startled, she looked across at him. She had forgotten he was even there. "I'm sorry. I was talking to myself."

"Quite all right." He smiled, then dipped his head to his chest and closed his eyes once more.

She turned her head toward the side of the coach and pushed aside the canvas flap that covered the door. The mountains still had a covering of snow, but a slow melt was starting. Soon the hillsides would be green and dotted with wildflowers, much like they had been when she first came here almost a year before.

A year. Was that all it had been? It seemed like too much had happened for it to have been only a year.

Once again she thought of Colter and the ranch. No, she never should have let him leave it. When she agreed to marry him, she should have sold the Ice Palace and moved to the Circle S and put Idaho City and being the Ice Queen behind her for good. If she had, how different things might have been. She and Colter wouldn't be fighting over the War Between the States, and she wouldn't be on her way now to rob the government of a gold shipment, perhaps risking her own baby's life.

And Althea would never have met Derek, she thought, letting the flap fall back across the opening.

It had been a month since Derek took Althea away, and despite what she'd said to Stella, Alexis was worried. Although she reluctantly believed Derek's affections for his wife were real, she still didn't trust him. If only the doctor had been able to tell her what was wrong with Althea, but Dr. Walters had done little more than shake his head and say it was a mystery to him. Alexis thought the doctor was a doddering old fool, yet she couldn't convince Derek to let Dr. Barker take a look at her sister.

Alexis rubbed her temples. Her head was throbbing. She was thinking too much. Her confusion was growing instead of lessening. She closed her eyes, hoping she would be released from her troubles by sleep.

Alexis was too worn out from the rough stagecoach ride to do anything but head for the hotel and drop into bed after a long, hot bath. When she awoke late the next morning, she dressed quickly and went down to the restaurant for breakfast. She was ravenous and, luckily, was not suffering that morning from a queasy stomach. Once she had finished her hearty meal, she went out, her first destination the house Derek had taken to live in while he and Althea were in Boise.

Her knock was answered by Mai Ling. The girl's eyes widened in surprise. "Mrs. Stephens!" she exclaimed.

"Hello, Mai Ling. Is Mr. Anderson in?"

She shook her head. "He is not here."

"Then I would like to see Mrs. Anderson."

Mai Ling glanced around nervously, then stepped aside to let Alexis enter. "Mr. Anderson lets no one see her," she said. "He says it's not good for her."

Alexis frowned. "I disagree, Mai Ling. Take me to her room."

Reluctantly, Mai Ling led the way.

Alexis was expecting to find her sister in the

same or worse condition than when she'd left Idaho City. She was surprised, then, to find her sitting up in bed, her hair carefully combed and falling softly over her shoulders. Althea's head turned slowly when she heard the door open.

"Althea?" Alexis walked over to the bed.

Althea smiled. "Alexis," she said in a strange monotone.

Alexis sat down beside the bed and took her sister's hand. For a brief moment, she had thought her sister was well again, but she could see now that her relief had been premature. Althea's eyes were dull. Even her smile was void of any real feeling. It went no deeper than her lips.

"Althea, how are you?"

"How am I?" Althea repeated. "I'm fine."

"I've been so worried about you."

"Worried? Why would you worry? I'm with Derek. Derek takes good care of me."

"Does he?" Alexis wondered aloud.

Althea's glance slipped away to the window where spring sunshine was filtering through the lace curtains. "Have you ever noticed how warm the color yellow is? I've thought about it often. Yes, it's a very warm color. You should wear more yellow, Alexis. It's so warm . . ." Her voice faded away.

Alexis had the feeling that Althea had faded away, too. She was sitting there, her eyes open, yet she wasn't really there. "Althea?" She tried to call her back, but there was no acknowledgement that she'd been heard.

She got up and went to the bedroom door.

She looked back one more time. Althea looked so pretty in her nightgown, pillows plumped all around her. She didn't look sick. Alexis swallowed the lump in her throat and opened the door.

"Mai Ling!" she called, and the girl hurried into view. "Where can I find Mr. Anderson?"

"I am not sure today. He left early this morning and said he would not return until tomorrow."

"And what is he doing for my sister?"

Mai Ling glanced toward the bedroom door. "He has the medicine the doctor gives him. And he tells me to comb her hair and dress her pretty. He says it will make her feel better. He checks to make sure she eats as she should."

Alexis nodded. It sounded right. It sounded as if he cared, as if he were making sure she had everything she needed. So why did she continue to mistrust him?

"Thank you, Mai Ling. Please tell Mr. Anderson when he returns that I am in town and will call on him and Althea again after his return."

Mai Ling bowed. "Yes. I will tell him."

Alexis stepped outside, then looked back at the girl. "Mai Ling, are *you* happy here? Is this a good place to live?"

Mai Ling looked startled. "Mai Ling is a good servant," she said hastily as she closed the door.

Alexis gazed at the door for a long time, thinking, *Mai Ling is a frightened servant, but why? What is wrong in that house?* Then she turned away and walked back toward her hotel, her thoughts remaining in the bedroom with Althea.

Colter sat easy in his saddle. His eyes roamed over the cattle dotting the range. He rubbed the bristle on his chin, then tugged at the brim of his hat. His leg ached a little, making him think of the day he got caught in the bear trap. That memory, like all his other memories, always seemed to lead his thoughts in the same direction. To Alexis.

Gads, how he missed her. He'd been wrong to come down here without her. This wasn't a solution. They had to settle this thing between them, and that wasn't going to get done with her in Idaho City and him at the ranch. He might as well give up and go back.

He turned Titan's head toward the bunkhouse, a slow smile curving his mouth as he thought of Alexis, her hands on her hips and her eyes flashing daggers at him, telling him he was wrong about the South being about to lose the war. You would have thought she hated him. But he knew differently. Fight they might, but they loved on. That's why he had to return. She needed him. She needed him by her side, even when they disagreed. And he needed her in the same way. Yes, he'd rather be trading words with her in their suite at the Ice Palace than here at the ranch without her.

Alexis sat in the parlor of the Houston home. Sadie was in the kitchen, making a pot of tea. The children had all been chased upstairs, leaving the adults to talk alone. The bustle of this household made Alexis feel good. It was a real home. There was warmth and love here. She wanted this kind of home for her children. Her hand moved involuntarily to rest against her flat abdomen.

"Here we are," Sadie said as she entered the parlor, tray in hand. "Can't tell you how good it is to see you, Alexis. Wish it were for a better reason than your sister." She shook her head as she poured the tea. "And I didn't even know she was in town. I would have called on her had I known."

"I'm not sure if she would have known you anyway, Sadie."

"It's that bad . . ." She clucked her tongue. "It's a shame. Not that I ever thought Althea had the spark you've got, but I wouldn't have wished her to be sick. She hasn't had an easy time of it since she went back to her plantation with your father. Losin' your mother and all." She paused a moment, watching Alexis. "Have you heard from Jonathan?"

"No. Not a word. And the news we hear from the South isn't good. I suppose he could even be dead." Her voice broke a little at the end.

Sadie patted her knee. "Now, you mustn't be thinking such things, Alex. Keep your chin up. That's my girl."

"Oh, Sadie," Alexis cried, setting her cup down so fast she slopped tea over its brim, "I wish I were a man. I'd be down there fighting right beside him."

Sadie gave her a reproving look. "It's a silly thing to wish for things that are impossible. You are *not* a man and you cannot fight beside your father."

"No, but I'll do what I can to help him," Alexis replied with a stubborn toss of her head.

Sadie was instantly alert. "What have you gotten yourself mixed up in, Alexis Stephens?"

"What makes you ask that?"

"I don't know, but I'd bet my right arm you're fixin' for trouble."

Alexis picked up her cup again, afraid to look at Sadie for the moment, knowing she couldn't keep the truth from showing in her eyes. "What possible trouble could I get into, Sadie?"

"Plenty, if I'm not mistaken. Now spill the beans to me. You're not leavin' here 'til you do."

"I'm sorry, Sadie. There's nothing I can tell you."

21

It was one of those April days that bursts upon the horizon, full of sunshine and the promise of warmer days to come, the sun's rays sending rivulets of melting snow streaming down the rutted, muddy streets. Spring beckoned to children and housewives to come outside, and the air was quickly filled with an increasing hubbub as neighbor greeted neighbor.

Colter smiled at folks as he rode into town. He felt the same surge of pleasure that he knew they were feeling, a sense of freedom, a release from the confines of small rooms and gray, snowy days. He was heading for the livery stable when he saw Stella and Sam walking along the boardwalk, Stella cradling the baby in her arms. He pulled back on the reins.

"Hello!" he called to them.

Stella squinted up at him from beneath her

bonnet. "Colter. What are you doing in town?"

"Nice welcome," he commented as he swung down from the saddle.

"You know I didn't mean it to sound that way. It's just I didn't expect you to come back from the ranch while Alexis is away."

"Away?" His eyes jumped from Stella to Sam and back again. "Where is she?"

Stella glanced at her husband. "She went to Boise City," she answered as her eyes came back to meet his. "I thought she would have sent word to you."

Colter patted Titan's neck. He tugged at the brim of his hat as he said, "No. She didn't send word."

"Listen, Colt," Sam said, "why don't you come back to our place and have a bite to eat? You're probably hungry after your ride up here."

Before he answered, Colter asked one more question. "Why did she go to Boise?"

"She wanted to see Althea, to see how she is doing. She said she hadn't heard anything from Derek since he and Althea left town. She was worried."

Colter felt the heaviness in his chest lighten. He'd been afraid, for just a moment, that she wasn't coming back. Now that he'd heard Stella's explanation, he could smile again. He nodded at Sam's invitation to stay and eat and turned Titan down the street toward the Wainwright home, keeping pace with Stella and Sam as they traversed the boardwalk.

The tiny home behind Sam's office greeted him with a homey, family feeling. The windows were open to let in the freshness of spring. The baby's cradle stood in the kitchen, and Stella went to it and laid Greta down. She paused for a moment, her eyes locked lovingly on the infant as her hand gently rocked the cradle.

"Coffee, Colt?" Sam asked, but his gaze was riveted on the mother and child scene before him.

"No, thanks," Colter answered. He pulled a chair out from the table and sat down. He grinned at his lawyer-friend. "Fatherhood agrees with you, Sam."

Stella turned around, her eyes still holding a dreamy quality. "It'll agree with you, too, Colter Stephens. Why, come Christmas..." She stopped suddenly, clamping her mouth shut in a guilty fashion. She turned back to the cradle.

For a moment, what Stella had said held no significance for Colter, but slowly it dawned on him why she had cut herself short. He got up from the chair, almost afraid to believe what he was thinking. He went over to Stella and put his hand on her shoulder, urging her to turn around and look at him.

"Stella? Are you saying what I think you are?"

"Oh, Colt," she answered miserably. "She'll never forgive me for letting it slip."

The stern set of his lips curved into a slow smile. His brown eyes twinkled with delight. "I'll be darned. A baby," he said, his voice low. The room was dead-still. Then, with a whoop, he picked Stella up and spun her around. Setting her down again, he planted a kiss on her cheek. "I think I'll head for Boise now. I can't wait to see Alexis and . . ." It was his turn to stop short. His smile faded.

What if she wasn't happy about the baby? With so much disagreement between them, maybe she was sorry to be carrying his child. Is that why she'd gone to Boise? Is that why she hadn't told him where she was going or that she was pregnant?

He studied Stella's expression as he asked, "What . . ." he began. "What did she say about the baby? Was she glad?"

A confident smile brightened her countenance. "She was in heaven. She wanted to tell you, but said she had to take this trip first. Maybe she was afraid you wouldn't let her go if you knew about the baby."

"I probably wouldn't have wanted her to, but since when could I have stopped her from doing what she wanted?"

Stella laughed and nodded. "You're right. I don't think you could've stopped her. She can be a little pigheaded."

It was Sam's turn to laugh. "Just a little," he said in agreement as he sat at the table. "Come on and sit down, Colt. There's no point in you rushing off this late in the day. You may as well have dinner with us and get a fresh start in the morning."

"All right," Colter said as he bent over the cradle to lay a gentle hand on Greta's diapered bottom. A baby. His and Alexis' baby. He would have to get the nursery ready in the ranch house. He'd build the cradle himself. Alexis would need a rocker...

"Colter" Stella stood at his elbow. "Sam offered you a drink."

Feeling a trifle sheepish, Colter pulled himself away from the baby's cradle and returned to the table. "Yeah, I think I'll have that drink. I feel like celebrating."

Alexis sat on the sofa in the parlor. She removed her gloves as Derek sent Mai Ling for tea.

"How is Althea today?" she asked as she laid the gloves on her lap.

"There's little change from day to day," he answered, taking a seat across from her. "But, as I'm sure you noticed when you came the other day, she has improved from when we left Idaho City. I'm encouraged. I think the change did her good."

"Yes," Alexis agreed, "she does seem better." She met Derek's gaze. "But she's so remote, Derek. It's like she's here but not really here. Do you know what I mean?"

He nodded. "Like I said, her progress is slow."

"And what have the doctors here had to say?"

Derek frowned. "She is still under Dr. Walter's care. I haven't sought any other opinion."

"But, Derek..." she began. She stopped herself.

"Mai Ling takes excellent care of her, and I do what I can." His words sounded hard.

Alexis swallowed a retort and forced herself to speak kindly. "Mai Ling has told me how good you've been with Althea. I didn't mean to sound as though I thought you weren't caring for her. But she's my sister, maybe even my only surviving family, and I'm so worried about her. I want to see her well again."

Mai Ling entered with the tea tray, stopping his reply. He motioned for the girl to set down the tray and leave.

"Will you pour, Alexis?" Derek invited.

Alexis filled a cup, then passed it to him. She noticed her hand was shaking as she filled the second cup. She had come to a decision last night in her hotel room, but she was finding it hard to reveal that decision to Derek.

"Would you like to see Althea now?" he asked, sensing her hesitation to speak.

"Not yet, Derek. There... there is something else I wish to discuss with you."

He waited silently.

Alexis set her teacup on the table, the hot liquid untouched. She looked up at him, forcing herself to ignore the intuition that screamed at her not to trust this man. She reached for her reticule and set it on her lap, slowly opening the drawstrings.

"I want you to see something," she said as she drew out the watch she had given Reckless. She held it out to Derek, watching his face for any sign of recognition.

He took it from her and turned it over in his hand, but the only expression on his face was one of puzzlement. "I don't understand, Alexis. It's a nice watch. In fact, I have one that looks much the same. Why are you showing it to me?"

As the air slipped from her lungs, Alexis realized she'd been holding her breath while she waited for his response. That was it, then. Derek didn't know anything about Reckless's death. The watch Stella had seen was his own, a near duplicate. Her instincts had played her false when it came to Derek Anderson. It was time she learned to trust her brother-in-law, to give him the benefit of the doubt. He really seemed to have changed from the man Stella had known.

"This watch belonged to T.C."

"T.C.?"

"To Reckless Jones. I . . . I guess I wanted to show it to you 'cause I want to talk to you about the Palace."

Derek leaned forward. His eyes sparked with interest. "What about the Palace?" he asked, his voice eager.

"I'm thinking about selling it, Derek."

Derek set his teacup aside. "You're going to sell it? To whom?"

"Well, you have offered to buy it in the past. I thought you might still be interested."

A jubilant expression passed over Derek's face but was quickly suppressed. "I'm interested . . . if the terms and the price are right. When did you think you'd want to sell it?"

"June, perhaps?"

"June . . ." His mouth turned up in a grin. "Yes, Alexis, I think we can probably come to an agreement of some sort."

Alexis stood up, feeling suddenly uncomfortable. She tried to squelch the feelings as she said, "You think about it, Derek, and we'll talk more when you come back to Idaho. May I see Althea now?"

"Of course. I'll take you to her."

Derek sat across from Alexis as she held her sister's hand and chattered a string of gossip. Althea listened with a placid smile, but Derek knew she didn't really hear what Alexis was saying. She was like a doll. Pretty but mindless.

His gaze drifted from his wife to Alexis. He felt the hungry stirrings of desire. *Damn* but he wanted that woman. One day, it would happen. Just like he was about to achieve his goal of owning the Ice Palace. He would own the Palace, and one day, he would own the Ice Queen herself.

He shook off those thoughts and looked again at his wife. It was time he withdrew her "medicine." He was tired of her like this. He preferred to have some response from his women. It was the conquest that gave him his sense of power. As it was now, there was no conquest, only meek surrender. Besides, now that Alexis was going to sell the Palace to him, there was no need to keep her sedated.

"Derek says you'll be coming home to Idaho City soon," Alexis was saying. "And I think we'll have a surprise for you. I know you've always liked the suite at the Ice Palace. How would you like it to be your suite, Althea? Would you like that? You could be the queen of the palace, Althea."

Althea as the Ice Queen? No, Derek thought,

she would never be able to be the Ice Queen. A poor imitation perhaps, but she didn't have that . . . that . . . Just what was it Alexis had that made her a queen and her sister a mere princess?

Derek pressed his lips together in a tight line as he felt anger wash over him. He got up and walked to the window, hiding his face from Alexis. He didn't know what it was she had that Althea didn't, but he meant to break her, he meant to rule her as he did her sister. No. More than he did Althea. He meant to make her sorry for scorning his attentions.

Patient, he reminded himself. I must be patient. I'll own the Ice Palace. Then I can extract my measure of justice.

"They're takin' the gold out of here tomorrow. They're usin' a Wells Fargo coach." Donahue leaned forward, speaking so low the others were forced to lean closer as well in order to hear what he was saying. "The guards are t'be dressed in ordinary clothes t'look like normal passengers. From what I learned, there won't be more than four men along."

"Can you be sure of your information, Donahue?" Meyers asked.

"Aye, I think I can. O'Reilly tells me they'll pull out o'here about noon tomorrow."

"And they're not expecting trouble?" one of the other men asked.

Donahue laughed aloud, then said softly, his brows drawn together for emphasis, "They're always expectin' trouble. This time, no one's to know about the shipment. They're hopin' if they look as if they're nothing but a coach filled with travelers that they'll pass the notice of cutthroats and thieves."

Alexis listened, her gaze moving around the table, noting the beads of perspiration on Meyers' forehead, the heightened color of Donahue's cheeks. Beneath the table, her hand touched her flat stomach. She wondered if what they were planning was worth the risk.

Donahue turned toward her. "Miss Alexis, you know what you're to do?"

"Yes." She recited the plans for good measure. "I'll rent a horse and go riding east of town. When I reach the wash near the grove of cottonwoods, I'm to wait for the stagecoach. I'll make it look as if I've taken a bad tumble from my horse and have hurt my leg. When the driver stops to help me, you'll show up and take the wagon."

Donahue nodded, continuing, "We'll threaten to shoot you should anyone interfere. That should keep them from firing any shots and risk any killings. We'll tie you up with them, so no one'll suspect your part in it." He turned his gaze on the men. "We'll ride out of town in twos after Miss Alexis has already gone. Don't forget to hide your faces when the time comes."

"I'm going to have dinner with friends tonight," Alexis said, sliding her chair away from the table. "I won't see you again until tomorrow."

The men murmured farewells as she turned her back on them and hurried out of the saloon.

Her stomach was churning, and she felt the

familiar dizziness creeping up on her. She paused, leaning against a building while the world righted itself again. Her vision clear, she walked in a more sedate fashion toward her hotel.

Once in her room, Alexis lay on her back on the bed. She closed her eyes, squeezing tears out of the corners. "I'm afraid," she said aloud. "Oh, Colt. I'm so afraid. What if something happens to your baby? I wasn't afraid before, but I am now." She rolled over onto her stomach. "But I've got to do it," she whispered. "I've got to help Papa if I can, and this is the only way I know to help." She sniffed and wiped the tearstains from her cheeks. "When this is over, Colt, we'll go back to the ranch and we'll never be apart again. I won't lie to you or argue with you ever again. I promise. I promise."

Midway between the ranch and Boise City, Titan pulled up lame. Colter spent a chilly night sleeping in the open, then began a slow trek into Boise early the next morning, leading his horse most of the way. The sun was just beginning to warm him as he entered the city. He went straight to Sadie's house, certain that Alexis would be staying there.

"No, Colt. She decided to stay at the hotel, though I don't know why. We'd have gladly made room for her." Sadie drew him into the house as she spoke. "She had supper with us last night. Seemed awfully quiet to me. Is something wrong between you two?" she asked, giving him a long, probing look.

"Nothing now, I hope," he answered, hanging his dusty hat on the back of his chair as he sat at the kitchen table.

"And what does that mean?"

"We've had a few fights lately, Sadie. But I think we're through with fighting now. At least, I think we will be as soon as I get to see her."

"Hmmm. I guess that would explain her moodiness. I thought it was more than just her sister. Coffee?"

Colter accepted the dark, hot brew in the cup Sadie handed to him. He took a quick gulp, feeling the hot liquid warming its way down his throat and right into his stomach. He let out a satisfied sigh. "Thanks, Sadie."

"Well?" she encouraged. "Are you going to tell me more or not?"

"We've been fighting about the war back in the states. She thinks I don't care about her father being in the middle of it."

"The war again, huh?"

Colter tipped his chair back on its hind legs. "Did she talk to you about it?"

"Not really. But I know her feelin's run deep about it 'cause of her father. She'd be fightin' in it herself if it weren't so far away. Said so herself."

"I know." He drained his cup and stood up. "Sorry to rush off, Sadie, but I want to find Alexis. I want to get it all straightened out so we can go home."

Sadie patted his shoulder, her eyes showing her understanding. "You hurry on then. I think you'll find her at the Boise Hotel. If not, she'll be at her sister's place. It's the one at the end of Grove. The one with the fancy trim and the white fence."

"Thanks, Sadie." He kissed her cheek. "We'll see you again before we head home."

"I'll hold you to that, Colt Stephens. And when the two of you come, I want to see you gettin' along the way you should."

Colter set his hat over his sandy brown hair and strode out to the street. He left Titan hitched to the post outside the Houston home, giving the horse a much needed rest.

As he walked toward the hotel, he thought he recognized Donahue and Meyers riding out of town. He wondered briefly what they were doing in Boise City together, but the thought was fleeting. He had something much more important on his mind.

He opened the door into the hotel, ringing the tiny door chime overhead. A clerk looked up from the register, tipping his chin down so he could look over the rims of his glasses.

"May I help you, sir?" he asked.

"I'm looking for my wife. I believe she's staying here."

"Her name?"

Colter leaned against the counter, trying to read the register upside down. "Mrs. Stephens," he replied. "Alexis Stephens."

"Ah, yes, Mr. Stephens. She is staying here with us."

"Where's her room?" Colter asked eagerly, ready to head for the stairs.

"Room 201. Top of the stairs, end of the

hall."

Colter turned away.

"But she's not here, sir," the clerk called after him.

He stopped and looked back. "Where is she?"

"I think she was going riding this morning. She was wearing an awfully pretty riding habit when she left here. Asked where she could rent a horse. I sent her to the livery around the corner."

"Thanks," Colter said as he bolted for the door.

The tangy smell of horse dung and hay, leather and sweat greeted Colter as he entered the stable. The bright sunlight behind him made the interior of the livery all the darker, and it took a moment for his eyes to adjust.

"Hello!" he called, waiting impatiently for the stablehand to appear. "Hello!"

"Hold on t'yer britches there, sonny." An old man with shaggy white hair and a beard came through the door at the back of the livery.

"I need to rent a horse."

"Fine. I got one I could let you use." He scratched his chin. "Tall fella, ain't ya?"

Colter ignored his chatter. "Listen. My wife took one of your horses this morning. Can you tell me which way she went?"

The old man eyed him suspiciously. "Your wife, huh? What proof have I got that she's your missus?"

Colter forced himself to rein in his impatience. "None, but I assure you I am her husband. I've just ridden down from Idaho City.

She didn't know I was coming to be with her. Please, if you'll just tell me which way she went..."

The old man turned away and went to a nearby stall. He led a sleek chestnut gelding into the light, tying his lead rope to a post near the door. "Will he do?" he asked, already lifting a blanket onto the horse's back.

"Yes. Now, where..."

"Don't know why you young folk are always in such a rush," he muttered. "That missus of yours seemed mighty impatient herself. Wears a body out. Wouldn't be so bad, but that young whelp of mine is off helpin' load that gold shipment. Humph," he snorted. "Never seen such silliness in my life, tryin' to keep somethin' like that a secret. Those government fellas must think this is a town full of fools. Everybody and his uncle knows what's goin' on, and there'll be more'n one hoodlum layin' for it. You mark my words."

Something clicked into place as the old man chattered to himself. Colter felt himself grow cold. "What gold shipment is that, old man?"

"Huh? Gold shipment? How'd you know about it?" He clucked his tongue. "Isn't that what I was just thinkin'? You can't keep somethin' like that a secret. Why, somebody will be after that stage 'fore they're twenty miles from here. You mark my words."

"Which way did you say my wife went?" Colter asked one more time.

"East."

Colter swung into the saddle. "My horse is at

Jasper Houston's house. Give him a good rubdown and check his left front leg. I'll pay you when I get back." The words spilled from his lips as he dug his spurs into the gelding's ribs. The horse shot out of the dim barn and into the daylight, and he galloped out of town.

"Please," he prayed under his breath, "let me get there in time."

Alexis sat on a rock alongside the road, twisting the leather reins in her fingers. Each minute seemed an hour long as she waited for the sounds of the approaching stagecoach.

She had spent a sleepless night. Several times she had decided to search out Donahue and tell him she couldn't go through with it. But then she would remember the stories she'd heard about the sufferings of the South, and her father's face would drift across her thoughts. She imagined him wounded or as a prisoner or, even worse, dead. She heard again Althea's tale of the burning of Willowind, and she knew she had to go through with it. This was the only way she could help. She had to help get this gold to the Confederate army. She had to keep those butchers, those plundering Yankees, from winning the war. She had no choice. No choice.

More than once, Colter's face intruded on her thoughts, too, but she tried to blank out his image. She couldn't wrestle with thoughts of him now. She felt too vulnerable. What she was doing was wrong. It could be dangerous for her and for the life that nestled within her. She might be imprisoned or killed because of it. Common sense told her she shouldn't do it, but stubbornness left no room for common sense.

Alexis drew Reckless's watch from the pocket of her riding habit and snapped open the gold cover. Noon. They should be pulling out of Boise by now. Her heartbeat quickened. There was no turning back. She chased the fear from her face. Her cool blue eyes watched the road with a detached stare.

The sound of galloping hooves reached her ears, startling her. It was too soon for the stage. She jumped up from the rock, her eyes scanning the sagebrush-covered landscape around her, wondering if Donahue and the others were out there and could see what was happening. Her mount's ears perked forward. He whickered, and Alexis stroked his muzzle.

The rider rounded a bend in the road at full speed. He was riding low over the saddle, obviously in a great hurry. Alexis knew the moment he saw her. He sat back in the saddle and eased up on the reins. Her hand moved to the small derringer in the pocket concealed in the folds of her riding habit, but she didn't make any move to mount her horse.

The moment of recognition caused her to wonder at herself. She should have known it would be Colter. She should have known he would come for her, even when he didn't know where she was or what she was doing.

He stopped his horse, his thoughtful brown eyes gazing at her in the silent moment while the road dust settled around them. Finally, he pushed his hat back from his forehead and said,

"Nice day for a ride."

She wanted to smile but couldn't. "Yes," she replied softly.

"I went to the Palace to see you. Had some things I wanted to say." He let his gaze drift to the blue sky overhead. His horse shifted beneath him. "Stella told me you'd come to Boise."

She wished he would get down from that horse and take her in his arms. It frightened her that he was staying so far away from her. What was it he had come to say?

"Alex, we can't go on like this. Scrapping and fighting over something so far away. Something we can't do a darned thing about." His eyes swung back to lock with hers. "Let's go home. I won't say anything else about the war, right or wrong. I promise."

She swallowed the *yes* that surged in her throat. She dragged her gaze away from him. "I can't go back. Not yet. Not today."

"I didn't mean today," he answered. "I meant right now."

Alexis shook her head. "I can't."

In a fluid motion, he swung from the saddle. Long strides brought him to stand before her. "Now, Alex." His hands rested on her shoulders.

She was forced to look up at him by his very nearness. "No," she whispered.

"You can't go through with this," he said, his jaw tightening, his voice deepening.

He knew why she was there. Somehow he had learned what she was planning to do. The surprise showed in her eyes. She felt something akin to relief. He had come to stop her. He wouldn't let her risk their love or their child.

"I forbid you to do this, Alexis. You're coming back with me now."

Unbidden and unwanted, her temper flared. "You *forbid* me? You have nothing to say about it. I'm a grown woman. I don't need you to tell me what I can and cannot do. I'm not your property, Colt Stephens."

"No, but you're my wife, and I'm not going to see you swinging from the nearest tree." With that, he grabbed her and tossed her over his shoulder like a sack of flour.

"Colt! Put me down!" she screamed, her feet kicking the air, her arms flailing at his back.

"Not until we get to Boise," he growled. "And maybe not until we get to the ranch."

"I'm not going anywhere with you, Colt Stephens." She continued to pound futile fists against his back. "Now, put me down this instant."

His answer was to step up into his saddle and turn his horse in the direction of town, never heeding her threats and protestations. Ever so slowly, she began to calm down, her anger lessening. She might even have forgiven him, perhaps even thanked him for stopping her, if they hadn't met the Wells Fargo coach while she was still draped ignobly over his shoulder. She heard the thunder of galloping hooves, the creak of leather and springs. Her head bobbed up.

"Colt, put me down," she cried, but it was too late.

The coach, gold shipment hidden from view, rattled by, and as she watched, she saw the grins of the men's faces as they looked at her and Colter. She seethed with indignation.

"You'll regret this, Colter Stephens," she hissed.

Grimly, he responded, "I'm sure of that, my dear."

22

Angry and humiliated—and too stubborn to admit he had been right to stop her—Alexis refused to speak to Colter. After gathering her things from the hotel, Colter hired a carriage and they left Boise City without delay. They spent a wordless night at the Circle S. Alexis wouldn't acknowledge Colter's suggestion that they forget returning to Idaho City and just remain at the ranch, so the following morning they resumed their silent journey back to the Ice Palace. Colter thought it was an appropriate destination for someone receiving the cold shoulder the way he was.

Wisely, Colter kept his peace. He never suggested that he knew anything about her pregnancy, nor did he berate her for her foolishness. He was confident that time would ease the strain between them, though he was impatient for that moment to arrive.

Alexis kept to herself, barricading herself in her office behind ledgers and business files whenever she wasn't in the saloon. The Ice Palace was once again filled to capacity, the spring runoff filling the miners' pockets with gold dust and nuggets which most of them spent as fast as they found it. Alexis moved among the men, her head high, her eyes unreadable, her smile cool. She knew Colter watched her; when her gaze met his, she could read his patient love in his eyes.

She was miserable. She wanted to admit she'd been wrong, but she couldn't. When they went to bed at night, Colter would reach out for her but she continued to turn her back to him.

He had no right to forbid me, she would think to herself. and then she would lie awake for hours, listening to his even breathing, sensing the closeness of his body, longing to nestle against him, but, instead, she hugged the edge of the bed all night long.

A week went by unchanged.

It was early in the morning. The saloon was closed. Unable to sleep, Alexis left the bedroom and went downstairs to her office. There was little work to be done, so she searched the bookshelves for something to read, something that would take her mind off her own problems. She pulled a book from the shelf and settled into the comfortable, overstuffed chair near the corner of the room. She opened the book and there it remained, not a word read, while she stared into space.

She was drawn back to consciousness by a rap on her door.

"Yes?" she called.

The door opened.

"Hello." Derek stepped into the room. "May we disturb you?"

She placed the book on the stand beside her. "I didn't know you had returned. How is Althea?"

"See for yourself," he replied as he held out his arm toward the opening. Althea stepped into the doorway, a tentative smile on her lips.

Alexis rose from her chair, her arms reaching for her sister. "Althea," she whispered.

Althea's glance seemed uncertain as she crossed the room to clasp hands with Alexis. "You came to see me in Boise, didn't you?" she asked softly.

"Yes. I was there." Alexis' initial joy at her sister's improved health dimmed.

"I don't remember very much of my illness. It's all rather like a bad dream." Althea looked over her shoulder at Derek. "But I'm much better now. Really I am. Derek takes good care of me."

Something was still troubling Alexis. Her sister was not herself, yet she couldn't deny that she seemed better. "Sit down. Both of you," she said, guiding Althea to the chair she had just vacated. "When did you get back?"

"Last night," Derek answered. "Sorry we came so early, but I wanted to catch you before you got too busy around here. I wanted to discuss the terms of the sale of the Palace."

"The sale?" In her turmoil with Colter, she had forgotten her decision to sell the saloon. Alexis glanced down at her hands, clenched in front of her. "Derek, I'm afraid I've changed my mind about selling. At least for now."

"But, we had an agreement..." Derek began.

She felt a hollowness in her chest. She couldn't tell him about the trouble in her marriage. It was too private. But until things were right again, she couldn't sell the Palace.

"I'm sorry, Derek. I really thought when I was in Boise that I was ready to sell. But ... but things have changed. At least for the moment. I hope you'll forgive me."

Her eyes moved to Althea, and so she missed seeing the flush of rage pass over his features, then his struggle to disguise those feelings behind a careful mask.

"I won't say I'm not disappointed," he said at last, "because I am. But you know I want the place, and when you're ready to sell, I'll be ready to buy."

"Thank you, Derek. I promise I'll let you know the moment I'm sure of what to do."

Althea walked slowly around the parlor, her fingers tracing over the furniture. Try as she might, she couldn't recall this room. In fact, she seemed to have no memory of anything that had happened to her in recent months. She remembered arriving in Idaho City, her whole world in tatters. She remembered that Colter and Alexis were married and that she had felt in the way, unwanted, the poor sister without a home. She even remembered that Derek had courted her almost from the day she arrived. But she couldn't remember her own wedding or the days following before she fell ill. Something kept nagging at her that she needed to remember.

Her first real memory during her convalescence was of Derek coaxing her to take her bitter medicine, and how she had obeyed, not because she thought it would make her well but because she was afraid not to drink it. Why was she afraid? What was it she couldn't remember that would tell her what she feared?

She wandered on toward the back of the house. Mai Ling was outside the back door, washing clothes. She looked up from the washtub as Althea stepped outside. The servant nodded, then pushed a stray lock of black hair away from her forehead as she bent back over the tub. Althea watched Mai Ling for a little while, trying to conjure up some memories of the girl at work in the past, but it was to no avail.

She shivered and folded her arms over her breast. The April sun wasn't as warm here as it had been in Boise. Still, she could see some persistent crocuses poking their yellow heads through the snow that stubbornly remained near the side of the house. She stepped off the porch and walked toward them, hardly aware of the voices drifting through the open window until she was standing directly below it.

"I'm not going to wait any longer, Tanner.

She said she'd sell it to me and now she's changed her mind. It's time I taught the Ice Queen just who she's dealing with.''

Althea stepped up against the house, afraid that she would be seen.

Derek continued, ''I want Stephens out of the way for good. Then I'll deal with Alexis.''

''Any preference how he goes?'' That must be Tanner speaking.

''No. Just get it done and report back to me.''

Althea sidled along the edge of the house, not daring to breathe until she reached the back. Mai Ling looked up once again. Althea thought she saw something flicker across the servant's impassive face, but she couldn't be sure. She wished she could trust the girl. If only she knew for sure just what was happening. She rubbed her forehead. Her head was pounding with tension.

''Do you need something, Mrs. Anderson?'' Mai Ling asked. ''Are you not feeling good again?''

Althea shook her head. ''I'm fine, Mai Ling. Please don't say anything to Mr. Anderson. He'll put me back to bed.''

She went back into the house and sat on the couch in the parlor. Once again she closed her eyes. She must have misunderstood what Derek was saying. He'd taken care of her while she was ill. He was a good man. Wasn't he a good man? Of course he was. He couldn't be planning to kill Colter. He couldn't want to hurt Alexis. She'd just misunderstood them. Yes. That was it. She'd misunderstood. She needn't say anything to anyone. She needn't be afraid. But she was afraid. Afraid of everything in this house. Why? Why was she so afraid? Oh, if only she could remember . . .

Colter stepped, unnoticed, into the doorway of their bedroom. Alexis was standing at the window, her forehead leaning against the glass. The soft light of late afternoon illuminated her sad features, and Colter's heart tightened in his chest. He wished there was something he could do or say to make things easier for her. It was a terrible curse to be so stubborn. She was suffering because of it. She was making both of them suffer. Without her ever telling him, he knew Alexis had wanted to back out of that doomed stage robbery even before he arrived. Somehow he had to get her to admit it to herself and then to him.

"Alex?" he said softly, stepping into the room.

She glanced his way, then turned back to the window.

"It's getting late."

"I know. I'll get dressed in a little while."

He moved to the end of the bed. "Can I help?"

She shook her head, refusing to look at him again.

Colter waited, watching the light fade from the window. Dusk settled over the bedroom. At last, shaking his head at the futility of the situation, he turned to leave the room.

"Colt."

His name drifted across the darkened room to stop him by the door.

"Colt, I'm . . ." She paused.

"Yes?" Hope surged in his voice.

"I'll be down shortly.

Colter nodded without speaking and left the bedroom.

Alexis blinked back the hot tears that filled her eyes. She had tried to say she was sorry, that she'd been wrong, but the words just wouldn't come. Why was she doing this to him? Why was she doing it to herself?

She turned away from the window, moving slowly toward the nearby stand where she lit the lamp. Then she sat down at her dressing table and stared at her reflection in the mirror. She touched her cheeks. She was pale. It was more than just the morning sickness. She wasn't sleeping. She wasn't eating. and it was all her own fault.

"It's not good for the baby, either," she whispered to herself.

She reached for the lamp and held it close to her face.

"Take a good look, Alexis Stephens," she said, her voice louder this time. "If you're unhappy, it's your own fault and nobody else's. You're the one who thinks she's the only one entitled to an opinion about the war. Unless, of course, he agrees with you. You're the one who got yourself mixed up with Donahue and the others. How would you have felt if it had been Colt? You wouldn't have liked it one bit, especially if he'd been caught and hanged." She leaned closer to the glass. "You are a first-class fool. You've got a man who loves you, and you're going to have his baby. Now it's time you started acting like a wife and mother instead of like a jackass. You're going to go downstairs and tell him you were wrong and that you love him and you hope he'll forgive you. And then you're going to get rid of this place and go back where you belong."

She set the lamp down with a thump and got up from her chair. She hurried to her wardrobe. Her hands pushed aside the elegant gowns one by one. At the back of the wardrobe, she found just what she was looking for.

When she stepped to the top of the staircase that night—clad in snug buckskin trousers and her sky-blue blouse with the silver braiding, spurs jingling from her knee-high leather boots—the usual admiring stares turned to surprise. The saloon fell silent. Then there were a few appreciative comments, followed by several hearty cheers.

Alexis pushed the slouch hat back on her head and smiled. Then her gaze swung across the room to the poker table. Colter was on his feet. Their eyes locked in a long look of understanding.

Colter's lazy smile crept into the corners of his mouth. He tossed his cards onto the table. "I'm out," he said to the others. He met her midway on the stairs.

"Colt, I . . ." she began.

But his lips stopped her as he pulled her against him. She was only slightly aware of the laughter and cheers of their audience. Her senses were too filled with the feel of his lips and the warm strength of his arms. It seemed forever since she had allowed herself this pleasure. Her arms wrapped around his neck. As she pulled herself even closer to him, her hat was brushed off, and it tumbled down the stairs. Colter's hand pulled at the ribbon that tied her hair, setting the blonde tresses free to flow over her back and shoulders.

Breathless, she straightened as his lips released her. Her blue eyes were ablaze with feeling. There was so much she wanted to say.

"Perhaps we'd better save it for later," Colter whispered, his own eyes smoldering with checked emotions. He offered her his elbow and she took it.

They had taken only one step when the door of the saloon burst open and a man raced inside, waving a paper over his head.

"It's over! The war's over!" he cried. "General Lee has surrendered. It's over."

Men were on their feet and surging toward the door.

"Surrendered? The South wouldn't surrender."

"Where'd you hear it?"

"When?"

"Lee, you say? I knew he wasn't the right general."

Colter's arm went around Alexis' waist. "It's

over," he said. "Your father will be coming back."

"Colt," she whispered, "it would have been too late anyway."

He knew she was speaking of the gold. "It wouldn't have helped even a year ago, Alex."

Her eyes were stricken with guilt. "But you don't understand. I risked so much for nothing. You don't know what I risked. Not just my life but . . ." She bit her lower lip as she shook her head. "You'll never forgive me," she continued.

"You mean because of the baby?"

Tears swam before blue eyes. "You know about the baby? You've known all along?"

"I knew."

"And . . . and you still love me? Oh, Colt, I've been such a fool."

He laughed low in his throat. "I knew what I was getting when I married you." He drew her close again. "We're going back to the ranch. Isn't that what your clothes mean?"

She nodded.

"And the sooner the better," he said as he bent to kiss her once more.

Alexis snuggled beneath the quilt, enjoying the feeling of happiness that surrounded her. The past weeks had been heaven. She and Colter had never been closer. They had kept to themselves, relearning the joys of sharing all their hopes and dreams. Several days before, Colter had ridden down to the ranch. The house was finished and would be ready to occupy soon. She expected his return today.

There was only one thing left to tie them to Idaho City—the Ice Palace. Colter had told her to be sure she wanted to sell it before talking to Derek. She *was* sure, and she planned to see Derek that very afternoon, as soon as her husband returned. And if Derek didn't want it, she would sell it to the next man with a ten-dollar gold piece in his pocket. Then she and Colter would pack their things and return to the Circle S for good.

Her stomach growled and her smile widened. Her morning sickness was gone. Her appetite was its normally healthy self, and she was sleeping soundly again. Her whole world was brighter, now that her life was back in order.

"So help me, I'm never going to do anything foolish again," she told herself as she scooted up on the pillows at her back.

Once more her stomach rumbled. She laughed aloud as she tossed the covers back and reached for her robe. She pushed her tumbling blonde locks away from her face as she crossed the room to her wardrobe. She was tempted to wear her buckskins but decided against it. She had best appear businesslike when she struck her deal with Derek. With this in mind, she put on a plain white blouse and a rust-brown skirt. She pulled her hair back into a chignon, seeking a firm appearance. It didn't work. Her smile continued to light up her face.

She rang for her breakfast, then went into the parlor to await Mona's reply. As she sat on the white and silver brocade sofa, her thoughts slipped back to the first time she had seen this room. How vastly different her life was now than she had thought it would be then. Despite herself, she was married to the man she loved and—miracle of miracles—he loved her in return. She had made the transition from buckskin-clad girl to elegant woman and found she was the same person inside. The clothes only changed how others perceived her, not who she really was.

She got up from the sofa and wandered around the room, touching things as she moved by them, admiring their beauty, yet strangely aware that she wasn't going to miss them. This had been her home for the better part of a year. It surprised her how easy it was going to be to leave it for good. Already she was thinking of the Circle S as home. It was so easy for her to imagine their children playing outside the new ranch house. Colter would teach them to ride and to rope. She would teach them to read and to write. They would be good children, strong and honest and beautiful. Of course, they would all have their father's big brown eyes and that same lazy smile of his that both delighted and infuriated her.

Mona arrived with her breakfast tray, interrupting her pleasant musings. Alexis sat down at the large mahogany table in the dining room. As Mona placed the plate before her, she noticed a glitter of tears in the woman's eyes.

"Is something wrong, Mona?" she asked.

Mona straightened and sniffed. "No, Miss Alexis. Only, I've been thinking how much we're going to miss you and Mr. Stephens here."

"Thank you, Mona," Alexis replied, her gaze dropping to her plate. "I'm going to miss all of you, too."

The maid left, and as Alexis began eating, she thought of all the friends she had made in Idaho City. She was going to miss them, even though she was eager to be gone. Stella, of course. And Sam. She didn't know what she'd do without them. Then there were all the people who worked for her here at the Ice Palace—Rafe and Joe and Hank and Jessie, Rose and Gertie and Mona and even Mrs. Roberts, the cook. She smiled as she thought of Rachel Cane. The dressmaker would be horrified to know how Alexis looked forward to days spent in the saddle, clad once again in the dreadful buckskin trousers.

Her plate clean, Alexis pushed her chair back and resumed her idle wanderings around the suite, her mind collecting memories to savor. She was startled once again from her reminiscing by the opening door. She twirled around, a bright smile ready to greet Colter, but it was Althea who stood in the doorway. Alexis' initial disappointment turned to concern as she noted the distraught expression on her sister's face.

"Althea, what is it?" she said as she hurried across the room.

"Where's Colter?" Althea demanded.

"Colt? He's gone to the ranch. Why? What's wrong?"

Althea's eyes closed as she whispered, "I'm too late."

Alexis grabbed her sister by the shoulders.

"Althea!" She gave her a shake. "What are you saying? What's happened?"

"If only I could have remembered sooner. I thought he was taking care of me. I told myself I had no reason to be afraid. Then I heard him talking to that man, but I wouldn't believe what I heard. I told myself I'd misunderstood. So I did nothing. And then it came back. It all came back. But I still didn't want to believe it. I was afraid."

Again, Alexis shook her. "Althea, you're rambling. What are you trying to say?"

Althea opened her eyes, revealing undisguised agony. "Derek," she whispered. "Derek is going to kill Colter."

"But why?" She couldn't believe what she was hearing. Was Althea sick again? Did she know what she was saying?

"I don't know. He wants to get even with you. He wants to own the Palace."

Alexis tried to calm her racing heart. She took her sister by the elbow and led her across to the sofa. "Slowly now, Althea, I want you to tell me everything. You must tell me everything."

Titan's hooves beat a steady rhythm against the road as he cantered toward Idaho City. Astride the saddle, Colter whistled a merry tune, confident that nowhere in the world was there a man more blessed than he. A wife he loved. A child on the way. A fine home and a ranch to be proud of. What more could any man want?

The bullet that sliced through his hat, knocking it from his head, couldn't have been more unexpected.

Colter ducked low and dropped to the side of his saddle as he turned Titan toward cover. An outcropping of lava rock provided the shelter he was seeking. His eyes scanned the area for his assailant, his gun ready. Another shot rang out, the bullet ricocheting off the rock just to his left. Colter aimed his revolver in the direction the shot had come from, then waited for the man to show himself.

23

As Alexis listened to Althea's tale, a cold dread crept through her veins. Dear God, protect him, she prayed silently.

But a prayer wasn't enough. She had to do something. She jumped to her feet and hurried to her bedroom where she pulled out her trousers and boots. She threw off her skirt and dressed with haste. Then she reached for her long discarded revolver and holster.

"Alexis!"

She heard Althea's cry and turned to find the reason. She was staring into Derek's eyes, his gun leveled at Althea's head.

"Drop it," he said, his voice cool and confident.

She did.

"Now, move over to the bed. Nice and slow."

"Derek, what are you doing? There's no

reason for you to do this," she said as she obeyed.

"Shut up, Alexis," he replied, his voice hardening. "I have plenty of reasons."

Alexis glanced at Althea. Her sister's face was deathly pale. "Please, Derek. Let her go."

"In time. If you do what I say."

"What is it you want, Derek?"

Derek moved closer to the bed, pushing Althea before him. "Listen to me very carefully, Alexis. You're going to put on Althea's clothing and then you're coming with me. As my dear wife, Althea Anderson."

"But . . . You can't get away with this."

"I can and I will." He shoved Althea onto the bed. "Now, start undressing."

Everything inside her rebelled against disrobing in front of this man. He had planned to kill Colter. In fact, Colter might even be dead at this moment. She wanted to hit him, scratch out his eyes, shoot him. She wanted to scream. Anything but obey him.

Derek cocked his gun and aimed it at her chest. "Now."

She thought of Colter's baby. If Colter were dead, the baby was all she had left of him. She had to do whatever she could to protect it. As long as she was alive, there was a chance the baby would survive, too. With shaking fingers, she unbuttoned her blouse. She wouldn't look at him. She refused to see the satisfaction in his eyes. She numbed herself to his presence as she donned her sister's dress.

Derek backed across the room to the wardrobe and pulled out one of Alexis' nightgowns.

"Put this on," he ordered Althea as he tossed it into her lap. "Now, get under the covers." As she did his bidding, Derek poured a glass of water from the pitcher near the bed. He pulled a small packet from inside his coat and tore it open with his teeth. He poured the powder into the glass, stirring the mixture with his finger. Then he handed the glass to Althea. "Drink it."

Althea looked at Alexis with terror-filled eyes.

"Derek, what is it?" Alexis demanded.

"Don't worry. It's not going to kill her. It's merely to put her to sleep for a good, long time." He turned a hard glance on his wife. "And Althea, my dear, if you want to live, I suggest you pretend to be Alexis when you awaken." He grabbed Alexis by the arm and jerked her to her feet. "Remember, not only your life depends on it, but Alexis' life as well. Now drink."

As Derek waved the gun in her face, Althea swallowed the liquid. It wasn't long before her eyes fluttered closed and her breathing slowed.

"Come along, *Althea*," Derek said to Alexis. "It's time we were on our way. Your sister seems too tired for visitors. We'll come another time. I promise."

"What is it you plan to do to me?" Alexis asked softly as she glanced at the still figure in the bed.

"You'll see soon enough."

Colter looked down at the man's body. He didn't recognize him. As far as he knew, he had never seen him before. Colter had no idea why the dead man had been trying to kill him. But there was no doubt that killing him was his sole purpose for being there. It was clear the stranger had been lying in wait for him. Colter looked through the stranger's things for a clue to his identity but found nothing. At last, giving up, he saddled the horse he'd found tied in the trees and threw the body across it. Then he headed for Idaho City once again.

Derek's buggy was waiting outside the Ice Palace's private entrance. He helped Alexis up with one hand, his other still holding the gun. As soon as he was settled beside her, he hid the revolver beneath his coat.

"Why don't you drive, Althea, my dear?"

Alexis grabbed the reins. "Where are we going?" she asked.

"I think a drive would be nice. It's a lovely day. Let's take the Placerville road." As they pulled out of the alley, he added, "I think you should smile. After all, you are recovered from a nasty illness, and today you and your adoring husband are out to take a little sun. Folks should see your happiness."

Alexis forced herself to obey, nodding at people as they drove by. Derek's free arm was thrown around her shoulders, but she could feel the cold muzzle of the gun against her ribs, belying his casual pose. She knew they must look happy and carefree, just as Derek wanted. And all the while her mind was screaming for someone to recognize her. Someone to see that it was Alexis and not Althea riding with Derek. Someone to read the terror in her blue eyes.

A few miles outside of town, they turned off the main road. Minutes later, Derek guided her off the road altogether.

"Get down," he instructed.

Amongst the trees, two saddle horses awaited them. With a wave of his revolver, Derek indicated she was to mount up. Her hopes soared. She was a good horsewoman. Perhaps her chance to escape would come on the trail. But her hopes were dashed as he tied her hands to the pommel.

"Don't go getting any ideas," Alexis," Derek warned. "If I have to, I'll shoot you."

She believed him.

Mounted on his own horse and leading her horse behind him, Derek pushed through the underbrush until they reached an ill-marked trail. Alexis dropped her head, assuming a position of defeat, but her eyes were alert to the passing countryside. When she escaped, she must know how to get back to town in a hurry. Her life and the lives of others might depend on it. They rode up one hill and down another, turning first left and then right, moving through dense trees and along swollen creeks. Alexis grew hungry as the sun moved passed its zenith, but Derek showed no inclination toward stopping.

The sameness of the trail became almost hypnotizing. It was hard to keep her thoughts on where she was. Instead, she found herself thinking about Colter. Was he alive? Had he escaped the trap Derek had set for him?

"Tanner's an excellent shot."

She looked up at him, hating him for reading her mind. Her blue gaze was filled with loathing.

"Be careful, Alexis. You've scorned me once too often."

The cabin was up a narrow canyon, hidden by trees and dense brush and a stubborn layer of snow. Alexis didn't even see it until they were almost upon it. Derek hopped down from the saddle and tied the horses to a tree, then unlooped the leather thong tying Alexis' hands to the pommel and pulled her from the saddle. Her weary legs barely kept her upright.

"Better relieve yourself. You might not get another chance." He laughed at her shocked expression. "This time, I'll turn my back. But remember. My gun is ready."

She chose to obey, moving behind a bush at the side of the ramshackle cabin. She could see his back and wondered if she might be able to slip away. If she moved carefully . . .

He turned around. "That's enough time. Inside," he ordered with a wave of his gun. She had no choice.

The shack had been deserted for a long time. Thick dust covered everything and cobwebs filled the corners of the ceiling. Tiny footprints disturbed the dust, mountain animals laying claim to what man had left behind.

Derek unrolled a blanket that had been tied behind his saddle and threw it over a pile of straw. "Sit down."

He handed her a canteen and she took a long

drink. As she passed it back to him, she asked, "Derek, why are you doing this?"

"Because of the Ice Palace."

"But I was going to sell it to you. Colt and I were leaving. We were going to offer you the Palace this afternoon."

His face darkened. Suddenly, he grabbed her bound hands and hauled her to her feet. His fingers pinched her chin as he forced her to look at him. "The Palace isn't enough. That was all I wanted at first. That's what I wanted from Reckless but he wouldn't sell it to me. Stupid old man. If he'd sold it, he'd probably be alive today."

"You killed him?" she said, knowing it was true. "I was right about you, after all."

"He killed himself. Over that watch you gave him. Wouldn't let me have it. Said it was his real wealth. Fool. I could buy hundreds of watches just like it. It wasn't worth that much."

"He meant me," Alexis whispered, feeling again the pain of her friend's death. "He meant our friendship was his wealth. Oh, T.C., you should have given it to him."

Derek didn't hear her. "The Palace would've been enough until I saw you. I wanted you from the first moment I laid eyes on you. We could have been a pair, you and I. We could have ruled that town together. I offered it to you and you turned me away. Too good for me. I could see it in your eyes." He shoved her back onto the blanket, then stood over her. "Well, I'm going to have you," he said, his words threatening, his voice low. "I'm going to have you when I want and as often as I want."

"You can't keep me a prisoner here forever."

He smiled. "No, I can't. But I can keep you here as long as I need to. You'd better hope that's not long. You'll grow mighty hungry and thirsty if it is."

She was afraid to ask what he meant. She didn't need to. He seemed to take pleasure in detailing his plans for her.

"You see, Althea is going to pretend to be you. No one will be surprised that the new widow wants to sell her saloon."

Alexis flinched at the word *widow*.

"The papers will be brought to you for your signature, of course. Wainwright is too good an attorney not to check your signature. Once the papers are signed, the widow Stephens will leave Idaho City for good. Of course, she'll never be seen or heard from again."

"You'd kill your own wife?" Alexis whispered, her horror growing.

"But my wife will still be at my side," he answered, squatting on his heels to see her better. He reached out and stroked her hair. "You'll be at my side, won't you, Althea?"

She was appalled. "You don't think I'd stay, do you?"

"Poor Anderson. His wife is sick again, you know? The doctor doesn't know if she'll ever be out of bed again. Too bad. She's such a pretty thing." He grinned at her. "It's not a bad drug, my dear. It just takes away all your cares and worries. Of course, you won't be able to enjoy our nights together as much. It seems to dim your senses more than I would wish. But . . . it's the only way."

Drugs. He had drugged Althea. He would drug her. Alexis fought the panic rising in her breast. She had to keep a clear head. She must keep her wits about her. It was her only hope. She was dealing with a madman. But he was so clever. He had figured out so many details. If she didn't escape before he forced the drugs on her . . .

Derek stood up and walked outside. She held her breath, wondering if he was going to leave her now. Perhaps he had forgotten that there was nothing to keep her from escaping once he was gone. He returned with a rope, dashing her hopes once more. He tied her ankles together, then secured the rope to a log of the cabin wall, slipping the rope through chinks between the logs. Alexis watched with sinking spirits as he turned and bound her hands even tighter, pulling her arms over her head and tying the rope to the opposite wall. She lay stretched across the blanket-covered straw, helpless, defenseless.

Derek stepped back from his handiwork. "I think that'll keep you until I get back. Shouldn't be more than a day or two if you're lucky."

"But Derek . . ." she began to plead, but he turned his back to her and left the cabin, the door squeaking closed as he left.

Hot tears streaked her cheeks as she lay still, listening to the silence.

Colter left the sheriff's office and hurried on toward the Ice Palace. The warm May sun was already kissing the western skyline. Alexis would be wondering what had happened to him. He had promised her he would be back today.

He met Mona coming out of their suite, an untouched tray of food in her hands.

"Don't tell me her appetite's gone again," he said with a chuckle.

But Mona's look was not amused. "I'm a might worried, Mr. Stephens. She's been asleep all day. She went back to bed after her breakfast. I just checked on her to see if she wasn't hungry. She missed lunch, you see. And I couldn't get her to wake up."

Colter brushed on by her, not waiting for the rest of the maid's explanation.

The bedroom was cloaked in shadows. Colter rushed over to the bed. Alexis was lying on her back, her hair spread over the pillows, sooty lashes brushing pale cheeks.

"Alex," he whispered, touching her shoulder. When there was no response, he shook her gently, calling her name in a louder voice. "Alex." He heard footsteps behind him. "Light the lamp, Mona," he said, not looking behind him.

"Yes, sir."

"Alexis, wake up. Alexis?" He gathered her in his arms, holding her limp form against his chest. "What's wrong with her?"

A flicker of golden light danced along the wall, then the lamp flared, bathing the room in its comforting glow. Mona carried the lamp across the room and set it on the stand beside the bed as Colter gently lowered Alexis onto the pillow once more.

"Mona, you'd better get the doctor," he said.

But before the maid could leave the room, he called, "Wait! Mona, this isn't Alexis."

"Sir?"

"It's Althea."

Mona stepped back to the bed. "Sir, are you sure?" she asked, staring hard at the woman in the bed.

"I'm sure. Mona, something's happened here." He thought of the gunman waiting for him on the road to Idaho City. "Who was here today?"

"No one that I know of, Mr. Stephens. Your wife, and I'm sure it was her, took breakfast this morning and seemed to be feeling her former self. She had quite an appetite. Finished her breakfast. Every bit of it. When I came back for the tray, she had gone back to bed. There were clothes thrown everywhere, so I picked up a bit."

"Clothes? What clothes, Mona?"

"Well, there was those trousers of hers for one thing. And a white blouse and . . . let me think. It was her brown skirt."

Colter tried to find a clue in those facts, but it led him nowhere. "You'd better go for the doctor, Mona. Whatever's happened to Alexis, Althea will know. She must or she wouldn't be here."

"Shall I send for Mr. Anderson, too?" Mona asked.

Colter was thoughtful, finally answering, "No. Tell no one else for now."

"Yes, sir."

Colter stared at Althea. Yes, she looked like Alexis, but he could tell the difference. Alexis had a finer jaw line, a trimmer nose. Her brows had a different arch. Her hair was more the color of wheat while Althea's had a golden glow. Where was Alexis? Who was behind this? If someone had harmed Alexis, he would search the world until he made the person responsible pay for it.

Derek returned to town after dark, stabling his horses and unhitching his buggy himself. He ate a quick meal, a smug smile on his face throughout supper, then left for an evening at the Golden Gulch. Every time the door of the saloon swung open, he expected Tanner to walk in. Once he knew Colter was dead, he could put the rest of his scheme into action. Of course, he was counting on Althea's silence.

He checked his watch. She should be waking up any time now, but Derek was confident that she would keep to her bed, feigning illness. She would be sufficiently frightened to hold her tongue until she knew what it was he wanted her to do.

It was only chance that brought him close to the faro table in time to overhear the two men discussing the shootout that had happened south of town earlier in the day. His pleased smile faded as he heard one man tell the other that Colter Stephens had brought the dead man into town for identification.

Damn! he thought, cursing Tanner for failing.

But Derek had no intention of failing, too, despite Tanner's ineptness. He would have to consider his other options. Nothing was going to stop him from owning the Palace—and the Ice Queen herself—but it was clear he was going to have to go about it differently than he had originally planned.

Colter didn't know what to do. He wanted to be out searching for Alexis, but he didn't know where to look. So he sat at Althea's bedside, watching her sleep, and waited into the night.

He was dozing when Althea's eyes fluttered open. "Colter?" she whispered in disbelief. "Is it you?"

Instantly he was awake and leaning close to the bed. "Althea, what's happened? Where's Alexis?"

"He's taken her."

"Who? Who's taken her?"

Althea rubbed her temples, her eyes falling shut for a moment as if to blank out the memory.

"Althea, please," Colter said as he took her hand. "Tell me what you can."

She opened her eyes. "Derek sent a man to kill you."

"Derek." He wouldn't have suspected him, but once Althea said his name, he wasn't surprised either. "His man failed," he told his sister-in-law. "Now tell me what happened here. We've got to find Alexis."

"You were supposed to die today. Then I was to pretend to be Alexis. That's all I know for certain. I came to warn Alexis, but he must have seen me and followed. He made me dress in her nightgown and drink something to put me to sleep. He had her wear my clothes so people would think she was me."

"Do you have any idea where he's taken her?"

Althea shook her head. "None."

Colter felt even more helpless than before. He knew who had taken Alexis but not where. And from the looks of things, he wouldn't hesitate to kill her if Colter brought in the sheriff. For now, Derek held all the cards. Colter would have to wait for his next move.

Alexis shivered in the cold night air. If only she could draw her knees up to her chest and hug herself, she thought she would feel warmer, but trussed up as she was, there was no way to escape the cold. She continued to work at the ropes and leather thongs which bound her wrists and ankles. She had torn the skin on her wrists, and she could feel a trickle of blood running down her arm. Still, she pulled and sawed at her bindings. There was no time to waste. She didn't know when Derek would return. She must be free before then. She must get loose.

Derek walked boldly up the stairs of the Ice Palace and knocked on the door to the Stephens' private suite. Colter himself opened the door and ushered him inside. Althea was sitting on the sofa in the parlor. He noted the widening of her eyes and the loss of color from her cheeks. He nodded toward her, then turned to face Colter.

"You know why I've come?" he asked.

"I'm sure you're going to tell me," Colter responded.

Derek wore a smug expression as he walked around the edge of the parlor. "I've wanted to own this place almost since the first stone was in place. Now it's going to be mine."

"Where's Alexis?" Colter demanded.

Derek shook his head and clucked his tongue. "All in good time, Mr. Stephens. All in good time. You see, before you're going to see your wife again, I mean to have the deed to this fine property, all nice and legal. Now, as I'm the only living soul who knows where she is, I can assure you she will die if I do not release her. Therefore, nothing must happen to me. Do I make myself clear?"

"You do."

"Then here's what I propose." He sat down on the chair near Althea and placed his hat on his knee. "It would have been better if Tanner had been a better shot than you, Colter, but I think this will work. I want witnesses to my obtaining the Palace. That way, there'll be no questions later, nobody wondering if there was some unusual reason that the Ice Queen sold her Palace to me. Once it's mine, you'll leave here. You do what I say and I'll return Alexis to you, unharmed. Cross me and she's dead." He looked at Althea. "Althea will fill in for the Ice Queen in her absence. You will need to be convincing, my dear. No one must doubt that you are Alexis herself."

Colter schooled his features to reveal none of his inner turmoil. He knew Derek would never let anyone survive who knew the truth. But he had no choice but to agree with his plans. He had to have time to find Alexis. Once she was safe, he could deal with Derek. But there was so little time. Each minute that went by pulled them closer to disaster.

"Just what do you mean by witnesses?" Colter asked as he leaned against the wall, assuming a relaxed stance that belied his taut nerves.

"We'll have a friendly little poker game which you will, unfortunately, lose. You will lose so badly, in fact, that you will wager the Ice Palace, trying to win back your losses. Of course, your loving wife will consent to your wager, certain that you could never fail her in this way. But, I'm afraid your luck won't change. You will lose that hand, too." Derek grinned and got to his feet, placing his hat back on his head. "The signed deed turned over to me, you and your wife here will pack your things and leave town, never to be seen here again. If there's no trouble, I will release Alexis in a few days."

"Do you really think you can get away with this?" Colter asked, his voice hardened by tension.

Derek laughed sharply. "I do. Do you know why? Because you love that wife of yours and you'd do anything to save her pretty little neck." He walked toward the door. "I'll see you at the poker table. Tomorrow night. And, Stephens," he added, "don't try to find her. She'll pay for it if you do."

The cabin didn't warm with the coming of day. Exhausted and shivering, Alexis slept fitfully for a short time. Upon awakening, she began to tug and saw at her ropes once more. Her wrists and ankles screamed with pain, but she was dauntless. She must be gone before Derek returned. *If* he returned . . . She tried not to think of that possibility. Could it mean he had left her here to suffer a slow death of starvation? What would be worse? That, or the prospect of his returning?

Perhaps it was the thought of him returning to use her as he'd suggested that gave her the extra burst of strength. Her arms flew forward, still tied together, but she had gained some freedom. At first she could only lie there and try to regain some normal feelings in her limbs. But she wasted little time. She sat up and reached for her ankles. Her bound wrists made it difficult to work with the knotted rope, but finally, her legs were free. Her body ached and protested as she got up from the straw mattress. She shook her legs, stretching her tired muscles and ignoring the pain of her open sores. She went to the door and looked cautiously outside, praying that Derek had no one watching the cabin for her escape. There was only the sound of silence to greet her.

Quickly, she moved from the cabin and into the forest, staying away from the trail they had followed into the canyon. Once she felt she was out of immediate danger of discovery should Derek return, she took a moment to relieve her protesting bladder, but she had to ignore her growling stomach.

She looked up at the sky. She had about eight

or nine hours of daylight left. She guessed the ride in had taken more than six. Now she was on foot. She couldn't make it before dark, even if she had no problems in finding her way back, which she couldn't be sure of. She glanced down at Althea's delicate shoes. They certainly weren't going to help matters.

But they were all she had and there was no time to lose. With determination, Alexis started walking.

"He's mad, Sam. There's no telling what he might do. If he thinks I've told anyone, he might..." Colter's voice broke and he moved across the room, his back toward Sam.

"I'll help all I can, Colt. You know that. But do you have any idea where I should look? Are you sure she isn't up at his house?"

Colter turned around. "I can't be sure of anything," he replied as he ran his hands through his hair. He felt helpless. The waiting was killing him. If only he knew where she was. "I... I told Rafe what was happening. He was on his way here yesterday morning and saw Derek and who he thought was Althea headed out of town toward Placerville. That's all I can tell you."

"Well, it's a start. Are you sure you shouldn't go with me? I'm not much of a tracker."

"I can't, Sam, or I'd be out there right now. He's told me not to look for her. He's sure to be watching me to see what I do."

Sam walked across the room and placed a hand on Colter's shoulder. "Don't worry, my friend. I'll find her. She means a lot to me, too."

Colter nodded but couldn't speak.

Alexis slipped and tumbled down the side of the hill. Unable to break her fall with her bound hands, she rolled and bounced without protection until she hit the bottom of the gully with a jolt. She lay still a moment, cursing herself for being careless. Then she pushed herself up. Her arms were bruised and her right ankle throbbed. Her hair was tangled with pine needles and brambles and traces of snow. Her face was smudged with dirt.

Tears threatened, but she blinked them angrily away. She wasn't going to cry. She wasn't going to give in. She had to keep going. She mustn't despair. Her baby depended on her. She must be more careful, but she must go on.

She stood and tested her sore ankle. She grimaced as shards of pain shot up her leg, but she took that first step and then another, climbing back up the hill to regain the ground she had lost. She began working again at the leather thong, determined to be rid of it, once and for all. As she reached the crest, her foot slipped out from under her again, and she nearly fell.

"That does it," she whispered as she sat down. "I'll be better off barefoot."

She removed the fancy slippers. She started to toss them down the hill but thought better of it. If Derek did come looking for her, she didn't want to leave him any clues. She would have to carry them.

Again the tears surfaced, this time escaping

her eyes to streak their way down her cheeks. "Colt," she whispered, laying her face against her knees. "What am I to do?"

She allowed herself a few minutes of feeling frightened and lonely. Then she sniffed back the tears and wiped her eyes. Sticking her chin out in stubborn determination, she got up from the ground. She glanced at the sky. She hadn't much time left. Shadows were lengthening, and soon she would have to take shelter for the night. She stuck the shoes under one arm and began walking, her feet already numb with cold.

"Althea, I want you to come down with me tonight. We've got to let Derek think his plans are going just as he wants them."

Althea looked up at Colter. She was seated in the dining room, her hands folded before her on the table. "I don't know if I can do it," she answered, her voice quavering.

"You've got to do it." Colter leaned across the table. "Please, Althea. It could mean her life."

Althea swallowed. "I don't know if you'll believe me, Colter, but I want to save her as much as you do. Oh, this is all my fault." Her head dropped to her arms as she began sobbing.

Colter came around the table and sat beside her. He put his arms around her and drew her against his chest. He dared not speak. The lump in his throat was too large.

Althea looked up at him, sniffing back the tears. "I hated you both, and I had no reason to. You were so good to me. Always."

"Shhh," he whispered.

"No, Colter. I must say it." She drew free of his comforting arms. "You never wanted to marry me. I maneuvered you into proposing because my mother wanted you for Willowind: It never would have worked for either of us. But then, when you were so happy with Alexis, I felt cheated. I always thought I deserved so much. If I hadn't been so greedy . . ."

"You couldn't have known about Derek. None of us knew."

"Didn't we?" Althea responded, speaking mostly to herself. "I wonder."

Colter stood up abruptly, almost knocking the chair over as he strode out of the dining room. He punched his fist into the palm of his other hand, cursing himself in silence. *He* should have known. Alexis didn't trust Derek, but he kept telling her they had no proof. Well, now he had proof and it might be too late for Alexis.

He pushed aside the drapes in the parlor, glaring down at the Golden Gulch across the street. Was he in there right now? Was he playing a game of cards without a thought for the woman he held prisoner? Or was he with Alexis? He slammed his fist into the window frame in frustration and rage.

"Alexis." Her name was a tortured whisper on his lips.

Althea's hand touched his back. "Sam will find her in time. I know he will."

"If anything happens to her, I'll tear him limb from limb with my bare hands. So help me God, he'll never be safe from me if he runs to the edge of the earth."

24

Alexis opened her eyes and looked about her. The canopy over her head was made of pine needles, as was the mattress beneath her. For a moment, she was confused. Then she became aware of other things. Her teeth were chattering from the cold. She was shivering uncontrollably. Her twisted ankle throbbed painfully as did the raw sores on her wrists. The physical realities cleared away her confusion, and she was forced to remember.

She closed her eyes again, whispering his name. "Colt."

It was easier to endure her physical pain than the ache that gnawed at her heart. All night long, memories of him had drifted through her mind, their presence a bittersweet reminder of what she feared might be lost to her forever. Derek's hired gun had been lying in wait for him.

Could Colter have had a chance against such odds? She prayed he had but feared the worst.

Why now? Now that they had put all their silly disagreements behind them? When they were finally going to do what they should have done long ago? Now that she was carrying his child, the son who would one day own the Circle S and make it an even greater ranch than his father before him?

"Please, Colt. Don't be dead," she whispered as she got to her feet. "I don't want to live without you."

Alexis brushed the pine needles from her wrinkled skirt, swallowing the lump that threatened to form in her throat. She didn't have the time to feel sorry for herself. It was daylight again, and time to travel. She had to get back to Idaho City before Derek killed someone else.

"No. Not someone *else*. Someone."

She wouldn't let herself think of Colter as dead. She would believe that he survived. Perhaps her very thoughts, her very wishes, would keep him alive.

She started walking again, her progress slowed by her injured ankle and bare feet.

Several hours later, she was lying on her stomach, drinking from the stream. Something—instinct, perhaps—made her stop and listen. Above the sound of the rushing water, she heard men's voices drifting toward her. Caution spurred her into a thicket on the edge of the hillside, the only shelter nearby.

Through the branches, she could see the two men as they came into view, leading their mules along the creek on the opposite bank. They paused directly across from her, passed a few words between them, then began to make a fire and prepare what seemed to be their midday meal. It didn't take her much time to assess their character and know she was better off staying hidden. These were the kind of men who would take advantage of her circumstances. Even promises of a reward would not help her. She would have to sit still and wait for them to move on. Her only hope was that their repast would be a quick one.

The smoke from their cookfire was carried across to her on a gentle breeze. The smell of food made her stomach growl. Alexis pressed her hand against her abdomen, ordering her body to be silent, the rumbling noise seeming loud enough to alert the men to her presence. Her muscles tensed, and she longed to be able to stretch but dared not move.

Not knowing how precious the hours of this day were to Alexis, the sun continued its trek across the sky, dipping into afternoon.

Sam had been all the way to Placerville yesterday. Now, as he returned to Idaho City, he was traveling as many trails as he could find, looking for some sort of clue. Even as he tried, he believed it was useless. What did he, a city-bred lawyer, know about tracking? What's more, he didn't know what he was looking for—buggy tracks, hoof prints, what?

Once more he turned off the main road, this time following a creek. If he didn't find something soon, he would have to make camp or try to ride back to Idaho City in the dark. Neither possibility was very inviting. He followed the creek for nearly an hour before he was ready to turn back. As he stopped, he caught a whiff of a campfire.

"Better check it out," he said aloud.

The cloak of darkness was settling over the mountains. In a matter of moments, Alexis would be able to creep from her cramped hiding spot. Several times during the afternoon, she had been tempted to announce her presence and ask for help, but her better judgment had prevailed. She had hoped the men would leave their camp for just a few minutes, giving her a chance to escape, but they seemed content to spend all day sitting around the fire.

Alexis was aware of the approaching horse even before the two men across from her. She moved aside the thick branches and stared across the stream, wishing back the daylight.

"Hello," the shadow on horseback called, announcing himself.

The two men were on their feet at once.

"Sorry to ride up on you this way. I'm looking for a friend of mine, but I seem to be lost. I'm not sure if she's up this way or not. Can you help me?"

Sam. It was Sam!

"Don't know this area," one of the men answered. "We're new around these parts."

"A woman, you say?" the other one asked. "Alone?"

"I'm not sure if she'd be alone or not," Sam answered.

He was looking for her. She moved carefully from behind the thicket, trying to remain unseen as long as possible. She hadn't liked the way the man had asked if she would be alone. She reached the stream before she called to him through the darkness.

"Sam! I'm over here."

She stepped into the icy water, holding her skirts above her knees as she fought her way across, trying to keep her balance. She paused as she reached the bank, thankful she had made it without falling.

"Alexis." There was relief in Sam's voice. "You all right?"

"I'm fine, Sam."

She glanced at the two strangers. The flickering campfire threw dancing fingers of yellow light over their faces, enough for Alexis to read the danger in their eyes. She prayed Sam was ready for trouble.

Deciding the best defense was a strong offense, she headed straight for them. "I can't imagine running into you here, Sam. I've been walking along the creek for hours. I stop to take a rest and there you are."

"Right pretty thing, aren't you?" the man closest to her said.

The other one started to step forward but the cocking of Sam's gun stopped him cold.

"Don't move," Sam uttered.

"Now, ain't a gun a bit unfriendly?" the fellow nearest Alexis asked. His hand darted forward to grab her arm. "Why don't you put that gun away?" he said to Sam as he yanked her toward him. "We don't aim to hurt her none. Just have a bit of fun. Wasn't that what you were lookin' for her for anyhow?"

Before Sam could decide what to do, Alexis drew her free arm back and rammed her elbow into his ample belly with a strength that surprised even her, especially after two days without food. He grunted in surprise and let go. She had no real hope of being able to get out of his reach in time, and she wasn't sure just how fast Sam would be able to react. With a split-second decision, she grabbed the frying pan lying on a rock near the fire and swung it around, catching her pursuer alongside the head. The hollow thunk of iron pan against skull was a sickening sound. The fellow crashed to the ground in a heap.

Alexis was stunned. It had all happened so fast. The heavy frying pan dropped to the ground as she turned toward Sam. He was still holding his gun on the other man, but he was wearing a weary grin.

"Nice work, Alexis. Care for a ride back home?"

"I'd love one," she answered, her voice shaking.

"Come on then. This fellow needs to take care of his friend, and we don't want to be in his way."

Alexis gathered her skirts and hurried across the camp. She put her foot in the stirrup, but Sam had to help her up behind the saddle. She didn't have enough energy left in her arms to do it herself. Sam turned the horse quickly and cantered off into the night. Alexis leaned against him, her arms wrapped tightly around his waist.

"How did you find me?" she asked once they had gained a safe distance.

"Chance," he replied, slowing the horse's pace a little.

She was afraid to ask the next question. "Colt?"

"He's worried sick about you."

"Thank God," she said breathlessly. "He's all right then. He wasn't shot. Is he looking for me too?"

"No, he had to send me, and believe me, I was a poor choice."

"Why, Sam? What's happening?"

"I'll tell you what I know," he replied, "but we've got to hurry back to town."

People were packed into the Ice Palace, but there was only one table seeing any action. A smoky haze hung in the air. For such a crowd, there was little noise, everyone straining to see and hear what would happen next.

Colter was wearing his black suit, his hat pushed casually back on his head. He studied his cards with nonchalance, ignoring the breathless hush that gripped the room or the rich pot that lay in the middle of the table.

They had been playing for hours, he and Derek, and word had spread fast that this was a grudge match of some sort. Only a few people in the room knew the whole truth. He glanced toward Althea. She was standing off to his left, wearing an elegant gown of blue and silver. She was doing a remarkable job of steeling her features, revealing none of the turmoil he knew she felt. He was confident that no one had guessed her true identity. She refused to speak to anyone, shaking her head when spoken to.

Colter looked back across the table at Derek. His opponent's hazel eyes burned with a fierce light. Derek wanted to win this game. Oh, it was fixed. Colter had to throw the game to save Alexis, but Colter also knew Derek wanted to win this game on his own. So far, Colter had frustrated him again and again. Soon, however, he would have to lose and lose big. He didn't think Derek could stand many more delays.

A slow smile spread across Colter's face. He wasn't ready to throw the game yet.

"Four queens," he said as he laid down his cards. The room erupted in cheers as Colter pulled his winnings toward him. "How about a break?" he asked Derek in a low voice.

"You're pushing me," Derek replied.

"A break would do us both good," Colter countered. "You're playing will probably improve after a drink and a good stretch."

Derek glowered. "It better."

Colter slid his chair back and stood up. "Drinks on the house," he cried.

His announcement was followed by a surge toward the bar, sending Rafe and Joe scurrying to beat the customers there.

"Come on, Alexis," Colter said as he took Althea by the arm. "Let's you and me take a break, too." He steered her toward the stairs.

"What are you doing?" Althea whispered anxiously as they climbed the staircase. "I thought Derek had to win this game?"

"He does. But he's never beat me before. I thought I'd better be convincing." His voice was artificially carefree, but it became serious as he continued. "Besides, I want to give Sam all the time I can."

Althea's hand touched his arm. "He hasn't got much of a chance, Colter. You know that."

"I know that," he echoed.

"Do you think she's . . ."

"No," he answered before she could finish. "I think he's kept her alive this long. But I do think he plans to get rid of all of us once he owns the Palace."

"But . . ."

"Don't worry, Althea. It's Derek Anderson who has to be afraid for his life." He ground out each word in suppressed rage. "He has taken my wife, and I mean to see him pay."

Althea watched in silence, her face pale.

"We'd better go back down." He took her once more by the arm. "I've asked Rafe to bring me a bottle of watered-down whiskey. I want you to hang onto that bottle. Don't let anyone drink from it but me. Just keep filling my glass. That way, it will look like I'm losing 'cause I'm drinking too much. Once I say I'll wager the Palace, everyone's going to look to you for confirmation. Can you carry it off?"

"I have to, don't I?" she replied, her eyes frightened.

"Yes, Althea. You have to."

It was about 9:00 at night. Derek was waiting for them at the table. As soon as Althea and Colter returned to the gambling hall, the crowd moved back around the table, everyone jostling for a better view as the game resumed. Colter made only small mistakes at first, but his drinking was noticeable. He still took a hand now and then, causing Derek to glower at him in muted fury. When Colter lost, however, his losses were sizable. His previous winnings dwindled. Perspiration beaded his forehead. His voice grew louder and gruff.

"I don't like the way you play," he muttered, tossing another losing hand onto the table. He reached for his glass and shoved it toward Althea. "Pour me another drink."

"Colter, do you think you . . ."

"Pour it, woman."

He could feel the tension rippling through the crowd. No one should speak to the Ice Queen in that tone. Not even her husband. He was becoming less popular in a hurry.

The minutes ticked by, taking with them all the money in front of Colter. He glanced around him, then swilled another glass of whiskey.

"One more hand, Anderson." He leaned across the table, staring straight into Derek's eyes. "Winner take all."

The room was hushed.

Derek pulled at his cuffs before answering. "Take what, Stephens? You have nothing left. Do you think I'd risk my winnings for nothing?"

"Nothing?" Colter turned to look at Althea, then back at Derek. "I've got something you want. I'll put up the Ice Palace."

Ripples of surprise spread across the room. All eyes turned toward Althea, including Colter's. He prayed she could play her part in this drama.

She gazed back at him, her expression remote, her eyes cold. Colter wondered at how he could see so many differences between these sisters, yet no one else seemed to guess. Still, she was doing a good job of mimicking Alexis' role as Ice Queen, her frigid glare convincing everyone as she nodded her consent.

"You see?" Colter said to Derek in a boisterous voice. "The Palace against all your winnings. Winner take all."

Derek smiled, saying loudly, "I have witnesses, Stephens. This hand is for the Ice Palace. And one more condition."

Colter lifted an eyebrow, wondering what his trick would be.

"If I win, you and your wife leave Idaho City and let me run the Palace without your interference in anyway. Go back to that ranch of yours. Agreed?"

He wasn't quite sure what that was all about, but he was sure it meant something. "Agreed."

"Then, if you'll get a new deck, I think we can start this game. Don't you?"

"Deal, Anderson."

"He's insane, Sam," Alexis said as her rescuer finished his story. "No one is safe as long as he's around." She shuddered as she remembered his threats of keeping her hostage to use as he pleased.

Sam pressed the horse as hard as he could in the dark. It seemed to take them forever to return to the main road, and even then they couldn't move fast enough toward Idaho City to satisfy either one of them.

Alexis had never seen anything more beautiful than the glow of lights pouring from the many saloons and gambling houses. Sam's horse trotted down Montgomery Street, stopping in front of the Ice Palace. Alexis slid to the ground, expecting to rush right inside, but she discovered her legs planned otherwise as they began to buckle beneath her. She grabbed for the hitching post to steady herself.

"Alexis?" Sam cried.

She lifted a hand. "I'm fine."

She took a deep breath and brushed at her skirt. Then she rubbed her hands across her cheeks, knowing how dirty they must be. She would like to march into Derek's presence looking as if nothing had happened, but she didn't have the time for that.

She stepped into the doorway and felt at once the fever-high tension that gripped the room. All eyes were glued on the action at one table, and she knew what was at the center of it all. Deftly, she began to work her way through the crowd. Even then, no one seemed to notice or recognize her. Their thoughts were too preoccupied with the high-stakes game in progress.

Finally, she slipped from behind the last spectator standing between herself and the poker table. She found herself behind Derek's chair. Her eyes fell instantly upon Colter. She saw his gaze lift from his cards, glancing first at Derek, then raising further. The corners of his mouth quivered, as if he were fighting a smile, when his eyes met with hers. He gave her a slight shake of his head, and she knew she should keep silent.

"Well, Anderson, this is it," he said.

"Indeed it is, Stephens."

Now he smiled. "I believe you're in for a surprise." He paused for effect, then laid down his royal flush. "I believe the winnings are mine."

Derek's chair tipped over as he jumped to his feet. "You'll regret this, Stephens," he hissed, his face turning beet red. He whirled around . . . and stopped. "You?"

"It's me, Derek. I'm here and you've lost." She spoke with a strength she didn't feel. All she wanted was to reach the safety of Colter's arms, but first she had to face down her foe. "You've lost it all."

She saw him move as if to strike her, but reason asserted itself in time, and his arm dropped to his side in impotent rage. He stepped around her. The crowd parted before him, puzzled murmurings rising in a steady hum. Alexis didn't even watch him go. She was headed around the table, ignoring the confused and staring eyes of all the men around them. She cared about only one thing. Reaching her husband.

Colter's arms reached out, and his hands

gripped her shoulders as his eyes devoured her. With one finger, he traced her cheek and chin. He rubbed gently at the dirt on her face, then pulled a piece of straw from her hair. Each action was an expression of love.

She fought the tears that welled up in her eyes. "Colt," she whispered. "Oh, Colt."

His arms pulled her against him. "Thank God," he breathed. "I was so afraid I'd lost you."

"Colt," she said into his chest. There were no words to tell him how she felt.

"Hey, everyone! There's a fire at Nell's and it's spreading fast. We need help!"

The saloon emptied in a rush—even Althea was gone—leaving the two lovers still embracing.

"Alex?"

She looked up at him.

"Are you all right? Did he hurt you?"

She shook her head. "No. Not really. But I . . . I don't want to talk about it now. I just want you to hold me." She buried her face in his chest as he ran his fingers through her tangled hair. "He told me you were dead," she said, her voice catching.

"He tried."

"I wanted to die too. But there was the baby to live for. He was all I had left if you were gone."

With a gentle touch, he lifted her chin and lowered his lips to hers, brushing them so lightly, so tenderly, she could scarcely feel them. Tiny shivers ran the length of her, and again she choked back a sob.

"You're a pair of fools."

Colter stiffened and Alexis gasped. She turned toward the door, Colter's arm still tight around her shoulders, and stared into Derek's gun.

There was a crazed glow in his eyes. "Did you think you could get away with this? Did you think you could do this to me in front of the whole town? I'm going to have the Palace. No one is going to keep me from it any longer. It's mine."

"You're right, Derek," Alexis said. Her voice shook. She cleared her throat and swallowed the fear. Louder, her voice now steady, she said, "It's yours. I'm giving it to you. Colt and I are leaving Idaho, just as you wanted."

His face reddened. "Do you think you can fool me again? I'll not be played a fool. I'm a man of means in this town. People look up to me. I *own* this town."

"Then you must own the Palace, too," Colter said, his arm slowly drawing Alexis behind him.

Derek cocked his gun. "Don't move!" he shouted. "You're not going to take her from me. The Palace needs its Queen. I've seen that. She stays, but you must go, Stephens."

Everything happened so fast. The door burst open and Sam ran in, yelling that the fire was spreading and had nearly reached them. Wild-eyed, Derek fired his gun. Alexis had seen what he was going to do. She pushed herself in front of Colter. The bullet tore through the sleeve of her dress. Her shoulder burned. Blackness rose from the floor to swallow her, but Colter's arms saved her from the abyss.

"Colt," she whispered.

His face and Sam's swam above her.

"It's only a flesh wound. Get her out of here, Sam. I'm going after Anderson."

Alexis pinched Sam's arm. "Stop him, Sam!"

But it was too late. Colter was already out the door.

"Come on, Alexis. We've got to get out of here. This whole town is going up in flames." He helped her to her feet.

She held onto her bleeding shoulder, ignoring the pain, as he hurried her toward the door. Her eyes were met by a terrifying sight. The world had turned into an inferno. Yellow-orange tongues leapt above the buildings, licking the clouds, then returned to consume another mouthful of pine board and pitch.

Althea met them just outside. "Sam! Alexis! I saw Colter chasing Derek into the Gulch. What are we to do?"

Alexis looked across the street. The Golden Gulch was engulfed in fire, great flaming sheets dancing from the roof of the saloon. "Colt!" she screamed as she tried to pull free of Sam's arms, but he held on tight. "Let me go! Let me go!"

"There's nothing you can do, Alexis. Come on. I've got to get you out of here," he yelled above the roar of the fire.

She struggled against him, but it was no use. He towed her down the street, their way lit by the fire that was sweeping away their city. As he turned the corner on Commercial, she looked back in time to see the Golden Gulch falling in upon itself. She stopped fighting him, no longer caring where he took her.

They took refuge on East Hill near St. Joseph's Catholic Church. Stella was there with Greta, and the young mother pulled Alexis into her arms as if she, too, were a child. Then they sat on the ground, watching helplessly.

A wind blew the flames onward. Businessmen scurried before the fire, trying to save what they could before everything they had worked for was taken from them. The fire gained strength as it swept along Main and Montgomery, devouring every building before it—the Wells Fargo Express Office, the Idaho Saloon, Taylor's Exchange, the City Hotel, Magnolia Hall, Harris's Drugstore, Donahue Bakery, the Umatilla Market. With unquenchable ferocity, it raged through Mix's Drugstore, Charlton and Langworthy's Brokers' office, Fred Bell's Saloon, the Washoe Saloon, Peff's Bakery, and Grans and Brothers Bowling Saloon. The Forrest Theatre's production of "Romeo and Juliet" had ended abruptly, and the Montagues and Capulets fled the stage for the relative safety of East Hill. Soon, the magnificent theatre was floating in flaming brands through the air. The fire lit up the sky for miles around, making it seem as if daylight had returned hours ahead of schedule. From throughout the basin, miners rushed toward town, many of them to loot and plunder what the businessmen could not save.

Alexis watched as forked tongues kissed the cloudy sky overhead. Dense, black smoke rolled in streams through the basin. The whole city from bank to bank was an inferno of boiling flames. And somewhere within the devastation was Colter.

An icy shower sprang up, checking the flames short of Wallula Street. But it was too late. By midnight, except for a few buildings around the edge of town marking where the city had stood, everything was gone. In two short hours, fire had leveled one of the most flourishing mining towns ever built west of the Rocky Mountains.

By the dim light of morning, the survivors surveyed the dreary, smoking mess that had been their town. Women, their faces mirroring tragedy, clutched their tiny ones to their breasts. Men built campfires and began organizing the job of cleaning up the smoldering rubble. Montagues and Capulets, in costumes singed and soaked, cooked breakfast in a can.

One by one, men descended the hill and wandered into the burned district, looking among the bed of hot ashes and cinders for the remains of what had once been their shops and homes. There was a look of devastation in their eyes to match the world around them. Many of them had been worth thousands of dollars when they sat down to breakfast the previous morning. This morning they were ruined.

In a daze, Alexis moved down what had been Montgomery Street. Sometime in the night, the doctor had bandaged her shoulder, but she was unaware of the throbbing pain that persisted. It was nothing compared to the torment in her heart.

All that remained of the Ice Palace was the

stone front. Like a skeleton, it loomed above the smoking ashes, a silent reminder of what had been. But it wasn't the Ice Palace that drew her eyes. Instead, she turned toward where the Golden Gulch had stood. There was nothing left. Nothing. Her heart felt like lead. If it had stopped beating, she couldn't have felt more dead inside. Tears fell unchecked down her smoke-smudged cheeks. She turned away and walked toward the Palace. The glass lettering was gone above the gaping doorways. She remembered the day she had first seem them. They had glittered like diamonds. She had thought this the most beautiful building she had ever seen.

But she'd been wrong. The most beautiful building was the tiny cabin at the Circle S, and if she had allowed them to return there after they were married, Colter would still be alive.

A sob tore at her throat, and she placed a hand on the stone wall to steady herself. The wall was still warm, holding the heat that had broiled around it during the night. In frustration and anguish, she began to hit the wall with her open hand.

"Damn you! Damn you! Damn you!" she cried, cursing the wall as if it were at fault for her loss. Then she sank to the ground and hid her face in the folds of her ragged skirt as she pulled her knees up to her chest.

She had no idea how long she sat there, crying and wishing. If only . . . If only . . . Those two words drifted through her mind again and again, increasing her sorrow tenfold. If only . . .

At last, her tears spent, she raised her head, knowing that she would never be the same. While Derek had held her prisoner, she had still believed that Colter was alive. When she and Colter were separated by her own foolish stubbornness and pride, she had still believed that their love would triumph. Now, there was no hope. It was all gone. There was nothing more to believe in.

She got up from the ashes, one foot moving in front of the other by instinct, leading her back through the devastation toward East Hill. She looked into the faces of those she met in the streets, seeing her own helplessness mirrored in their eyes. So much despair.

She stopped, fighting tears once again. She refused to cry anymore. Tears wouldn't bring him back. She wouldn't cry. She wouldn't.

And then she saw him hurrying toward her from the far end of the street. His black suit was turned gray with soot. His head was wrapped in a bandage. But it was him. It couldn't be, but it was. She started running, and now she didn't care if she cried.

"Colt. Colt. Colt."

He caught her up and held her close. "It's over," he whispered in her ear. "This time, it's really over."

EPILOGUE

Dusk was settling over the ranch, bringing with it a gentle silence, disturbed only by the occasional lowing of the cattle. Alexis, clad in her trousers and fitted shirt, the heels of her boots resting against the rails, sat on the fence and whistled. Lucky perked her ears forward and nickered, then tossed her head as she cantered across the pasture, sliding to a halt in front of Alexis. Alexis hopped down from the fence, carefully cradling the baby in her left arm.

"Evening, Lucky," she said, scratching the horse behind her ears. "And how's the family?"

As if she understood, Lucky craned her neck to the side and whinnied. A young colt on spindly legs peeked at Alexis from behind the black mare. Alexis laughed, and he ducked back into hiding.

"Not very friendly, is he?" she said.

Lucky poked at the infant in Alexis' arms with her muzzle, as if trying to make up for her own offspring's shyness.

"Crystal is fine, thank you." She pulled the light blanket back from her daughter's face. Bright blue eyes stared back up at her. She kissed the blonde fuzz on the baby's head. "Have you ever seen such a beautiful little girl?"

Lucky nickered obligingly.

Alexis lifted her eyes across the fields. She could see the horses galloping toward the ranch. She raised her free arm and waved, then ducked between the bars of the fence and hurried to meet the riders.

Her father was the first to dismount. Jonathan removed his hat and wiped the sweat from his brow. His hair was gray and his face was creased with the lines of age. He would never look young again. The war had taken his youth from him as the years before it had been unable to do. But his eyes still twinkled, and nothing could stop him from smiling when he gazed upon Alexis and his granddaughter.

Alexis kissed her father's dusty cheek. "I was beginning to worry if you'd make it back before dark."

"And not get to see my Crystal before she was tucked in for the night?" Jonathan said, his brows arching over gray eyes. He took the baby from Alexis.

Alexis turned toward the other horse, her own contented smile greeting her husband and the young boy who straddled the saddle in front of him.

Colter lifted the boy from the saddle into Alexis' waiting arms, then hopped down himself. "Young Jon helped us bring in several strays today," he told her, dropping a kiss onto her forehead.

"Is that right, Jon?" she asked.

The boy turned solemn brown eyes—so much like Colter's, she thought—up toward his mother. He nodded. "Four," he answered, holding up three pudgy fingers for her to inspect.

"That's wonderful, darling." Alexis set him on the ground. "Why don't you run on after Grandpa. You can tell baby Crystal all about it," she told him, patting his backside. "Mommy and Daddy will be along in a minute."

Little Jon raced across the yard to the house, his short, chubby legs churning up a cloud of dust behind him.

Alexis sighed as she nestled into Colter's arms. It was her favorite place to be.

"Something wrong?" he asked softly.

"No. Just feeling a little nostalgic."

All day long she had been thinking over the last few years, marveling at how wonderful her life had been. After the fire, they had returned to the ranch, at last building the life they had both known they wanted. Little Jon was born in the new ranch house that fall, healthy and noisy, changing their lives once again. Her father had shown up the following spring, thin and haggard, but alive. His wanderlust was gone for good, and he had settled with them, domesticated at last. Even Althea seemed to have found happiness. She had married a shopkeeper in

Idaho City and had two children of her own.

This spring, when Jon was two-and-a-half, Alexis had given birth to Crystal. Colter had chosen the baby's name, reminding Alexis of the night he had told her she was like a crystal, catching the sun and throwing a glittering rainbow against the world.

"That's how our Crystal will be," he had told her. "She will fill the world with warm, bright colors of the rainbow."

And he was right. That's just what Crystal did.

"Do you miss it?" Colter asked now.

She looked up at him, surprised out of her reminiscing. "Miss what?"

"The Palace. Being the Ice Queen."

She smiled and shook her head. "Not ever."

"I'm glad I played the gambler for a little while," he said, his eyes holding hers in a loving gaze.

"You are?" she whispered, feeling a trifle breathless, her heartbeat quickening as his hand slid up her back to tangle his fingers in her hair.

He nodded. "I gambled for love..."

He drew her close. She could see his curly chest hairs peeking from the open neck of his shirt. He smelled of cattle and dust and sweat, but it was an honest, masculine scent, and she liked it. She could feel the steady beat of his heart in his muscular chest as his sinewy arms tightened their hold. His mouth descended with deliberate slowness toward her waiting, eager lips.

"...and won."

AUTHOR'S NOTE

The Boise Basin gold rush, which began in 1862, became one of the greatest the world has ever seen and was the richest strike in America, greater even than the California '49er or the Klondike in Alaska. It is estimated that over $340 million in gold was removed from the Basin. At today's prices, that represents several billion dollars.

Thousands upon thousands of miners poured into the Boise Basin in those first years, and boom towns sprang up everywhere. Idaho City, the "Queen of the Gold Camps," quickly became the largest metropolis in the Northwest and was the bawdiest and lustiest of the towns in the Basin. Any holiday was an excuse for a party, a picnic, or a parade. The stars of the entertainment world performed in its theatre and opera houses. The Dan Rice Circus (the world's largest at the time) visited the city. The rougher element filled the saloons and gambling houses (of which there was an abundance). Murders were frequent. Of the first 200 men and women buried in Idaho City's boothill, it's believed only 28 died of natural causes.

The fire portrayed in *Passion's Gamble* was the first of several fires to strike and nearly level the city. Few mining towns ever suffered as much from fire. But Idaho City rose again each time, and gold continued to be mined from the area well into the 20th Century. It's said that untold wealth remains hidden in the mountains of the Basin to this day, and miners are still panning the many creeks that rush to swell the Boise River.

Today, Idaho City, once the "Queen of the Gold Camps," has become the "Ghost Town that refuses to die." Each year, thousands of visitors pour through the historic sites in Idaho City and the surrounding Basin, perhaps slipping back for a short while to a time when the night skies were ablaze from the miners' fires as they worked round the clock to line their pockets with gold.

At the time of this story, Idaho City had officially been awarded that name by the legislature; however, it's probable that most people would have still called it Bannock, its former name. To simplify matters, I chose to refer to it only as Idaho City. I ask the tolerance of historians. In addition, the Ice Palace and the characters of this work are fictional, but I have tried to stay true to the times.

As a personal note, I would like to add that I am a native of Boise and have spent many hours (in my youth and as an adult) in and around Idaho City, swimming in the natural hot springs, riding horseback through the rugged mountains, and camping beneath the stars. It's fun to imagine—as you sit alongside a gurgling creek, named for the man who discovered the gold, or as you gaze at the crumbling remains of a wooden sluice, or as you stand inside a dimly lit saloon, the walls tilting precariously—what it must have been like to be a part of life in the Boise Basin over a century ago. I hope I have succeeded, for at least a little while, in taking you back with me to that time. I enjoy hearing from my readers, and personally answer all letters. Please feel free to write me in care of my publisher.

All my romantic best,
Robin Lee Hatcher

Winner of the *Romantic Times* reviewers' choice award for Best Indian Series!

Madeline Baker
RECKLESS DESIRE

Cloud Walker knew he had no right to love Mary, the daughter of great Cheyenne warrior, Two Hawks Flying. Serenely beautiful, sweetly tempting, Mary was tied to a man who despised her for her Indian heritage. But that gave Cloud Walker no right to claim her soft lips, to brand her yearning body with his savage love. Yet try as he might, he found it impossible to deny their passion, impossible to escape the scandal, the soaring ecstasy of their uncontrollable desire.

_____2667-8 $4.50US/$5.50CAN

**LEISURE BOOKS
ATTN: Customer Service Dept.
276 5th Avenue, New York, NY 10001**

Please send me the book(s) checked above. I have enclosed $ _____
Add $1.25 for shipping and handling for the first book; $ .30 for each book thereafter. No cash, stamps, or C.O.D.s. All orders shipped within 6 weeks. Canadian orders please add $1.00 extra postage.

Name _____

Address _____

City _____ State _____ Zip _____
Canadian orders must be paid in U.S. dollars payable through a New York banking facility. ☐ Please send a free catalogue.

Passionate tales by one of the country's most cherished historical romance writers...

CATHERINE HART
Leisure's Leading Lady of Love

____2661-9 **ASHES & ECSTASY** $4.50US/$5.50CAN

____2791-7 **FIRE AND ICE** $4.50US/$5.50CAN

____2600-7 **FOREVER GOLD** $4.50US/$5.50CAN

____2732-1 **NIGHT FLAME** $4.50US/$5.50CAN

____2792-5 **SATIN AND STEEL** $4.50US/$5.50CAN

____2822-0 **SILKEN SAVAGE** $4.50US/$5.50CAN

____2863-8 **SUMMER STORM** $4.50US/$5.50CAN

LEISURE BOOKS
ATTN: Customer Service Dept.
276 5th Avenue, New York, NY 10001

Please send me the book(s) checked above. I have enclosed $ _____
Add $1.25 for shipping and handling for the first book; $ .30 for each book thereafter. No cash, stamps, or C.O.D.s. All orders shipped within 6 weeks. Canadian orders please add $1.00 extra postage.

Name _____

Address _____

City _____ State _____ Zip _____

Canadian orders must be paid in U.S. dollars payable through a New York banking facility.   ☐ Please send a free catalogue.

"Cassie Edwards is a shining talent!" — *Romantic Times*

EDEN'S PROMISE
CASSIE EDWARDS

Beautiful, wild-eyed and golden haired, Eden Whitney was the most delectable woman Zach Tyson had ever found trussed up in the hold of his pirate ship. As dangerous and turbulent as the dark seas he sailed, Zach knew a priceless treasure when he saw one — and he had no intention of sharing this plunder with any man. One taste of Eden and he knew he had found his own private paradise of love.

_____2780-1 $4.50

LEISURE BOOKS
ATTN: Customer Service Dept.
276 5th Avenue, New York, NY 10001

Please send me the book(s) checked above. I have enclosed $ _____
Add $1.25 for shipping and handling for the first book; $ .30 for each book thereafter. No cash, stamps, or C.O.D.s. All orders shipped within 6 weeks. Canadian orders please add $1.00 extra postage.

Name _____

Address _____

City _____ State _____ Zip _____

Canadian orders must be paid in U.S. dollars payable through a New York banking facility.   ☐ Please send a free catalogue.